Warda

Warda

A Novel

SONALLAH IBRAHIM

TRANSLATED FROM THE ARABIC BY

HOSAM ABOUL-ELA

YALE UNIVERSITY PRESS ■ NEW HAVEN AND LONDON

A MARGELLOS
WORLD REPUBLIC OF LETTERS BOOK

The Margellos World Republic of Letters is dedicated to making literary works from around the globe available in English through translation. It brings to the English-speaking world the work of leading poets, novelists, essayists, philosophers, and playwrights from Europe, Latin America, Africa, Asia, and the Middle East to stimulate international discourse and creative exchange.

English translation copyright © 2021 by Hosam Aboul-Ela.
Originally published as *Warda* (Cairo: Dar al-mustaqbal). Copyright © 2000 by Sonallah Ibrahim.

Yale University Press books may be purchased in quantity for educational, business, or promotional use. For information, please email sales.press@yale.edu (U.S. office) or sales@yaleup.co.uk (U.K. office).

Set in Electra and Nobel types by Tseng Information Systems, Inc., Durham, North Carolina.
Printed in the United States of America.

Library of Congress Control Number: 2020951709
ISBN 978-0-300-22865-6 (hardcover : alk. paper)

A catalogue record for this book is available from the British Library.

This paper meets the requirements of ANSI/NISO Z39.48-1992 (Permanence of Paper).

10 9 8 7 6 5 4 3 2 1

CONTENTS

The Egyptian writer Sonallah Ibrahim was born in Cairo in 1937 into a lower middle-class home at a time of historic change, as Egypt began to free itself from British colonialism. While still a teenager, he was arrested for political activity and saw one of his mentors tortured to death in prison. These experiences must have permanently marked someone so young, thoughtful, and idealistic, advocating for the most radical social vision in that promising era of the revolution led by Gamal Abdel Nasser (1918–70, president of Egypt 1954–70). His literary career was launched in the aftermath of this blow. His first published work was a short, experimental novel that flirted with existentialism in depicting the disillusionment of a young man released from prison into a society that had been made apathetic and trifling. Appearing in 1966, *Tilka al-ra'iha* (*That Smell*, in Robyn Creswell's updated translation of 2013) shocked Egyptian readers with its frankness and gave its author a reputation as the Cairo literary scene's *enfant terrible*.

Since those beginnings, Ibrahim has published thirteen novels, young-adult science fiction stories, a picture book, travelogues, and translations. He has worked as a journalist in East Berlin, studied film in Moscow, and taught literature in Berkeley, California. Within Egypt, he has gone from prisoner to exile to senior presence, still maintaining something of the impish rebel in his public persona, resulting from his independent spirit.

Warda, his seventh published novel, is the only one that combines the visions of the youthful rebel and the mature public figure. Published in Arabic in 2000, it represents a highpoint in his decades-long career. By this time, Ibrahim had become an author who invented a new way of writing with each novel. What was this new way in the case of his seventh novel?

First, there are its two distinctive voices. Rushdy, the main narrator, is an alter ego of the author, and as such, is a character familiar to those who have read other Ibrahim novels. Rushdy's life experiences parallel Ibrahim's in many respects, and his critical view of the posh comforts of Gulf Arab petrodollar society that he observes seems consistent with attitudes of Egypt's aging leftist intellectuals. In this case, however, another voice intrudes on Rushdy's tendency toward feckless cynicism. "Warda," which means "Rose," is the *nom de guerre* adopted by the title character at a crucial moment in her life, several decades before the middle-aged Rushdy comes to tour her homeland. After she grows up in an elite Omani family, she becomes radicalized while a student in Egypt and Lebanon, ultimately committing herself to armed revolution in solidarity with downtrodden countrymen and women. The strategies used by the author to portray her mark the novel's second innovation. Although the character is adapted from actual historical personages, Warda emerges here as a unique figure in both Arabic and world literature. Both hearing news of a revolutionary movement thousands of miles away and falling in love with a fellow guerrilla can move her profoundly in equal measure. Thus, she is unusually complete as a feeling human being, to a point that some readers will find her unimaginable.

The main outlines of the history behind this tale are based on a general leftist revolutionary spirit that captured the Arab region in the 1960s and 1970s. Specifically, the novel focuses on a revolution launched against Anglo-Sultanic rule of Oman by impoverished residents of the Dhofar region in the 1960s. Unlike the parallel movement in nearby southern Yemen that led to the British being replaced by an independent revolutionary government, the People's Democratic Republic of Yemen (1967–90), the Dhofar revolution was eventually put down by the combined efforts of the British-led Sultan's Armed Forces, local militias trained and directed by the British, international mercenaries, and army and air force units brought from Iran and Jordan. Put in simple terms, this is a story of people opposing colonialism and proposing a radical vision as a replacement, only to find their dream crushed by a far less idealistic version of independence. In this sense, the story of Dhofar is the story of the young Sonallah Ibrahim in Nasser's Egypt.

Readers interested in the worthy project of understanding this historical background more completely might consult the author's historical sources in the appendix to the novel, or the recent, authoritative account *Monsoon Revolution: Republicans, Sultans, and Empires in Oman, 1965–1976,* by the historian Abdel Razzaq Takriti, who cites Ibrahim's novel in his bibliography and takes inspiration from its imaginative account. The novel's influence on such scholarship results from Sonallah Ibrahim's own deep interest in who makes history, how history is presented, and how it might be recaptured. But the main contribution to historical discussion out of the novel springs from its innovative portrayal of the title character, who somehow manages to embody both the historical and the unimaginable.

Warda

Chapter One

Once I decided to take the trip, her nocturnal visits ceased. She had been coming to me in dreams repeatedly for a while. I would always meet her amid a crowd of people reclining on couches, as in pictures of ancient Rome, or of paradise. Sometimes in a long hallway, other times on the deck of a ship. On each occasion, she would turn toward me, and in her eyes I would see an obscure look: questioning, sympathetic, inviting. I would approach, surprised at her responsiveness, until I found myself close. The hint of a smile on her lips encouraged me. I drew closer until my leg pressed against hers. Then she turned to face me and, with no care for those around us, pulled me into her embrace. While I looked furtively at the others, fearing that someone might notice what was happening, my pleasure surged until it started to overflow. Before my desires peaked, the scene suddenly changed. Only a few times was my desire so impassioned that it came to fruition. Those times ended in my waking, right after that moment, soaked, glistening, and filled with emotion.

The vision of her was always strong, strikingly clear, exceedingly moving. It pursued me even after I woke, and I remained under its lingering, vivid influence. I lost all sense of consciousness, finding myself unable to tell the difference between waking and dreaming. And I stayed for a while under the illusion that I was recapturing a memory of something that had really happened. What was strangest about her visits was that even though our acquaintance had not been substantial, she resurfaced through all the other events and women I'd experienced since the last time I had seen her. In fact, it had been more than thirty years. No, it was but a fleeting acquaintance. In reality, she had never connected with me in the way the vision of her did in the dreams. So why had she chosen—or wait, I had chosen for her—that her vision should appear with such vividness at that exact moment, as I stumbled awkwardly toward middle age and mortality?

Chapter Two

MUSCAT, DECEMBER 1992

1.

As Fathy pulled the seat belt across his chest he said, "Please fasten your seat belt or we're doomed. Traffic cops here are tough, nothing like in your country."

I almost said that it wasn't our country anymore, but I didn't want to start off with an argument. I did as he asked while he sped out of the airport. I had to fumble around with the fastener, giving him a chance to make fun of me.

He was a little older than me—heftier and certainly more cheerful. He never stopped humming all types of music: Arabic, Western classical, opera, and things he had written himself while working. He was wearing a short-sleeved shirt, and I looked odd next to him in my suit. I started to take off my jacket, but he stopped me.

"Keep it on. The car's air-conditioned," he announced.

I told him I hadn't expected it to be so hot, so I'd only brought winter clothes.

"No problem," he said. "Tomorrow, we'll buy you whatever you need."

He drove his Japanese car down the silky-smooth highway. The way was lit by high streetlamps and had no trace of life. Prominent speed bumps slowed him. He turned the wheel a little to take them at an angle as the manuals recommend. After a few intersections, modern houses started to crop up on both sides of us, most of which were no more than one story tall.

"Always, remember this road," he said. "It's the main road. It's called Qaboos Street. It's the longest street here and it ends at the harbor, Qaboos Port." He continued: "In a second, we'll pass by New Qaboos City on the right."

"Everything's named after him?" I asked.

"Same as happens back home," he answered. "Anyway, he has the right. This country was nothing before he took over."

I noticed that he drove cautiously, allowing a number of cars to pass us, even though in Cairo I had known him to be reckless. He stopped at a red light, despite there being no other cars near the intersection, nor any sign of someone coming the other way. Only when I noticed a police car nearby did the mystery become clear.

As he started to move again he said, "If you want to drive here, you'll have to take a serious driving exam and get a new license. They won't accept the Egyptian one."

"I have an international license," I told him.

"It doesn't matter," he said. "You have to have an Omani license. They know we just give them to anyone back home."

He started in humming the latest song by the French Algerian singer Cheb Khaled, then stopped and said, "I wasn't surprised that it took them so many months to issue you a visa. That's normal around here. What surprised me was that they actually gave it to you."

It wasn't really all that strange, though. And by now, in any case, it was all water under the bridge. I stared at the wall of darkness surrounding us for a moment, before we came upon another modern residential area, well lit and organized, a Sheraton hotel looking down from on high.

"We're here."

The streets were quiet, lined with parked cars and glitzy, illuminated storefronts displaying electronics, toys, clothes, and designer eyeglasses. We had to continue far down before we found a parking spot.

I liberated myself from the seat belt and he helped me get my bag out of the trunk. He asked me to wait a second while he set his car alarm.

"Are there many burglaries here?" I asked.

"Not too often. The police are vigilant. Besides, a mere whiff of a theft sends the thief off then and there."

I was surprised. "Sends him off where?"

"Back home," he answered. "The thief could never be Omani because they don't need anything. It would have to be one of the guest workers, an Indian, a Pakistani, a Filipino. They're the ones who take low-paying jobs."

We each grabbed a handle of my suitcase and started along the street. We entered a modern building, five stories high, with a travel and cargo office occupying the ground floor. The elevator took us up to the fourth floor.

He fetched a key out of his pocket and said, "Shafiqa went to sleep two hours ago."

He opened the door without making a sound and we entered a small living room with a dining table in the middle. We went into a room to the right that was dominated by an entertainment center holding a few books, some souvenirs, and an enormous television set. I threw myself into a chair as he picked up the remote and turned on the television. A portrait of Sultan Qaboos hung behind an announcer reading the last newscast of the day. It was an item about a flower show someplace in Europe that featured a red flower named after the Sultan. Fathy wanted to change the channel, but I told him to wait.

The announcer talked about the history of the flower, how a Dutch flower society had cultivated it after two years of trial and error. It was marked by the brilliance of its color, the purity of its smell, and the length of its stem. Its name, "Qaboos," was an acknowledgment of the Sultan's personal commitment to developing international relations, and His Excellency would be given this namesake flower during the celebrations of the twentieth anniversary of his rule.

The announcer moved on to the sports report and Fathy turned off the television, then started humming a contemporary American tune, shaking his full figure along to the beat with enviable grace.

"Come. I'll show you your room."

I picked up my suitcase and followed him to a room at the end of a long hallway. There was a couch with pillows and covers and a small desk with a computer and a big stereo. At the back of the room was a wide picture window, a piano, and an armchair.

"I'm sorry there's no place to hang your clothes," he said.

"It doesn't matter. I can leave everything in the suitcase."

"Good night," he said.

"You too," I answered.

I put my carry-on atop the desk and took out a pair of pajamas, slippers, a towel, and my shaving kit. I realized I had lost a wool scarf that I'd packed in anticipation of windy evenings. I remembered I had put it around my neck on the plane and hadn't taken it off while changing planes in Doha's cosmopolitan airport. I had it in my hand when I went into the plush restroom, but I couldn't remember having it after that. Could I have forgotten it in the restroom?

I began to replay my trip, starting from the moment I had boarded the plane at Cairo airport. I repeated it several times. Each time it went into slow motion when I got to the moment in the men's room at Doha airport when I stood washing my hands next to a plump young man with dark Bedouin features and a shaved head, wearing a silk shirt and baggy designer pants. He was engrossed in shaving his face and had spread out before him—in a scene of complete chaos—a collection of tubes of cream and jars and bottles of cologne and aftershave of all different sizes and colors, so that the sink looked like it was the makeup shelf for some starlet. He kept pulling out ever more paraphernalia to make himself even more fragrant.

Those disorganized movements, I now realized, had reminded me of Yaarib, who was about that same age when I first met him over thirty years ago. He, too, always took up space around him, scattering books, cigarettes, and fruit, while he waved his hands and kept barking, "Can you imagine?"

After changing my clothes, I took my shaving kit to the bathroom, where I washed up and brushed my teeth. Then I went back to the room and collapsed into the chair by the piano with a yawn. I flipped through the local papers that I had collected during the trip, unable to read anything more than the headlines. An editorial said that Kuwait had escaped the catastrophe of Iraqi occupation only to find itself in the claws of a war of attrition that was more damaging and insidious, sucking the nation's blood drop by drop. It was shelling out billions of dollars for what was called security, cooperation, training, and defense. Another quoted the British magazine *The Economist* on British efforts to sell Saudi Arabia forty-eight "Tornado" bombers worth about 7 billion dollars, the second biggest sale of its kind in history. The first such deal had been worth over 15 billion — in other words, thirty-three thousand jobs for British workers in the two countries. As for the new deal, it promised to create nineteen thousand British factory jobs in order to fill all the orders by the end of the year.

I yawned again and put my newspapers to the side. I slid the window open, instantly feeling the warm breeze. I looked over the quiet street, devoid of all life, not a single movement or sound aside from the humming of the AC units. The light from the streetlamps faded a short ways off, leaving a thick blot of darkness beyond.

When, finally, my eyes adjusted to the darkness, I could just make out a range of mountains, tall and wild.

2.

In the light of day, the city revealed its modern buildings and wide highways with their monotonous overpasses, manicured greenery scattered throughout. The whole was surrounded by barren mountains.

Fathy said as he drove, "This trip that's taking us a few minutes used to take half a day. The hills used to completely divide the neighborhoods of the capital. Then Qaboos built this thoroughfare that cuts straight through."

Nearing the sea, the road narrowed and there were people. We turned left and drove along the seawall, where the crowds, mostly Indians, became thick. A strong, penetrating fish smell came at us. We passed a small building on the beach, a big group gathered in front.

"I have to bring you here sometime to see all the strange kinds of fish and hear the songs the fishmongers chant while they are cleaning them. You'll find some who remember the British colonial times along the African coast. Maybe even some who saw Gordon Pasha's campaign in Sudan."

He nodded toward a big gate on our left. It was next to a supermarket and led to a bunch of dark side streets. "That's Al-Lowatiya District," he said.

When he saw the expression that came over my face, he added, "Hang on. These are Shiites who immigrated from Hyderabad long ago. They put them in their own ghetto back then and wouldn't let anyone else in."

He wanted to show me the Sultan's luxurious yacht docked in the port, but my vision was stuck on something more enchanting. In what looked like a small square a woman stood, wearing a long dark skirt that went down to her ankles and a sky blue, short-sleeved blouse with black ribbons along the shoulders. Her head was wrapped in a white scarf, on top of which squatted a small blue cap. A gun was tucked in her waist, and she was vigorously directing traffic with her arms.

We pulled into a parking lot and walked along a neatly paved symmetrical sidewalk, like the ones in the finest capitals of Europe.

We were in a bay surrounded by the mountains above, and below there was a cluster of small houses built in an old style but with brand-new exteriors. Most were no more than three stories tall, with front façades consisting of long blue windows set against a white background, with a decorated arch through which a sloping entrance descended. We cut through a passage between two houses and found ourselves in an area like the Hamidiya Souk in Damascus or the Khan al-Khalili in Cairo.

"Of course, you don't want to pay one or two hundred pounds for a shirt," he said. "That's why I didn't take you to the shops that sell Benneton, Lacoste, or Jovial. Here you can find a shirt for one or two riyals." I multiplied by eight to approximate the price in Egyptian pounds and nodded approval.

We walked through the arcade with its shops perched a couple of steps up on either side. Some had glass window displays; others were of the traditional style, the owners relaxing on cushy pillows atop built-in benches in front of their open shops.

The scent of perfumes and spices surrounded us as we moved from one section of the market to another, avoiding the lanes that would lead back to where we started. We passed by shops stocked with canes, staffs, daggers, coffeepots, gold and silver craftwork, incense trays, brass and porcelain pitchers, imported clothes, electric appliances, and local sweets. I noticed the many Indian tailors.

As we looked over the men's European suits in front of one such shop, Fathy remarked, "Don't think those are for sale. It's just like a catalogue: You choose the style you want after you've bought your material. The Indian tailors it to precise specifications in a few days."

I changed a few dollars at the bank rate from a money changer working at a small desk along the way, then bought myself several light, short-sleeved shirts, while my cousin looked around in a shop that sold silver. I waited for him outside, observing the shop owners, whose faces seemed about to disappear behind their beards, aside from the sparkle of their shrewd eyes. I imagined the lives of such merchants during the classical past. A typical one might spend the whole day in his fixed corner, sitting on a comfortable pillow with his right leg propped up and leaning on one arm, watching customers, passersby, owners, and sellers in neighboring shops. He would record it all in the archive of his mind to draw upon later, to get an upper hand over the competition. His eye might linger on a woman passing by, drawing upon his imagination to picture the body underneath the enfolding *abaya* while he took a puff from his narghila and sipped at a cup of tea or coffee brought to him by an errand boy. He might also have the boy buy some fruit, some fish, or whatever the shopkeeper wanted to purchase from his day's earnings. He would never leave his place except to pray at the nearby mosque or run a very small errand, until he went back to his house at the end of the day with the boy carrying his purchases. At home, he would find a hot meal waiting for him, along with his harem of wives and handmaidens and his children. Was this a picture of stability and contentment generally, or just a kind of contentment for the lucky few with full bellies, surrounded by dirt, disease, flies, vermin, hunger, and poverty?

Fathy bought a tiny silver jug about the size of a finger that the silversmith had decorated with precision. We retraced our steps, got in our car, and headed back down the road we had come on. Instead of turning onto Qaboos Street to get back to the house, though, we followed the seawall in the opposite direction until we came to a road that cut through the hills. Suddenly we were going down small, narrow roads lined by modern buildings. He pointed to a row of old houses a single story high, looking like they were made from stone or mud brick, and said, "That's how people lived way back when."

Not everyone, I thought, since in what you could call the heart of the old city the houses announced the wealth and luxury of their inhabitants.

We parked the car and set out on foot, looking at the houses that resembled fortresses: plain façades without balconies, long thin windows topped by traditional Arab arches and, in turn, by tiny windows like cannon wells. The outer gates were thick, with ornate frames embedded with metal spikes; their wooden surface was covered with delicate engravings, some of which looked inspired by Indian style.

"This little quarter served as the capital only twenty years ago," Fathy said, pointing to two stone columns that blocked off the road. "They would close up the area from here at sundown, cutting it off from the world until the next morning. The gate couldn't be opened for any reason. Many times the sick, coming from the far north to visit the only hospital in the area, died because they arrived after the sun went down."

I remembered Yaarib and the way all his stories started with, "Can you imagine!" "Can you imagine that wearing prescription eyeglasses is forbidden at home! So is smoking!" "Can you imagine that anyone who enters Muscat has to take off his shoes and leave them at the city's gates!" "Can you imagine that in these times when all children go to school, children in the Gulf states work as house servants instead!"

I commented on the severe cleanliness surrounding us: "So far I haven't seen a piece of paper in the street, much less a pile of trash like you'd find back in Egypt."

"Well, first notice that there's not that many residents," he said. "The length of Oman, which goes on for three hundred thousand kilometers, doesn't hold more than two million. The whole country has fewer people than a few neighborhoods in Cairo. And anyway, the Indians are responsible for maintaining cleanliness."

"What do you mean?"

He gave a sarcastic laugh as we approached a two-story building. "Don't go thinking that the Omani cleans up after himself. There's plenty of Indians to go around; they do all the menial labor."

I glanced over at an Indian in yellow overalls pushing a trash cart and asked, "Why don't they bring in Arab workers? We have plenty of unemployed."

"An Indian will sleep in the open, and if he gets laid off, he quietly goes out and looks for other work. The Arab, in contrast, loves to complain and stir things up."

"How so?"

"Well, he might demand his rights, for example."

We entered a small villa. Fathy was humming an old Arab religious hymn. We met a young man in traditional clothes who was wearing glasses and an old kind of turban that we used to call *almosara*. Fathy introduced him to me as one of the first cohort that had graduated from a university founded just six years ago.

"Looks like they observe the dress code," I said as we moved on.

"The daggers they wear are each different," he said. "They all wear a kaftan and a small turban or fez, but the ones who hold a high position wear daggers also. Oh, and Qaboos issued a decree forbidding workers to take off their turban during work hours. He seems to have done it to save the necks of the shop owners and the weavers who make and sell headgear."

"It's a very egalitarian decree," I said. "That way you can't tell the difference between the rich and the poor."

"Anyone with experience will pick out the person's status from his clothes right away. There's the type of cloth, for example. Some turbans are made from cheap cottons, others from wool or thick silk. The price of a really fine one could reach a few thousand pounds. Then you have the cloak worn only by the important people, made from the finest camel hair, woven until it becomes transparent, and decorated around the borders with silver or gold."

He lingered before a shop whose shelves were full of music cassettes and VHS tapes, where he said hello to a young man in traditional clothes sitting in front of a computer. In the next room another youth, engrossed in writing something, was wearing big headphones plugged into a huge recording machine. He pulled off the headphones and came over to us, accompanied by a co-worker who wore eyeglasses with tinted lenses. They both stood and stared at me in curiosity until Fathy, pointing at the picture of the Sultan hanging on the wall, said, "Now there's four of us. Let's get going."

As we climbed the stairs to the third floor he explained the law, going back to the days of communist rebellion in the south, that forbids any gathering of more than three people.

"Wasn't that revolt put down a long time ago?"

"But the law still stands."

I glanced at an old Omani with a black beard so thick that it almost covered his face and said, "You seem to have your share of Muslim Brothers around here."

"But they're a minority," he said.

We entered a room full of musical instruments. Accompanying the customary piano were all shapes and sizes of drums, some made of wood and others of light metal or plastic. Then there were trumpets made from animal horns and enormous seashells, and other instruments made out of brass, silver, or fine metal.

I sat in a chair beside the desk while he grabbed some video cassettes piled high in a storeroom. A young Indian brought me a spoon and a plate with some kind of white pudding on it. I noticed he seemed to be wearing red lipstick. Fathy picked up on my surprise and said, "It's a red gum that Indians are always chewing on, until it reddens their teeth and their lips and they go around spitting red juice everywhere."

The Indian returned with cups of coffee. Fathy asked him if the director was in the office, and he answered with a strange movement that I couldn't immediately decipher. His head went down slightly, then to the left, then up high. It was like he started to nod "yes" but then quickly switched to "no."

I laughed and said, "What was that head movement?"

"It means he's not here yet."

"Maybe it's like in Egypt when you ask a question and someone answers, 'Sort of.'"

I took a spoonful of the pudding, which tasted strongly of cardamom and ghee. Then I picked up the local paper on the desk. Its masthead featured the name of the minister of information in his capacity as editor in chief. Its lead was a color photo of the Sultan as he reviewed the Omani armed forces that had helped liberate Kuwait: the Sultan's tank corps, the Sultan's paratroopers, the Sultan's air corps. At his side was Yusuf Bin Alawi, the foreign minister. Underneath, another picture showed the Sultan meeting delegations from various tribal communities. The bottom of the front page gave prime space to an article on communal riots in India. Next to that was an article about Palestinians who had had their houses confiscated by Israeli authorities and been expelled to Lebanon, but were stopped at the border by Lebanese authorities and ended up in a makeshift refugee camp.

Most of the pages were in color and crowded with glossy ads for perfumes: Armani, Calvin Klein, Fahrenheit for Men. But a different type of ad caught my eye: "We offer Filipina maids for 250 riyals or Sri Lankans for 150."

I was about to put the paper down when I noticed an ad on the last page for a play being staged at the university titled "Baghi Got Married." The ad announced that the actors were men and that they would present two performances, the first open to male students and the second to co-eds.

A skinny young man with glistening eyes appeared in the doorway. He nodded at me, and Fathy told him to come in. He sat down in a chair across from me, smiling.

As he was stacking up tapes, Fathy said, "Qaboos is a connoisseur of classical music. He put together a symphony orchestra of young Omanis so they could play him his favorite symphonies. After gathering all these thousands of cassette and video tapes of Omani music and traditional dance, he's asked that we collect great symphonies for him."

I sipped from the bitter coffee and asked, "You mean just for him?"

He laughed. "Would anyone else around here care about that kind of music?"

"Has the symphony orchestra done anything?"

He frowned. "Not yet. Do you think such things are easy?"

"I don't know," I shrugged.

"Arabic music is a melodic musical genre that depends on one voice presented by the lead musician through his instruments. But symphonic music is made up of competing and contested tunes. How can we make such music using our traditional melodies and rhythms? That's the problem. Especially in a place like this that has such a rich tradition of folkloric music and dance. Luckily, Qaboos thinks of everything: he commissioned us to record this heritage before it's wiped out by modern media. It's a hard job because the tribal dialects are so different. It's the one thing he took from the communist countries."

The youth with the glistening eyes suddenly stood up, excused himself, and walked out wearing a crooked smile. I looked up at Fathy and pointed inquisitively.

Fathy said tersely, "I'll explain him later." He put the tapes he'd gathered on top of the desk and sat down behind it.

I asked him, "Have you found the right songs?"

Shuffling through the tapes, he said, "I'm still looking. I want pretty, simple tunes that will also be rich enough to inspire new songs. I'll give you an example. Certain rhythm instruments like the tar drum or the tambourine are essential to Omani traditional music, so you can find all kinds of drums here. We have to find symphonic pieces that feature the drums. Still, if you go too far with the drums you could drown out some of the beauty of the other melodies."

He stood up, tucked some tapes under his arm, and said, "We are going soon to make a recording in a village in the interior. Want to come with us?"

"Of course," I said. "I have nothing else to do."

We left the building and were suddenly exposed to the broiling sun. As we got in the car he said, "That young man who came in is named Zakariya and he wants to marry Heba. He saw her when she came to visit last summer. Of course, she didn't like him."

I said, "Because his eyes are watery?"

"No. He's got old-fashioned ideas. He thinks I can force it on her, so he never stops coming around."

I laughed. The man had not yet been made who could force anything on Heba, Fathy's daughter.

He hesitated, then added, "He makes me uncomfortable. He is outspoken against all the modern developments that Qaboos put in place. That makes us scared of him, since he could be doing it on purpose."

"So, you mean he . . ."

He nodded just as we shot out onto the road leading to the port. We turned onto Qaboos Street until we caught the traffic circle, then headed to the left through the modern houses in the Roy neighborhood.

"Notice anything about these houses?" he asked.

I gave a look, but couldn't tell what he meant.

"They basically preserve elements of the traditional Arab style," he said, "but with modernizing touches. Even so, the mix doesn't really clash or seem strange. It's a lesson to all Arabs in solving the problem of the traditional and the modern. I'm trying to do the same thing in my music. Luckily, Qaboos understands this problem well. Once someone put up a tall building like those in Abu Dhabi, Kuwait, or even Egypt: all glass and steel. When he saw it, he ordered it to be demolished and for all buildings to adhere to the municipal code. The upshot is this harmony that gives balance. In fact, it's relaxing to look at. Just what your friends were calling for."

3.

The smells from the kitchen greeted us. Shafiqa extended her hand to me in that conservative way now common among middle-class Egyptian women: she put out her hand with the ends of the fingers firm and rigid, ready to be pulled back in an instant, as though you might grab her by the wrist and drag her to bed if she weren't careful.

I casually took her hand and gripped it, hanging on for a moment despite her effort to let go. With a ceremonial smile, she said the exact words I would have expected: "Praise God for your safe arrival. You finally remembered us."

I answered in the same tone of reproof: "You two are the ones that haven't been home for so long."

She was full-bodied like her husband and a few years younger. Her face was completely unadorned and encircled by a white scarf. Her two eyes, like a falcon's, peered out.

Within familial relations, there are always little strains with no explanation, and perhaps even no reason. My connection to Shafiqa was this way. As hard as I tried to figure out the source of the tension, I never could. For a while, I thought it was a sense of superiority stemming from her lighter complexion compared to our darker-skinned branch of the family. Then I started thinking that she felt inadequate because they hadn't had any sons, whereas we had two. Finally, I decided the tension between us was just there but impossible to explain.

She had prepared a table covered with traditional Egyptian dishes: stewed okra, moussaka, rolled cabbage, grape leaves, sautéed beef.

I made a crack in a querulous tone: "I was expecting Omani cuisine."

"All they eat here is different types of biryani," she said.

Feeling thirsty, I stared at a jar of cold water for a moment, then looked away. She asked me, "Do you want something to drink? Shall I bring you some juice?"

I looked over at Fathy, who smiled slyly but remained quiet. Finally I said: "I don't suppose you would have any . . ."

She answered immediately, "No. No way."

My cousin stepped in. "Later on, we'll solve that problem."

But she responded just as decisively: "Later, shmater. I said, 'No way.'"

Trying to de-escalate, I turned to the food, remarking that she had become an expert at making complicated dishes. She answered with false modesty: "What else can I do? The only hobbies around here are food and cooking."

"What do you mean?" I asked. "Don't you have movie theaters and such?"

"Very few cinemas, and they only show Hindi films."

After my compliment to her cooking, she decided to pay off her debt by saying, "How is the writing going?"

I tried to close the door to this line of questioning. "Don't remind me. I'm here on a break. How is your radio job?"

"Okay."

We began eating and I answered her questions about Egypt, repeating what she already knew of the news of her daughter, who was studying in the United States. She skirted the topic that was actually on her mind, but then finally asked directly: "Is there any new news about the Islamic investment firms scandal?"

I suppressed a smile. She had fallen into the clutches of the money-laundering firms founded in the mid-'80s by one of the former leaders of the Muslim Brotherhood, handing over all her savings. When the scandal broke, the savings flew away.

"There's nothing new," I said. "Just that the founder married off his daughter in a soirée at the Cairo Hilton worthy of Haroun al-Rashid in some *Arabian Nights* fantasy."

She sighed, then changed the subject. "What's the story behind the prime minister resigning? Or did he get fired?"

"There's a bunch of rumors," I said. "One version of the story is that it's a plan to get him out of the way because he talked in a closed meeting about notables being involved in arms dealing. Another says that he was too closely tied to some high-level police officers who were caught dealing drugs."

The conversation moved on to all the jokes circulating about the prime minister. I told them the joke about the budget that had to be distributed: The Syrians started the fiscal year with a plan, and the Saudis had a plan. Finally, Egypt had to come up with something. The prime minister decided to go and stand in the center of Midan Tahrir, throw the money up in the air, keep whatever fell to the ground, and let the rest go to the Egyptian people.

Next I told them a real story that I had heard straight from the source, a friend of mine working as an interpreter at the United Nations. It happened that in New York he met the PM, who asked him if he was happy. The young man answered that he was homesick and anxious to find a job back in Egypt. The PM shouted at him, "God forbid! You'll go hungry back there. I'm hoping myself to find something here in America."

Shafiqa frowned, and I thought for a second that her sense of nationalism had been offended, but then she put her hand up to her head in pain.

"She always has these headaches," Fathy said.

I studied her silently, comparing in my mind the hijab she had wrapped around her now with pictures of her from just a few years ago, or from the early '70s, when she showed herself off—like everyone else—in a short skirt that exposed her knees without drawing anyone's approbation. In no time, the headache bug had spread to me.

I helped Shafiqa clear the table and put the dishes into the dishwasher. When I asked if she had a maid to help her, she looked unhappy. "You mean pay half my salary to a Filipina or Indian woman? No way. Besides, there are only two of us. And you know I don't like bringing strangers into the house." She put a kettle on the stove and added, "You can't imagine how they waste money here. A family sometimes has a different nanny for each of their eight children. The Filipinas, especially, work hard as servants. I know an American woman who insists on making her maid take off her shoes for her. Hunger is a monster."

We took our tea in front of the television. As she stared at me watching a Western music video with young women swaying to the rhythm of the instruments, she asked: "Do you ever think about getting married?"

"Once is enough," I answered.

"But your life isn't settled like this."

"Am I complaining?"

We saw that the dancing women in the video were Russian, and Shafiqa threw out a comment: "They fill up the markets and sidewalks in Dubai, and they'll sell you anything, including their bodies."

Fathy broke in. "Russians buy anything. Especially electronics. They can sell them back home."

She answered victoriously, "Their country has famine. That's what happens to communists."

I pretended I didn't hear, then Fathy came to my rescue. "Wouldn't you like to go for a walk? Come, I'll show you around a bit."

His wife followed us to the door and stood there until we had entered the elevator and turned to face her again. "There's only one God . . ." she said; and quickly, before the doors closed, Fathy answered: ". . . and Muhammad is His Prophet."

I looked at him in shock. Such a show of religiosity wasn't normal for our family.

"Exile has influenced her," he explained.

I examined him carefully. "What about you?"

He started humming a Faiza Ahmed song and said, "I am what I am."

"It seems like you're happy here," I said.

He wouldn't say yes or no or even maybe. As we stepped out of the building, he said, "Life here is totally unbearable from May until mid-September. The humidity will choke you."

We got into the car and fastened our seat belts, then he drove down to the sea.

"The Egyptian woman gets it from both sides here," he said. "Because she's educated and liberated, she is sought after by the local men but subject to the envy of the women. As an answer, she goes out of her way to show off that she's religious. Shafiqa has to deal with plots against her coming from her Omani co-workers every day. And it would only take a word from her boss for her to find herself back in Cairo."

"It's that easy?"

"I have an Egyptian friend who works in one of the banks. He had the bad luck to observe a mistake on the part of his boss and to take it to the bank manager without realizing that they were related to each other. The next day, they informed him that he had a seat reserved on a flight out the following day. Just like that, without any warning . . . Of course, he had his apartment, furniture, and other affairs here. We took it on ourselves and managed to salvage most of it, but it was a huge pain."

He steered the car toward a parking lot connected to a hotel overlooking the port. I heard a familiar howling. When I turned around, there was a black Mercedes coming up behind us surrounded by motorcycles. The entourage slowed in front of us and I looked toward the passenger seat, expecting to find curtains drawn over the windows, as would happen with this type of entourage in Egypt. But this passenger went out of his way to be visible. I turned my eyes to the back seat and espied a character who seemed to have stepped out of *The Arabian*

Nights. The borders of his *dishdasha* were embroidered with gold lace; on top of his head sat a crown of white cloth; and around his waist was a wide belt from which dangled a dagger with a silver handle tucked in a decorative sheath.

We got out and walked along the boulevard. The promenade was full of Asians, many of whom were unmistakably Indians. We watched as first cement mixers, then Land Rovers and Toyota pickups, and finally a bus packed full of Asians passed by. I asked Fathy about the Egyptian community, and he said there were many—doctors, teachers, engineers. He said he was friends with some of them.

He went on: "Pretty regularly, I pick one of them up and we drive out to the airport and back, or go to a new quarter called Al-Qorm to sit in a cafe or a shop owned by a Syrian friend on the beach."

"What about the women?"

"What you see is what you get."

"But I haven't seen a thing."

"As a general rule here, the Filipino barbers are pimps controlling the Filipina women who work in low-paying service jobs or are unemployed. One will cost between twenty and thirty-five riyals."

Darkness had fallen, so we decided to head back to the house, where we'd leave the car—Fathy explained that the police can be harsh with drivers who have alcohol on their breath. Once there, we hailed an orange taxi that made me think of Alexandria's cabs. The driver was Omani, but he didn't utter a word the whole trip. Fathy paid him 200 baisas. Then he led me to a spacious, multi-level bar. The waitresses were all Filipina and all average-looking. One brought us two mugs of beer and a small plate of green olives. The customers were all Omani, aside from a table with two Europeans whom Fathy greeted as we sat.

As he sipped his beer he said, "The guy on the right works for PDO—that's the Omani national petroleum company. The other is an English consultant for the Omani Ministry of Environmental Affairs, and he speaks Arabic, both classical and local dialects."

The customers all sipped from their glasses in silence, throwing occasional glances toward the bare legs of the parading Filipinas before directing their stares back into the distance. The waitresses moved around as though suffering from stress. I felt like the silence was concealing boisterous tensions roiling just beneath the surface.

"Do you know any members of the Front?" I asked out of the blue.

His expression changed; he suddenly looked stern. "Listen. Anything having to do with politics is pretty sensitive around here. The Sultan and his coterie monopolize political activities, not to mention commerce, academia, oil, and everything else. The secret police are powerful and they have advisors from both England and America."

"I just asked a simple question," I said.

He took a sip of beer then went on in a voice less rigid, as though he were mollifying a stubborn child. "There are no more Front members or sympathizers. Socialism is dead now, and money is all that's left. Money and riches are the only spice of life."

"I agree," I said. "In fact, that's the precise reason that wealth has to be distributed fairly, so that everyone can have some spice in their life."

Before the exchange turned heated, we were saved by a young man in a white silk dishdasha with Saudi embroidery who came over to our table and asked: "Brothers, are you from Egypt?"

We nodded. He presented himself as a journalist from Riyadh, and Fathy invited him to sit.

"Do you live here?" I asked.

"No," he said. "I came a week ago to cover the latest discovery of ancient ruins."

Fathy explained to me that foreign experts had discovered a hundred human skeletons dating back to 4000 BCE about two kilometers from the hotel.

"They also found a twenty-six-million-year-old petrified stone pine in Hima province," the Saudi threw in. He ordered a whiskey and went on: "Now I've become interested in the Sultanate's foreign policy."

"And what exactly is the connection between foreign policy and archeology?" I asked.

"I just have many friends here," he said, "so I suggested the topic to my editor. We just want to write about what people here think."

"And what have you found?" Fathy asked.

"It's still not clear," he said. "There seem to be two groups. One won't say a thing; the other agrees with the Sultan straight down the line."

I laughed. "That's just like in your homeland."

He laughed along with me. "Exactly."

"Are you planning on staying long?" I asked.

"I'm in a waiting period," he said. "I've requested meetings with the information minister and the foreign minister. No one has responded so far. Things are a bit tense."

"You mean between Saudi Arabia and Oman?"

"The Sultanate wants to pursue a neutral policy acceptable to all sides," he said.

"Their position is that all the Arab countries can set the policy that they see best," Fathy interjected. "So they don't try to influence decisions of neighbors or get involved in intrigues and conspiracies."

"You could say it's a tightrope act," the Saudi said. "During the Gulf War, they refused to join the forces against Iraq, sending only a symbolic force to Hafr al-Batin."

"What do you mean by 'symbolic'?" I asked. "American air strikes took off from air bases here."

"That's historically the Omani policy," Fathy said. "It goes all the way back to Ali, Muawiya, and the first wars in Islam. They follow the Ibadite school, which refused to take either side in the split that created the Sunnis and Shiites."

"Maybe it's geographical location," I said. "They have the Iranians on one side and you Saudis and Yemenis on the other. In the middle of it all is the Strait of Hormuz that controls the flow of oil."

The Saudi turned to me. "Have you ever seen an Omani map? It doesn't mark off any border with the United Arab Emirates."

Fathy shrugged and said, "All of these Emirates were part of Oman."

"The problem is that no one knows exactly what Qaboos wants," the Saudi said.

Fathy said, "Maybe he just wants to be left in peace to pursue his modernizing projects."

I lifted my eyes to the portrait of the Sultan hanging over the bar. His black eyes glistened and his white beard was immaculately trimmed. In this portrait, he wore a blue turban.

The Filipina waitress came and asked us if we wanted anything else before the bar closed. We ordered two more beers and the Saudi ordered a double shot of whiskey.

4.

I decided the next morning to walk around the neighborhood. I left the building and headed up the main road until I arrived at Mattrah. From there, I walked in the opposite direction toward the Sheraton. Once I made it to the corner occupied by the Defense Ministry, I turned left and cut across Said Ibn Sultan Street toward the intersection with the street leading back to the house.

I passed a cheap Indian restaurant, then a Lebanese shop selling falafel sandwiches for 200 baisas. I came to a large supermarket and headed toward its entrance. I almost bumped into two young women who, judging by their accents, seemed to be Omani. One of them was dark-skinned, her hair uncovered, face exposed, and wearing a blouse and jeans.

The shelves of the market were stocked with imported products from everywhere. I purchased some Egyptian-style foods, a can of fava beans, and a package of Egyptian-style feta made in Holland, as well as a few more sundries, then headed back toward the house.

The Pakistani doorman stood at the entrance to the building. When I asked after my cousin and his wife, he said they were both out. I stayed and chatted, mixing Arabic phrases, Urdu words, and hand gestures freely.

Fathy had mentioned to me that there were special shops in the Al-Qorm neighborhood that sold alcohol to foreigners who carried permits, mostly Europeans, but also a few Indians and Filipinos earning higher salaries, such as those who drove heavy equipment. These customers sometimes turned around and sold their product on the black market to Omanis, from whom they made a nice profit. They might, for example, purchase a bottle of gin for 3 riyals, then turn around and sell it for 5.

Jawhar, the doorman, had a huge frame, a thick beard, and kind features, and in no time I found myself sharing his wooden bench and having a meandering chat. I learned that the locked apartment next door was leased by an Omani who lived in the interior and visited infrequently. He used it as what Egyptians might call a bachelor pad. From there I managed to steer toward asking for a solution to my problem. He seemed to get it. His look became sympathetic and he promised in the end to find me some beer. The normal price of a can was about 700 baisas, but I offered to pay a full riyal to help compensate for his trouble, as long as he agreed to store the beers in his refrigerator for me, bringing them to me when I asked and keeping the whole thing secret from my cousin's wife.

I left feeling proud of myself for solving the problem and took the elevator up to the apartment. I went into the kitchen and set down what I had brought in a prominent place, so that Shafiqa could easily find it when she got home and hopefully feel reassured that my presence would not drain any of the few riyals that she was so carefully accumulating.

I had barely made it to the living room and flipped on the television before the doorbell rang, and I opened up to find Jawhar. At first, I thought he was bringing me what I had ordered, but instead he handed me a thick envelope with my name on it, which someone had just delivered.

I shut the door and immediately opened the envelope. I pulled out a thick notebook encased in glossy shrink wrap, which I tore off. As I opened its covers, there looking up at me was an image of a dinner plate, fork, knife, spoon, and wine glass. Above these was a musical staff and an inclined piano.

I went back to the living room, tossing aside the wrapping, and delved into the notebook. It turned out to be a small magazine, modestly produced. It seemed like a clandestine printing, with the thick banner *Voice of the Revolution* and a date of June 1992. I flipped through the whole thing, then went back to the first page. A strange headline announced that the magazine had decided to terminate its publication for good, after a twenty-year-long struggle for justice, in order to make way for another voice that might speak to the new stage of the struggle in light of the challenges of the last four years. A special section of the magazine was devoted to what it called "the fourth conference of the Popular Front for the Liberation of Oman" that had convened in early June of the previous summer, brought to order by the secretary general of the Front, comrade Abdel Aziz al-Qadi. The article said the conference ended with a resolution to pursue a new political path and the consecration of a new name: the Omani Popular Democratic Front.

The magazine reported on the various achievements of the conference, following an analysis of the setbacks that had beset the Front. These included military failures, the collapse of the socialist bloc globally, the withdrawal of several cadres, the broad modernizing campaign undertaken by Qaboos, and his pragmatist policy adopted in recent years on both the internal and the foreign fronts, including cooperation with the Islamic Republic of Iran and with Arab countries that had opposed the American invasion during the Gulf War, such as Yemen and Jordan. Finally, there was the government's gradual evolution toward allowing popular participation in government. The Omani Counsel of Advisors had become a Shura Council, its members selected not directly by the Sultan but rather through a process whereby each region offers three nominees from whom the Sultan chooses one.

The article concluded that the central goal of the movement was no longer to overthrow the regime, since the Front no longer had the capabilities or the vision to bring that about, besides which it wasn't even a demand of the people anymore. Rather, it would call for reform of the regime on the basis of sensitivity to the will of the people and commitment to nonviolence. The article emphasized the issue of national sovereignty as a priority of the popular will. It called for the annulment of the pact made with the United States in 1980 and renewed for another ten years in 1990, which extended to the US a broad set of military privileges. Finally, it called for agitation by peaceful means to bring about the unification of the historical state of Oman, presently partitioned into the Sultanate of Oman and the United Arab Emirates.

But the general tone of moderation did not stop the magazine from deriding in sidebar articles what it called "continuation of arbitrary, clannish rule" and "the systematic abuse of the human rights of Omanis." There were claims that the opposition had faced surveillance, imprisonment, and both physical and psychological torture. They had also been denied legal due process because of the absence of a modern court system. The magazine also attacked the continued siege on villages and towns around Jebel Akhdar and on Rakhiut and Dhalkut in the Dhofar region, and the imposition of stringent restrictions such as forcing the residents of these areas to carry permits and travel documents in order to enter and leave.

I set down the magazine and considered. I was used to seeing this sort of publication circulating in Cairo, both through the mail and furtively by hand. Still, my question was how whoever sent this could even know I was in Oman, much less pinpoint my address after only three days.

I went back to the packaging and found a few lines written on it in both Arabic and English: "Ashrah al-Sadr cordially invites you to forget your troubles every Saturday as we offer you an exquisite variety of dishes, the finest wines, and tunes from the era of Glenn Miller in the Intercontinental Hotel's Al-Qorm Restaurant."

I had never heard of this Glenn Miller before. But okay, still, what could he have to do with this revolutionary front? Could it be a kind of camouflage, covering the magazine as though it were something else? Also, how could my correspondent know that I was in the apartment alone at just that time? Or maybe it didn't matter if it fell into the hands of regular occupants of the building. This last thought led me to a different question: What should I do with it? Should I throw it out or keep it? I had a flashback to the time I took refuge at Fathy's house in Cairo, trying to avoid capture and imprisonment, and I remembered Shafiqa's harassment, including inspecting all my bags and sending their daughter to tear buttons off my shirt until I was forced to leave.

I went into my room and stuck the magazine into the folds of a jacket packed inside my luggage. Then I went into the kitchen, lit the oven, and took last night's leftovers out of the refrigerator.

5.

An American van with video and recording equipment and two technicians were waiting for us. Behind it, a Toyota jeep carried two young men in traditional garb. One was wearing those tinted prescription sunglasses I kept seeing.

I climbed into the van and took a seat next to Fathy. After passing in front of the ornate Qaboos Mosque, we headed out to Qaboos Boulevard near the Sultanate's police headquarters. When Fathy pointed to a green, leafy square behind the building, I said, "That must be Qaboos Park."

"Indeed," he laughed. "But it's an amazing project. It ends up being a preserve for native flora and fauna."

We continued on Boulevard Qaboos until we had passed by Qaboos City on our left and come up on an automobile exposition, announced by a huge banner with the name of one of the ministers. When I asked Fathy about it, he answered, "Here, they don't mind if a person is both minister and businessman at once."

I was about to respond with disbelief until I thought about all the Egyptian ministers who do the same thing in secret.

Arriving at the roundabouts on the outskirts of the airport, we stopped to get gas at a British Petroleum station. Then we turned left and headed down a smoothly paved stretch of road past rising smoke from factories. We passed a group of small stone houses of a similar style, all one story and free-standing with a small yard and a fence separating them from each other. Air conditioning units stuck out from the sides, and large water tanks sat on top. Fathy said they were public housing units for less wealthy citizens who could choose between living there or receiving a 6,000-riyal grant to refurbish their older houses.

After about a hundred kilometers we arrived in a town called Samail, where we stopped for a break. We walked to a dusty square where there was a noisy market offering everything from palm dates, fresh honey and beeswax, and dairy products like cheese and butter to lambs and calves, some of them newborn. Here, the majority of sellers were women, many of whom wore pointy leather masks, like the iron masks worn by knights during the Middle Ages. Their brown eyes, full of strength, gazed out from behind; in some cases, their lips were also visible. Others left their faces completely uncovered.

We then headed on for another hour to Nizwa. Fathy took me to the covered market housed in a modern building in the shadow of the old prison with its large round citadel. We went in through the nearest entrance and found ourselves in the midst of adjoining modern shops selling clothes, carpets, wooden boxes, sweets from Muscat, and perfumes from India and the Far East.

Fathy lingered over the engraved metal: bracelets, anklets, rings, and necklaces, all with detailed designs of flowers and leaves. Some of the bracelets had an opening, making for a partial circle, and they were decorated with prominent studs like the ones I had seen over the ancient wooden door frames, while the gold and silver necklaces had medallions inscribed with Quranic verses or silver Maria Theresa coins like those that served as common currency at the start of the century.

Fathy commented on the crude craftwork: "All the inscriptions and patterns on this jewelry that you are looking at is recent. People just bring in old pieces of metal and have them shaped and inscribed. It's the influence of the Gulf countries."

He glanced at his watch and we left the market to go back. This time we rode in the jeep driven by the young man with the sunglasses, heading down zigzagging roads past houses with treetops peeking over their stone fences. We followed the van back to the highway.

"Salem studied television production with your pals," Fathy said.

I gave the driver an inquisitive look, but he sat stone-faced, focused on driving. I looked back at Fathy, who explained: "He studied in the socialist state of Bulgaria. That's why he couldn't get a job in government TV. It's our gain."

We were traversing a mountainous region surrounded by towering hills covered spottily with thick vegetation. Then the road inclined slightly toward the left and we passed over a paved side road. Fathy signaled for Salem to stop and said, "Come, let me show you Tanuf."

We backtracked and turned onto the side road, following it for another fifteen minutes or so until we found ourselves overlooking a gathering of old houses. Getting out of the car, we followed Salem into an isolated area through scattered rocks and brush until we came upon some walled-in plots that were either partially covered or open to the sky.

Salem pointed at holes in the tops of the walls and said, "The British strafed the village with fighter jets in 1956, destroying most of it. Then they arrested all the villagers. Only these ruins are left."

I looked around in confusion. "Shouldn't there be a marker to commemorate what happened? There's not even a sign with the name of the place."

He tilted his head toward the ground and said, "The authorities don't like to dig up the past."

"We must be close to Jebel Akhdar," I said.

"It's just above us."

After taking a thorough look, we climbed up some steps until we met the other car on the ridge above a town called Bahla. A little further along, still on foot, we came to Jabrin Fort and looked down on its high stone walls and enormous entrance gate. Walking through a narrow courtyard, we came to another, smaller entrance that framed a small wooden doorway where a liveried guard stood holding a classic rifle. He stepped to the side to let us through, and we entered a covered passageway that led us to an interior courtyard. There we found a row of low buildings to the left that had once served as horse stables, storage space, slave quarters, soldiers' barracks, and the servants' wing.

We climbed a long spiral staircase to the roof, whose perimeter consisted of narrow openings that held old, rusted cannons with iron balls stacked next to them.

Salem pointed to a hole at the edge of the roof. "That aperture looks directly down to the front of the fort. There are seven of them on every level, and they all provide a view of the main entrance and the smaller entrances leading up to it. The system made it so anyone trying to infiltrate the fort had to face death several times. Even if they survived the first door, they could never survive all the ones behind it."

He led us to another opening covered by a wooden lid. He lifted the lid to reveal a net of iron rods running crossways, covering a deep sunken room enclosed in smooth walls. He said, "Whoever was condemned to death was thrown down here after being tortured. Their sentence was not carried out until they confessed."

With some effort, he replaced the heavy cover and fastened the latch. Then he commented, as though either explaining or apologizing: "Omani history is full of convulsions, rivalries, and invasions. Every tribe has wanted to be selected to lead, and every family in every tribe has wanted to be leader of all the other families."

We went down toward the courtyard and entered the castle. Inside we were swallowed by spacious, airy rooms full of light, even though they had thick walls. There were rooms for the Sultan and others, with galleries for counselors and judges. The ceilings were adorned with floral patterns, influenced by Persian and African design. A fan hung from the ornate wooden ceiling; its shaft was made of brass, and cloth leaves hung from its middle. There were small chambers between each floor that amounted to bathrooms, each with side windows allowing water to be hauled up from the palace well. Underneath the wide staircase, a narrow chamber with a short thick wooden door served as a men's prison, which paralleled a similar chamber on the next floor for women.

I imagined life in its heyday: men busy with their weapons and battles, women who saw the outside world rarely—if ever—and who experienced life entirely from within this palace. Inside, they moved among the shadows, exchanging visits and erupting in minidisputes. Servants and slaves, meanwhile, gathered around their own quarters on the outskirts of the fort. Maybe they performed duties like spinning the shaft of the ceiling fan for hours. Naturally, should they make any kind of mistake, they would be punished.

We went down to an underground area and stood at the entrance of a chamber that housed the tomb of Sultan Bilarib. According to Salem, Bilarib's father had built the palace over a twelve-year period 350 years ago, bequeathing to his son a flourishing sultanate. But the son was generous, good-hearted, and naive, and a mob of cutthroats seized the chance and came after him. Bilarib's brother Saif conspired with court advisors and counselors, and a series of fratricidal battles followed, claiming many victims. The final battle took place north of Nizwa, and Bilarib was defeated. When he tried to retreat to the city, its notables blocked him, so he took refuge here at the fort, where he lived in seclusion. But the brother, not satisfied, came after him and laid siege to the fortress, attacking relentlessly in an attempt to invade. Bilarib pushed back with his whole entourage, including all his wives and servants. But he finally capitulated and, taking refuge in this chamber, dug his grave, lay down in it, bid his family farewell, and called upon God to let him die. And God answered his plea.

"What a tragedy," I remarked.

Salem answered without emotion: "The real tragedy is that the murderous brother Saif went down in the history of Oman, and for that matter all of Arab history, as an important leader. He is said to have united the Sultanate, achieved peace and justice, and expelled the Portuguese from Mombasa and Zanzibar. He built a powerful fleet with advanced weaponry that imposed its sovereignty on regional trade routes. History only really cares about the final result."

As we left the fortress and headed back to the car, I thought about Salem's summation. I waited until we turned the car around in the direction we had come from, then asked, "How did you end up in Bulgaria?"

He didn't speak for a moment, then he finally said, "A fellowship."

Taken aback, I asked, "Did Qaboos offer fellowships to study in communist countries?"

His brow furrowed as he answered, "It was the Front that paid for it."

I was still surprised. "You mean the Dhofari Front?"

His tone was defensive. "I had a cousin in it who helped me get to Aden in the People's Democratic Republic of Yemen. There, in 1974, I received a grant to study in Bulgaria."

"When did you come back to Oman?" I asked.

"About eight years ago."

I did a quick calculation and said, "You mean you stayed there for ten years. And there were no problems when you came back?"

"None at all. The revolution had ended. The Sultan had issued a general amnesty."

"And what about the Front? Did it end as well?"

"There was no more mention of it," he said.

"Would you know any of its members? Is it possible to contact one?"

He shook his head no.

I changed the direction of the conversation, asking him whether he was married. He answered that he was and that he had three children, two boys and a girl.

We stopped the car on a broad plain, verdant and covered with trees, and stepped out to stretch our legs. Salem pointed out a long canal whose waters sparkled in the sunlight. "That's the *falaj* irrigation system. One of the miracles of Oman. Of human history and civilization, in fact. Like your pyramids."

"What is so miraculous?"

"It's more than an irrigation ditch. It's a complete system of complicated interlocking canals." The driver of the van joined us and stood considering the canal. He was short and skinny and his head was almost swallowed up by his turban.

"Who built this?" I asked.

The driver volunteered: "The prophet Solomon laid the foundation in ancient times, and then they copied what he had done."

"The prophet Solomon came all the way here?"

"God bless you. He came in a ship borne by the winds."

"But who did the construction?"

"The djinns. Solomon stayed ten days. Each day his djinns dug one thousand canals."

"Makes sense. They had no consideration for earthworms in those days. What about the new ones? Did the djinns build them as well?"

Salem laughed and said, "No. Now we have specialists in the construction of irrigation ditches and falaj networks. In fact, a whole tribe called the Awamer grooms specialists in underwater systems. They call them diviners and they have the ability to examine the ground, detect water under the surface, and know how far down it goes. Following their lead, crews dig falaj canals, extending under the ground through tunnels, over a distance extending several kilometers."

Fathy added, "There's a modern falaj system being built now in the Emirates. To build a canal just one and a half kilometers long has taken eighteen years of continuous work."

"The Persians first conceived of the falaj system back when they occupied the region during the Sassanid era," Salem said. "The word *falaj* has Semitic roots. It means the division of the kingdom into provinces. In this case it refers to the system to distribute the water among all who helped build it."

"Completely equitable."

"Not exactly. The rich benefited in that the feudal lords oversaw its construction and administration, and they ended up controlling its waters. Water from the falaj system was supposed to be proportioned for the common good."

No one said anything more and we walked in silence back to the vehicles. Our driver stopped to take a long look at a gaudy Jeep Cherokee with several floodlights and a flock of long antennas. He kept following it with his eyes until it disappeared, then said, "I'm going to buy one of those for myself."

I asked him if he could afford it on his salary from the ministry, and he said, "I'm getting ready to leave this ministry work to go back to the private sector."

"What will you do?"

"Broker."

"I don't get it."

"I will bring workers from abroad and rent them out to local employers at a rate of twenty riyals a month per head."

"Like a bondsman?"

"Right."

We drove on to Bahla and stopped at its hotel for the night. There, we gathered for our main meal at a large table near a circular pool. A crew of Indians waited on us. The driver sat next to me, and when I asked how old he was, he laughed and said he hadn't made it yet to thirty-five. I took a good look at his wrinkles and missing teeth. Then I asked if he was married.

"Two," he said. "An Omani girl and an Indian." He picked up on my surprise and added, "Men in Egypt marry two wives too, don't they?"

"Four," I answered, but then added: "But that was in the past. These days no one can handle even one."

He gave a satisfied smile and agreed: "Especially an Egyptian woman."

"But why an Indian?" I asked.

"God's will," he answered. "I was going back to India every year. I started out as a cloth merchant before I joined the ministry. I would stay in India for a month. One can pretty much just buy an Indian woman."

"Does your Omani wife know that you married in India?"

"Of course. We all live together now."

"Here in Oman?"

"Yes indeed. The Sultan had issued a decree forbidding that we marry foreigners, because too many men were overlooking Omani girls to try to marry educated and liberated women. He allowed for a grace period during which we all had to follow certain procedures to codify foreign marriages that had already happened. I had to bring my Indian wife here. I couldn't just leave her with our children."

"Both wives are in the same house?"

"Of course. They have a perfectly good relationship."

I remarked as I was peeling my shrimp, "You must be very even-handed."

With an air of total confidence he answered, "I don't give them any chance to complain."

"Have you given any thought to a third one, like an Egyptian, maybe?"

He answered with a straight face, "Not right now. Maybe in the future."

"Just be careful. Egyptian women don't compromise. One wouldn't accept living with a couple of co-wives." But his self-confidence appeared immovable.

I looked around and commented on the luxuriousness of the hotel. Fathy said, "Just wait until you see Qasr al-Bustan."

"Is that a hotel?" I asked.

"Its construction took two years and cost two hundred and eighty million riyals," the driver said. I multiplied by eight yet again and let out a whistle: "Two thousand two hundred and forty million Egyptian pounds—two and a quarter billion. Seven hundred fifty million dollars."

As though trying to justify the insanity of it, Fathy said, "It serves as the center for summits of the Gulf Cooperation Council."

In a neutral tone, the driver added, "After the hotel opened, His Highness noticed that its official insignia closely resembled that of the Sultanate, and He ordered that it be changed. That alone cost three million riyals."

I whistled again. "Twenty-four million Egyptian pounds to change an insignia."

He maintained his neutral tone: "It required them to change all the plates, forks, knives, glasses, bedspreads, sheets, curtains, and so on."

I poured a glass of mineral water and, thinking of glasses, noticed that it bore the name of the village we had just visited that had been destroyed by the British. Turning the side of the glass that bore the name in both English and Arabic toward Salem, I said, "History is not forgotten."

He studied the glass, then turned to me and said, "Wouldn't you like to go up into the hills?"

We rose and, stopping only long enough for me to wash my hands, headed for the jeep. Back on the highway, we took off in the direction of Nizwa.

"I once had an Omani friend from this area," I said. "He always spoke of Jebel Akhdar and Nizwa. Wait: I remember that he spoke of a village that was named after something to do with the left. We used to laugh about it. It was something like 'the leftist' or 'the vanguard' or 'the international.' I can't remember exactly."

"There's a famous village near here called 'Red.' Is that it?"

"Can we go there and ask about my friend?"

"We'll see," he said. Soon we turned onto a side road to the left that went up. We kept climbing for about ten kilometers. As we did so, I realized that the earth was gradually turning red. We paused near a phone booth on the side of the road, then turned and entered the village.

"What's your friend's name?" he asked.

"I don't remember," I said. He looked at me in surprise. "That was a long time ago. More than thirty years."

"I was barely born then."

"What year were you born?"

"Nineteen fifty-seven."

"That's about the time that I knew Yaarib."

"Is that his name?"

"I'm not sure."

"What do you mean?"

I chose my words carefully: "Well, I came to know him under very special conditions in Cairo. He tended not to use his real name. I think it was Yaarib, but I don't remember exactly."

"You haven't seen him since then?"

"Not even once."

"I'm not sure how we can find him when we don't even know his name," he said. "People here are rooted in their families and tribes."

We took clean roads past a central park with children playing, surrounded by several modern buildings that housed a grocery store, a school, a medical clinic, and administrative offices. We parked and walked through a narrow lane until we came to a small mosque. Salem went to the entrance and leaned inside without stepping over the threshold, then shook his head and came back to us. He headed over to a small, one-story house adjacent to the mosque and knocked on its new wooden door, which had been painted gaudy colors. The front of the house had windows with laminated wooden frames and horizontal steel bars. He kept knocking until a bald man, possibly in his forties, looked out the window. Salem greeted him and asked how his father was doing.

The man just stared at us in silence, then he disappeared inside, closing the shutters behind him. Some minutes passed. I was about to suggest that we knock again when the door suddenly moved and an old man with a thin frame, bulging eyes, and a long white, wispy beard that hung all the way down to his chest appeared in the crack. He studied me with care before turning to Salem and offering him a formal greeting: "Hello."

"Hi," Salem said.

"How is everyone doing?" the old man asked.

"Everyone's fine, praise God," Salem answered.

"How is your family, and your children?"

"They're all fine, praise God."

The old man went quiet. We waited. Finally he said, "Where is our brother visiting from?"

"From the capital," Salem answered.

"Welcome, please enter," the old man said.

"That's okay. Thank you anyway," Salem said.

"How are things in the capital?"

"Fine," Salem said. "Our brother here is visiting from Egypt and he wanted to ask about a friend." The old man raised his eyebrows and once again studied me with care. Salem went on, "He had an Omani friend in Cairo. That was thirty years ago. He's not sure of his name."

"My memory is not what it used to be," I offered apologetically. "His name might have been Yaarib."

"Was he from here? From Hamra?" the old man asked.

"Yes," I said.

He thought for a while and then said, "There are so many people by that name."

I sighed, then added, "He must be almost sixty years old by now. He was a university student in Egypt."

The old man slowly shook his head. "Who were his family?"

Salem broke in: "Unfortunately, we don't know."

I suddenly thought to say, "He had a sister with him. She was also a university student."

"Do you remember her name?" the old man asked me.

Did I remember? I said, "I think it was Shahla."

Salem jerked his head toward me and opened his mouth, but then closed it again without uttering a word. The old man bowed his head and spoke decisively. "Those two are not from here. I don't know any pair of siblings with those names. Please enter for a visit."

"Thanks anyway," Salem said. "We should be going."

The old man turned and walked back inside after saying goodbye. The front door was closed in our faces and locked before we had a chance to move. After we'd walked a ways from the house, I asked, "Have you met him before?"

"Never," he answered. "He's the sheikh that runs the mosque. If he doesn't know, you couldn't find anyone who does."

"What about the town council, for example?"

"We would not get anywhere with them. They're all too young, and they focus on minutiae, like street cleaning, pest control, and inspections."

"So one can't find either here or in Muscat anyone who participated in the revolt?" I asked.

He stopped walking and turned to me. "What revolt?"

"The revolution in 1957 led by an imam whose name I can't remember."

"Imam Ghalib," he said. "Of course, they can be found, but I don't know any of them." We started walking again and headed back to the car, with him ahead of me by a step as though an invisible barrier separated us.

"We can try one more time in the next village," he said.

The car took off up the mountain. The paved road ended, giving way to a smooth dirt road with some bumps. It twisted through curves, bringing us along the edge of a steep cliff above a valley. A thick forest spread out in front of us and then a green plateau. I clutched at the door as we curved around a narrow road overlooking two gorges. Finally, we came to a stop at a small square among some houses and parked next to a large pickup truck. We stepped out of the car.

Several men were gathered nearby at what looked like the entrance to the village. Some were sitting on a stone wall and the rest were standing. From the first glance, I was struck by their faces. They appeared old—even antiquated—although they were mostly middle-aged. Old and somehow malformed or distorted, as though they were elongated, imbalanced, unusually skinny, or with a disproportionate brow, excessively broad or narrow. They wore traditional jellabas, and one had on a short Western-style vest as well. They had noticed us, but they kept talking anyway in a dialect I didn't understand.

We walked over and greeted them. The ones who had been sitting stood up to acknowledge us, and the traditional salutations came out: How are you? How is everyone and how is your family and children? Then, finally, the traditional invitation: "Please enter for a visit."

Salem gave the expected response. "Thanks, but we're just passing through."

They nodded as though understanding the only thing that might bring travelers to their modest village. As we headed down a narrow road between shuttered houses, I asked Salem: "Do they know you?"

"Not at all."

We walked past a large water tank labeled Ministry of Electricity and Water; fancy pipes were coming out of it, connecting it to a concrete basin with a public tap. Passing through a dark tunnel underneath one of the houses, I almost lost my balance on some narrow stone steps that had been worn away by thousands of feet over the years. The village seemed to have been built up on pillars on the side of a hill. It had several levels and its small houses were spread around them in a haphazard manner, with bare, sloping patches of ground interspersed here and there. I stood in front of a house built on a canted rock that seemed like it was about to slide off, even though another two-story house, with fancy jars for cooling water set in its windows, had been built on top of it.

A boy and a girl, both in their early teens, passed us. They were running and laughing, but they were skinny and I detected a pallor in their faces. I glimpsed at the top of some steps, between the broad green leaves of the banana trees, a cove crossed by shadows where sounds echoed of water flowing and birds chirping. Two old men sat there chatting, taking no notice of us.

Salem walked over to them, while I stayed where I was. I heard the sound of greetings being exchanged, followed by silence. Then I saw the men shaking their heads no. The call to pray the Maghrib prayer sounded loudly through the trees. Salem came back to me as I meditated upon the descending pathways winding down into the valley. "We'd better go before it gets dark," he said, and we headed back toward the car.

6.

After breakfast we left the hotel and went out to the central square of the town, where the townsmen were gathered wearing traditional dress and carrying long, curved Yemeni swords, rifles, and the now familiar to me red, white, and green Omani flag. They had formed into ranks of only a few, leaving enough space in front of them to swing their rifles and swords. There were ranks of drummers, each carrying a different type of drum, and a bugler next to them.

Salem and his helpers went to work setting up their video equipment and measuring distances. He took aside a couple of the sword bearers and talked with them in a low voice, turning back toward me every so often. Finally, he returned to his place behind the camera. The bugler puffed his cheeks and let out staccato blasts to call the men to attention and initiate the march. The troupe took their paces while the drums beat out a rhythm in double time. The march then set off with bold strides, advancing in rapid, precise, synchronized steps. Some chants rang out; at first I couldn't understand them, but as they continued I made out a few words, though their larger meaning remained elusive.

They arrived at the square and divided into two ranks facing each other. The drummers began to move between the ranks, beating out a quick rhythm, while the marchers chanted the same lines back and forth: *First I salute my manor, And upon you blessings of God, Our fortress has raised its banner, Woe to the betrayer of the pact of God.* Salem moved the video equipment; I realized why soon thereafter as two men came down to the square, each with a large sword in his right hand, and in his left a small, conical metal shield. They commenced to fight. It started with them circling each other. Then they showed off their consummate skill at parries, thrusts, and dodges. Once each had taken the measure of the other, they sped up and became more violent, the sound of the swords clashing in rhythm with the drumbeats coming faster and faster. Their contest was harsh and forceful. For a moment I thought they weren't acting after all, that the match was real, that each of them was trying to harm the other, and that it would not stop until one had plunged his sword into his rival's chest.

I realized then that Salem was turning the lens of his camera toward me from time to time, as though he wanted to capture the alarm in my expression. I could feel the tension rise in the crowd as they locked in on the combatants, eager for a winner: would one of them end in defeat, even destruction? A song started gradually. The dust floated up around us. I just made out these lines: *Our fortress has raised its banner, Woe to the betrayer of the pact of God.*

I understood that the first line indicated the raised flags and guns, while the second directly threatened the betrayers of the pact. The battle became more violent. Perspiration poured off their faces. The rhythm of the drumbeats sped up and the chants narrowed down to the last line, "betrayer of the pact of God" repeated in a breathless bark.

Now the combatants had spun around each other until they were directly in front of me. I could smell their sweat. They spun once more so that one of them had his back to me. Their bodies and swords locked together—then suddenly came back apart. The combatant with his back facing me staggered back a step so there was only a foot or two between us. Then he suddenly jumped to the side just as the other prepared the decisive blow. The rhythm of the drums picked up and the last lines of the chant echoed violently as I felt blinded by the sun's rays bouncing off the sword of the fighter who faced me. My eyes latched onto the sword as it was thrust toward me, but I still felt numb until it flew in front of my face and came to a stop a hair's breadth from my chin.

The drumbeats and chanting ceased suddenly. Silence prevailed. Fathy rushed to my side, apoplectic. Once the sword had been pulled back, he bent over me asking if I had been hit. I brushed my hand across my face and raised it up before my eyes, half expecting to see blood, even though the blade never touched me. Then I got up, took a step back, and said, "I'm fine. It was nothing."

Fathy spun around furiously toward the combatant, who rushed to apologize, and I repeated, "It was nothing."

Looking around for Salem, I found him still behind the camera, capturing the expressions on my face, and I heard him ask, "Do we need to do another take?"

"No," Fathy answered. "We couldn't capture that same rhythm in a second take."

He added, suppressing a smile: "And at least we've put together a dramatic ending."

Therein, the ending . . . but what about the beginning?

Chapter Three

It was only a few months after the Tripartite Aggression of '56. I was barely nineteen and up to my ears in postadolescent rebellion. I had stopped attending my classes at the university and was dedicating all my time to political activity, considering myself engaged in a struggle alongside others who rejected bourgeois life for nobler goals. I thought I had hit upon the ideal lifestyle, the proper way to correct the various types of darkness and oppression that surrounded me. My view of the world was clear, grounded in a scientific analysis of history and economics, never thinking at the time that such a scientific analysis might require extensive life experience as well. Furthermore, my unique role put me immediately on a level above my cohort, as well as those adults immersed in their lives of narrow, banal concerns.

Still, what started as a rich adventure built on secret meetings with clandestine figures, on clever attempts to identify and deceive the secret police, and on strategies to reach out through revolutionary slogans and ideas to the masses quickly lost much of its glory and sex appeal. At first, the priority had been to overthrow the military dictatorship, described by the communist movement as clients of the Americans and enemies of the working class. The proof came when it executed two strike leaders a month after the 1952 coup. But now it had gradually moved to the forefront of the Arab nationalist movement. It had clashed with imperialist forces several times, finally nationalizing the Suez Canal, which provoked the invasion by the two traditional colonial powers plus Israel. When Abdel Nasser nationalized the economy, liberating it from foreign hegemony, building a productive public sector, closing off opportunities for comprador capitalists in league with the West, and committing to a comprehensive program of economic development based on national popular goals, there was no choice for any true patriot but to stand behind him.

Thus, my days came to be made up of making lethargic rounds to the assembly rooms in the Dokki neighborhood. These included associations from the Coca-Cola factory, the beer distributors, the agriculture ministry, and the pharmaceutical and research laboratories. At each place, I went looking for elements to enlist in secret cells that could be mobilized to defend national policy. My lethargy grew more out of the impossibility of explaining a clear Communist party policy than from not feeling like doing the work. The party's secret work and its public policy had become too incoherent.

Abdel Nasser preferred not to cooperate with the collectives made up of intellectuals, even though, compared to the military officers, they possessed a higher level of consciousness, superior talents in organization, the ability to interact with regular folk, and an even greater readiness to sacrifice themselves. (They had proved this often during the time of resistance to British occupation in their work opposing class exploitation, fighting the cholera epidemic of the 1940s, and even organizing armed resistance during the Tripartite Aggression.) Another problem was that these intellectuals, armed with their elevated consciousness, never could overcome their differences, and so ended up spreading themselves among several different groups, including groups that showed pure naiveté in their applications of theoretical principles. As a result, we stayed a secret organization, and this created problems both for our struggle and for our credibility. How many times did I succeed in enlisting someone to our cause only to realize the reason he'd signed up was that he presumed, since we were a secret organization, that we must actually be working to overthrow this regime which threatened his interests. I'll never forget the day I just started passing out a secret publication to anyone and everyone because I realized there was nothing in it to justify secrecy. In fact, it called for protecting the regime, even defending it to the death. A little imp figured out what was going on and called out, "Commie!" A group of clueless stiffs gathered to help him grab me and turn me in to the police.

The situation wasn't our fault, really. Abdel Nasser, in his drive for absolute authority, had abolished all types of political organization, except for one group established after the revolution called the Foundation for Liberation, which was a huge joke. As for us, we kept our secret structure, committed as we were to staying engaged. After all, we thought, this is everyone's country, so why should any one person have the right to monopolize its thinking and activity? In fact, we considered ourselves, rooted as we were in theoretical analysis, the most enlightened about the future and the most prepared to sacrifice for its sake. Likewise, we believed in the importance of engaging the people in political work, having recently seen the dangers of casting them aside.

Then, on a day I will never forget, after a long wait in front of the Coca-Cola distribution plant to meet with a worker who never showed up, I left and went to meet the officer in charge of the branch office of the Foundation for Liberation, a man who would later become one of the biggest video cassette salesmen in Egypt. I had met him during the Tripartite Aggression, when I went to him to put myself at his disposal, without hiding my politics. Later, I had wanted to find some way to work together.

That day, he picked me up in his little Fiat and spun me around the quiet streets of Dokki as he threw questions at me, all of them designed to reveal the number of members in our local chapter. I almost laughed out loud at his ignorance when he came around to asking directly: "Are there fifty of you?" The truth was, our members could be counted on one hand. Growing irritated, he turned curt and proclaimed that he saw no need for any kind of cooperative work, since everything was going fine; indeed, the main thing we might do to help would be to stay home and let the revolution take its course.

I left him feeling down and headed to a coffeehouse in the square, where a colleague who later became a famous poet was waiting for me. I found him sitting with a short, wide-bodied youth with a dark, broad face and Bedouin features. I noticed a book about Arab nationalism by Sati al-Husri on the table next to a pack of Marlboro cigarettes. That tipped me off that he wasn't Egyptian. In those days—and for that matter still today—Dokki was the central neighborhood for students from other Arab countries because it was right next to Cairo University, so one found there political refugees from Yemen, Morocco, Palestine, and Sudan. They were easy to spot: they all carried around books about politics or literature and smoked foreign cigarettes.

My friend presented the young Arab man to me as a student from Bahrain called Khalifa. In no time, we were arguing. He opened up a fierce attack on communists, accusing them of being lackeys of the Soviet Union and traitors to the Palestinians. I said that Lenin had critiqued the Zionist project from the beginning, but the Soviet state changed its policy in 1948, accepting the partition, which seemed like a reasonable move at the time, since the alternative would have been a war that would play out to the advantage of reactionary Arab groups and the Zionist movement. I reminded him that Arab rulers had marginalized Hajj Amin al-Husseini, undercutting his call for a Palestinian state. We found common ground in the end by placing responsibility for the disaster on Arab leaders, and as we parted he gave us his home address, insisting that we visit.

The next day we headed to his quiet, tree-lined neighborhood of Agouza. Apartments in the area regularly rented for 8 pounds a month, a big sum at the time. We walked as far as the agricultural museum, then turned left onto Nawal Street and carried on until we crossed Al-Duri Street, at the edge of a green space. We stopped in front of a modern four-story building. The doorman tried to tell us there was no one named Khalifa living there, but then he threw in that there was someone from one of the Gulf countries living on the third floor. Khalifa opened the door and cleared a path for us to enter, apologizing that he had neglected to tell us his real name: Yaarib. His country of origin also was not, it turned out, Bahrain, but Oman. He explained that he had concealed his true identity in case his meeting with us might be noticed by the Egyptian secret police. They themselves had organized his coming to Cairo along with his sister and a number of other young Omanis and Yemenis in order for them to get an education and plan a revolt against English colonial rule in their homelands.

We saw nothing strange in this. At that time, almost every young man had his personal *nom de guerre*, if not two.

Then his sister entered.

Shahla was smaller than her brother, but her bronze complexion had greater depth. Her eyes were beautiful, her lips delicate, and her chest ample. She greeted us and then brought us fruit and tea, as her brother burst into a discourse about Oman, repeating every so often, "Can you imagine?"

And we could not, for what he narrated about life in his country was beyond belief. He told us of how he had memorized the Quran as a child and learned to read and write under a tree, sitting in a group with other boys and girls. How they would sit together holding books printed in Egypt with the teacher in front of them, hatless with his long beard, writing with a piece of reed dipped in ink on a slate made of animal bone, keeping a substitute reed between the toes of his right foot.

"Can you imagine? The list of things forbidden by Sultan Said includes smoking, riding motorcycles, playing football, opening restaurants, barber shops, shoes, radios, and immigration."

He related how his father had started a trading company in Oman, then lost all his money and moved his business to Aden. During the war between Indonesia and Japan he heard about an 8,000-ton sugar shipment for sale out of Sumatra for next to nothing. He bought it and contracted a Chinese ship from Hong Kong to transfer it. He waited three months for the shipment without any sign of it, during which time a sugar crisis hit the Yemeni market. Finally it appeared; its contents were unloaded in one night, and by the next morning the entire cargo had been sold and he made a fantastic profit.

Yaarib's sister interrupted to explain how their father's profits had multiplied after that. He had cornered the market in leather and coffee by working with small farmers who transferred their product to him via camels, after which he sold it to traders in the port of Hodeida, who exported it from there. I still remember the way she stopped and looked at me with wonder in her eyes and said, "Do you know how much money he made? He bought one hundred kilos of coffee from the farmers for twenty riyals, then sold it to the traders in Hodeida for a hundred."

I asked a naive question: "Why did the farmers have to go through him?"

She laughed. "Once they were in debt to my father, they couldn't send their goods straight to Hodeida but had to go through him and sell at below wholesale. It's the same story in Oman. All the merchants have to buy from a middleman, because all those who work the land are in debt to wholesalers to whom they end up selling their products for dirt cheap. The small traders are all in debt to the retailers, and the retailers are all in debt to the big wholesalers. Meanwhile, the regular citizen owes every one of them."

I wasn't surprised to hear her slam her father. We were all always trying to outdo one another in our sarcasm about our parents. To us, they were backward, ignorant, ruthless, and lacking humanity. I myself often gave it my all by criticizing my father's suffocating affection, telling the story of how he spent an entire wintry night outside a police station where I'd been detained following an opposition protest. Or there was the time he found the hiding place where I had stashed a Communist party communiqué and a pamphlet called "How to Be a Good Communist," by the Chinese philosopher and revolutionary Liu Shao Chi. He wanted to set them on fire. I threatened to kill him if he did.

I left their apartment that night in a strange state of bliss, so much so that I found an excuse to go back two days later. On arrival, I found that my friend had hit upon the same idea. For the first time in my life, I could now appreciate a family atmosphere. The apartment was kept clean and organized, and there was always food prepared by their Egyptian housemaid, as well as fruits and foreign cigarettes. Both Yaarib and his sister had study grants from the Egyptian government that paid them nine pounds a month, and that, next to the extra spending money from their father, made them quite rich by the standards of our circle. It was just a simple apartment; still, the one I had grown up in didn't compare. That place of ours had become more and more sparse, until in the end it only had the small iron cot that I slept on (which almost touched the floor after it was unfolded), my father's large iron bed, a cheap storage closet with barely enough space to open its doors, a wooden couch where the roaches frolicked, and a few broken-down chairs.

But the biggest thing that distinguished Yaarib's apartment was the presence of his sister. She was two years younger than him but more enlightened. When she commented on a topic, he listened to her attentively. Before offering his opinion on any matter, he instinctively looked to her—his looks always seeming to settle on her chest. My friend and I tried to make it seem like our purpose was to discuss political and intellectual topics with Yaarib, but our real interest was her. She was probably the first young woman in our lives who connected with us socially in an atmosphere that was warm and open. A joy infused my being each time I saw her, and despair struck me whenever I arrived and found she was not at home. She always welcomed us and encouraged our visits. Nor was it just the two of us who visited regularly. In fact, we discovered that they had a number of Arab student friends who did not bother to hide their special interest in her.

A particularly harsh winter hit that year, and we ended up over there almost every night. Mostly, we sat around the electric heater on their comfortable new armchairs with their sturdy legs and embroidered upholstery. Sometimes we took the heater into Yaarib's room and gathered on top of his wide bed, wrapped in blankets, sipping tea, and listening to classical music. We engaged topics carefully chosen not to inflame our differences. For example, we would all make fun of the Baath party, with its romantic talk of the eternal mission of the Arab nation. They said this mission would appear in a new guise during the various stages of history, always seeking to revive humanistic values. Their founder, Michel Aflaq, had been compelled at gunpoint by the Syrian dictator Husni al-Zaim to sign a commitment not to engage in political activity.

During these sessions I homed in on her every expression and emotion, obsessing over the slightest indication of some special connection between her and any of the other regular visitors. I carefully studied that elusive look in her eye that struck me first as questioning, then as gently mocking, and finally as challenging. She would crane her neck and her cheeks would go crimson, either from the warmth emanating from the heater or from the looks being directed at her. If her eyes were to land on me, the blood rushed to my face and I had to turn away. At the end of the evening, I would bring her specter with me back to my room, and right into my bed, where I pulled her close until I almost drowned in a sexual ardor that ultimately had nothing to do with her.

That time was like a dream. So, as with all dreams, it came to an end.

One day I found a young Jordanian at the apartment, who had just arrived from Beirut. His name was Shehab, and he was not only handsome but also immaculately dressed. He was studying at the American University in Beirut, and he made a point of visiting Yaarib and Shahla when he was in Cairo. It came out that he was an adherent of the Movement of Arab Nationalists; he spoke with us of their ideas, which struck me as vague and uninformed. Relying on loose and flowery language, they sang the praises of unity, liberation, and revolution. I was against what he was saying, but I checked myself when I saw the respect with which they listened to him. That alone could have made me anxious, but then I realized that the names Shehab and Shahla both started with *sh*. Surely that did not bode well. Still, nothing prepared me for what happened next, as the two of them walked into another room by themselves.

Yaarib was visibly annoyed, but he carried on with the conversation. I was just as annoyed and focused all my attention on that room. I knew it to have a wooden desk, two chairs, and a small couch. Although the door was ajar, I couldn't hear anything that helped me divine what was going on in there.

I lit a cigarette with trembling fingers, then went on to smoke several in the one hour plus that passed before the two appeared again. Shehab seemed like he was waking up from a pleasant nap, with a dreamy look in his eyes and a satisfied smile on his lips. I looked at Shahla, who walked behind him. Her cheeks were rosy and her hands were clasped in front of her. I left the apartment that night on the verge of tears.

This same scene repeated itself several more times. At first, I rationalized to myself that they were involved in activism together. Gradually, it became clear that their connection was not based on politics.

So I suffered in silence. But I took perverse pleasure in tracking the outward signs of their relationship: the way she greeted him when he arrived at their place, for example, or the way she said goodbye to him when he left before I did. I even started trying to go at different times of day, using any pretext to divine how often he was there. I was falling apart and had no idea how to handle it, so I satisfied myself by seeing her but without daring to show her my true feelings.

Then one day, Yaarib greeted us in a state of acute agitation. "Can you imagine? A revolution has started in Oman!"

The spring of '57 had been extremely tense. In Egypt, preparations were under way for the first democratic elections since the revolution. In Algeria, resistance against French rule had entered a crucial stage. Then there was Jordan. King Hussein had been forced by popular pressure to expel the British general (and de facto ruler) Glubb Pasha. He had held democratic elections that brought to power a nationalist government, which he promptly kicked back out of power. The nationalist response had been a violent series of bombings.

The summer heat had barely flared before Omanis everywhere received a message from Imam Ghalib announcing the start of the armed struggle and calling on them to return to the homeland and help liberate it from the Sultan in Muscat and his English sponsors. The Imam's call spread quickly, and the major towns began to accept his authority, including Nizwa. The Sultan, besieged in Muscat, called on the British to rescue him. The British entered the fray, bombing the fortress of Nizwa from the air, which forced the mujahideen—as they began to call themselves—to abandon the fort and take refuge around Jebel Akhdar. Yaarib was on the verge of tears while talking of the fall of Nizwa. He had decided to go. With his decision, my dream was crushed: he would move Shahla to a girls dormitory.

He flew first to Bahrain and from there to Dubai. He continued by car to Muscat, bringing with him medicines needed by the liberation forces. We kept up with his news through a scattered stream of correspondence that he sent to his sister, whom we managed to meet regularly in spite of obstacles. The girls dorm restricted visits and prohibited her from going out at night. Our meetings took place in the afternoons at Midan al-Misaha, near the dorm, where we sat around in its wide green spaces. Sometimes, when Shehab was in Cairo, she wouldn't show up, but I never asked about him. It was as though I hoped I could erase his existence by ignoring it. When we did meet, she told me about Yaarib's letters with their stories of the struggle and its battles. I never forgot a story he told of an Omani woman whose husband had been arrested on charges of helping the nationalists. The same night of the arrest, she was shocked to find an English officer breaking into her house. She grabbed a knife and stabbed him twice, knocking him down, then escaped into the darkness.

In one of his letters, Yaarib mentioned that word had spread of Salah Salem, one of Nasser's right-hand men, who came to be nicknamed the "dancing captain" after he visited the south of Sudan and danced practically naked with the tribes hosting him. It was said that he had arrived at Jebel Akhdar to lead the revolution. British officials believed the rumor and started to search for him everywhere.

The correspondence was disorganized, brought over by travelers or transferred by the Egyptian secret police, but we were able to follow events through the radio station Voice of the Arabs, which devoted a segment to Oman every Thursday night. We felt a special rush as we imagined men and women sitting in the Omani hill country also listening to the broadcaster Ahmad Said's fervent calls for Arabs to rise up, from the Atlantic to the Gulf. In fact, Yaarib assured us in his letters, these broadcasts were not just being heard on the hilltops of Oman, but fighters often learned from them what was happening in surrounding areas.

When I talked about these broadcasts with Shahla, her face would flush and her eyes would gaze off into the distance, shining with a strange light. Sometimes she would start to talk about her childhood. From these conversations I pieced together a picture of the old Sana where her father had taken refuge and she had spent her childhood: mud-brick walls adorned with high towers on each side and solid wooden doors that were slammed shut every night; tall houses that touched each other, covered with decorations and bearing white inscriptions and minarets; broad, high windows with wooden shutters, decorative arches, and stained glass that reflected the sunlight; souks with everything from Japanese porcelain to Indian or Syrian cloth to eastern European ceramics to Italian medicines; its central square overlooked by a large poster of King Ahmed flooded with light. The city's shopkeepers left their shops wide open at midday and headed to the mosque for prayer, long sleeves protecting their hands that they had just washed. After prayer, they lingered in the mosques to talk because coffeehouses were banned, and as they chatted, the calls of the qat sellers filtered in. Then they all headed home for naps and the streets emptied out.

On one of these occasions, Shahla told me the story of qat, a bush with large green leaves that had noteworthy properties. Yemeni men habitually chewed on the leaves, storing them in their cheeks for hours as they sat with others, feeling happy. I asked her if she had tried it, and she laughed: "Of course. Women also had their gatherings that they would dress up for. Lipstick, rouge, nail polish, eyeliner. Hands and feet decorated in floral patterns with henna. Everyone threw off their wrap and their shoes and kissed each other's hands when they walked in. The windows were all covered by curtains, but light from outside infiltrated through the glass arches. They would start smoking and chewing qat right away, then a little later everyone would dance, once they had cleared out a space in the middle for a singer with a tambourine and one of the women reached out to another to start things off."

"So the people there were happy?" I asked.

She laughed sarcastically. "You haven't witnessed anything like the common scenes in our cities. Such as a man walking down the street with shackles on his ankles. Anyone with power could order the binding in metal chains, for several days or even months, of someone who displeased him. The poor person, who was usually a slave being punished by his master, would have to go about his normal workday as though being shackled were nothing."

Her mention of slaves caught my interest, since I had never crossed paths with one in my short life. So I pressed her. She said that in Harad province in northern Yemen there was a slave market where one could buy a person for 1,000 riyals. She told of how the Saudi ambassador had asked her father to help him buy a white slave girl from one of the princes in Sana, so that he could offer her as a gift to his mentor. Her father worked it out and the deal was completed at his house. There, Shahla had spied through the latticework in the door while a foreign woman doctor conducted a medical exam. The young slave, who couldn't have been older than fifteen, had resisted the inspection until the prince forced her to submit.

I noticed Shahla always avoided any reference to her mother, so I asked directly. Her expression changed, her features hardening. She spoke tersely, saying only that she was dead. It took a while, but finally she opened up: "She was pregnant for the tenth time. The first time had been right after she married, at age fourteen. She had complained of weakness and abdominal pain from the time I was born, and the doctor had warned her to stop having children, but my father showed no concern. After another pregnancy, she had a miscarriage. On the tenth one, my father brought an Italian doctor from Taiz in the highlands to see her. You had to have been there: The doctor is walking up the stairs with a translator behind him, and in front of him a young man is calling out, 'Allah . . . Allah . . . ,' so the women in the house know to move out of sight. My father is upstairs next to my mother, with the door of the room ajar. The translator stands behind the door. Then the questions begin, but in a whisper to make sure his esteemed wife only hears her husband's voice, and that only her husband can hear hers. So the doctor whispered to the translator, who translated for my father, who whispered the question into his wife's ear. Then she answered him, he told the translator what she said, and he passed it along to the doctor. After this went on for a while, the doctor gave his judgment that surgery was necessary. The operation was done and the child was born. Everyone was happy except my mother, who spent the next several days lying in bed indifferent to the world, until finally God took her life."

Whenever I left her, I wandered a long time along the Nile, careless of the cracks that had worn through my shoes, going back over in my mind her words and expressions, trying to detect some indicator of any special connection she felt toward me. A deep sorrow engulfed me whenever I overheard a song by Abdel Wahab, Abdel Halim, or some other crooner. How many cigarettes did I smoke in a daze, listening to ballads like "You've Wronged Me" or "I Adore You," or complaining to one of my friends about unrequited love?

Around this time, talks began exploring unification of the various Egyptian communist organizations. The initial talks were successful, and the birth of a unified party was declared on January 8, 1958. A month later, the unification of Egypt and Syria was announced, and Abdel Nasser flew to Damascus, where his car was mobbed by adoring crowds. From that point, events spiraled. In July, the Iraqi monarchy fell, and within moments of Abdel Karim Qasim taking power, the Baghdad Pact was defunct. The dream of Pan-Arab unity seemed on the verge of being realized. Abdel Nasser was just about to return from a visit to Yugoslavia when he turned back around and flew to Moscow, fully aware of the volatility of the situation. Sure enough, the next day the Americans landed marines in Lebanon.

But the real danger came from a different direction.

All these victories had Abdel Nasser's head spinning. Especially important was his success in imposing on the Syrians his own concept of democracy, bringing both the Baathists and the communists into the process. Abdel Karim Qasim followed his lead and declared himself the central authority. The two autocrats began to compete, and Nasser's Voice of the Arabs radio soon challenged the Iraqi leader. Meanwhile, the British and the Americans shrewdly seized the chance to exacerbate the two men's differences, recruiting allies from among advisors to the two leaders and prominent journalists like the Egyptians Mustafa and Ali Amin.

Then the communists became caught up in the rivalry.

In Iraq, the Communist party, which had played a central role in the overthrow of the monarchy, insisted on their right to continue as an official entity, fearing that Abdel Nasser would successfully impose his concept of unity on Iraq and thereby make himself the only legitimate political movement. As a result, they encouraged Qasim to oppose Abdel Nasser's push for one-party rule. The Iraqi position actually resonated with elements of the Egyptian Communist party, which had just managed to come back together a few months earlier.

When Egypt united with Syria, Abdel Nasser had taken sides with the Syrian Baathists to push aside the country's communists. Now he made a similar move within the recently unified Egyptian communists. The supporters of unity could not keep together a party split by old rivalries, nor could they agree on a unified policy. In the end, two factions joined forces to expunge the third. Support for Abdel Nasser became a main source of division. In no time, the newly unified party had split into two, with one group supporting democratic forces in Iraq and Syria, and the second supporting Abdel Nasser and calling for the unification of all nationalists in the fight against the dangers of imperialism.

In the midst of all this, Yaarib suddenly came back from Oman.

When we met at the old apartment that he and his sister had rented again, the change in him alarmed me. I found him sitting on the balcony with a bottle of beer before him and his usual pack of Marlboros next to him. He seemed sullen and he didn't speak. When he finally opened his mouth, the first thing he mentioned was the difficulty of life in Jebel Akhdar, where disease proliferated and medical professionals—*dukhterz*, as they called them there—were impossible to find.

"Can you imagine," he said, "that we extracted bullets from the bodies of the wounded with string?" He added bitterly, "We had to put it into the wound and play with it until we harnessed the bullet and pulled it out. Of course, infection usually set in."

He told us unbelievable stories that night about the naiveté of the freedom fighters. Some of it seemed more like farce. Such as the rumor which circulated that Major Waterfield, the leader of the English battalion at the Nizwa fortress, had called the rebels cowards for taking refuge in the mountains instead of coming down to Nizwa and confronting him face to face. When word of this challenge reached the freedom fighters, five of their leaders actually left their camps and headed toward the fort, determined to invade the outer walls and stand before its front gate so that they could call out the major by shouting, "We are here, Major. Open your gate." At that point, they thought, either he would come down and they would finish him off, or else his truly cowardly nature and that of his forces would be on full display.

The five came back telling a tale of having knocked on the fortress gate but hearing no answer. So they kept knocking harder until they heard the major's voice calling to the guards, "Don't open the gate for anyone or anything. We are safe as long as it is closed." Finally, the five guerrillas decided to leave. As they did, one turned to the closed door and cried out, "Guardian of this fort, tell your master that we came and he would not come out to us!"

I had to control myself to keep from bursting out laughing, until Yaarib went on plaintively: "The British attacked people's houses and dive-bombed the entire area with their air force. Even sources of water were bombed. The people took refuge in caves. But the British sent in paratroopers, and they managed to occupy parts of the hill country by coordinating with a double agent who had fought alongside them in Kenya before joining the freedom fighters. They managed to take several rebel leaders prisoner and put them in a dungeon under Al-Jalali fortress. They burned the crops of everyone else, destroyed their houses, and confiscated their property."

I remember he went quiet for some time, not daring to speak to him, until Shahla—who had been staring off into space—turned to him and said sarcastically: "And the others escaped."

I sensed they were picking up on an earlier conversation. He answered her in a perturbed tone, "Only a few of the freedom fighters were left in the hills, and those saved themselves, fleeing to Saudi Arabia, Kuwait, or Bahrain . . ."

She cut him off: "Or they came to Cairo."

A passion suddenly came over him. "I did not run away. I came bearing a letter requesting military support from the Egyptian authorities, and I had orders to organize a Cairo office of the rebellion."

But watching him over the next few days, I found this hard to believe. He spent most of his time sitting on the balcony with a bottle of beer. At the time, I didn't blame him, because the news from Oman made clear the decisiveness of the defeat. Differences emerged among the leaders of the revolt, and the tribal chiefs flipped and began to favor a cease-fire, with some even helping the enemy find the rebels' weapons stashes. From this, Yaarib concluded that the re-volt had not ushered in a new consciousness. Thinking was still tribal, and if the chief of the tribe did not move, neither did any of its members.

By then, he had joined the struggle going on among Egypt's communists. The Movement of Arab Nationalists supported Abdel Nasser down the line, even calling on him to crush those that they called "populist demagogues," who opposed immediate unification with Iraq. They welcomed the abolishing of all political parties in Syria and set up a council in Kuwait to oppose communist influence. I had expected that his position would be consistent with MAN's be-cause of his close connection to Shehab. I was surprised that he instead took the side of those we still considered on the left, who took up slogans in support of Abdel Karim Qasim and called on Abdel Nasser to follow his lead. Meanwhile, Muhammad Hassanein Haykal, Abdel Nasser's spokesperson, used his news-paper column to threaten both the right and the left should they try to handcuff the president. Finally, at the midnight hour on the first day of the new year 1959, pretty much everyone—including me—was arrested and sent off to prison.

That was the end of the stage of my life that included Yaarib and his sister.

Chapter Four

MUSCAT, DECEMBER 1992

1.

"Total and eternal faithfulness to all creatures of the universe on the condition that all of humanity joins together and recites: '*Nam—myoho—ren—ge—kyo.*' Spiritual development that is seamless and without limits for all creatures of the universe, those visible and invisible, can only be realized if all of humanity adopts the *no—ko—do* mantra and recites it before the very holy T'ien Tan, servant of Tien Tao." The TV commercial ended with the announcer holding up a book entitled *Four Steps to Total Peace: Selected Writings of Professor Hisatoki Komaki.*

I liked the rhythm of these Asian words. They reminded me of the pamphlets we wrote back in the '70s for the Great Leader, Kim Il Sung, "the rising sun over North Korea."

Opening a can of beer that Jawhar had snuck up to me, I fantasized about Shafiqa standing in front of me, so I could say to her as I swallowed the forbidden elixir: "*Nam—myoho.*" I was alone in the house, waiting for her to come back with Fathy so we could eat our late lunch that I had volunteered to make with only the best intentions. I was done cooking the rice and had just put a pan of potatoes with tomato and onion in the oven. Now I was back in the living room, relaxing in an armchair in front of the television with my can of beer at my side, and I started to flip through the various channels: an Arabic channel, a channel from the Emirates, BBC, another English-language channel from Hong Kong, and finally a channel devoted to Western pop music videos.

The telephone rang. I said hello, but no one responded. I thought I heard breathing, then the line dropped and I hung up. Distracted, I grabbed one of the volumes of *The Sultan Qaboos Encyclopedia of Arab Names* from a shelf next to the television. The back cover described it as "A unique experiment with no precedent in modern Arab history," the first attempt to gather and record common Arab names, including their etymologies and historical usages. The volumes' practical use was to help the ordinary Arab understand exactly why he had named his son Zayed, for example, or Amro. I started to look through the names starting with *sh*, like Shafiqa, but was interrupted by another phone call. The same thing happened, and I hung up again. When it rang again, I just stared at it without moving. It rang and rang until finally I lifted the receiver. Now, I was surprised to hear a strange voice.

"Mr. Rushdy?"

"That's me. Who's asking?"

"You don't know me, but I want to see you regarding something important." He sounded like an Omani trying to imitate an Egyptian accent.

"What is this about?" I asked.

"I can't talk about it on the telephone. It's better that we meet."

I thought for a moment. "You're welcome to come over," I said.

"No. It's better that we meet outside."

"Where?" I asked. "I'm not familiar with this city."

"We can meet in front of the main entrance to Masjid Qaboos," he answered. "It's not far from your house. Just ten minutes' walk."

"When?" I asked.

"At noon prayer."

"How will I know you?"

"I will be the one to come to you. Okay?"

I didn't answer right away, so he said, "This is a matter of interest to you."

"All right," I said.

"One important thing, though," he added. "Please don't let anyone know about this meeting—even your relative." I hesitated again, but he wrapped up the conversation: "See you at noon."

The line went dead and I slowly replaced the receiver. I finished off the last few sips, put the empty can in a plastic bag, and stuffed it for the moment under my chair as I returned to the encyclopedia, inattentively resuming my search for the name Shafiqa.

As soon as the sound of the call to prayer wafted in, I got up, fetched my plastic bag with the can, and left the apartment. I passed a trash can and tossed the bag as I headed toward the Chamber of Commerce building that sat on the corner, then turned down the street with the footbridge and walked past the Plaza Cinema and Kentucky Fried Chicken. I kept walking, turned right, and saw the mosque where we were meeting right in front of me.

Those who came to pray, including many Indians and Pakistanis, were still collecting at the entrance. No one seemed to take any interest in me. A memory of Cairo and its bustle came to me as its microbus driver passed by shouting their destinations to potential passengers.

I waited awhile at the entrance without anyone coming near me. After half an hour I decided to leave; aiming toward the end of the street, I passed a row of government buildings that ended with the Yemeni embassy. At the main intersection, I turned right. Then I took a long stroll before heading home.

The ringing of the telephone came through the front door as I was unlocking it. It stopped once I stepped inside, but then started again soon after.

His voice sounded apologetic. "I came," he said, "but I couldn't manage to talk to you. I'll explain the whole thing when we meet."

"I don't really have time for all these games," I answered.

"Sorry," he said, "please bear with me for just a bit."

"You are making a very big deal of this, no? If you want to see me, just come to the house."

"Give me one more chance," he said. "This will be the last. You won't regret it."

I sighed, and he asked me, "Will you be going out tomorrow?"

"Maybe."

"About what time would you go out—if you do?"

"No earlier than 10 A.M."

"I'll call before then." And he hung up.

I smelled something strange and remembered the pan of potatoes. Rushing to the kitchen, I pulled it out of the oven. As I considered the steaming, charred lump in front of me, I cursed the telephone caller, the encyclopedia of names, Shafiqa, and the beer. I tossed the black lump into the trash can and ran water over the pan. Flipping on the kitchen fan and opening the window, I then dedicated myself to making a new pan of potatoes.

This time I concentrated on what I was doing, not leaving the kitchen until the pan was fully prepared. Then, as I lifted the cover so I could salt it to my taste, I heard the sound of my cousin and his wife returning home. When I brought a pot of rice to the dining table, I was surprised to find a strange woman wearing modern clothes that showed the skin on her arms up to the elbows. Not only was her hair uncovered, but it had been styled at a hair salon, and there were even signs of makeup on her face.

When I asked her what had happened, she made no answer, so Fathy offered an explanation: "A Pakistani doctor told her that the hijab was causing her migraines, and that instead of wearing it most of the time but taking it off at night, it would be better for her not to wear it at all. That way, the total exposure of her sinuses to the air conditioning stays level."

She then spoke for herself in a confrontational tone: "That's what I decided to do. True Islam does not force all women to wear the hijab."

"O learned one," I said, "who made this decree?"

Fathy answered, "Here, the aristocratic women cover up everything, but the women of Zanzibari origin don't cover their heads."

I brought the potatoes and we sat around the table while I worked to understand this theory of adornment. Finally, Fathy distracted me by saying that Fendy, the director of the music center, wanted to invite us all for dinner.

"At his house?" Shafiqa demanded.

"No," he said. "At the Inshirah Hotel or the golf club."

"Will his wife be with him?" she asked.

"I don't know," he said. "I doubt it."

"You two go," she said. "I was planning on fasting anyway."

He seemed unenthusiastic about the whole thing. "This invitation is going to be very expensive."

"Well, won't he be paying?" I asked.

"But it has to be reciprocated," he explained. "In fact, we should outdo it. Omanis are very generous, but they also look down on anyone who doesn't respond with at least the same level of generosity."

"Half of our salary goes to gifts and pleasantries," she said.

"Is it possible to decline?" I asked.

"No. Fendy doesn't let people off the hook. Anyway, the whole thing is for your sake. He wants to get to know you."

2.

The voice called the next morning, as promised.

"Can you meet me in half an hour?" he asked.

"Where?"

"At the National Museum," he said.

"You've forgotten. I don't know my way around."

"There's no way you can get lost. You know the Masjid Qaboos and the Kentucky Fried Chicken? One block further is the Ruwi roundabout. Keep going after that to Qaboos Street headed toward the airport. The museum isn't far; just four more blocks. Take a taxi and when the driver asks you, '*Injaj?*' say yes, so he'll know you don't want him to take other riders."

"What was that word?"

He laughed. "It's our version of the English word 'engaged.'"

"All right. See you in half an hour."

The taxi let me out—after my exclusive, *injaj* ride—in front of a scruffy building. I entered a wide hall with a statue of an antique sailboat on display at the front, while on the walls on either side posters hung showing the historical evolution of the region. Ancient pottery, storage chests, decorative plates, clothing, and arms filled out a timeline stretching all the way back to prehistory. The display convinced me that the first steps of civilization had been taken here and that Oman was probably the gateway through which the first human had passed.

Coming from central Africa to Asia?

Is this reality or an exaggeration?

The display documented the desertification of the Arabian peninsula in ancient times, with many of its tribes migrating to Oman as a result. After the Maarib dam collapsed, the Azd tribe from Yemen also migrated over. The leader Malik Ibn Fahm established a powerful kingdom, probably the first Arabic kingdom in human history. The kingdom had stood tall for some time already when the Prophet sent Amr Ibn al-As with a personal letter, calling its people to Islam. The Prophet's call was accepted.

This historic document was preserved in a sealed glass case, and its inscriptions, produced by a companion of the Prophet, appeared like talismans. The one thing that was clear was the Prophet's seal: Muhammad is the Prophet of God.

In no time, a half hour had passed without my mysterious caller showing himself, so I walked outside. I was standing on the sidewalk looking around for a taxi when a dark blue Japanese sedan pulled up directly in front of me. The driver was a short man in traditional dress, his face clean-shaven and dark, with African features. He leaned over to the passenger side door and opened it, then gestured for me to sit, saying, "If you please."

Although I recognized his voice, I didn't move. He smiled, flashing bright white teeth. "I apologize for being late yet again. Please come along."

"Where to?"

"We are not going anyplace in particular. Just going for a drive, so we can talk." Seeing my hesitation, he added: "Don't worry. Nothing will happen to you."

I got in the passenger's seat. By then, it was automatic for me to pull the seat belt across my chest. As he shot out recklessly into the traffic, he said: "At least my tardiness gave you a chance to learn about the history of Oman." He drove out to Qaboos Street and headed off in the opposite direction from where he had come as he continued talking. "There is something strange and particular about this history. Maybe it's because of the location. We've always been desired by foreign powers."

Aren't we all?

"More importantly, our weak local leaders always aligned with foreign powers against their rivals at home, even against their fellow Arabs. One partnered with the Persians and occupied the land. That was a long time ago. More recently, the Qassem tribe of Ras al-Khima became a maritime power. The Sultan al-Sayyed Said feared them, so he made an alliance with the French, then the British, then finally the new rising power: the USA. He made a pact with them in 1833 and tried to confederate with them to occupy the port of Mombasa."

He paused while stopped at a traffic light, but soon picked up again. "Another characteristic is all the patricide. The son of al-Sayyed Said and his Caliph, whose name was Thuwainy, imposed a tax that bred resentment. The grumbling increased, and eventually the opposition recruited to their side his oldest son, Salem. The son went to the father in the afternoon as he was resting in bed by himself. Salem asked his father to cancel the excise tax, but the father held firm, explaining why the extra revenue was needed. The son felt he had no other choice but to pull out his loaded gun and shoot his father, and he killed him. . . . Did you see the portrait of Malik Ibn Fahm in the museum? Did you know that he, too, died by his son's hand?"

I had failed to pick up on this detail. He kept spinning the tale: "Legend has it that Malik's children took turns standing guard at night. The one he loved most was Salima, whom he had drilled in marksmanship from the time he was young. The father's love made the other children jealous, and they organized a plot to sabotage their brother's standing with the father by telling him that Salima was sleeping during his guard duty. What do you think Malik did? He decided to investigate their accusations himself. He snuck out in disguise and found Salima sleeping at the guard post on top of his mount. But the horse heard the king approaching and let out a whinny that startled Salima, who pulled out an arrow, drew his bow, and aimed it at the father. When Malik heard the arrow being released, he called out, 'My son, don't shoot! I'm your father.' And the son answered, 'Too late, O my father, the arrow has found its home.' This became a well-known saying. I'm sure you've heard it. The arrow hit Malik in the heart. He collapsed on the spot after muttering something that also became well known: 'I taught him marksmanship every day until his arm grew strong and he shot me.' Of course you've heard it."

A moving tale that invites interpretation and reflection.

"Life can't go on without the killing off of fathers," I said.

He shook his head, contemptuous. "Freud."

As we came to the first roundabout, he turned left. By then I was already mixed up. I noticed he couldn't stop looking in his rearview mirror at cars coming up behind us. I almost smiled. Surely the Sultan or his apparatus could find a way to observe him secretly, since Qaboos's modernizing project had to include the arts of surveillance and tracking.

"Shall we get to know one another?" I asked. "You know my name and telephone number and maybe much more. I, on the other hand, know nothing about you."

"I'm sorry I haven't mentioned my name," he said. "It's for the best. Besides, it's not important. I could tell you any name I wanted. You'll understand soon enough why I take precautions. I was close by yesterday, as I said, but I didn't dare speak. I wanted to make sure first that no one was following you. Same thing today. I have actually been watching for the past hour."

Remembering the Sultan's encyclopedia, I said to him, "Shall I call you Zayed, or would you prefer Amro?"

He laughed. "Zayed is better. It's more common around here. The only thing that really matters is for me to help you find your friend."

I was stunned. "What friend?"

"That old friend of yours that you're looking for . . . the one with the sister."

"But how did you know I'm looking for someone? How did you even know I'm here?"

"It's a small town," he laughed. "Nothing's hidden."

I wasn't sure what to say next. Finally I came out with, "Why do you want to help me?"

"I just feel like doing a good deed."

"Do you think that answer is good enough?"

"Of course not. Don't worry. I'll tell you everything. But first let me ask: when was the last time you saw this friend of yours, or his sister?"

I hesitated a moment, then said, "Thirty years ago in Cairo."

He studied me with interest as he said, "Isn't that strange? You are looking for someone you haven't seen in thirty years?"

Indeed strange, he's right.

"Do you remember his full name?"

"No."

"Doesn't the whole thing seem weird to you?"

"But you just said that names are meaningless."

We had been twisting and turning through side streets, but he still kept checking behind him. I realized that we were going back and forth across the main highway.

"What about the sister?"

"I haven't seen her or heard from her in all this time."

"What about now?"

"Well, I'd like to find her."

He examined me carefully. "What for? She could no longer be that same young student you knew."

I didn't answer at first. Then I said, "Maybe I'm looking for a topic to write about." He reached for the glove compartment, pulled out a plastic bag, and pushed it toward me. It was light and branded with the slogan United Colors of Benetton. I went to open it, but he stopped me. "Not now. Read it when you get home."

"Is this another magazine?"

He looked at me questioningly. "What do you mean?"

"Is it you that sent me a copy of *Voice of the Revolution* through the doorman?" I asked.

He let out a long whistle. "So they got to you already."

"They? Who do you mean?"

"You'll know everything once the time is right. Here you'll find copies of papers that will interest you. You'll even find your name mentioned. Read it. Then we'll meet and I'll explain everything." He added, "I needn't remind you not to let this fall into the hands of the authorities."

We had made it to the Ruwi roundabout, where he turned right. He dropped me off before the corner with the Kentucky Fried Chicken and, in an instant, shot off. I walked back toward the house swinging the bag on my arm, remembering the old days of the underground pamphlets. The cell's printing press had fallen into the hands of the authorities, so we rented a shed on top of the roof of one of the buildings around Al-Qobba. There, we set up our own makeshift printshop, advertising it with a couple of wooden placards shaped to the size of a magazine and covering one with a sheer cloth. Our first pamphlet announced support for Abdel Nasser upon his return from the Bandung Conference. It described his government as "righteous," a term that stirred up jokes for some time because of its Islamic connotations. It was up to us members to do the distribution, and we were always looking for ways to avoid surveillance. We collected grocery bags made from heavy paper, filled them with pamphlets, then carried them down the street hugging them to our chests like an office worker who has made the rounds to the green grocer and deli and is heading home at the end of the day. In those days, we had not yet discovered plain plastic bags, much less Benetton and its "colors."

I shook the bag in front of Jawhar's face, and he dropped in my daily beer. I put it in the cooler as soon as I walked in, then sat and opened up the bag. The two sets of papers in it each consisted of Xeroxed notes stapled on the side like a notebook. I flipped through them quickly and realized that I had in my possession diaries written out in a clear, bold hand, although the words were smeared and faded in some parts. Both sets had their dates printed in red ink on the front page. The smaller of the two was labeled with the years 1960 to 1965, so I decided to start with that one. The other set of papers I took into my room and hid in my suitcase.

It was still early, and I decided I had plenty of time to get some reading done before Shafiqa came home. At that time, the diaries would go back into hiding, for I had no doubt that what was in these notes would earn the censure of that rigid authority under whose dominion I now resided.

Chapter Five

September 5, 1960

I love this city. Is it because I feel free here? I still don't understand how Yaarib convinced Father to put aside his idea of marrying me to my cousin and let us both enroll in the American University with a $1,000-per-year allowance. He must have played on his conscience. Either that or he talked him into it while Father's mind was wandering, because when that happens he can forget we exist. I imagine part of him is happy to not have to think of us for several years. His new wife is younger than I am.

September 6

I have moved into the girls dormitory. Yaarib is sharing a flat nearby with two roommates, an Iraqi and a Bahraini. They each pay 300 lira per month.

My roommate's name is Mai. Her Arabic is weak, even though she is the daughter of a well-known Lebanese writer, who lives in the mountains and never leaves his house.

We took a twenty-minute walk to the Alhamra area and sat at a cafe called Elissar on Bliss Street. Students nicknamed it *al-yissar*. I had to explain to Mai that the nickname means "the leftist" in Arabic. We had dinner in a restaurant called Faisal. We were a big group, including students from Afghanistan, Ethiopia, and England, not to mention all the Arabs. Shehab tried to get me to go with him back to his place, but I had to get back to the dorm. We cannot come back any later than 8 P.M.

September 7

Beirut is both a hotbed of Western intelligence operations and a hub for revolutionary movements. Almost everyone is affiliated with some political group. I really love the classical coffeehouses around Alhamra, always full of large groups debating everything imaginable. There's a rich translation scene.

The poetry of Nazim Hikmet and Mayakovsky. Rock music and Elvis Presley. Films of Truffaut and Godard. Cairo, although so enormous, is a village in comparison. The Lebanese comrades have a greater consciousness when it comes to equality between women and men.

September 9

Shehab introduced us to one of his comrades. We organized ourselves into a cell directed by a Lebanese woman, also a student, living in a tall building on Alhamra Street. In spite of the group's democratic spirit, we maintain total secrecy. Many comrades come from rich families that own big companies and drive fancy cars. The university's organization calls itself "the union."

September 10

Shehab showed me the pool hall where the first meetings of the Movement of Arab Nationalists were held, among lots of flags and swords, after the 1948 disaster. Most of them were students who wore black shirts wherever they went and practiced strange rituals to control themselves and become pure. They opposed Marxism and communism. Bands of guerrillas were organized out of that group, and it included young men who later became well known, like Jihad Dhahy and Constantine Zurayq. Later, the Palestinian George Habash broke away to form a group called the Young Arab Nationalists, made up of students at the American University, like the Palestinian Wadie Haddad, the Kuwaiti Ahmad al-Khatib, the Syrian Hani al-Hindi, and the Iraqi Hamid al-Jabori.

Details have come out regarding the killing of Shuhdy Attiya, the imprisoned leader of the Egyptian Communist party, one of the first communists to be thrown in jail back in the time of the monarchy. He was beaten to death. Apparently, he was calling out pro-Nasser slogans even as they tortured him. Here, the movement seems to accept the purge of communists in Egypt. I wonder what is happening now to Rushdy. I have not heard a thing of him since they began to round people up at dawn on the first of last year. The struggle between Qasim and Nasser goes on.

September 11

The streetcar reminds me of Cairo. Two open-air cars like the ones in Sayyida Zainab. Two classes: *primo*, with cushioned seats, and *secondo*, with wooden ones. I rode it from Bliss Street to the end of the line in Ras Beirut.

I bought new high-heeled shoes from a shop on Souk al-Tawila Street.

September 12

The film *Psycho* by Hitchcock. Fascinating. I also want to see Fellini's *La Dolce Vita*. Mai and I went swimming at the beach in front of the campus.

September 15

Yaarib has decided to buy a transistor radio. We will try to send one to Father.

September 19

A visit to Place al-Burj. It's like a souk with prostitutes for sale. They have to receive work permits from the government and health cards. Between 5 and 20 Lebanese lira. There's a police station right at the entrance. Posters are lit up in red: Marika, Sonia, Firecracker. Alhamra Street itself has prostitutes that you can order over the telephone. We must liberate women from the need to sell their bodies.

September 22

We organized a large protest in support of the struggle of the Algerian people. As we passed by Joan of Arc Street, we covered the street sign with a new one that names Djamila Bouhired, the courageous woman leader in the Algerian resistance.

September 30

People do not understand existentialism correctly. The existentialist is to them a bohemian without morals or values. But the essential point in Sartre's philosophy is the individual's responsibility to himself and to society for his actions. I am impressed by his principled stances. He lives with Simone de Beauvoir in a free relationship that strikes at the heart of the whole institution of bourgeois marriage, including childbearing. They agree that the love that binds them should not tie down the freedom of either of them, including freedom to pursue other relationships. Indeed, no one owns the body or the soul of anyone else.

October 1

A horrid event in the building where Yaarib lives: the guard killed his sister when he found out she was pregnant outside of wedlock.

October 7

When I told a Lebanese comrade how much I admired Lebanon's economic miracle, he explained that the phenomenon is artificial, since the Lebanese economy depends not on productive sectors but rather on its services to the tourism sector or on financial instruments — including transfers to foreign banks — that are offered to neighboring countries. Also, this so-called economic miracle only benefits about 4% of the populace, who also control a third of the country's income.

Yaarib said that the Lebanese press has freedom and stands up for nationalism. Our Lebanese comrade laughed and said that most of the national press is bankrolled by the Egyptian embassy, and the others are all financed by either the petrodollar sheikhs or foreign secret services.

October 12

We have decided to boycott American-made cigarettes in protest of US imperialist politics and the relationship of US companies to the apartheid regime in South Africa. We've switched over to Bafra, a Lebanese cigarette.

October 30

There must be twenty factions in Lebanon . . . I don't see how they can coexist.

The woman who had organized it asked us to attend an important symposium on Arab unity at the Arab Cultural Club. They gave the microphone to a young man. At first he spoke softly, but then his words came out like an avalanche. He focused on the need to subordinate oneself for the sake of service to the nation and Pan-Arabism. He lit us on fire. When he pumped his fist, the group went wild.

November 4

I asked the organizer of the symposium for the name of the speaker. She refused to tell me because she said they were a secret cell. Shehab told me it was George Habash himself! I couldn't believe I had seen him with my own eyes.

I have transferred out of medicine over to the College of Social Sciences, which includes politics, economics, and philosophy.

November 18

The Arab man is a strange being. I was the one at first who decided to assert my freedom. He was the one who seemed reluctant. I was excited by the carnal urge in his eyes when he gazed at my naked body. But then I didn't enjoy it as much as I expected to. Although I didn't feel pain. Still, I really enjoyed it more in Cairo when we stopped at kisses. Afterward, he started apologizing to me. Why? I didn't get it. Then he started saying that he was ready to marry me right away . . . as though he had violated me and owed me something in return. I laughed.

I studied myself in the mirror for a while—nothing different. I have never been comfortable with my looks. My shoulders are too wide. My breasts are too big too.

I think all the time about our apartment in Cairo, and Rushdy, who was always looking at me all dazzled. He never had the nerve to tell me his feelings. He was also a strange one.

I read a novel by Layla Baalbaki. Had not imagined I would find an Arab woman who wrote with such courage.

November 25

I still cannot enjoy it.

Last night, I came home late from Shehab's—by the time I made it back to the dorm, it was nine. The administration decided to forbid me from going out next weekend.

December 3

The American University is a center for vital cultural activity. There are many professors committed to nationalism: Yusuf Sayigh, Constantine Zurayq, Hana Battatu, Walid Khalidi. They do not hesitate to attack American foreign policy, right in front of the officers from its embassy who attend film screenings.

I discovered a very sensitive spot on my back. Whenever Shehab touches it, I completely melt. Competition for my breasts.

December 6

Yaarib's relationship with Shehab seems tense. Could this be because of me? I can't explain the way Yaarib is acting. Mai also doesn't care for Shehab.

December 28

Survived several tough days. My period was late. I became afraid of intercourse. Shehab doesn't like condoms, and neither do I. Read several books about it today and then explained to him the rhythm method.

January 1, 1961

New Year's party at the university. I danced to rock music with an English student in order to learn how. Shehab became angry, so I stopped. Danced with Mai instead.

January 25

Shehab and I argued about Um Kalthum's new song. I told him that she exemplifies feudalist aesthetics—that the music is reactionary and the lyrics meaningless. I piled it on. Told him his enjoyment of her contradicts his other commitments. Pretty sure I was trying to goad him. Something has changed in our relationship.

I read the novel *The Latin Quarter* by Suhayl Idriss. Fascinating.

February 13

They have assassinated Lumumba . . .

We discussed our relationship. He reassured me that he loves me. He never says much about his childhood, though he loves to talk about himself.

. . . Will the Arab foreign ministers be able to back up their stand and stop Israel from redirecting the waters of the Jordan?

February 22

We gathered to celebrate the anniversary of the unification of Egypt and Syria. Different factions started to fight with each other. Military forces came and arrested us. They released us at the end of the day.

The movement needs monetary support. We decided to cut down on spending. No one's expenses should exceed 200 lira per month. I suggested we save money by wearing cheap jeans. Shehab and Yaarib refused, saying they were not respectable.

February 28

Fought once again with Shehab. He bought black shoes to get ready for the winter season, even though he had gray winter shoes from last year and two other pair of light-colored summer shoes. It would have been nice if he had donated the money he spent on the new shoes to the movement. He said that gray shoes are inappropriate for the winter. I accused him of lack of commitment.

March 1

Week packed full of meetings and demonstrations in Beirut, Tripoli, and Sidon.

We visited camps full of Palestinian refugees. I volunteered with some of the other women in the movement to teach English in their schools.

March 2

Yesterday was a historic day. We were together. He was in a sweet mood after several drinks. I even drank a bit myself, though I normally don't enjoy it. I got on top and he gave himself up to me. I felt a wild, new pleasure. He whispered that he was my servant. Suddenly, I was adrift. I no longer knew where I was. I think I lost consciousness for several seconds. That part I didn't like. It reminded me of the one time in my life when I was drunk and lost my self-control.

April 2

He refuses to be underneath me. Insists on being on top. Because I reminded him of the need to hold onto his manliness? As for me, I don't get much out of being fastened between his strong arms. I enjoy it more on top.

April 12

A great victory for humanity! Gagarin has circled the earth in an hour and 48 minutes.

The movement has nominated Yaarib for a leadership position.

April 19

The Cuban revolution remains strong and solid. The American landing in the Bay of Pigs has failed.

May

I have had my first birthday as a total woman.

I rejected Yaarib's idea of spending the summer in Yemen. I was afraid that we might not be able to get back out, for whatever reason. Father could change his mind or the king could issue a decree forbidding travel. Mai invited me to spend the summer at her father's house.

I think Yaarib has a crush on Randa.

June

An anonymous letter warning Yaarib to stay away from Randa. I suspect it is from her family, which is Christian.

We celebrated the announcement of Kuwaiti independence and the end of the British protectorate.

July 1

Kuwait has called for British protection after Iraqi threats.

Training drills in the Lebanese hills of Sofar. They nominated me as a member of the Thought and Ideas Committee. Yaarib has been demoted to a regional cell because of his conduct: blatantly pursuing a love affair.

July 5

Abdel Nasser calls for the withdrawal of British forces from Kuwait.

July 18

Randa forbidden from seeing Yaarib.

July 20

Nasser's nationalizations create confusion and raise questions. Shehab says that it's the logical next step in a program to reassign foreign capital and dedicate it to national development.

I am writing this from paradise. Mai's house in Chtaura. Shehab is in Amman visiting family. I feel like his view of me has changed because of what happened between us. Although he pretends to support equality between the sexes, he cannot overcome the effects on his mind of centuries of tradition. Jealousy devours him and he suspects that I'm ready to surrender myself to any man, the way I did with him. I think his respect for me has taken a hit.

I read Sartre's new book, *Critique of Dialectical Reason*—an attempt to join together existentialism and Marxism. He argues that the ideology that sets out to defend whichever social class has the potential to revolutionize society at a given time ends up being the most important philosophy of that time. It has to be a dynamic philosophy specifically for its time, and for that reason, Marxism can be recognized as the philosophy of the twentieth century. Marx has said that development takes place dialectically and that it is both cyclical and linear. The cyclical sense is the perpetual struggle, but there is also the linear—or progressive—movement. Struggle is the most prominent characteristic for development, historical change, and dialectical progress. It is what prevents stagnation. At the same time, Sartre rejects the Marxist principle of historical determinism because it contradicts the dialectical nature of history.

July 29

The first Arab nuclear reactor in Egypt.

August

I didn't think Yaarib would be so weak. He cries all the time since Randa left him. That's even though it doesn't seem like his feelings for her were that strong.

September 14

A new quarrel with Shehab. Ever since he came back from Jordan he has bombarded me with questions. If he sees me exchange hellos with someone, he asks: How do you know him? Has he kissed you? Has he slept with you?

September 28

Egyptian-Syrian unification has collapsed, brought down by factionalists.

October

Wide-ranging discussions around the goals and priorities of the revolution. Which is more important: unity, freedom, or socialism? Severe disagreements and divisions.

My underwear keeps disappearing. I have no idea how.

November 1

Rents have been lowered in Egypt.

November 10

I have discovered that Mai has been stealing my undergarments over and over and then wearing them. I confronted her with proof and she cried. She said she loves me. I did not know how to answer. Finally, I told her that I loved her as well, but not in that way. She begged me not to tell anyone.

November 28

There is tension in our room. She avoids me. She does all her studying in the common area. Should I move to a different room?

December

Just as Djamila Bouhired is the woman who fought for liberation in Algeria, I want to be the woman who liberates the Arabian Peninsula.

Two amazing films: *Last Year at Marienbad* by Alain Resnais and *Wise Guys* by Claude Chabrol.

January 3, 1962

She did not come to the New Year's party. She went to her house and stayed there for several days. She has been curt with me since she came back. Has she started to hate me?

February

We almost can't speak to each other.

I read a summary of Karl Marx's book *Das Kapital*. He affirms the inevitability of the collapse of the capitalist system and the transition to socialism in its role as the ultimate consequence of capitalist oppression. The capitalist system is nothing more than a system of class exploitation imposed by the bourgeoisie. At the same time, it produces the class that is able to place limits on the system and eventually end exploitation: the proletariat. This class does not control the means of production, so it only produces through the sale of its labor as a commodity that contributes surplus value to the wealth of the capitalist. I found the concept of "surplus value" hard to understand, but then I realized that neither Yaarib nor Shehab understood it either.

Amad explained it to me: "surplus value" is the difference between what the worker receives as wages and what he produces as value, since of course he could never receive something equal to what he produced. Only the dialectical materialist method allows one to divine these laws of capitalism, for it's the one method that can study the phenomenon as an objective reality independent of an individual consciousness or personal interest. Only such a study allows a full view of its movements, contradictions, and manifestations. He gave me Henri Lefebvre's books on Marxism. Amad is very well read because he writes poetry, and he seems to be a communist. Shehab makes fun of his big nose and the pimples on his face. Jealousy?

March 1

I meet with Amad often these days. He's also often hanging around outside the dorm as I go out.

March 9

I made a date to meet Amad in front of the campus. I was delayed three hours, but when I came out I found him still standing there waiting for me. It gave me a rush.

March 17

Castro brought the communists into a unified party and then launched a violent crackdown on them.

May 2

For the first time, Cairo is celebrating May Day with the rest of the world.
I had my birthday party at Shehab's. By the time everyone left, he was drunk. He ripped my clothes. I saw a strange look in his eye that frightened me. I tried to push him off me, but he held me by force. For the first time, he enjoyed it completely alone . . . I totally disengaged.

June

Shehab has decided to stay with me in Beirut this summer.

July

Comrade Samer has taken charge of our group. Very serious personality. Skilled presenter of ideas. Not unattractive.
The revolution has triumphed in Algiers. Independence has been announced after 132 years of imperialism.

What Engels calls the dialectic is the science of the general laws for the movement, for natural development, for human society, and for thought. No thing or phenomenon in the world is permanently fixed. The dialectical approach examines the world in its movement, with attention to change, and its permanent development. The old fades away and constantly leaves the new in its place. What is meant by the new is the progressive ideal. Greater mastery and power over life. That which constantly develops and evolves and comes to fruition as an inevitable response to the demands of political economy.

The basic laws of dialectical materialism:

1. The law of synthesis and the struggle between contradictions. In every phenomenon there are contradictory aspects that contend with each other in constant struggle. This struggle is the primary engine of development.

2. The law of transformation from quantitative change to qualitative change. The world changes through upheaval and revolution.

3. The law of negating the negation. The progressive structure is like an evolutionary spiral. It must dismiss the form of its previous existence while at the same time preserving what is positive in the preexisting form.

The dialectic is a method of complete interdependence between things and developments. It is necessary to comprehend every development—as Lenin says—and to study each of its aspects and interrelationships.

September 7

Mai has chosen another room. An American student is living with me now. She has a crush on a Kurdish boy.

September 26

A historic day. What a world we are living in! The revolution in Yemen has begun. The Imam and the family of Hamid al-Din have gone into exile. I only wish I were actually there to hug Sallal, the champion of the revolution. I almost agreed to Yaarib's idea that we travel to Sana, but I was afraid that Father wouldn't let me come back to Beirut.

I saw the Imam Ahmad once in Taiz. He was always there. He was wearing a red shirt and a white turban with two pendants hanging from it to identify him as the Imam. He wore blue eye shadow and his beard was died black. He had this ferocious smile that showed his gold teeth. He was sitting around with two of his four wives and they were playing with an electric train set. If an engineer is summoned to Taiz, it can only be to fix the train set of his Majesty.

The strange thing is that the people believed in his supernatural powers. There exist people who swear they have seen him throw his staff on the ground and change it into a serpent. Some said that he retired to his room some nights, turned out all the lights, gathered all the djinn in the area, and gave them his marching orders. He and his family—and the whole class of Zaidi sharifs—are responsible for Yemen's backwardness and for its isolation from the world. Since the end of the ninth century, they've occupied the seat of the Imam, with each new Imam killing off the one before him, only to be assassinated in a revenge killing on behalf of the previous one by the one to follow.

November 12

Five Saudi pilots have defected to Cairo, taking their planes with them. Refused to bomb the forces of revolution in Yemen. Two Jordanian pilots followed their lead; then the head of the Jordanian air force himself. The nationalist forces move gradually toward victory.

November 22

A stunning surprise. I went to a meeting at comrade Samer's house. He met me in his pajamas and I realized he was alone. He said he had told the others that the meeting was postponed. When I asked him why he hadn't let me know, he said he wanted us to discuss a personal matter. He asked me about my relationship with Shehab, calling him immature. Then he said these exact words: "How do you feel about having sex with me?"

I looked at him in shock. I had never thought that I might be the object of his desire. He has a charismatic personality, and all the women have crushes on him. In fact, I'd had a crush on him. But once I processed what was happening, I felt insulted. He remarked with this twisted smile that he knew how to make me happy, that I would experience total pleasure, and that women always had a good time with him. He was going to show me things that my Jordanian boyfriend could not. I thought about leaving, but then I changed my mind. I took off all my clothes and stripped away my stockings and panties. I lay across the couch and quietly said, "Help yourself." He looked confused for a second, but then took off his clothes and came to me. I held my frozen look on him while he tried to do it. Of course, he couldn't do anything since I was so dry. Suddenly, he came onto my bare thighs. I said while I was putting my clothes on, "I didn't enjoy it. Did you?" He didn't answer, so I said, "Wouldn't it have been better to just bring home a prostitute from Place al-Burj? You might have had a better time."

December 3

Samer disappeared completely, and the group came to our meeting with a different comrade in his place. I didn't utter a word.

Consideration of forming a committee responsible for activity in Oman. Comrade Ahmad Ali (his movement name) met with us. He's an Omani from our same region, Jebel Akhdar. His family are farm workers. Here, he involved himself in a broad set of activities with peasants on the Akkar coastal area in the north. He had trouble speaking, stuttering most of the time. There's a new movement in a highland area located between Oman and Yemen called Dhofar. A group was formed called the Dhofari Benevolent Society. Egyptian or Saudi intelligence forces might have been behind it. Its members are collecting money, using the ruse that they are building mosques and helping the poor. Their real goal is to organize armed resistance to oppose the Sultan of Oman.

For the first time, Shehab, Yaarib, and I all agree on something. We came together over the understanding that the pact that Nasser agreed to placed our movement at a crossroads. The old slogan "Blood, iron, fire — Unity, liberation, revolution" no longer goes along with our times and their events. Amad speaks with admiration about George Habash and his socialist tendencies.

The National Front for the Liberation of Occupied Southern Yemen has been formed out of a group of secret organizations. Qahtan al-Shaaby organized it from some workers returning from the Gulf plus students, teachers, and workers at the British base in Aden.

January '63

The Saudi reactionaries fear the influence of a revolution in Yemen, so they are trying to suppress it. Nasser proved he is a real nationalist by sending 30,000 troops to help the rebels. We learned that the Dhofari Benevolent Society was formed by Muslim Ibn Nofel, a sheikh from the Dhofari village tribe called Qarra, who had escaped to Saudi the year before. It's a revolutionary separatist movement and its slogan is "Dhofar for the Dhofaris."

February 8

Abdel Karim Qasim is dead, killed in a military coup. Could Nasser be behind it?

The Egyptian secret service started a new front opposed to the nationalist front in Aden. They have called it the Liberation Front.

This must be faced up to: I no longer enjoy myself with Shehab. Our fights are ongoing and about all things. If I say east, he says west. He's always trying to establish his strong character. Then there's his severe jealousy, spoiling my life. He's asked me to stop meeting Amad. I told him it was not his right to infringe on my freedom to meet whosoever I wish. Had I ever told him that there was anyone he couldn't meet?

I am tired of this.

February 25

There's a Baathist struggle in Baghdad between Ali Salih al-Saadi and al-Bakr. The latter is relying on the help of Saddam Hussein, who's known by the name the ready-made executioner.

March

Fatah is branching out. We had critiqued its isolationist tendencies in our pamphlets.

May

Decision by student elements to enter the popular movement. We laid out a plan to conscript circles in Shiyah and in the Palestinian refugee camps.

August

Nationalizations are ongoing in Egypt . . .

Mohsin Ibrahim and *Al-Hurriya* magazine are calling for all to commit to Nasserism and help build Arab socialism. A struggle within the leadership. There's a new spirit among us. Class issues are on the table.

October 14

The armed struggle has broken out in southern Yemen under the leadership of the National Front. The tribes of Ben Rajih and Ben Ghalib fought next to Egyptian forces in the north. When they went home to the Radfan Hills, the British forces cut them off and demanded they surrender their weapons, but they kept up the fight until the tribal sheikh died in the fighting. That lit the first spark. The National Front transformed the revolt into an armed revolution and opened multiple fronts in the south.

Faisal Abdellatif al-Shaaby and a number of others from the leadership of the Front were not too zealous about armed struggle. They preferred a political resistance that calls for the right of the poor tribes in the southern region to represent themselves and supports their aspirations for a good life and self-reliance. Naturally Faisal would take that position, considering he was a minister in the government appointed by the British.

November 18

The Baathist regime in Iraq has fallen. Coup d'état by Abdel Salam Arif with support from our movement and the Nasserists.

December

I have asked to be sent to Aden to participate in the armed struggle.
The film *Tom Jones* by Tony Richardson is amazing.
Three meetings in one week. I have taken responsibility for the cells in the Lebanese University. Also the branch at Alexandria University.

January '64

We celebrated the new year in a mansion owned by the father of a comrade. Shehab danced for a long time with a Lebanese journalist called Nahla. A white woman, with full lips.
The Syrian Baath party publicly released a clarification of its use of Marxism as its foundation. They have started talking about the "Arab path to socialism." Used to be just "Arab socialism." A military bloc formed there made up of Umran, Salah Jadid, al-Assad, and Abdelkarim al-Jindy.

February

Read an article by Nahla in a fluffy weekly magazine.

March 23

Abdel Hakim Amer appointed vice-president by Nasser. Could this be a silent coup? Some claim he represents the progressive camp in the Egyptian government.

April 14

I participated in a conference of the Movement of Arab Nationalists. Comrade Samer was there, but he ignored me. A group came from the Aden National Front, with Qahtan al-Shaaby as their leader. It's clear now that there are two distinct camps. The Lebanese are true revolutionaries. They raised the issue of social class and gave the class struggle in the Arab world prominence. Stressed the issue of the petite bourgeoisie. They called for a people's war to liberate Palestine and emphasized the need to apply the concepts of scientific socialism creatively. The leadership forced the orthodox revolutionary position on the rest of the conference. One of them told us with some bitterness, "Nasser stole the ground we stood on from under us, especially after all the nationalizations. Everyone's competing now to get to his left."

April 17

Comrade Qahtan al-Shaaby had a private meeting with us (attended by comrade Samer) to go over in detail the experience of the armed struggle in southern Yemen. It was tough at first. Aden has the shape of a small peninsula or bottle neck, so a not very big force was able to easily take control and secure its ports. The English countered by surrounding it with checkpoints and setting up a barbed-wire perimeter. Our forces had not been trained in urban warfare. They imported some weaponry using camels that were bringing in grain and vegetables. From inside, the fighters made plastic bombs. After a few months of round-the-clock agitation, they started to throw hand grenades and fire bazookas at the houses and clubs of the British officers.

He described a mortar attack on a military airport. As they were going back, an attack helicopter started to chase them and they fired back with assault rifles before they ducked for cover in some side streets. The helicopter came down very low, but even so they managed to hide, even with heavy weapons.

I knew that Samer was Yemeni, but I hadn't realized he was connected to the armed struggle. I listened to him in disbelief as he told how he led an assault in the Tawahi district, where the British had their high command for the Middle East. They climbed a hill that overlooks the British broadcasting station and fired a bazooka. It destroyed the building and killed a number of British soldiers. Then they walked back into town by cutting through the hills and met people in the streets to see what the popular response had been.

As he spoke, he glanced at me from time to time with this smile of proud disdain.

April 18

The two groups came to a compromise agreement that mixed their ideologies. The conference was considered a stage in the process of building an Arab socialist movement united under the leadership of Abdel Nasser.

The release of communists from Egyptian jails has started.

April 19

Something weird happened. A communist prisoner killed one of the guards at a desert camp for political prisoners in Egypt. Is this an attempt by some party or other to start a new conflict between Nasser and the communists?

I wonder what has become of Rushdy . . .

May 1

I am thinking so much of Cairo and our house there in Agouza. The late-night gatherings with friends. The visits of Shehab, also.

May 20

Release of all communists imprisoned in Cairo over the last five years. They were all let go just days before Khrushchev arrived to attend the christening of the completion of the first stage of the Nile High Dam. Khrushchev's remarks fueled more debates here. He praised Egypt's path of development without capitalism. The Nasserists consider his statement the final nail in the coffin of regional communism. The right sees it as new evidence that Nasser is throwing himself into the embrace of global communism.

June

We celebrated my graduating with high honors. I had my hair done at the salon. Shehab didn't invite me to his place as I expected.

July

Yaarib and Shehab joined forces against me twice: the first when they saw me wearing a miniskirt and the second when I decided to join an armed group. As always, I managed to overcome Yaarib's opposition.

Acrimony between Shehab and me.

August 3

Our group has 16 members. There are three other women besides me, a Lebanese and two Palestinians. We went for training at a remote farm in the Beqaa Valley.

The trainer is an old former military officer. He left the Jordanian army in 1957, after the Nabulsi government resigned; then he went on to set up a physical fitness school. Our training was harsh and arduous, demanding the utmost in discipline and endurance—an almost ascetic life. He trains us from sunrise to sunset and sets rigid schedules for going to bed and getting up. He saw me one morning carrying my toothbrush and towel on my way to our shared bathroom. He ordered me to go back, saying I had to get used to a life with no bathrooms or toothbrushes. We are learning marksmanship, map reading, camouflaging, silent movement, explosives manufacturing, hand grenade use, reconnaissance, and first aid—for broken legs and open wounds. We take long marches in all types of weather.

August 5

We trained on the Kalashnikov. Fires both individual shots and automatic bursts. An officer in the Soviet Red Army by the same name designed it in 1919. Amazing weapon. It rarely sticks, and a person could even throw it in the dirt and stand on top of it and it would keep firing.

The revolutionary fighter in an armed conflict: "He comes in like the whirlwind and destroys everything in his path. He has no mercy except under special circumstances. He kills if necessary, deals responsibly with the vanquished, and respects the dead. The wounded are sacrosanct and must be given medical attention. He doesn't take prisoners. He risks his life whenever necessary. He is bold, analyzing dangers and possibilities coldly. He displays sufficient capacity for adaptation and adjustment. He never leaves a wounded comrade to the mercy of the enemy, nor does he ever complain. He can bear all types of suffering, from thirst to deep wounds, and most of the time can suffer all the way through until the wound heals without any treatment, for he carries nothing beyond the barest necessities. He keeps ammunition dry and makes sure none of it is ever lost. He eats whenever and whatever he can, and can even go two or three days with no food. The sky is his ceiling, and between him and it there's never any more than a slip of nylon to guard against the rain." Che Guevara.

Guevara considered heroic behavior the norm. Anything short of that had to be rejected.

September 11

The Arab Summit decides to start work immediately on a project to divert the waters of the Jordan River and protect them with armed forces. The goal is to cut off Israel's path to control of its headwaters.

September 25

Comrade Samer showed up to give us our diplomas. He gave no sign that he knew me. When my turn came, he asked me to demonstrate how to crawl through the mud while carrying a rifle without getting it wet. I rolled around in the mud in front of him and then stood. I noticed something like a smile of victory on his face. He asked me, "What would you do if you suddenly found the enemy in front of you, but you had no time to point your weapon at him?" I said, "I would grab his throat with my bare hands." He smiled and said, "But your hands hold the weapon. I don't think you would be able to do anything. You're a woman. Come on. Let's see what you would try to do. Pretend I am the enemy." Without thinking, I raised my foot and planted it right between his legs with all the strength I had. He fell on the ground writhing, his hand covering the place I had kicked. I was so happy I could have danced.

September 26

I went to Shehab's house as soon as I arrived back in Beirut. He had left, even though I'd written to let him know what time I would get back. I wrote him a note.

September 28

We met. I went to his house. He pulled his clothes off the moment we got there. I did the same. What came next lacked any passion.

October 1

In Egypt, national health insurance has been put in place.

October 29

Tough endurance drills and political training: codes, radio signals, rules of covert operations.
I've devoted my life to the struggle for the liberation of humanity.

I read *Fontamara* by Silone, *Mother* by Gorky, and *The Knight of Hope* by Jorge Amado.

"The revolutionary devotes himself entirely to self-sacrifice without any recourse to consideration of the self, and he never engages in bravado, exposition, or exaggeration," Guevara says.

November 10

Explosions aimed at the British in Aden continue. Al-Asnaj has shown his true colors, taking the position that many countries achieved independence without war, including Zambia, Malawi, and Sudan.

November 27

I led a march in solidarity with the demonstrations in Cairo that set fire to the library of the US embassy. They were protesting the new round of American and Belgian military aggression in the Congo.

December 24

Nasser launched a blistering attack yesterday on the United States, responding to the attitude of its ambassador in a meeting with the Egyptian minister of resources. He said the Ambassador hopped in and announced in a threatening tone of voice that he refused to address any agenda items in the meeting because he did not like the behavior of the United Arab Republic. Nasser commented bluntly, "If they don't like our behavior, they can go to hell."

Levi Eshkol: "Israel considers water tantamount to the blood that runs in our veins, and we'll conduct ourselves on this basis."

So far, West Germany has given Israel reparations and grants worth 10 billion US dollars.

December 27

National Front guerrillas in Aden have assassinated an Arab officer working in the British secret service. The operation took place during the day in the crowded neighborhood of Kraytar. It was led by Abdelfattah Ismail (a former oil refinery worker who became a schoolteacher), Muhammad Salih Mutia, and Ali Salem al-Baidh.

The Dhofar Liberation Front has been formed. The leadership is a council of five working for the initiation of an armed struggle that is authorized by the Movement of Arab Nationalists based in Kuwait, the Dhofar Benevolent Society, and a secret group of Dhofari armed resisters. Muslim Ibn Nofel is the contact person between the Front and the tribes inside Oman. Egypt is pressing for unity between all parties as a condition for any aid and assistance.

December 28

Ben Bella tries to take control of the Algerian oil production that is still held by French companies.

Socialist textbooks in Africa by the Sudanese Communist party secretary Abdelkhaliq Mahjoub say that socialism can often be constructed without a socialist party and proclaim full support for Nasserism and its noncapitalist way. The Sudanese Communist party has come out into the open in the past month after operating in secret for eighteen years.

January '65

I confirmed my suspicions about Shehab. I spotted him yesterday sitting in Alhamra with Nehla, his hands wrapped around hers. When I confronted him today, he coldly answered that our relationship was an open one.

I didn't sleep.

January 5

The new Dhofar Front consists primarily of two elements: the Dhofaris who have migrated to the hills from the Gulf, and the local tribal herders with their long history of revolt against the Sultans of Muscat. The resentment of the latter against Sultan Said Bin Taymur spiked after the announcement that oil had been discovered in Dhofar. He became insistent that the locals would not benefit in any way from it, even issuing a law that forbade residents of Dhofar from working for any foreign oil company.

January 8

There is a substantial need for political and military work in Dhofar, especially among the women.

Dhofar's significance is that it is located at the edge of two-thirds of the West's reserves of crude oil. It suffers from a twofold exploitation, in that while Oman is under British hegemony, Dhofar is under Omani hegemony as well. The taxes: one goat per year for every five goats in possession; same for camels; one cow for every ten. The fisherman pays 120 riyals to the governor of the region for the right to fish during the high season, which lasts three months. Taxes on imports are 300% of what they are in the rest of the Sultanate.

America has gone crazy. Johnson issued orders for air attacks along the North Vietnam border. Vietnam's National Liberation Front now controls two-thirds of the area that makes up South Vietnam, waging a successful guerrilla war against that government, which is supported by the US and its 27,000 troops.

January 20

Shehab and I agreed to end our relationship. We will remain friends.

February 3

The discussions within the executive council of the Union of Egyptian Socialists around a working plan for political action really make you laugh. Abdel Hakim Amer is saying that the organization is the principal agent. Nurredin Turaf answers that the organization can't take action. Abdel Nasser takes the position that it only exists on paper. Hussein Khallaf then says, "So how can we do anything? If we want to act, we have to have people, and how can we gather people from paper?" Abdel Maguid Shadid admits that, just counting the main ones, there are as many as 7,000 cells and the problem is that their secretaries don't know what to do. Nasser is now saying that there has to be a socialist party inside the larger Socialist Union.

February 24

Amer announces that Egypt has lost 105 officers and 1,053 soldiers in its Yemeni operations. The cost of the operation was equal to three million pounds sterling over two years.

After his return from Cairo, comrade M told us that Abdel Nasser is underwriting a secret organization called the Vanguard Group. He said he felt the need for this group during the Tripartite Aggression in '56, when Cairo appeared vulnerable to foreign occupation, and started planning to put it together after the breakup of the union with Syria. He stipulates that in order to be a member of this advanced group, one may not own private property. That way, they can work toward the erasure of any differences in socioeconomic class. He also wants it to remain secret so that other groups can be watched over more efficiently.

Comrade M commented that from his meeting with Nasser he got the feeling that Nasser didn't really feel deep down a need for the group, since he has the ability to mobilize people and bring them into the streets merely by going on television and giving a speech. The proof of Nasser's superficial commitment was the way he imagined the role of the group, as he explained things to comrade M. He saw it as nothing more than a communications network that would mediate between leaders and base, bringing any information about the base—all its crises and problems—quickly, securely, and comprehensively, so that nothing could ever happen outside the view of the leadership.

March

Guevara is in Cairo. I wish I was there to meet him. I read an interview he did with a group of Egyptian intellectuals. He talked about the Cuban experience of uniting the five major revolutionary organizations, headed up by the group led by Castro, who had put in place a leadership that was from those petits bourgeois with revolutionary ties. There were two wings: the highlanders and the coastals. The highlanders talked about a revolutionary battle that depended on the peasant masses, while those from the coast talked about general strikes with revolutionary goals. In the end, it was the highlanders who managed to overthrow Batista and take power. The second force was the communists, who had long experience going back over forty years in revolutionary struggle. They had committed grave mistakes. They were isolated from the mass of the people as a result of being suppressed, so they were unable to spread the foundation of the revolutionary movement, and that meant they kept lagging behind the mass movement being led by Fidel Castro. This seemed to prove his legitimacy as leader. Guevara said, "We started working together, and we made a compact with Escalante, one of the communist leaders in the organization of the unified party. Of course, Escalante chose his forward comrades to run the directing centers, and many of them went on to direct institutions of production. Instead of forming a party of the avant-garde, they formed a party of administration, and Escalante supervised all authorities cavalierly, not allowing the formation of a national popular party. Again, his men made mistakes because they were isolated from the masses. They had been through so much during the struggle and then found themselves as heads of organizations enjoying all sorts of benefits— personal secretaries, Cadillacs, air conditioning. Out of this experience, the opportunist faction was exposed. Escalante had 17 telephones in his office. That didn't mean he was a traitor. He was a smart man with a revolutionary spirit. But he committed fatal errors, and he benefited from his position. He was neither a traitor nor a saint. Fidel resolved to review his position in March of '62, and at that point the new party was formed."

What struck me in all this was his definition of communism. During the interview he said, "Must one be an atheist, or can one be a believer? Is it possible to ask of him a normal amount of work, or must he work extra? Must one remain in the rear, or is it okay to take the lead in battle? Should we protect him, or may we send him to the front to face danger directly . . . These questions are still waiting for a final answer. But it is my opinion that he is the last to sleep, the last to eat, and the first to lay down his life for the cause."

April 1

Amad wrote a new poem. He says I inspired him. Even asked me to marry him while we sat under an oleander tree. What a romantic! I told him I was flattered and that he's a wonderful human being, but I wasn't ready to marry anyone, and that there are many other things I want to accomplish. Love is the last thing I'm thinking about at the moment. I don't want anything to tie me down at this stage of my life.

Amad is so tender, he's almost effeminate. I feel comfortable when we're together. But I'm not feeling attached to him.

April 5

Egypt's two main communist parties decided to disband their organizations and go forward as individuals to ask for membership in the Socialist Union, considering it the single revolutionary organization aligning itself with the popular working forces.

Saudi Sheikh Abdullah al-Tareeki is calling for the nationalization of the oil companies. Petroleum companies in the United States have increased profit levels at a rate of 7%. The rate is 18% in Venezuela, 81% in the Arab region. Aramco has achieved this level of profit from its Saudi operation since 1961.

April 7

Through an Iraqi comrade, we met a leftist journalist from Egypt who was passing through Lebanon. Yaarib wasn't excited about the meeting, saying that people cannot leave Egypt today unless they are close to either the authorities or the secret police. We talked about the current atmosphere. There are hidden power struggles going on at the top. We asked the journalist about the vanguard group and whether Haykal was representing the reactionary wing in his confrontation with Ali Sabry. What was Abdel Hakim Amer's stance toward the socialist transformation? He attacked the communists, saying they are a spent force with no vision for the future. He spoke very carefully and looked around while he talked. Later, the Iraqi comrade would explain to us that this fellow exemplified the "terrified Egyptian."

After half a bottle of arak, he relaxed and the conversation started to flow. We learned from him that the Egyptian vanguard group had been formed in a strange way. There are a few collaborators in whom Nasser has personal confidence, like Haykal, Ali Sabry, and Sami Sharaf. Each of these is responsible for the conscription of ten people in whom they in turn have confidence. These recruit ten more people, and so on. Abdel Nasser insisted that they had to do the recruiting outside the view of the secret police and the intelligence agencies. When we couldn't hide our surprise and disbelief, he laughed and said that he himself was a member of the organization. In fact, a number of journalists had become involved. He explained how a recruiter would make an appointment with one of them someplace isolated, then tell him there that he was a messenger from a group around President Abdel Nasser, that the president wanted him to know that he trusted him and that he wanted him to join a secret organization whose goal was to defend the gains of socialism. All the while, he's watching out for the gaze of the secret police and intelligence.

After a while longer, the knot in his tongue came completely undone. He told us Haykal had gotten together a group of people who worked at *Al-Ahram* newspaper, and Ahmad Fuad and Ahmad Hamroush had put together another group of former communists, who had moved away from political work at the beginning of the '50s in the face of a harsh police crackdown. They were coming back now to raise up their heads and satisfy their desire to join an organization like ones they had joined when they were young, but without being exposed to any real danger. It satisfied their need to feel important and soothed their tortured conscience. Made them feel they'd been right all along and had never really given up. Later, every minister formed a group of the bureaucrats below him in the chain of command: the minister, his general manager, and so forth. The sheikh of Al-Azhar formed a group with former members of the Muslim Brotherhood.

When we asked him about the story of the two communist parties that disbanded, he said they had come up with a clever scheme. They were told from the start that Abdel Nasser would go along with an organizational union between them and the vanguard group. So they, in fact, sketched out a plan to join together all the members of the three organizations. At the last moment, they were told to join the Socialist Union individually, without following through on joining the vanguard group. Then a small number that you could count on one hand was picked out, excluding all the workers. At the same time, the secret police started calling in the communists for questioning, asking them accusatory questions about their activities, and soliciting information from them about the vanguard group!

April 10

Something's going on with Guevara . . . The international press is talking about his disappearance . . . Could the CIA have assassinated him?

Last night, I dreamed that I was with Guevara, up in the mountains.

April 12

It's decided that we'll travel to Dhofar to initiate the armed struggle there.

Supplies required: oil, jars of preserves, condensed milk, sugar, salt, onion, garlic, coffee, and tea. Enough spoons, and knives with different types of blades. Grease to lubricate rifles, or maybe sewing machine oil as substitute. Cloth to keep the weapons polished at all times. Canteens. Medicines like penicillin, aspirin, tranquilizers, cold medicine, antidiarrheal pills, tablets for parasites, antidotes for poisonous venom, and first aid kits. Cigarettes, matches, and lighters. Radio batteries. Dishwashing soap. Books. Small benzene canisters to light a fire when the firewood is wet. Leg wax, if possible. A notebook or something to write in. A pen. Needle, thread, and extra buttons. String. Can't do without a blanket, because the nights in the hills can get very cold.

I hesitated over birth control pills, then decided to take them. How much should I take? Suddenly, it occurs to me that I don't know when I'll return or how long this mission will last. A year? Two?

I cut my hair and trimmed my nails. Goodbye to nail polish.

The future is ours.

I have to remember to bring Dramamine pills for sea sickness.

I have chosen a brand-new code name: Warda.

Chapter Six

After my *injaj* taxi dropped me in front of the Intercontinental, I walked past a young African woman in a blouse and skirt manning a small table, then turned into the hotel's open-air entrance hall, its floors stretching skyward, and went looking for the reception desk. A coffee waiter leaning on a pillow stood up and stopped me to offer a small brass tumbler of dark coffee. Taking a sip, I pressed on until catching sight of a young man in Omani robes who looked over at me with a big smile. His face seemed familiar. When I headed toward him I caught a good look at the card he held up: "Environment Ministry," it read. He told me to come along.

"Where to?" I asked.

He seemed annoyed. "Aren't you a participant in the conference?"

His smile broadened when he realized the mistake, and I left him without another word.

A glass elevator in the open reception area was slowly bringing down a European woman with puffed-out hair and a short skirt. Gradually, her bare thighs came into view in all their radiance: firm, toned, and nicely proportioned. I headed toward the side of the hall with the Al-Qorm restaurant in search of Mr. Glenn Miller, but I found it closed with a strictly evening and late-night schedule posted on its door, so I kept going toward the swimming pool. A collection of virtually nude bodies—European all, of course—were scattered about.

Oddly, this variety of bare thighs, leaving nothing to the imagination, captured not a bit of my attention. I was still under the spell of the firm, toned thighs covered halfway by the miniskirt. In fact, I didn't even notice when a woman came toward me calling out my name.

It was Julia. She was one of those foreigners that pass through Cairo regularly. They reside for periods of time on various pretexts—academic study, a journalistic investigation, participation in a conference—then suddenly disappear. But after a while, they always pop back up. Julia carried a Danish passport, and I had been with a writer friend when I met her. She had appeared at our door wearing an authentic gallabiya, stain covered, and carrying a baby over her shoulder. She slipped off her sandals at the door and walked in barefoot. We were mesmerized by her milky white skin, her blue eyes, her long frame, and her skill at both standard and colloquial Arabic. While we talked, her child started crying, so she took him to her chest and began to rock him gently. But he kept crying, so she undid the buttons on her gallabiya and extracted a round white breast like a ripe pear that she stuffed into the mouth of the child, continuing to talk without pausing or even moving her gaze off us, just as would a peasant selling vegetables at the souk.

Now, noticing small wrinkles around her eyes, I asked, "What brought you here?"

"What brings *you* here?"

She spoke with her glance averted—as she always had—adding that she had visited an old Jewish cemetery a mile and a half from the provincial capital Sohar, north of Muscat.

"Jews in Sohar!" I remarked with wonder.

"Wilstead documented the presence of twenty Jewish families in the area in the first decade of the nineteenth century," she said. "They seemed to be Iraqi Jews fleeing the repressive regime of Daoud Pasha, who governed Baghdad at the time."

"Are any of them still there?" I asked.

"No, not one. The only thing left is the graves. But I saw with my own eyes those Jewish names written on the stones: Moses, Joseph, Jacob—all written in Arabic." Then she pulled me by the arm and exclaimed: "Don't you want to be enlightened? Come along."

She led me to a ballroom with a banner over the entrance announcing an international conference to address the water crisis in the Middle East. It was a conference I had reluctantly considered attending. Now it had started without me. About thirty attendees were scattered around, facing a dais where several speakers sat, two wearing Omani dress and two Europeans, while a fifth had features suggesting he could be Egyptian.

I noticed the Saudi journalist sitting in the front row playing with the buttons on his small tape recorder. A speaker was presenting the various dimensions of the water problem in fluent English, and I picked up from his accent that he hailed from that erstwhile empire on which the sun was never supposed to have set.

"The Middle East is in need of twice as much water as is currently available in order to sustain its populace. The same is true of Egypt, which imports half the foodstuffs it needs for sustenance. Certainly, there is a crisis, but it has a simple solution in my opinion, to be found in buying up low-cost grains from the international market to be put in reserve. One needs a thousand tons of water to irrigate one ton of wheat, for example. Yet to transfer a ton of wheat is much easier than to transfer a ton of water."

The Saudi raised his hand to make a comment, but the English professor just smiled and went on: "Indeed, when countries like the Saudi kingdom decided to cultivate a surplus to hedge against price spikes, prices remained stable. There is too much emotion in our way of viewing this problem. Lebanon, for example, wants to benefit from the waters of the Litani River to develop its agricultural production. Israel, for its part, wants to purchase water from Lebanon. But the political situation causes an emotional response from Beirut, pushing it to think of ways to use access to water as a weapon. So it refuses to sell, even though to do so could benefit Lebanon economically, especially since international lenders look unfavorably on this type of protectionism and tend to withhold loans where they find such practices."

The Saudi gave up his effort to break in and sat silently. It struck me that no one was paying close attention, so that the English expert's mistakes were flying over all their heads. The proceedings dragged on quietly like this until the Egyptian presenter stood up and stunned the room by proposing a project to desalinize seawater that would cost several billion dollars, further suggesting that all countries in the region—including Israel—cooperate to bring it about. He understood the minefield he was navigating, otherwise he wouldn't have ended his talk by saying, "Cooperation—not political equality—will mark the road to regional peace."

An attendee with a Levantine accent responded with agitation: "The essential reason for the '67 war was Israel's decision to redirect the waters of the Litani. By the end of the war, the Israelis had increased by 25 percent the country's freshwater supply via the lands that it occupied. Now it proclaims ownership of not only the Litani but also the Jordan and Yarmouk—basically all of the water of its neighbors—and whenever there are peace negotiations, it asks that no one bring up what it calls 'past grievances,' meaning all the water it has taken by force. Now it wants to start discussions based on present circumstances." He stood quietly for a moment, catching his breath, then finished: "A half-century-long history with Israel leaves us no room for trust in agreements and cooperation. Instead, it persuades us that any joint projects need to be preceded by a just peace settlement, and not the other way around."

This declaration seemed to stoke the attendees. A young Omani stood up and proclaimed: "There is a bias in the region's distribution and consumption of its waters. The Israeli citizen consumes five times as much water as any individual living in a neighboring country, and the settlers in particular fill up their swimming pools with water stolen from neighboring Arab countries."

Another attendee stood up, announcing that he was a hydrogeologist who worked for the Egyptian Nuclear Energy Commission, and posed a question to the entire panel: "Israel obtained one billion square meters of underground water in Sinai worth two billion Egyptian pounds. It dug two hundred wells on the Egyptian border to withdraw a million square meters every day from the basin of Wadi Um Garad. What does international law have to say about that?"

A Dutch expert in international law volunteered a curt reply: "Israel has a need for more water than it controls in its lands."

This answer raised the temperature in the room, and the hands of attendees wanting to comment shot up everywhere. But the Omani organizers intervened to call a short break. Julia and I headed toward a table full of pastries and hot and cold drinks.

The Dutch professor, who knew Julia, caught up with us and, after she made introductions, said: "Egyptians are wise; they know how to stick to a sound policy."

I realized he was talking about the peace treaty, and I said, "You mean the Egyptian regime."

He thought for a moment before answering in a sagacious tone: "The condition for remaining historically relevant is to acknowledge reality on the ground. It's a basic law, about which Native Americans, for example, seemed unaware . . ."

I cut him off and asked, "Whoever plunders the land of another and continues to occupy it and refuses to . . ."

He waved a hand to halt me. "The reality on the ground is today in Israel's favor. If you can't accept that, you are unrealistic and not pragmatic and you have no place in history."

As I looked up at him, I imagined scraping off his fat, white skin that seemed full of racism. As though he'd been reading my mind, he turned to Julia and asked to exchange addresses. She pulled out a huge notebook filled with several pages of addresses and flipped through until she found an empty space to record his, then handed him her card as he headed away.

We filled our coffee cups and set them on the table. I asked her about her next projects, and she said, "What do you know about Sayf Ibn Dhi-Yazan?"

"I think he's one of the heroes of Yemeni folklore," I said.

She gave me a mischievous look and said, "Did you know that he was Jewish?"

"Good God! Maybe I'll find out tomorrow that I'm Jewish too," I said.

She laughed. "Here's the story: During the sixth century BCE, the Aksumite kingdom collapsed, and the Himyarite empire rose up in its place, lasting for ten centuries, all the way to the fifth century CE. When the Maarib dam collapsed, the last of their rulers imposed Judaism on the Christians who had been living side by side with the Jews and pagans. A civil war broke out during which the Christian community asked for help from their Abyssinian brethren. The latter managed to assert sovereignty for half a century, until Sayf Ibn Dhi-Yazan made an alliance with the king of Persia, soliciting help with the liberation of Yemeni land. The Persian armies descended on Aden, driving out the Abyssinian forces. The Persian king shared power with Sayf for a time, but then took control for himself."

"How does that prove that Sayf was Jewish?"

"What I'm interested in is, there could have been a Jewish state in southern Yemen at the beginning of the common era."

"If you could prove that, it would be catastrophic."

"Why?"

"Because Israel will turn around and demand that Yemen and Oman be annexed to the rest of its land."

She laughed. "That's a good one. Although I guess it's possible. Did you know that the Yemeni island of Socotra was discussed in 1939 as a possibility for establishment of the Jewish state instead of Palestine? Luckily, it didn't happen."

"Maybe lucky for the Yemenis, but not for the Palestinians," I said. "Maybe Egypt could demand the Kaaba shrine or the annexation of Saudi Arabia."

"How so?" she asked.

"There are those that say the family of the Prophet emigrated from Memphis in Egypt, which would make the Prophet a descendant of the Pharaohs."

"Okay. Why not?"

She suddenly stood and announced, "I feel all sticky. I'm going up for a shower."

"What about the conference?"

She slid her hand around my arm. "Come on. I want to talk."

I asked her about her child, and she answered that he was ten now, no longer a baby.

"Is he here with you?"

"No—with his father in London."

We took the glass elevator up to the third floor, and she led me toward her room with rapid steps after pulling the key out of her purse. There was something striking in her stature and bearing; her posture suggested a soldier at attention. Once she got the door open, she turned around and said, "Please come in."

"Ladies first."

She insisted I precede her and waited until I was all the way in before she followed and closed the door. When I turned to her, I noted her gaze surveying the room quickly. Then she stepped over to the bed, tossed her handbag down on it, and sat on its edge. She gestured toward the armchair, and I threw my briefcase on the floor and sat down.

"What would you like to drink?" she asked. "Scotch?"

"It's still early," I said.

"Do you care?" she responded. "Anyway, the minibar is there. I'm going in for a shower."

She opened her suitcase and closed it again quickly. Her eyes surveyed the room once more, then settled on the handbag. She bent over, took something out of it, and headed to the bathroom. I noted that she left the door ajar.

I stretched my legs and looked out the window through its parted curtains. She returned after a while wearing a white cashmere robe, a towel of the same material wrapped around her hair like a turban. She sat near me on the edge of the bed and asked me to light her a cigarette. She took a long drag off it, then put it in the ashtray, untied her turban, and began drying her hair with the towel.

"Tell me what you're really doing here," she said.

I couldn't control my laughter. Her robe was running up her leg to above her knees and my gaze had settled on her thighs, but when I raised it to her face I found her studying me intently. It was curiosity more than desire that spurred me to lay the palm of my hand on her knee, then gradually move it up without shifting my eyes from hers.

She put her hand over mine, wrapped her iron grip around it, and pulled it away as she said, "If you please."

I caught a hint of triumph in her stare, so I stood up and took hold of my briefcase, then said, "I have to go."

She crossed her legs, and the robe fell away completely. "Aren't you going to attend the rest of the conference?" she asked.

I answered on my way to the door: "I don't have time. How long will you be here?"

She threw the towel aside and answered, "A few days."

As I opened the door, I said, "Well, I'll see you again then. Ciao."

I headed down to the lobby. Looking around for the coffee shop, I spotted it off to the left of the entrance. It was empty except for a European man intently reading an English newspaper. I understood immediately why Fathy had suggested the place as a spot to be alone or to escape from Shafiqa, who was stuck back in the flat with a cold. I picked a place in a far corner and pulled from my briefcase the second set of diaries.

Chapter Seven

DHOFAR MOUNTAINS, 1965-1968

May 1, 1965

Everything happened with firm smoothness. The trip was tough, especially the part we made by car over unpaved roads. There were three comrades, plus Yaarib and myself. The Kuwaiti Ghazal, a Bahraini, another Omani. We took a motorboat from Basra, disembarking near Dubai after four days. I could hardly stand the ocean waves. Yaarib was even worse, vomiting the whole trip.

May 5

We stayed two days in Jebel Akhdar, then Ghazal and I left Yaarib, the Bahraini, and the Omani behind. A Dhofari comrade named Amar had joined us there. Serious and earnest. Seems very old, even though he's still in his twenties. He's the opposite of Ghazal. Gets excited easily but has a kind heart. Smokes like an oven, is always making wisecracks. We continued the trip along the road that takes the southern route from Nizwa to Salalah, stretching nearly a thousand miles. Getting into Salalah was hard because the main gate was well guarded. We managed the crossing with a herd of camels carrying firewood to disguise us. The roads were long and straight, lined by clusters of one-story mud-brick buildings. Then we came to a big clump of palm trees, a cluster of buildings, and finally, the prison. There was an English civilian there who, in a drunken haze, had run over a person with his car. The victim died and the foreigner was in jail waiting for the amount of blood money he owed the victim's family to be set. We each took refuge in a different house. I was given a room in the house of Amar's sister. She and her husband, a clerk in the city commissioner's office, support our struggle.

May 10

We met with two Dhofari comrades. Fahd, a 36-year-old army corporal, had been arrested after a failed assassination attempt on the Sultan. He pulled off a heroic escape from Al-Hisn prison. Stocky and quick-witted, at times to the point of devious. Sports a thick mustache that he keeps stroking. Never says much. I suspect that behind his sharpness and aggression lurks an extreme shyness, especially toward women. Rafie, 28, dark-skinned, African features. He was a slave.

I handed them the letters I had brought charging them with their duties and we divided up the money that had been donated. They unfolded a map and I bent over it. Its distances were marked in miles, which I had to convert to kilometers in order to get a better sense. Dhofar stretched out on the table before me: 230 km in length, or around 58,000 square km. It divides naturally into three provinces. The coastal region stretches up to the mountains over a distance of about 15 km. The hill country forms a crescent across the top of the coastal province and contains three large mountains: Samhan in the east, Al-Qamar in the west, and between them Al-Qarra, the tallest, with an elevation somewhere between 1,000 and 1,500 meters above sea level. The third region is Al-Nejd, a rock plateau in the interior that separates the mountains from the Empty Quarter that stretches into Saudi Arabia.

The population of the region is around 60,000, comprising three main groups. Bedouins roam in the desert area to the north. Their various tribes, like the Rawashid and the Awamer, are spread out up to the Empty Quarter. The highlanders herd livestock and grow crops during the rainy season. They actually descend from various ethnic groups, even though they are usually lumped together as highlanders. Most of them identify with one of three different tribal communities: the Qarra, the Mahra, and the Shahra. The third population is composed of the coastal peoples who subsist on herding, farming, fishing, and commerce.

The populace can also be divided into those that produce and those that live off the productivity of the others. The second group includes merchants, officials, and some of the more wealthy sheikhs. The working class is made up of the herdsmen, the slaves, the fishermen, the peasants, and the porters. Social classification is arranged along the same lines. The Saada are the elites, who say they have descended from the Prophet. After them come the more elite tribes, like Qarra and some of the Mahra. The other tribes are below these. The slaves are the bottom rung. Livestock ownership is more familial than individual but still plays an important role in the social hierarchy between the tribes. The structure is preserved through marriages within the same class.

Tribal relationships are what shape daily life here. These are complicated and very sensitive. At times, the stronger tribes act as protectors for weaker ones. This is how the Qarra treat the Shahra, for example. These relationships, in turn, have important economic effects. For example, the Mahra were able to acquire absolute water rights throughout the lands of the Bitarha tribe in exchange for a precious dagger and 11 goats! Or in another case, the Jannaba complain that the Harasis occupy their area. The tribal sheikhs act as mediators between the people and the authorities, even to the extent at times of acting as agents providing labor to the oil companies.

We agreed to divide the region so as to break up the traditional tribal divisions. Fahd will take responsibility for Jebel Samhan in the east, Ghazal the western area around Jebel al-Qamar, and I the middle region around Jebel al-Qarra. Rafie and Amar will stay in Salalah to supervise clandestine activities, replenish supplies and ammunition, and coordinate between the different sectors.

May 13

I dreamed last night that my body was soaring over Dhofar . . .

A woman in the mountains enjoys a position distinct from that of her sisters in the cities. She is able to hold on to a certain independence because she participates in production. Married women own livestock and inherit. They are able to obtain divorces more easily, and they can go on to remarry without it affecting their social standing. Travel is permitted without the consent of a guardian. Men participate in childrearing, and the society generally sees the roles of the two genders as less separate. There's no preference for marrying a cousin, nor do they fixate on virginity. Their customs are more like those of the Daham tribe in Yemen. There, if a wife places a piece of red cloth on the door of the home, she signals the need for privacy, and the husband would not dare to enter lest he bring shame on himself and his family.

Still, women are forbidden from going to school, and their first marriage—unlike later ones—is agreed to between the bride's father and the bridegroom. Marriages are also arranged between child brides and old men, and the practice of polygamy proliferates. So does radical clitoridectomy.

Spring runs from March 12 to June 21 and is called the hot season.

May 18

We lost the element of surprise. In an announcement to news agencies in Beirut, the politburo declared the start of armed struggle in Dhofar before we were prepared. An Iranian patrol intercepted one of our motorboats that was transferring weapons, men, and plans from Iraq. It delivered them to the British authorities in Muscat.

May 19

The authorities in Salalah captured forty fighters just arriving from Dubai. Another blow to us thanks to the double agent Said Ibn Jeej. He had picked up a weapons shipment for us in Saudi Arabia, but delivered it to the British intelligence service instead. He let them know that a car caravan was on its way from Saudi Arabia led by Muslim Ibn Nofel, and their attack planes bombed it.

Swelling in my breast. The usual signs. I hate the stickiness, having to change constantly . . . I wish I were a man.

I made a list of radio stations, the times of their news broadcasts, and their frequencies.

May 20

We snuck out to the mountains in darkness. A group of guerrillas met us and led us to the temporary camp. It has a big cave, large enough to house several men, and we camouflaged its entrance with tree branches. A little further on I found a smaller opening in the rocks that I set up for myself. I hung a curtain made of burlap over its entrance and put up a mirror. Set up my radio. Made a pillow out of straw.

I was surprised by all the frogs hopping around in the dry desert. I had a shock when I had just settled into my sleeping bag and one jumped right onto my chest. Their croaking makes it impossible to sleep. Around the standing water there are insects as big as tadpoles swimming around. Swarms of flies never stop. I spat, and one came out of my mouth. There are dozens of kinds of beetles, some really huge, like the kind that fly over the tents and the bathing areas until they wear themselves out and collapse. Black and red ants have a stinging bite. Giant wasps come out of nowhere and fly at your head. You have to duck to get away from them. There are spiders and scorpions too.

In the morning, I walked around on my own until I found just what I was looking for: at the edge of the valley, a small recess with a natural rock covering. I went back in the evening with my rifle and some newsprint. I stopped at the rock covering and had a shock when I looked inside the space: someone else had stolen my idea. I walked a little further, found another place, pulled down my pants, and squatted. Right then, I spotted a scorpion nearby. I clung tightly to my Armalite and looked around in fear, sure that I would be overtaken by either men or scorpions.

I met with Fahd and Rafie before they left us and agreed on how to stay in contact. I will be in charge of 25 fighters divided into five smaller groups. We have 20 rapid-fire Belgian rifles, 5 Russian Simonov semiautomatics, and a modest stash of ammunition.

While we were talking, I heard a strange voice. Fahd jumped up and ran to the corner. He bent down, then stood back up with a snake in his hand. It was almost half a meter long. He had grabbed it by the tail and its flat head dangled down. He lightly passed his hand down its body to its neck, then choked it to death. He looked at me with pride and said, "Here, our enemy is not Great Britain as much as it is the great serpent." Rafie was smiling as he pointed out that it was a type of rattlesnake indigenous to Africa. Moves slowly, but very deadly.

I was so frightened at night, I couldn't sleep. Decided to listen to the radio for a while. We get more than 30 different Arabic language stations: Peking, Sofia, Tirana, BBC, Voice of the Arabs, Voice of Oman (out of Cairo). I made notes on the headlines to use when I teach the politics class. Finally, I lit a fire and slept on top of my sleeping bag without taking off my boots. I imagined for some reason that my feet were most vulnerable, so I kept the boots on and slept with them close to the fire. The fire burned my boots.

May 21

I was the only one dressed in military fatigues. I ordered the unit to gather, and they fell in where I had commanded, dragging themselves without passion. I understood why they had on civilian clothes: most of them were poor young men who didn't even have a shirt to wear. Some wore nothing but a loincloth or a colored cloth skirt called a *mauz* that covered them from the waist to the ankles. They went barefoot. A few of them hung their weapon on their shoulder. Their faces were largely the same. A few had very dark, African complexions. Their yellow teeth were broken and worn down. My voice came out sounding feeble: "Attention." They looked at me, and I could tell some of them felt contempt. A few did adjust their stature, but still nowhere near the stance we had learned back in our Bekaa training camp. Some stared straight at my breasts trying to picture them, even though I was fully clothed in my uniform. I was, I thought, facing a crucial test that had to be confronted head on.

I gathered myself and said, in the most authoritative voice I could muster: "We are all members of a democratic organization we call the Dhofar Liberation Front, but from today forward all of you are also soldiers in the People's Liberation Army, and I am your leader." I hesitated for a moment, half expecting someone to talk back. No one said a word.

Encouraged, I raised my voice: "The Liberation Army is a force of free volunteers without rank, but each of you will execute what you are commanded to do to the letter. No one has the right to dispute his orders. The military way of life may be harsh, but it is also the one proven method for fashioning a fighting force and achieving victory."

After that, I talked of the political situation, the nature of our enemy, the balance of power, and I asked them: "Can we lose this war?" I assured them that we would win the war without a doubt, that defeat was impossible, that our destiny was already fixed. Either we would all die here, down to the last revolutionary, or we would conquer whatever stood in our way.

I explained that I was against acts of terrorism carried out impulsively, because they leave so many victims without bringing us any closer to achieving our revolution.

I ordered all who had experience with weapons and combat to step forward. Most of them jumped up. Only those without weapons held back. I surveyed what I was working with. I could tell by the way they carried their weapons which of them had real experience. Out of those, I chose the group leaders and called them to one side. Looking over the others, I tried to hide my anxiety, and hoped I could avoid staring at their bare chests.

There was a young black boy named Masrif, who was probably 12 at most. Four hand grenades hung down from his waist, and he carried a machine gun as big as himself. At least one and maybe more of them were my father's age. The oldest man had a short white beard and was so skinny you could see his rib cage. He had strange scars around his chest, and he gripped his weapon by the barrel with his left hand while he leaned its stock on the ground. He stared straight ahead, as though avoiding my gaze, but I felt he was watching me from the corner of his eye. He tried to stiffen in order to look more official and strong. I asked his name. He gave no sign of understanding or even hearing me, so I repeated the question, and he shouted: "Alsees!"

Next to him was a short young man who might have been anywhere in his 20s or 30s. Hard to tell because of his baldness. His broad chest didn't fit with his skinny waist. His rifle was slung over his left shoulder, and his ammunition belt over his right. Giving me an intense look, he called out his name: "Bakheet." I struggled not to stare at his wide, hairy chest. I had the strange sense that his eyes were smiling at me—almost as though he were showing off his manliness—and I felt repulsed by him.

Both he and Alsees wore a light red mauz decorated with tiny squares. Bakheet had a rubber hose for a belt. I was bothered by the thought that it might suddenly fall off and reveal him completely naked. I couldn't keep from blushing.

The third, Hamd, seemed younger than Alsees and Bakheet because of his thick beard and full head of hair. He was taller than Bakheet, but less muscular. He had slung his rifle over his shoulder and was letting it rest in his arm. He had a wool sweater around his neck and an ammo belt around his waist. His mauz was blue with square dots and stretched from his waist to his heels, unlike that of the comrade toward the end of the row, whose mauz stopped at his knees. It reminded me of the short skirts I used to wear. I realized that this one—Abdullah—was the only one wearing a khaki shirt. It was unbuttoned, exposing his skinny, hairless chest. The veins in his legs bulged. He seemed meek and servile, and I could not place his age. He stuck very close to the last comrade. That one was the tallest of them. He had a thick build and his long mauz fell from his navel almost to the ground. His left arm had a dark tan, and it was folded across his chest to support the rifle he carried in the other arm. Bulging muscles. The only one who wore a wristwatch. His scraggly beard didn't quite connect with his mustache, and his temples were already graying. He might have been in his forties. He kept staring up over my head, avoiding my gaze, as if to say that he didn't need my training, that he could kill like an expert when the time came, and that he doubted that I—his leader—would do as well. His name was Soweid.

I told them that our first concern was hygiene—keeping away the swarms of flies and fleas. I made myself a provisional latrine from brush and tree branches some distance from our caves but with exposure to the breeze. The others had to find remote areas and bury their waste. I ordered that all fires be extinguished and their embers smothered with dirt to keep our location secret.

May 22

I left a group of six comrades on guard under Soweid's command while I took the others through a marching drill to check their stamina. Also to get a sense of our surroundings. I ordered silence during the march, issuing commands via hand signals, whispers. I marched in the middle of them, in accordance with our standard procedure. Although I was wearing boots—the ones that had burned—my movements were halting. Meanwhile, my barefoot troops moved quickly and easily.

We walked without stopping for several hours under the punishing heat of the sun. We passed several houses made of stone that could be used as shelters in the winter, when their inhabitants moved to caves to escape the harsh north winds. We left the valley and climbed 500 feet to a rocky area with very steep cliffs. Yellow fields where hay comes up to a person's waist. Scattered thickets with giant trees whose leaves have fallen. Behind and beneath us, the blue sea, while all around are cliffs covered by trees. Butterflies, grasshoppers, and locusts. Suddenly, a beautiful valley with a creek cutting through it. Two large fig trees.

Three hours of climbing made us all thirsty. We met a group of shepherds with a strange-looking flock—skinny rear ends, very fine wool like human hair, delicate and narrow faces almost rivaling a gazelle in their beauty, their prominent eyes, their gaze.

We asked them how they were, using their local salutations, and they answered us in kind. They didn't seem surprised to find us there, but neither were they welcoming. There was a collection of tents nearby with dozens of camels resting next to them in the sun as birds picked at the insects in their coats.

We went and sat next to an old woman, whose face was painted with yellow and green that streaked down onto her neck and shoulders as well. She had on a loose black robe and covered her head and shoulders with a cloth. She offered us a porcelain bowl filled to the brim with fresh, frothy camel's milk. A young man came over, kissed her on each cheek, then on the top of her head and on her chest. Then he turned and gave us a fixed look. I could see a small fenced-in area to the side, barely big enough to fit two people, with a front gate that you would have to crawl to get through. The ground was covered by a straw mat, and there were pots made from reeds where they stored milk, honey, and butter.

We walked for a while under shady sycamore trees that grow wild there. They grow fruit that can be eaten if there's nothing else.

When we arrived back at the end of the day, some were completely worn out, but I felt a kind of rapture from the exertion. I commanded a group to clean up and make us our one meal for the day: rice and field peas. But I told them to wait for dark to light the fire, so the smoke wouldn't give away our location.

When I got back to my space, I was surprised to find my radio was gone. I found it in the big cave with Soweid. Those on guard duty were listening to music. Rebuked them and made clear that the radio was our only way to know what was happening in the world. Explained the need to save battery power. Then I promised to set aside special times to listen to music whenever we had a large reserve of batteries.

May 23

The muscles in my thighs feel sore from yesterday's march. Hard night. I couldn't sleep. The faces of the guerrillas came to me and I found myself replaying our exchanges. Every now and then I'd see Bakheet's bare chest or the forlorn face of Soweid.

Stepped out of my sleeping bag and was attacked savagely by a swarm of fleas. I lit a candle, and then the flies came at me. I pulled out my books on guerrilla warfare: General Giap, *People's War, People's Army* . . . Mao and Guevara as well. Started to flip through them, shooing away the flies as a set of piercing questions spun around in my head: How could these eager Bedouins be transformed into revolutionary fighters? How could these people who live life so freely be convinced of the need for a regimen with precise, tight schedules? How would I get them to boil their milk? Above all else, how would I convince them to follow a woman? Somehow, I needed to penetrate the hearts of these highlanders.

A guerrilla managed to hunt an aging mountain goat. Its meat was smelly and tasted awful. We boiled it and charged Soweid with dividing it up. He divided it into five equal portions. Each troop took its section, and a new round of dividing followed—except that a problem came up in Masrif's group. One of the soldiers claimed that he had been given a small piece. Soweid stepped forward to settle the dispute, taking it upon himself to do the portioning. He made five skewers out of straw and wrote a name on each one. Turning his back, he placed one of the skewers on a piece of meat and said, "This is for whoever is best." Then he placed a skewer on another and said, "This is for whoever is worst." The third one was for whoever woke up late. Everyone laughed. The tension was broken. I joined in with the group as we gathered around the platter of rice, each one having his own piece of meat. I had been having trouble lately eating rice the traditional way, even though I'd been used to it as a child. You have to stretch out the right hand, ball the rice up in your palm, then drop it in your mouth with your fingers.

I gave a lecture after the meal on imperialism and neo-imperialism. I talked about the people's struggle and the road to victory. I talked about the long marches of Luís Prestes in Brazil and Mao Tse Tung in China. I asked if they had heard of China. Alsees spoke up and said, "That's the land of waqwaq." I asked him why they called it that, and he said there are trees there whose fruits look like humans, and if you picked one off, it called out: "Waqwaq." I decided to ignore this and go on with the lesson. I talked about being organized and the consequences of disorganization. I went over the need to take care of one's weapon, cleaning it always, counting your bullets, making sure never to lose any, and to always be ready to use it. I spoke of revolutionary principles. Then I turned to the issue of flies and reminded them all to bury their excrement far from the camp or burn it in order not to attract them. Finally, I reminded them that disloyalty and abandonment were crimes punishable by death and that chewing qat was forbidden.

I then turned my attention to basic needs for a good life, things like healthy sleep, how to maintain supplies, and how to build a fire and cook. Since our supply of fresh water was dwindling, I ordered that it be devoted exclusively to drinking and that we all forgo using it to bathe or for cleaning until we could replenish our supply at the nearest well. I had noticed that we were running out of salt, and I also mentioned preserving our stock of sugar. I ended by setting up a system for night watch duty: one guard for every five sleepers, in rotation. Then I dismissed them all and went back to my cave. I pulled the curtain shut and turned on the radio. I lit the candle. A mosquito started to buzz in my ear. I smelled my own sweat and felt my clothes clinging to my body, and I found myself wishing I could shower, shampoo my hair, and spray myself with Chanel No. 5. The BBC came in just as its news broadcast began.

I started to hear people talking, so I put out the candle, turned off the radio, and came out. I had made it clear to everyone that we needed to have set times to lie down and to wake up. My anger boiled at the sight of a group of guerrillas who had lit a fire and were sitting around Bakheet near the entrance to the big cave listening to him tell a story in a language I couldn't understand. He stopped talking, and they looked at me in silence. They sat frozen in place. Not one of them stood up. The language did not sound like Hadhramiya—that, I know a few phrases of, or at least how to count from one to ten, *tad* to *ashroot*. Nor was it Ahmeriya, a closely related dialect also spoken by the people of Hadhramaut. There's also Bathariya, spoken by the Batahara, but I didn't think it was that either. Bakheet asked me if I needed anything. I shook my head no. He said that it must be hard for me. "You mean because I am a woman?" I asked. He did not answer and his gaze settled on my chest. I could feel the blood rushing to my face as the flames of their fire bounced off their bare chests. A cool breeze gave me a tingle and I folded my arms across my body. I managed to speak in a neutral voice: "It is time for bed, comrades." I waited for them to get up and move away, then I went back to my cave. As I pulled off my shoes, I held my breath so I wouldn't smell my feet, then I unbuttoned my military shirt and felt a rush of cold. Unrolled my plastic sleeping bag and curled up inside.

May 24

Today a sudden strong storm kicked up and the wind spread dust along the coast. I found Bakheet staring quietly at the clouds and rain. He said that the air was upset by a battle among djinn. I could not conceal my disbelief. "Look at its shape," he said. I observed the storm. It was conical and it twisted and swung, like a dancer. I told him that such folktales were made up by reactionaries. Science had shown that . . . blah, blah. This made him mad and he turned away in silence. I tried to change the subject. I asked what they had been talking about around the fire the night before. He said they were talking about sorceresses and how they can possess people, especially women. He told the story of a person he knew whose mother and sister hated him. They made a pact that one of them would turn into a snake and bite him. But they spoke of their pact in front of a cat who was really a disguised djinn who was in love with the man, and this djinn killed the enchanted snake. I couldn't say anything. Was he thinking I was the cat or the snake?

Two of the guerrillas had served with British army troops in the Gulf. One had been on security patrol in Qatar and had taken part in putting down the intifada of 1963 there.

Several of them are from Salalah itself. Most are highlanders, some from villages near our camp. Many of these are married, unlike those from the city.

May 25

I woke up at sunrise, but it was hard to stand. Diarrhea. Do I have some kind of microbe? Should we boil our water? I took two tablets of Entroform. Went to brush my teeth, but the toothpaste made me throw up. Can't allow myself things I forbid to others. As I came out of the cave, one of the guerrillas with African looks met me. To my surprise, he raised his hand to his forehead in an abrupt military salute and shouted in English, *"Good morning, Sir!"* For a second, I thought he was mocking me, but as I looked closer I could see his manner expressed high respect and admiration. He had worked in a mess hall at an air base for English officers.

Long- and short-term goals for hitting the English are set. We started our rifle drills. I showed them how to use Molotov cocktails to assist rifle squads. None of them had seen this before. I taught it to them. That pleased me.

I sent out two patrols on reconnaissance and asked them to seek out the best spots for an ambush. Also a special patrol to hunt for fresh water.

We must make our drills precise: rigorous marches day and night, a bit longer each day — just to the point of exhaustion.

A very stupid situation today. I had come back from a trip to the provisional latrine we had set up half a kilometer away. I aired out my sleeping bag, folded it, and put it away. I opened my suitcase, and something jumped up and hit me in the face. I let out a scream before realizing it was a frog, hopping away to escape. I suspected one of the young guerrillas had put it there. Bakheet, for one, always gives me strange looks that I don't know how to interpret. Was he angered by what I'd said about the djinn? I will avoid one-on-one conversations with him from now on.

Soweid still stares at me with that same arrogance.

When the first patrol got back, I found one guerrilla's foot covered in blood. Something had stung him. They plunged it in the blood of a sheep slaughtered by a group of shepherds. He refused to let it be cleaned or treated with any type of antiseptic, saying that sheep's blood is enough to heal any wound.

May 27

Our fighter's foot has not improved. I convinced him to take antibiotics and I cleansed the wound.

The Sultan's air forces consist of three divisions, distinguished from one another by their hats: a red beret for the Muscat division, green for the desert force, and gray for the mountain division. During their missions, though, they all wear a cloth headcover with green, black, and maroon stripes. Most of the troops are from Baluchistan, and the majority of their officers are British, with a few Asians and Arabs mixed in.

I heard a fighter encouraging his comrade by using this strange word: *shobash!* I discovered that among us there are a number of Baluch who trace their roots back to India, including one named Jumaa. He cannot be older than 20. His first wife died in childbirth when he was 15. He remarried and has already had two more children. Another, Muhammad, also married at 15. There's Khamees, who was born into slavery 30 years ago, but escaped to Muscat at 14 and was freed there. He married six years ago and has a boy and a girl.

May 28

I have ordered a fighter stripped of his weapons for not following orders.

We don't have the capacity to put soldiers in prison. If they do something wrong, we withhold food for a day or two. It is absolutely forbidden to discipline any comrade using corporal punishment.

I finally seized an opportunity to talk about djinn during today's political lesson. I said that I personally do not believe they exist, but I respect the opinion of whoever does. I think this reassured Bakheet.

I asked the old man about his hometown and he told me that he comes from Beit Handub in the west. He left his wife and children there. I asked him why he had joined us. He smiled and said right away that he joined to recover "honor and dignity." For a second, I felt very proud, but then something seemed not right. It seemed like a prepared answer that he had recited many times. What did it mean? I tried asking the same question to Soweid, and he smiled that sarcastic smile of his and said, "I'm a tax dodger." Was this mockery or the truth?

May 29

About 25 km from Salalah to the north, a rock ledge overlooks a deep lagoon through which bird calls echo. I must try to go back there one day for a swim. The best time of day for swimming in warm waters is right at sundown.

The guerrilla with the swollen foot finally improved. He became convinced of the value of modern science. I took advantage of the chance to discuss superstitions.

During our rifle drills, I noticed that Soweid was frazzled. His Armalite had jammed and he fumbled while trying to fix it. I realized what the problem was right away: he had filled the magazine beyond its capacity. I told him, "There are two things to be very careful about with this rifle. First, you can't try to load it with more than 17 bullets or you'll find that it can't fire. Second, it will jam if the cartridge explodes while it's still in the barrel. When this happens, dislodge it with a metal rod." When I started to demonstrate, he looked embarrassed at his ignorance. I couldn't help but feel satisfaction.

A disturbing event tonight. I was settled in listening to the radio when I heard gunfire nearby. I ran toward the noise, where I found Bakheet gripping a gun and Hamd trying to wrestle it away. Bakheet said he had been cleaning the gun when it misfired. Hamd backed him up, but something in the way he said it made me suspicious. I took the weapon from him and turned it over in my hand. A Makarov 9 mm. The red spot on the left side was not covered, so the safety was off. Were they fighting?

May 30

I could not resist any longer. I gave in to its call. Just after sundown, I snuck out to the lagoon, took off my clothes, and dove into the water. Glorious. I sensed some movement on the land. I dove completely under. My weapon was up on the bank on top of my clothes. A being of some kind was out there. Animal or human? Friend or enemy? I stayed where I was without moving. The being did not move either. I swam toward the bank and it started to move away. I dressed quickly. A strange feeling that I was being watched overcame me. A spy? A passerby? Or perhaps . . . the thought that frightened me most: one of the men from our troop.

May 31

I found my wrist swollen when I woke up. Hard to clench my fist. By mid-day, a wound had appeared that was of a blood red color moving gradually up my arm. Something must have bitten me without my noticing. I took an antibiotic.

June First

Arm has started to improve. Redness of the wound is fading. There's a type of wasp whose sting causes swelling that lasts several days.

Bakheet and Hamd come from rival clans within the Al-Katheer tribe.

June 2

We have convened our first conference of the Dhofar Popular Front's central Dhofar branch. A successful conference. No obvious fissures. Everyone enthusiastic. We voted unanimously to start the armed struggle right away. Rafie, Fahd, Amar, Ghazal, and I were elected to the leadership team made up of 18 people, including Yusuf Alawi, who has strong Cairo connections.

From the conference communiqué addressed to the Arab masses in Dhofar and beyond: "A revolutionary vanguard has come forward from among you by the grace of God and the national spirit. This government of Sultan Said, the foreign agent, has rented a formidable foreign mercenary army. But the desire for freedom instilled in us by God will conquer this army of vermin."

The front is responsible to provide for its guerrillas. It provides them with food, clothing, weaponry, and transportation. Each fighter, regardless of rank and including the leadership, will receive a 10-dinars-a-month stipend for personal use. I have donated back my allowance to the cause and encouraged my platoon to follow my example. It's not as though we have cafes and cinemas to spend money in. Our finances look good thanks to the donations coming in from supporters all over the Gulf region.

June 4

Divided my forces into three divisions: Division based in the camp assigned to protect it. Division charged with surveillance of the British camp on the way to Hamrein, with Soweid in charge. Third that would take the British air base, with myself in charge.

It was a deep black night with no moon. We stepped out from the mountains without anyone noticing. There were seven of us. We carefully advanced in two lines using zigzag formations, then spread out around the base and lay down in the dirt. I put my binoculars and walkie-talkie to the side and started to dig sand barriers all around. Suddenly, something was moving next to me. Dozens of crabs were trying to share my foxhole. I crawled forward to get a better view. I gathered some bramble into a pile and slowly lifted my head to peer around it, but I saw nothing. My senses were keen. It seemed like hours passed before finally I heard a sound to my left. I heard it again. I went back into my hole to join the crabs and raised the FN rifle. The weapon, I suddenly realized, was not fully assembled: its safety valve was missing. The way there had been full of rocks and potholes, so I had put off assembling it to avoid an accident. If I tried to put it together now, the noise might give us away. All I could do was wait until my target exposed himself and then quickly assemble the weapon and fire in one motion as fast as possible. I aimed the barrel with my right hand and gripped the trigger with my left. I was ready. I could get off two shots and then roll over to the right. The rifle had begun to weigh on me. Suddenly, I sensed movement. I checked my aim, reminding myself to be patient until my target exposed himself fully and gave me a better shot. I was about to fire when someone jumped on top of me and pressed their hand over my mouth. Bakheet. I wrestled myself angrily out of his grip. He put a finger to his lips, signaling for silence. We pulled back, pressed close together. He was wearing a short mauz that left his thigh bare, and the heat of his body washed over me. I stiffened my leg to make space between us but then I felt a pain in my back. We were squeezed into a narrow place, impossible to move apart. Finally, I relaxed and left our legs touching each other. We stayed there pressed together until the sun came up. I climbed up out of our foxhole and crouched behind the pile of bramble. I pointed the binoculars toward the enemy base. A barbed wire fence surrounded it. At the main entrance, a guard post manned by British and Asian MPs carrying Sterling submachine guns and wearing gray berets. One hundred yards past the fence, two heavy cannon, their 40-gallon barrels capable of firing 25-pound shells. The airstrip was unpaved. In front of it and to the right was a deep, encircling trench. An area surrounded by a barbed wire fence was guarded by local soldiers wearing bright red berets. Empty oil barrels surrounded Strikemaster jets and Skyvan cargo planes.

I gave the order to retreat at midday. Soweid and his group returned before sundown, and I recorded their observations.

Avoided Bakheet during the evening meal. Again, couldn't sleep and spent the night tossing around. My insides were boiling. Tried sticking a pillow between my thighs and pressing. Bakheet holding me came back into my mind. I felt frustration; I flipped and flopped. I remembered Rushdy's face and his forlorn looks . . . and Amad's raging emotions. Shehab, that time he drank too much and said he would be my slave. I thought back on the swim at the lagoon, imagining that Bakheet and others were watching me naked. I tried to recall that saying of Guevara: "The revolutionary who prepares for war in secret must be a complete ascetic." Did he mean to include clandestine work in cities to prepare for insurgencies, or just during fighting? And then what about a war that goes on for months . . . or years?

June 6

Two comrades came up from Salalah to bring us supplies and ammunition—even a bunch of landmines stolen from English warehouses. They brought old Arabic newspapers, too, and instructions from the leadership. They had news to share about the first conference of the National Front for Southern Yemen that had just convened in Taiz. Disputes erupted around different issues, like what position to take with respect to the clerics and notables and whether to coordinate with the Egyptian secret service. The conference issued a communiqué stating that the south is passing through a stage of national liberation right now, and it will be followed by a stage of social development through socialism. Workers, peasants, soldiers, revolutionary intellectuals, and students make up the driving force. The communiqué was not satisfied merely to leave the bourgeoisie off the list of revolutionaries: it named it explicitly as an enemy instead. One of the comrades commented sarcastically that the signatories didn't seem to understand the socialism that they were trying to build. He said the leftists issued 38 demands to the leadership, then insisted that no one leave until they had all been agreed upon. One of the demands was that another conference be convened in January.

We had a discussion over what to make of this new information.

The papers are full of competing conjectures about the fate of Guevara and news of American defeats in Vietnam.

Shortages roil Egypt: notebooks, cigarettes, matches, fruit.

No news from Yaarib.

June 7

We have set the day after tomorrow for our attack.

June 9

The revolution in Dhofar is under way.

I led an attack on the road to Hamrain. We were all so anxious that we dripped with sweat. I had to force myself to keep my knees from knocking. I issued the order to fire on the camp. The English fired back with a rocket that lit up the whole area. The guerrillas were afraid they had been seen, so they stopped their attack and ran. But I caught them and told them to turn around, saying otherwise they could face court martial. When they hesitated, I went back to my position and started to shoot. The English did not return fire. Then we saw cars speeding away from the camp, and I kept firing at them. After a while, it became obvious that the English themselves had run away. When my troops realized it was true, they ran back. I felt a new spirit rising in them. Our enemy's air of invincibility had been shattered.

I gave way to the spirit of the moment and ordered that each division could open a can of Blue Beef for dinner.

I have been born again on this day.

June 10

Like human Land Rovers. The highlanders here can cruise through the mountains at blazing speed, way faster than us urbanites. A group came back with news this morning. A second group led by Fahd left on a mission to sabotage an oil supply convoy run by British Petroleum. A third launched an attack on the fortress of the governor of Taqa. We confirmed over the radio in the evening that both were carried out.

We decided to plant an olibanum tree inside the camp to mark the occasion. They take ten years to bloom.

The guerrillas wanted to throw a second party like we had done last night, but I was firm that I would not allow it. I noticed that Masrif had disappeared. He came back to camp smiling just before dinnertime, carrying a string of birds. Then he showed me how he had hunted them: he put a pinch of rice down a small hole and set up a stone cover propped up with reeds that would collapse at the slightest movement. We used our iron supply case to cook them and had a nice meal.

June 12

Masrif and I agreed that he would teach me some of the language of the highlands and I would help him learn to read and write in Arabic. Results for today very basic: *tith* means woman, *gheikh* means man. *Yol-hut:* how are you? *Min holun hut:* where are you from? *Hut* is masculine you, *heetee* feminine. Greetings depend on the time of day: *Yul sabahuk* means How are you this morning? and *Yul ghamduk*, How are you tonight? I Learned words for boy, girl, water, and go. My first real sentence is what the herder says to the camels when watering them: *Allun huk, aheer bik*, meaning Come, my beauty, drink to your content.

One must confront laziness in so many areas.

To start with, we lack the patience and determination that must form the foundation of our struggle. We also need clarity or ideology and consciousness.

June 14

Tomorrow we will attack the British airfield that we have just discovered. I will take Abdullah and Hamd along with me.

June 15

We closed in on the airfield before dawn, avoiding the main gate. Instead we made a breach in the barbed wire to slither through. Our goal was the group of aircraft in storage. We realized that they were defended by circular trenches around airplane hangars watched over by a couple of guard posts. I signaled to my two comrades that each of them should draw the attention of one post while I made my way to the planes. We crawled forward carefully. The hand grenades they tossed exploded in a clap of thunder, answered by a fuselage from the enemy. I zigzagged my way to the nearest hangar and jumped inside. A soldier inside lay on his back with his face covered in blood. I looked away. No time to figure out whether he was still alive, nor his nationality. A burst of gunfire erupted from a new corner. I listened as I crouched, trembling. A huge explosion rumbled at the edge of the trench. Cannon fire from one of the two cannon a hundred meters beyond the barbed wire fence. A cloud of desert sand kicked up and clung to my face and hands. Explosions continued. If the assault kept going, the enemy would surround us and there would be no escape. The attacks had to be halted at their source. I dared to lift my head. The cannon was in plain sight. I raised my rifle and put the soldier manning the cannon in my sights. Then I fired. But I missed. He didn't seem even to realize I'd fired at him. I could tell by his movements that he was going to turn his cannon on Hamd.

I fired again but missed a second time.

I concentrated, trying to collect myself. I forced myself to be composed . . . deep breath . . . ready . . . aim . . . a touch of pressure on the trigger. The shot fired and he fell. I started to tremble. I threw up. I was in a daze as we made our retreat.

June 16

I can't forget the face of that soldier covered in blood inside the hangar. Nor the head of the soldier manning the cannon who was struck by my bullet. It's my first time to spill the blood of another person. I imagined it would be a simple exercise. I hope they were saved. We aren't killers. But they force us to defend ourselves. It's either us or them.

June 18

The nights and early mornings have turned good and cold. During the rainy season, the livestock are fed dried fish and the stench of their stored feed fills our caves and our tents.

Yesterday afternoon, black storm clouds gathered in the skies to the south. Then they came suddenly upon us. In the evening the rain was still pouring down. By the time we made it back to camp, our comrades had lit a fire. We sat around it to dry off our clothes. The rain poured harder, and we had to raise our voices to hear each other over the din. The claps of thunder sounded like cannon firing. The lightning strikes lit us up; everyone seemed frozen in place for a full second before disappearing back into darkness. The rain turned into a cold river running through the grounds. I had to escape, but when I climbed up on a dry rock, I found a scorpion had beat me to it, trying to escape the water.

June 19

A shock. In Algeria, Boumediene has led a coup that has overthrown Ben Bella and imprisoned him. This coup does not make sense. These are the same political movements. Boumediene even announced that he would adhere to the old policies of socialism and the one-party state. Why then lead a coup?

June 21

Autumn has started and will continue until September. Temperatures don't get above 80 degrees. Trade winds come in off the Indian Ocean with light rain, and a thin fog gives the air a touch of magic. Stinging insects multiply: blood-sucking fleas and bedbugs that live in the clothes and stir in the dark just when we are trying to rest, and bite us until it's impossible to sleep. It seems to take a month of washing and drying in the sun to get rid of them.

I have had two more lessons in Dhofari highlander language: green grass — *sha'r*, cow — *hati*, butter — *mash*, bull — *fiyur*, clothes — *ku*, sickle — *mezrab*, rainstorm — *mishoun*, smoke — *dikhan*, beans — *dajur*, cucumbers — *hashiba*, tobacco—*timbiku*, winter—*shataa*, autumn—*khuref*, goats—*aroun*, camel—*ambreek*, stone pipes—*fijeer*, olives—*meetan*, son of so-and-so—*bir* so-and-so.

Illnesses: stomachache—*sheefa*, facial paralysis—*bu berqa*, skin rash—*hizaza*, swelling in the neck area—*selua*, child's rash around the mouth—*busha*, watering of the eyes (may cause blindness)—*nazul*, a hard boil—*hiba mashauma*.

June 23

Results of reconnaissance surveying the Um Jawarif air base that contains headquarters for the Sultanate's air force:

A large camp surrounded by a barbed wire fence wrapped around lookout posts, with moving sensors that are spaced out around the circumference. In the middle of the camp, an old fort raises the Omani flag. This must be the headquarters. Rows of portable sheds are separated from each other by thickets of dark trees. These are the soldiers' barracks. There's a well, augmented by a pump, near the main entrance; it is guarded by local soldiers armed with 7.6 mm F1 rifles. Behind the well is an officer's mess, and behind that are their quarters and some storage sheds. Transfer operations in which Skyvans transported mortars, cans of grease, and empty jerricans for fresh water were observed. A British soldier is mounted behind a Browning machine gun in a dugout area surrounded by sandbags and barrels. Others are there also, wearing short pants and short-sleeved shirts.

June 25

An example of international solidarity: the Soviet Union turns a shipment of wheat headed toward its territory around toward Egypt.

June 27

We hid behind some boulders overlooking the Um Jawarif air base until we had a chance to scurry down to a low lookout point. Two convoys came toward us across the plain. Three camels bearing wood were being herded toward Salalah. Then two Packards came out of the base and cut their way slowly upward, out of the valley. We opened fire on the lead vehicle. It made a sharp turn before its driver lost control and flipped. The second one backed up, turned around, and sped back to the safety of Um Jawarif.

We left our hiding places and advanced, curious to inspect the wreckage of the first vehicle. The name Salah al-Din was painted on it, and a Browning heavy machine gun was mounted on it. We pulled out the bodies of the occupants. One was English. Luckily, they were dead, so we didn't have to worry about transporting them or treating them. We stripped them, then we took the Browning and the box of ammunition and headed back toward the mountains. Because of heavy rains, it took us three hours to cover just 1 km.

July First

We made a plan to mine the roads leading into the bases of the enemy. I inspect my body every night.

July 15

We lost one of our comrades when a mine we were planting exploded. The explosion cut him in two. Depressed atmosphere fell over us. Our first human casualty, without any direct combat, caused by our own weapons. I gave an order that we fix our marches over paths with footprints left by humans or animals, or else over large borders where mines cannot be hidden.

July 24

American losses in Vietnam continue apace. American and Southern armies lost 8,000 soldiers in just one confrontation with the liberation forces. Afterward, an American official called the soldiers "missing in action," as though the earth had opened up and swallowed them.

Flora of Jebel al-Qamar: the *atira* is half tree, half cactus. The *hobouk* produces poison leaves that should be avoided, though a very small dose can work as an excellent purgative. The gum of the *zirote* can be used as a salve to dab on wounds, like iodine. Its wood works for making tools and building structures. The *bedah* is a type of gladiolus whose tubers when roasted over camel dung taste like chestnuts.

August 25

Nasser and King Faisal signed a peace agreement yesterday that commits to a plebiscite in Yemen to determine its form of government after the Egyptian forces pull out.

Yaarib has surfaced in Beirut. I don't know why he left his post. Perhaps the Omani heat was too much for him.

September 1

We have decided to attack the British air base before the rains end.

Alsees is throwing up blood. Admits he's been sick for years, tried to treat himself by branding his chest with a hot iron. I explained that he had tuberculosis and that it was a serious illness. He didn't seem convinced. Our medical supplies are lacking and I don't know what to do. I had to isolate him from the others but am afraid this will break his spirit.

One of the guerrillas asked if he could go down to Salalah to see his mother. I said no. I feel my decision has angered the group. I explained that security must be airtight in the lead-up to our next operation.

September 3

Naseeb, whom I had forbidden to go down to the city, has disappeared. I decided to cancel the operation.

When I opened the issue for discussion among the group leaders, they insisted on following through, and they became angry when I warned them against dissension in our ranks.

September 8

We have barely avoided a disaster. The British discovered our movements and set up an ambush in coordination with the Sultan's air force. Their plan was to send a troop to lie in wait under cover of darkness until they caught us out in the open plain where they could start shooting. At the same time, the Omani heavy weaponry had repositioned to stations near the air base so they could strike us as we tried to retreat. Then the air force would come in to finish us off. Only luck saved us. Before we ever made it to the open area, the Omani heavy artillery misfired. We realized a trap had been laid and beat a quick retreat before we could be ambushed.

September 9

I called a general meeting of the unit. We discussed in detail what had happened. I reaffirmed that I had made the correct decision in forbidding Naseeb to leave. Made the same point regarding my decision to cancel the operation after he disappeared. But I also said we could not presume he had become a traitor. He might have simply spoken freely to the wrong person — or been captured and tortured.

I offered my first public self-critique: I should have been more firm in my decision to cancel the operation, asserting my leadership authority. Then I explained the concept of self-criticism, making the point that this practice was what distinguished the true revolutionary.

We now had to move our camp, I told them, but I could feel their resistance to the idea. They began to list all the advantages of that place, but I suspected they were really thinking only of its being close to their home villages. Soweid said that we were safe there because the herdsmen looked out for us and let us know whenever a stranger came into the area. I told him they could also be informing to the strangers that passed through, pointing us out to whoever asked about us. In the end, we made the decision to look for a new location after a few days, as soon as the rains ended.

September 12

In the morning, the guard finishing his rounds brought a woman who had been searching for our camp all night. She was carrying a small child that had been bitten by a snake. Her family had treated the girl in the traditional way: they cut out the spot where she was bitten with a knife. Then the mother sucked out the poison and spit it out. But the wound got infected, and the child's fever rose. I put a cold compress on her head. The wound had left a deep hole in her ankle, so I cleaned it and gave her an antidote for the snake venom. Then I gave an order that we reinforce our guard forces. If this mother had managed to find us, what would prevent the enemy from doing the same? But there was a positive side to this incident that could not be ignored: the people of the area had started to accept us and were coming to us for help.

October 1

The rainy season has come to an end. Local plants are blooming, like the *bith* that the highlanders use as an herb. The other local flora is gathered and cooked, like mushrooms and other bushes whose fruits resemble figs and have a sweet taste. Flowers are blooming in abundance along the banks of the valley. We added an extra camel to our herd.

Military coup in Indonesia. Bloodbath. Massacre of communists. The leader of Sukarno's guard force is supervising strange maneuvers on the orders of right-wing generals on the pretext that communists are trying to overthrow the regime.

In a general meeting of the Cuban Communist party, Castro read passages from a letter Guevara sent him at the beginning of April just before he disappeared. In it Guevara said that he had completed the responsibilities the Cuban revolution had charged him with, and for that reason he was stepping away from all affiliated positions, including minister, party member, leader, and Cuban citizen. He addressed Castro directly: "Other nations are requesting my services and I must leave you at this time . . . I remain prepared to offer myself for the cause of liberation of any nation in the Americas if called upon for that purpose. As I say this, I leave behind the most precious of memories and people most precious to me, and I carry with me the spirit all of you instilled in me as I move to new sites of struggle against imperialism, and if I come to an end in one of these sites, I carry with me always the supreme example you have set for me."

October 2

We scrubbed our camp clean and erased every last trace of our presence. We loaded the camels with the little bit of supplies we own plus the ammunition, water cans, and baskets of medicine. We set out marching, most of us barefoot and with our rifles slung across our shoulders, and kept going for three hours. At a pond near the foot of the Qarra mountains, we untethered our herd to let them graze and spent the night underneath the fig trees. Swarms of insects chirped loudly. Tree beetles flew from one branch to another over our heads. At the tops of the trees, flocks of white and brown storks settled for the night. We made a hearty dinner from goat meat, boiled rice, and a hearty broth. The harsh cold air kept us awake. Alsees cannot stop coughing. After the victory, we will give him full medical treatment.

October 3

The calls of the kingfishers woke us at dawn. We continued our march across rocky pastures and steep inclines. To our left, deep valleys extend down to the coast. Green lemon trees collected around a water source. After a while we made it to the edge of a valley of thick trees, rising 1,600 feet above sea level.

October 4

We visited a camp on a small plateau. A family lived there in a small cave whose ground had been lined with goat dung. A nearly blind old woman sat on a wicker chair with a leather covering. A young man brought us a frothy tumbler full of warm milk. It had a salty taste, like camel's milk.

October 5

We snuck our way up the Kasmim Pass. The peaks there are covered with green, jungle-like vines, shrubbery, and shaded pathways. We climbed down toward Jerbib—on the coast—Salalah, and the Indian Ocean, opening out onto another world. Just to the north, an incline of black rocks and yellow sands stretches toward the Empty Quarter.

October 6

We went down in the morning to Al-Ayoun Pool, some 200 feet above sea level at the head of the Ghoudoun Valley. Someone warned that it was full of deadly snakes, that one had swallowed whole a goat while it was grazing. We rinsed ourselves off and filled our water cans.

October 7

Slowly we headed north, following the Ghoudoun Valley, one of the five dry riverbeds that branch out from the coastal chain. It was hard to walk through the dry beds because of the piles of sharp rocks. Our path crossed with two families from Kathir that had camped under the trees. A young man who had been bitten two months ago by a snake had a swollen leg with a wound that oozed pus. I washed the wound and gave them some medicine. He had a very thin wife who suffered from a chronic cough. All that they owned was strewn on the sand: some pots, a cloth pouch, a bag made from goat leather half-filled with flour, piles of sardines wrapped in torn rags. The powerful stench that enveloped the place drew swarms of flies. They had an old rug and some rags to wrap themselves in at night. Two saddlebags and a leather bucket to carry water. An old single-barrel rifle.

October 9

We found a spot that will work about half a km away from a well. Two large caves for the men and a smaller one set apart for me. We are surrounded by fields of wild beans. We could walk in them for hours without seeing the sun.

November

Sultan Said has ordered the major cities and towns of Dhofar to be fenced in with barbed wire, and he has imposed a curfew on the region. Fewer highlanders now take the chance to go down to the coast for work or to trade, and just getting basic food supplies is harder. The Sultan's forces have carried out revenge campaigns involving the abuse of women and children. Their infantry burned down straw huts and blew up water wells. They resorted to taking family members hostage in order to force those accused of cooperating with the Front to surrender. We made the decision to respond boldly.

I put in place a plan to attack supply and ammunition caravans heading from the base at Um Jawarif for Taqa. A simple trap on the outskirts of the city. I confidently offered the plan to comrades on the leadership council. But Fahd opposed me and offered a competing plan. He said the enemy knew that we had put mines down on the main path that leads to Taqa, so the best way for their convoys to go was along the beach after the tide has gone out and the sands are dry and packed. We would have to aim for the precise moment that they left Um Jawarif. They could not leave early, or they would be stuck on the beach until the tide went out and become sitting ducks for our attack. If they left late, they could be overtaken by the incoming tide. We just needed to pinpoint the time between the two tides. Plus, when they did go out, it would probably not be from the main gate that they usually use, but from the other side leading to the sea. Then they would turn left and take the path along the wall that becomes a road extending all the way to Salalah. The path leads to a barbed wire fence guarded by two soldiers armed with 303 rifles, at the head of a road made of a hard-wire grid covering a path of loose sand. Seventy-five meters farther on, the packed sand starts. Over those 75 meters, they are forced to march slowly and cautiously. That's our chance.

He gave a logical presentation, informed by his superior knowledge of the area, but the way he spoke and watched me while he was talking made me angry. It was that classic male position. He thought the mere fact that he was a soldier made him a military expert.

I went back over the key points in Abdel Nasser's speech. He said whoever was not benefiting from their experience and dealing with the reality on the ground was losing an opportunity for substantive change. He said the struggle was just waiting for those who are committed, and the only thing blocking them is human exploitation. He noted that the Eastern Bloc countries loaned money to Egypt with an interest rate of 2%, while the West's loans were at 7%. In other words, the interest that Egypt paid the West was equal to the construction cost of two new factories. He described with precision the basis of capitalist exploitation: How does someone make a million pounds? It's very simple. He starts with his principal, he brings his workers, and the workers start to produce. He gives them part of the profit they produce and keeps the rest for himself. He *must* steal from them.

He announced the presence of a political organization inside the Socialist Union that would be called the Socialist Vanguard.

November 28

Fahd won. The ambush we set outside the base at Um Jawarif worked. We didn't suffer a single casualty.

December

My boots fell apart. I acquired a pair of sneakers.

The fate of the Moroccan leader Mehdi Ben Barka is still unknown. Has he been kidnapped or assassinated? Why is this happening right now? Is it because he has defined a popular socialist path to economic development, or because he's chairing the organizing council for the Tricontinental Congress that will convene soon in Cuba. The United States has five air bases in Morocco.

At a speech in Port Said, Abdel Nasser attacked the policies of the Muslim Brotherhood, including the imposition of the hijab on ten million women and the call for women to stay at home instead of working. "Work protects women from atrophy and self-absorption." He called for the nationalization of wholesale trade.

The Iranian Communist party has called for a broad nationalist front that would include elements of the bourgeoisie and the clerical leaders like Khomeini, all uniting against the status quo imposed by imperialist British and American forces.

The Sudanese parliament has decided to dissolve the Communist party.

There's a strong current inside the Sudanese Communist party that is pushing to transform it into a socialist party. Ahmad Suleiman, a well-known lawyer and member of the party's political committee, is the leader of this movement. He's supported by others who have worked in ministerial posts since the October revolution.

I am truly fortunate to have been born into and be living my life during this age when I can witness the definitive transformation of human relations from relationships of exploitation to ones of cooperation, solidarity, and equality. The main struggle revolves around the individualist principle in conflict with the communal principle. The exaggerated emphasis on the value of the individual leads to the ascendance of egotism. The economic equivalent to the principle of individualism is the valorization of the profit motive, this idea that the strongest motive driving the individual is personal interest—even at the expense of others.

The claim is that the human is naturally selfish and that the consideration of values or ethics cannot, therefore, be a sufficient driver in human progress.

I am walking barefoot now that my sneakers have torn. At first, the bottoms of my feet were covered in blisters, but then they became calloused and tough. Walking is easier now.

Listened to the new song by Um Kalthum and Abdel Wahab called "The Hope of My Life." I am feeling nostalgic for Cairo. I wonder what Rushdy is doing today?

No news from Yaarib.

The northerly has begun—a hot, dry wind from over the hills.

I have finished off the last of my supply of Tide powder that I was using to wash my underwear. This made me almost want to cry. Masrif brought me a branch from an okra plant. Here they call it *qamrut*. He showed me how to chop its leaves into a powder, dissolve it in a bit of water, and stir until it becomes a foam exactly like Tide.

January 1, 1966

I helped prepare a report for the occasion of six months since the start of the revolution. There's a new spirit in the mountains. At first, the response of the locals was cautious, even hostile, in the face of harsh pressure coming from the sheikhs and the regime's agents. But then we gradually broke through the ring of isolation. The first to make common cause with the revolution were members of local tribes and poor families from Qarra and Kathir. We also managed to keep rivalries among the different tribes from infiltrating the Front's work. We did it by dividing regional camps up according to geography and conscripting soldiers based on individual choice rather than tribal affiliation. We also chose our leadership based solely on merit.

January 13

In Aden, a program—under the supervision of the Egyptian secret service—to integrate the National Front and the Organization for Liberation was announced, bringing together Asnaj and Mikawi. The plan was to cut out the leftist current under the leadership of Abdelfattah Ismail. Meanwhile, a delegation made up of George Habash, Mohsin Ibrahim, and Hani al-Hindi arrived in Taiz for a meeting with Ismail. Qahtan al-Shaaby was in Cairo, where he argued against the merger. The Egyptians thanked him by forbidding him to leave the country.

For the first time, Nayef Hawatmeh criticized the leadership of the movement. He called it a petit bourgeois leadership.

January 14

We lost Masrif.

January 18

Only today am I able to write again. We were returning from a march as part of our drills when we were caught in an ambush. I heard that hollow metallic sound of a rocket and yelled out, "Mortar!" We threw ourselves onto the ground with our hands over our heads. The shell exploded at the top of a hill. The booms of rocket fire intensified. They came every half minute, as though the explosions were coming from short range, something like 400 meters. Masrif got up and began to run, shouting hysterically. His shouting called the attention of the enemy to our position. I experienced a moment of sheer terror. Our entire troop faced annihilation. My only option was to silence him, even if it meant firing on him directly. I raised my head carefully and lifted my machine gun. I saw him covered with blood, his insides hanging out of his stomach. He stumbled toward my position and I managed to pull him by his waist until he was next to me. I hugged him tightly, putting my hand over his mouth until his shouting ceased. He died in my arms.

February 2

An historic victory for the people. A Soviet space station has landed on the moon's surface. For the first time, humanity visits a heavenly body that is not the earth.

The Egyptian national legislature has issued a law declaring that the president and his cabinet may not earn more than 5,000 pounds per year.

I am not sleeping well. Keep waking up imagining Masrif running toward me.

February 23

Bloody coup in Damascus carried out by a wing of the Baath party led by Salah Jadid and Hafiz al-Assad. Michel Aflaq and Salah al-Bitar under arrest.

America announces publicly its latest arms deal with Israel.

Coup against Nkrumah following the economic boycott by Western companies that had been buying cacao from Ghana.

March

The French poet and communist Louis Aragon has written an article in the party's newspaper opposing the trial of two writers in the Soviet Union who have been accused of smuggling anticommunist writings out of the country.

Another bloody coup in Indonesia. Military government now in place led by Suharto.

April

An extremely dangerous development: American warplanes bomb a suburb of Hanoi for the first time since the start of the war.

I prepared a report on our health and medical needs: serum for snakebites, inoculant against tuberculosis and other respiratory ailments. Our barber can treat psoriasis himself by shaving the head and massaging the scalp with lemon. How to convince them that it is necessary to boil milk? The most widespread problems are malnutrition, dysentery, malaria, leprosy, scabies, and conjunctivitis. We really need morphine, bandages, and antibiotics.

May 3

In his Labor Day speech, Abdel Nasser threatened to bomb the Saudi bases targeting Yemen. He went back to the topic of exploitation in the form of capitalist appropriation of the surplus value extracted from workers—in other words, the theft of their hard work. "The worker who does one pound worth of work is given a fourth of a pound by the employer, who then takes three fourths for himself."

The Beirut press: Saudi king Faisal has asked the United States for help.

June 9

Anniversary of the start of the revolution. I feel depressed. We are still so far from the final victory. It seems I have had no clear sense of how long the killing will have to continue . . . or for that matter, the degree of general backwardness. Life in Sana is like paradise compared to here. How I yearn for the smell of fresh coffee in the streets of Beirut. Nights here are particularly hard. So much violence and killing. One must stay determined. Tomorrow, I will start a new round of marches and drills. We formed a committee to raise awareness around health issues.

Three new volunteers, but one of them is unfit for combat. Salem Hassan, age 17, worked as a fisherman in Salalah. He was earning 25 riyals per month from the owner of the boat during the three-month fishing season. The rest of the year, he carried rocks at a construction site for less than half a riyal a day in 10-hour shifts with no lunch break. He tried farm work, renting a vegetable garden for 5 riyals per six months and another half riyal for every hour of irrigation. Then he came down with trachoma and began to lose his sight. A charlatan convinced him he was a doctor and sold him eyeglasses. When those didn't help, he applied for assistance to travel to the Gulf for treatment. When the Sultan turned down his request, he escaped to the mountains. We have promised to give him duties that don't require good vision until we have a chance to send him away for treatment.

June 11

The second congress of the Aden National Front has elected new leaders, headed up by Abdelfattah Ismail, leader of left-wing block. Also Ali Salem al-Baidh, Ali Antar, Salim Rubai, Ali Salih Abad, and Muhammad Ali Haitham. Yaarib attended. The new leadership is revolutionary to the core, as seen in the class background of its members. Abdelfattah Ismail, for example, worked in an oil refinery before becoming a teacher. Ali Antar was a goatherd who became a porter in airports in the Gulf. Salih worked as a water carrier before joining the army, which he had to leave after he killed an English officer. Haitham worked as a tailor in one of the villages.

Abdel Nasser commented on the assassination of Salah Hussein in a Delta village, carried out by rural comprador capitalists goaded on by feudal landlord families: "There must be a vibrant and ongoing revolution, for the exploiters will not simply give up. The capitalist sector is expanding, and if we want to pursue socialism, wholesale trade must revert back to the public sector."

A Supreme Council for the Liquidation of Feudal Practice has been struck in Egypt under the leadership of Abdel Hakim Amer.

The Egyptian National Congress has agreed to a government initiative to amend the Agricultural Reform Law. Renting land is now the exclusive right of those who work the land themselves. This will eliminate sharecropping.

The rainy season: for the next four months we will be able to move, while the enemy will be stuck in their bases and will try not to engage us.

July

A major confrontation in Rabidhat al-Kilab. We lost two fighters, but we also blew up seven of their military vehicles and we killed or wounded at least 58 of them.

The Supreme Council for the Liquidation of Feudal Practice made an interesting discovery in Egypt. Between the years 1954 and 1966, feudal ownership of land actually increased from 60 feddan to 1,413 due to a combination of expropriation of alluvial lands and restrictions on the fellahin, resulting from indentures and various regulations. According to the cooperative system, the old landlords control distribution of cotton production, deducting expenses and then keeping half of the profit. On top of that, they control the mortgage banks and the co-ops.

The process of political purification is ongoing in China. Mao Tse Tung has given the orders. He has decreed that the system of higher education be revised so students spend two years only in scholarly activity before completing their degrees, with another two years devoted to practical work among laborers, peasants, and soldiers in order to gain the kind of experience that might directly benefit the revolution. Chou En Lai described these policies as a "great cultural revolution" on behalf of socialism. Defense Minister Lin Bao, who has established a new center for the study of Mao's work and is presenting his own strategy for a world revolution built around it, commented: "If one considers North America and Western Europe the world's metropole, then Asia, Africa, and Latin America are its hinterlands, and the contemporary global revolution consists of these hinterlands besieging the metropole."

Guevara's new book attacks financial incentives because they make it possible for capitalist values to take over. He calls for social incentives instead. The commodity is the economic nucleus of capitalist society, and its influence over production and consciousness has not abated. Because the economically underdeveloped countries still have such a long road to travel, there are powerful incentives enticing them toward financial motivations and economic quick fixes. Here we see the danger of dead ends resulting from efforts to achieve socialism by way of the rusty instruments inherited from capitalism: the commodity as the primary economic unit, the profit motive, self-interest, etc. We find ourselves at this roadblock looking for shortcuts around the long road, ones that allow economics to play the role of hindering the raising of consciousness. Building communism requires not only a change in the foundations of economics, but also a change in the consciousness of the individual. Thus, the means by which the people are enlisted in the cause must be social means, though without ignoring the proper use of economic incentives when it incorporates the crucial social element. Society must be transformed into a type of grand school. If humans are going to recover their true nature, it is inevitable that the tie that has made humans into commodities be undone. The state must begin to provide them with social services equal to their value. Once the individual's mentality has been freed from the anxiety of having to work in order to meet basic needs, and human labor is connected to human dignity, we will relearn our own value as humans through our strength and creativity. Once work no longer involves conceding part of one's being through the commodification of one's labor, the individual will recapture a sense of life's communal values.

August 15

A second Israeli attack on Syria because of the progressive direction taken by its new government led by several young physicians—Attasi, Zaeen, Makhus—who have been boldly developing Arab projects to profit from the tributaries of the Jordan River.

I managed to get some jeans that fit me—just a little bit tight . . .

September

A note of discord in the midst of the revolutionary rush toward the unified push of Arab progressive forces. Ahmad Said on Voice of the Arabs radio network has attacked the call for a unified progressive front in Iraq that would bring together nationalists, communists, and Baathists.

The youth brigade of the Chinese Red Army have taken into their own hands the revolutionary question. They have challenged the clothing worn by Chinese youth and their Western hairstyles. They have forbidden the drinking of tea in tea salons, considering it to be a bourgeois luxury. Beethoven and Bach are being attacked. True communism embraces a pure, abstemious life, facing up to the most arduous burdens.

We received a package of three books in Arabic from Peking. Collections of articles translated from the daily papers of the liberation army. "Mao's thought represents the highpoint of Marxism/Leninism in the current age." "Lin Biao is the first military person to decisively address the issue of arts and letters in the struggle." "The Soviet Union has fallen back down the road toward capitalism."

Each sentence of Mao's writing is true. His words have a weight to them that go beyond tens of thousands of normal written words.

Writers and artists are always the source of problems and perversions.

I cast aside my jeans. Their zipper had a hardness that rubbed against my body and caused distraction.

October 14

A coup in Abu Dhabi against Sheikh Shakhbut. The British authorities called him reactionary, stubborn, and stupid. His brother Zayed has taken over. He is being called open-minded.

After a successful ambush, Soweid found a dead Pakistani and an injured Dhofari, who was clearly on the side of the regime. He finished him off right there. I went mad when I heard. Our rule is that we treat the enemy's injured. I yelled at him that we are not murderers. Then I decided I would call him before a military tribunal to face the death penalty. Abdullah begged me to consider the circumstances. He said that the man who was killed had helped in the torture of Soweid's family members just to get them to pay unjust taxes, and that his father had died in the incident. That was what led Soweid to join the revolution in the first place. I remembered him telling me that he had joined to dodge taxes, but he had never said anything about what the authorities had done to them. I gave it much thought, then finally decided to call a council meeting. I spoke to them of the substance of our struggle—that this was not about individuals taking revenge. We were searching for a solution that went to the heart of all types of the oppression and injustice that our people were subjected to.

Then I pardoned Soweid once he had engaged in self-criticism of his actions.

November 13

An Israeli raid carried out by a full brigade with 30 tanks backed up by cannon and fighter planes overran a defenseless village near Hebron. They must be looking for something.

November 21

New volunteers, but with the same downside as before. Our troop is now made up of 80 men.

Jordanian authorities are carrying out widespread arrests of individuals active in the nationalist movement in Hebron and Nablus. The king has called in battalions made up of Bedouins to put down protests.

The supreme court in Sudan has ruled that the dissolution of the Communist party is illegal. The parliament decided that it won't let communists attend its sessions in spite of the court's ruling.

December

The National Front has had its third congress, in Qaataba, northern Yemen, where it has taken the decision to break with the Liberation Front. They elected a new leadership made up of Qahtan al-Shaaby and Faisal Abdellatif al-Shaaby. Under the leadership of George Habash, the Arab Nationalists are resisting the movement's drift to the left and condemn the decision to leave.

We have to purge the troops of men with low morale.

An example of the negative influence of tradition: the Indian Congress party moves to ban the slaughter of cows in the midst of widespread famine, acting under pressure from extremist religious groups.

January 5, 1967

Amazing scene: the arrival of three submachine guns with stands, three Madsen lightweight rifles, nine M16s, ten semiautomatics, and 6,000 rounds of ammunition.

Yaarib is in Muscat.

A British report confirms that over the past year there have been 500 operations in and around Aden, resulting in 583 killed or injured. Amnesty International has exposed the styles of torture used by the British authorities: removal of fingernails, breaking of bones, filling up internal organs with water, hanging upside down by the ankles.

Three-fifths of Britain's total petroleum reserves come from the Arabian Gulf. The British are actively working to form a federal confederation that would unify the sheikhdoms of the Gulf.

History is definitely on the move over all of the Arab lands. No act of imperialist tyranny will stop the triumphant march forward.

January 9

A confusing situation in China. Chou En Lai in defending the cultural revolution has denounced Liu Shao Chi and Deng Hsiao Ping. Placards accuse him of speaking from fear of the revolution.

The US troop totals in Vietnam have reached 400,000. In one of their raids on a village, they surrounded 42 villagers and mowed them down with their machine guns. Before killing one of the women, they pulled her young daughter from her arms and split her in two right before the woman's eyes.

January 16

A general strike in Aden in response to a call by the National Front to commemorate the anniversary of British occupation that began in the 19th century. Demonstrations cheer Abdel Nasser.

February

Lutfy al-Kholy declares that Abdel Nasser's latest speech raises him above the status of a simple political leader and into the realm of the master leading his pupils in the thought and practice of revolutionary activity. Is this harmless hyperbole—or are we watching the birth of a personality cult?

We have executed a confessed traitor after we caught him smuggling papers and weapons.

Strikes and curfews throughout Aden.

February 20

I finished going through the news and threw myself down on the bed. I lit my lamp and reached for the radio tuner. I found a light music station and the melodies made my mind wander. As I was loosening my pants, I heard a noise at the entrance. I lifted the screen to find Fahd. No one had told me he was in camp. I sat back down, seething. Meanwhile, his gaze enveloped my entire body from head to toe, then settled on the radio. He sounded like he was trying to be seductive as he said, "What are you doing alone?" The flame of the lamp flickered across his face. Unnerved by his brutal masculinity. "What if we married?" he said. With that, I found words, and I answered angrily: "The answer to the first question is that no one has the right to break in on my solitude. As for the second question: please leave!"

February 27

The Egyptian minister of justice has issued an order to halt all police efforts at enforcement of the marital obedience law. Resistance is coming from opponents of women's liberation in the National Assembly.

Personal conduct laws have always been a site of struggle between progressive thought and backwardness. The man's legal right to four wives, for example, or his right to divorce as he pleases. He is given the right to the custody of small children without regard to their own interests. And he has the right inside his home to force a woman to submit to him. The radical reworking of these laws will correct the male's notion that a woman is a piece of property, replacing it with her status as a full partner—equal in her rights and responsibilities.

An explosion in Aden, killing three of Abdel Qowa Mikawi's four children. The imperialist forces blame the National Front. 10,000 attend the funeral. Guerrilla operations accelerate.

February 28

Bakheet tells me he has found evidence that Hamd is a spy. He says he saw him hiding papers in a tree trunk. Then he gave me the papers. They were full of strange numbers and drawings. I made out the King of Yemen's escutcheon. A note underneath said that it was lucky for marriage, love, making money, and sales. Also useful for the bites of scorpions, snakes, and lizards. Also, Solomon's seven covenants that protect whosoever adheres to them against all calamity.

March

Dhofari broadcast over Radio Cairo: Our goal must always be to undercut the enemy. We must avoid engaging in battle on their terms. Strike and run, O brother!

The schools in Peking have reopened after being closed for nine months so that students could participate in the cultural revolution. Rafie says that the on-going struggle in China is the result of economic difficulties in the aftermath of the failed "great leap forward."

April 7

Seventy-two Israeli fighter planes cross Jordanian airspace to get to Syria and circle Damascus. It's the first such action since the '48 war. Meanwhile, President Johnson makes an odd declaration: "We are taking direct, concrete action with respect to the situation between Israel and the Arab countries."

April 8

We carried out a successful operation on the road to Thumrait. Hamd was hit by a bullet in the thigh. We had to carry him on a makeshift stretcher. Now we will have to try to smuggle him into Salalah for treatment.

April 12

An open letter made it to us that Guevara had written to the Organization of Solidarity between the Peoples of Africa, Asia, and Latin America. It was called "A Treatise on the State of Global Revolution," and in it he condemned the isolation of Vietnam that was resulting from the dispute between the Soviet Union and China. He blames the American imperialists for their aggression — and also those who did not act at the proper moment to prevent the territorial division of the country and the blocking of its socialist aspirations, even to the point of risking a global war. No doubt he refers to the Soviet Union. He says that exploiters should be made to fight everywhere and that the struggle must be global, so that the enemy cannot rest, even for one minute. He calls for the development of an authentic proletarian internationalism, with the worldwide proletariat forming its armed wing. Our brigade is on a sacred mission to save humanity or die under the banner of the people's fight for equality in Vietnam, Venezuela, Guatemala, Laos, Guinea, Bolivia, and Brazil — all united by a common hope for the Americas, Asia, Africa, and for that matter, Europe itself.

May 16

Levi Eshkol announces: A confrontation between Syria and Israel is inevitable.

Egypt has asked for the UN's peacekeeping troops to withdraw from Sinai and Sharm al-Sheikh and has decided to block Israeli traffic in the Gulf of Aqaba. The Arab masses have taken the initiative.

In Saudi Arabia, 70,000 amputees and 600,000 victims of human trafficking have been brought from every Arab country, as well as other parts of Asia, Africa, and Europe.

May 17

Field Marshal Amer has appointed Lieutenant-General Sidqi Mahmud as commander of the air force. Wasn't he arrested fifteen years ago on the morning of the July 23 revolution on the charge of being a stooge of the king? After being rehabilitated and appointed second in command over air squadrons, he left the attack planes under his command sitting on the tarmac in 1956 during the Tripartite Aggression, and the whole fleet was wiped out in a day. Strange, this Egyptian order.

June 5

I've been sitting at the radio since early morning. Has the moment finally come for the decisive confrontation with forces of imperialism? Everyone is on edge, full of zeal. We have postponed an operation. Voice of the Arabs radio is glorifying the march toward Tel Aviv.

June 6

Something is not normal about these news broadcasts.

June 8

Israel has occupied Gaza, Al-Arish, and the Arab neighborhoods in East Jerusalem. Its forces are advancing in Sinai. Its bombers have pounded Damascus, and it has announced that its troops are advancing toward its suburbs. What should we expect from these petit bourgeois Arab leaders? I have not left my place at the radio — even for a second.

June 9

The blow of his resignation. Does this make sense? I argued with Fahd when he said he was content with Abdel Nasser resigning.

We decided to carry out an operation to commemorate the first anniversary of the revolution and to exact revenge for what happened on June 5th.

June 10

State of total shock. Can't believe what has happened. I cried, overcome with happiness at the news that Abdel Nasser had withdrawn his resignation based on the demands of the masses. Tomorrow, we do our reconnaissance of the English airport.

Sharp discussion with Fahd. He criticized Abdel Nasser's accepting the cease-fire. Abdel Nasser is being denounced from all directions — especially by Iraq, Algeria, and Syria.

June 11

I took my spot behind the dark curtain surrounded by a ring of stones and loosened my Chinese leather ammo belt that was buckled around my waist, putting it on the ground next to my machine gun with its long curved cartridge. Drops of sweat ran down my back and front and dripped onto my pants belt. I pulled a date out of one of the pockets and tossed it in my mouth. Taking a sip of warm water from my goatskin flask, I stared toward the enemy camp. A Caribou transport plane had brought in a 40-gallon shipment of fuel. There was a Land Rover. One of their mercenaries climbed through an open door at the back of the plane. Crates of beer and cigarettes were unloaded. Once its doors were shut again, it started up and headed to the end of the camp's runway. Halfway to the end, it stopped and the pilot got down. As the mercenary came to pick him up in the Land Rover, he pointed to one of the plane's tires. The mercenary looked at it, then spoke into his wireless phone. Was he asking for help? Had they spotted one of us? The two stood there awhile, smoking and staring up at the sky. Finally, a helicopter arrived. It landed near them and someone got out with a tire and a tool box. If only we had a rocket launcher.

June 20

The comrades in Aden were able to set up an authority run by the National Front in the Kraytar district, where they raised the flag of the Front. At the same time, fighting broke out between the National Front and the Liberation Front.

Newspapers describing the dark days made it to us. I studied the photo of Abdel Nasser's despondent face. What happened to that familiar image of him, exuberant and beaming, with his familiar smile and eyes sparkling with confidence?

June 22

Fighters led by Ali Antar have liberated the emirate of Dhala in Yemen.

July 5

I have learned that comrade Samer, my commander in Lebanon, played a heroic role in the attack carried out by our comrades in Aden on the Khormaksar airport. They were able to wreck several warplanes as they sat on the ground, and then retreat. While retreating, they were pursued by attack helicopters. They fired back and brought one of them down.

July 7

The comrades in Aden have retreated from Kraytar district after having occupied it for more than two weeks, during which they set up a local administration. A turning point in the armed struggle.

August 11

The nationalist liberation forces in southern Yemen have carried out 90 attacks over 24 hours.

A packet of Beirut newspapers has arrived . . . new information about the situation in Egypt and the reasons for the defeat. Employees in the office of Field Marshal Amer were using warplanes to smuggle commerce. High officials were changing their tactics the way they changed clothes. Some of them made a big show of being ardent socialists. The newly powerful made their presence felt all over the place, especially in the committees that ran the newly nationalized companies and in key positions in the foreign ministry and at *Al-Ahram* newspaper, where there was also the highest concentration of figures from the old guard, with whom the editor Haykal felt comfortable. A smarter class of operatives went into the import-export sector, figuring out how to work around any barriers thrown up by the transition to socialism and exploiting any holes in the new laws.

September

Change in the weekly Dhofar Liberation Front radio program. Muhammad Ahmad al-Ghassany, one of the leaders of the group's nationalist faction, has replaced Yusuf Alawi as the representative of the Front presenting the broadcast. He has issued this call: "To the people of the Gulf in Muscat, Nizwa, Sharjah, Dubai, Bahrain, and everywhere else, the Dhofar Liberation Front calls on you! The liberation movement in Dhofar is also your revolution."

A new round of killing between the National Front and the Liberation Front in Aden after the former declared itself the sole legitimate representative of the people in southern Yemen's negotiations of the handover of power from the imperialist forces. The British prefer to negotiate with the National Front in order to undercut Abdel Nasser, who has closer ties to the other group.

October 21

The Egyptians have retaken the initiative, sinking the Israeli destroyer *Eilat*.

His voice breaking in sorrow, Castro announced that Guevara has been killed by Bolivian army forces.

We received declarations issued by the fourth congress of the Sudanese Communist party: Marxism is a complete program, rather than a collection of fixed slogans. The priority is formation of a broad front against counterrevolutionaries and encroachment of the right wing that wraps itself in religion.

November 2

The British have suddenly abandoned two neighborhoods on the outskirts of Aden. The Liberation Front has taken over both areas. Clashes with heavy arms — mortars, bazookas, grenades — between the NF and the LF are ongoing tonight.

My pencils are all used up and my pens are out of ink. Bakheet brought me bunches of small red fruit that look something like doom palm, but smaller. We boiled its seeds and it made a red ink — revolutionary ink!

November 5

The results of the defeat are coming into focus: Egypt has halted all aid to Yemen and withdrawn its troops.

The Popular Front for the Liberation of Palestine has been formed under the leadership of George Habash out of three organizations, the biggest of them being the Palestinian/Jordanian branch of the Movement of Arab Nationalists and Ahmad Jabreel's group.

November 9

Coup d'état in Yemen against al-Sallal while he is away in Moscow.

The LF and the NF are still fighting around Aden. 100 dead and 300 wounded.

Royalist forces with the support of Saudi Arabia launch a vicious attack on the Republican army in Yemen. Colonel al-Amri in command of democratic forces.

November 30

Declaration of independence by the Democratic People's Republic of Yemen, ending British occupation that has lasted since 1839. The National Front has declared itself the sole governing authority over an area covering 25 different former emirates and sheikhdoms. Qahtan al-Shaaby has been appointed temporary president. He has formed a government made up of Ali Salem al-Baidh as defense minister; Muhammad Ali Haitham, interior; Abdelfattah Ismail, culture; and Faisal Abdellatif al-Shaaby, economy.

Here in Dhofar, the government's stooges have arrested 550 youth in the towns. They made up the majority of the cells that were supporting the revolutionary movement in the mountains.

January 1, 1968

Egypt was able to shoot down three of the four Israeli planes that violated airspace over the Suez Canal.

January 16

Vietnamese revolutionaries have mounted an offensive on all fronts.

February 3

Changes in the ranks of the Movement of Arab Nationalists: In Lebanon, the socialists have left to join Fawaz Trabulsi's group. In Aden, the movement has split in two: a right wing led by Qahtan al-Shaaby calls for a moderate pace, arguing that the revolutionary stage came to an end with independence, while a revolutionary wing led by Abdelfattah Ismail is calling for deeper strategic thinking regarding workers and poor peasants, the dismantling of old state structures, and redistribution of land to poor farmers—without any compensation to the rich, feudal landlords—as ways to bring about national-popular revolution. They feel the land belongs to whoever works it and should be understood within a framework of new relations of production being constructed along the road to socialism. Also, they are for a transformation of the economy from a services-based system to one of production. 90% of the country's industrial production has been tied up in the oil refineries owned by British Petroleum, while foreign agencies with a monopoly on the local production of salt for global export rake in huge profits.

February 5

We made a pact with the comrades in Aden. They put Mahra, the sixth province, at our disposal. The port of Hawf will be used to support our struggle. We threw a wild party to celebrate. All our problems with supplies and medicine will soon be over. We are going to send Alsees and Salem for medical treatment in Aden—or possibly abroad. We can get new weapons, recent news, and plenty of batteries for the radio.

February 25

The National Front is preparing for its fourth congress. Nayef Hawatmeh will represent the revolutionary wing of the party. Demands of the revolutionary group: nationalization of all local companies owned by foreigners or big capitalists; closing of the free zone; realignment of the salary gap between office workers and laborers so that the former earn no more than four times as much as the poorest of the laborers; redistribution of land so that land ownership is limited to five feddan of arable land and ten of nonarable land; no burdensome fees on poor peasants as lands are redistributed; creation of cooperatives; establishment of popular councils made up of workers, poor peasants, and soldiers, who eventually are to be given full authority.

March 1

First results of the Vietnamese offensive that has continued for a month and a half: one-quarter of a million US soldiers killed or wounded.

March 9

Last night, the congress of the National Front that had convened in Zanzibar, Abyan province, concluded. The revolutionary wing was victorious. A new leadership team was elected, including Ali Antar, Abdelfattah Ismail, Ali Nasir Muhammad, Salim Rubai, Salih Muslah, Ali Salem al-Baidh, and Muhammad Salih Mutia. The front has fully committed to scientific socialism.

March 12

This time, the plane was ready to take off. I followed it with my eyes, a little sad as it sped over the tarmac. Then I heard movement behind me in the valley. I spun around and aimed my Kalashnikov in the direction of the sound. Soweid repeated my name, then whispered: "The anti-aircraft gun. The big one. It's almost here." I was so happy I almost kissed him. He left me and crawled off at a distance. The plane made it to the end of the runway. At that moment, I looked behind me and saw three men leading a galloping camel, the long barrel of the gun rocking on its hump. As their leader drew near, he surveyed the distant runway. The plane took a turn in preparation for takeoff. "It's too far away," he said. "We have to get closer." "There's no time," I said, and he said, "Okay," and turned around to his two comrades. "Load the gun." The Caribou engine grew louder, pushing forward as the plane accelerated. The comrades unfastened the rope binding the gun to the camel's back. They planted its base on the ground, attached the long barrel quickly, and loaded it with a frighteningly large shell—close to rocket-sized. Their leader pulled the trigger and the shell went flying toward the moving plane. Explosion. Plumes of smoke. The mercenaries ran for their foxholes. But I watched in frustration as the airplane lifted off. I looked over at the military personnel carriers parked to the side, then ordered the men to quickly dismantle the gun and put its parts back on the camel's back. Our group moved down a bit onto a rocky flat. We kept going for a few more meters until we found a rock pile to shield us and the gun. Finally the weapon was assembled, mounted, reloaded, and aimed toward the vehicles. I told the group leader, "Wait until the soldiers get into the vehicles, so we can hit as many as possible." He answered, "We can't wait too long. The fighter jet is going to circle back looking for us soon." I begged him to wait. He took a look up at the sky, then nodded his okay. Tense moments. Flies driving me crazy, swarming around my eyes. I spit one out of my mouth. Finally I saw someone walking toward the vehicles. Our wait was finally over. I gave the order to take aim. Their man put his rifle on the front seat of the personnel carrier. I gave the order to fire. He was caught right in the chest, and his buttons popped as he screamed and fell forward onto his knees. His arms reflexively went up to cover his head as the sand kicked up around him. He managed to climb into the driver's seat and turn the ignition; the vehicle moved out onto the tarmac, bouncing from side to side. I looked over at the smoke streaming off the empty copper shell that had spilled onto the sand. The gunner pushed another shell down into the barrel. The plunk of its release gave a thud in the air. The gun was quickly dismantled, and we threw it onto the camel's back without even knowing if we had hit our target. We ran, descending an incline toward the valley, then flying like the wind until we made it to a narrow opening in the face of a rock that passed through to a dark, shaded platform. We led the camel into the shade, pulled him by the front reins until he kneeled, then gathered up some thistle and stacked it up around us. It wasn't very long before the jets started flying over the valley looking for us, but we shrank ourselves under our camouflage until the sound of the jets died out. I prodded the camel to stand up and gave the order to move out. We headed back toward camp.

March 13

The popular council of Hadhramaut has issued its revolutionary declarations: nationalization of a number of properties owned by rich capitalists and conversion of these properties into schools for the poor; lowering of rents by at least 30%; shortening of weddings from eight days to three; an upper limit on bride-prices of 250 shillings; and brides' gifts reduced to three gold bracelets from eight. Hadhramaut is an ancient cultural center with a 1,500-year-old farming tradition. It has recently reintegrated 8,000 workers returning from Zanzibar and Indonesia after the bloody repression of the communist movement there.

March 15

We received copies of several articles by Nayef Hawatmeh in the Beirut-based magazine *Al-Hurriya*. He describes the movement in the salons of Hadhramaut as the real pursuit of revolutionary goals, compared to the authorities in Aden settling for a reformist Nasserist line.

The central committee of the Cuban Communist party has brought before the revolutionary court three members of the old Communist party. It's charged them with opportunism, isolationism, and promoting ideas that take a pseudo-revolutionary line toward the Latin American region. Most of the older communist parties seem not to support Castro in his drive to spread socialism through Latin America via guerrilla movements. Their hearts beat for Moscow, more than for their own common people.

March 18

Anxious developments in Aden. The old tribal army unleashed a show of strength in support of the congress's policy statements. They have arrested several leaders of the Liberation Front, including Muhammad Salih Mutia, Salem Salih Muhammad, and other representatives of the left wing. Rumors that Salman, al-Baidh, and Ashtal have escaped to Maqtaba on the border between the North and South.

News of a bloody massacre carried out by American soldiers in the Vietnamese village of My Lai.

March 20

Military coup in Aden. Announced goal of saving the country from communism. Qahtan al-Shaaby sides with the coup in an official radio broadcast.

March 22

Arrests ongoing in Aden. The number of political prisoners has exceeded 300, including 8 members of the LF's leadership council. Demonstrations calling for the prisoners' release.

March 23

We have heard that Ali Salem al-Baidh, Salman, Ali Antar, Muhammad Salih Mutia, and Salih Muslah all managed to escape and make it to the third province. Also, Qahtan al-Shaaby's announcement in support of the coup was made under duress after the coup plotters beat him and dragged him to the radio station.

March 27

The right is losing ground in Aden. President Qahtan al-Shaaby has issued a decision to enforce to its full extent the agricultural reform law. It covers all the landholdings of the old sultans and ministers, setting the upper limit for ownership of agricultural lands at 50 feddan. It distributes the leftover plots to infantrymen, indigent peasants, and new militias made up mostly of factory workers. Reports are that the US military attaché supervised the failed coup attempt.

Economic situation now difficult. 25,000 dockworkers have been laid off because of the closing of the Suez Canal.

March 30

Systemic changes in Poland and Czechoslovakia under the slogan of democratization. The revisionists are having their day.

May 5

A second full-scale assault by Vietnamese liberation forces. For the second time, they have penetrated the capital, Saigon.

May 12

The UN Security Council has asked Israel to rescind its annexation of Jerusalem.

June 5

The uprising of French students proves that revolution is on the march. Guevara's words are inspiring young people in the West: "The priority during this current transitional stage is the preparation of the global socialist revolution and the building of its materialist foundation. This stage is not just a time to try to build a socialist economy in one large state."

June 9

Celebration of the anniversary of the revolution.
The revolution currently consists of ten armed units that control 80% of the

mountains of Dhofar. We are up against 6,000 soldiers, mostly from Pakistan and Iran. We will take advantage of the rainy season to move in shipments of weapons and ammunition from South Yemen.

There's no news from Muscat. Why not? Is Yaarib just enjoying a drink somewhere?

July 17

A military coup in Iraq has brought to power the right wing of the old Baath party, represented by Ahmad Hassan al-Bakr, who has been chosen as president of the republic.

Preparations for our second congress. I helped put together a communiqué called "Thought Should Control the Rifle" that discusses the meaning of organized revolutionary violence. First, we distinguish between our movement and earlier tribal uprisings. Tribal violence is random, lacking a system or a goal. It produces not revolutionaries, but rebels: people who take up arms against the authorities but lack the thought that controls the arms. They have no revolutionary vision. (Neither, by the way, does the majority view of the armed Palestinian struggle, which gives the weapon almost magical powers in the process of building a revolutionary consciousness: "Abu Ammar has declared the rifle the supreme leader of the revolution in Palestine.")

Armed revolutionary force consists of revolutionary consciousness plus an organized system. How can the transition from blind tribal loyalty to sound revolutionary allegiances come about? That goes back first of all to making sound connections between general Marxist principles and the particular situation of Dhofar, which is distinctive from that of either China or Vietnam, for example, in that it is less developed and it has not yet produced a large class of landlords or a comprador bourgeoisie, like the ones in the Gulf States.

August 3

Campaign against the Shiites and Kurds of Iraq, carried out under the supervision of Saddam Hussein, the regime's second in command.

August 21

Warsaw Pact forces invade Czechoslovakia to put down the revisionists' subversions.

September 1

We held the second congress of the Dhofari Liberation Front in Hamrein in the central province. Sixty delegates came to represent the liberation army, the militia, and the secret organization in various regions of the Gulf. Guests from Aden including comrade Samer, who completely ignored me. We lodged in nearby farmhouses and stables—round and oval-shaped buildings with domed roofs. I counted 50. Walls made of large rocks and ceilings fashioned out of tree branches covered with a thick layer of straw. Each house has one entrance about a meter high and less than a meter wide, with a swinging wooden door. One large room inside, half of it furnished for lounging or for sleep. The other half of the room is used for storage: household items, fabric, food, firewood, dried fish. An open stove is near the entrance. A revolutionary family hosted comrade Huda and me. Huda is the daughter of a businessman based in Bahrain and was also a student at the American University of Beirut. I had heard so much about her, and I realized that she was respected by everyone. Just a few years older than I am.

September 3

I convened the meetings in the big cave that is used for livestock during the rainy season. Comrade Salih announced our political declaration: "Historically, the only social class with the ability to fight imperialism has been the class of workers and poor peasants in solidarity with soldiers and revolutionary intellectuals. The bourgeoisie has managed to carry out revolutions of democratic nationalism in advanced capitalist nations, but not in the colonies. Thus, what we need is a connected revolution. These colonized lands will not pass through a bourgeois capitalist stage. The working classes will serve the function of the revolutionary bourgeoisie; its ascendance will usher in the dictatorship of the proletariat. The working classes in the advanced capitalist countries, meanwhile, will have to give up the myth of a 'peaceful transition to socialism.'

"On the Arab front, the petite bourgeoisie's movement for national liberation has failed to solve the problem of how to execute a nationalist democratic revolution, because its theories are vague and its policies are wishy-washy, as evidenced by their disastrous defeat in the June War. The unity of the revolutionary Arab forces is the only precondition to fashioning a solid Arab unity built upon the principles of scientific socialism."

September 5

Comrade Fatih explained the position on the discussion currently taking place within the global communist movement. It is not that different from positions held by factions within the revolutionary left here in our region. They condemn revisionism while supporting the third way in the global communist movement as represented by Cuba, Vietnam, and the Democratic People's Republic of Korea.

September 7

One of our Palestinian guests asked me the secret of Mao's popularity and his influence over the revolutionary movement. I answered that Maoism was the most advanced school of Marxist thinking and that it managed to crystallize the main issues of the nationalist and socialist struggles in the colonial and neocolonial worlds.

I heard that Rushdy has become a journalist.

September 10

Comrade Huda has a very strong personality. We weren't able to get along.

September 15

I played an active role in the discussions. There's an outspoken opposition coming out of the right-wing elements.

Suddenly, Yaarib showed up. He had come through Aden. He has changed somewhat. The tension and anxiety show on him. He hugged me violently, and it almost felt like he became hard—even ejaculated. I presumed he was beside himself that we were meeting for the first time in over three years. Still, I felt uneasy around him.

September 16

Fahd has asked Yaarib for my hand in marriage!! I told Yaarib I could never marry anyone that I had not chosen for myself.

September 18

One of the fighters said to me, "We will win victory over the Sultan by God's grace, and once we're done with him, we'll turn our attention to the communists." "Why? What about them?" I asked in surprise. He heated up as he answered, "We will cleanse this land of them." I asked cautiously, "Why do you hate them so much?" He said, "Because they're atheists who screw their own mothers. They have no morals and no religion."

Then I thought that as recently as three years ago, if we had been having this discussion, I might have even agreed with him that they all had tails like monkeys.

The problem is that the traditional communists can lack the required revolutionary vision. They are not good for much besides talk. Guevara said of them that they could commit to sacrifice their lives fearlessly, as long as they never had to leave their houses, but they are unable to form an armed group strong enough to penetrate a post office.

September 20

Discussions have gone on up through today. Final declarations: build scientific socialism, foster political leadership in each unit of the popular liberation forces, train militia groups, abolish slavery, undertake agricultural reform, rename the movement the Popular Front for the Liberation of the Occupied Arabian Gulf. This is more than some minor name change. Indeed, it distances us from the local, separatist character of the older name, replacing it with commitment to the unified destiny of the whole region.

A significant resolution: Total equality between men and women.

In a side conversation, Rafie admitted to me that he's not comfortable with our current direction, even though he supported all the resolutions. He is afraid that we will lose our broad political appeal by working toward Marxist Leninism. He said that the liberation front in Vietnam did not come out and announce that it was a Marxist-Leninist movement. That helped it lay down a broad populist foundation. He also said that so few Dhofaris have even a basic understanding of the meaning of contemporary nationalism that he couldn't see any use in emphasizing Marxism to them. I answered that people do learn and that life and the struggle are about developing consciousness. But he cut me off sarcastically: "Any one of them starts off by saying, 'I'm from so-and-so tribe.' How are you supposed to get them to think about their class standing?" He is reading a book by Lenin called *Left-Wing Communism: An Infantile Disorder.* He promised to lend it to me.

September 21

The congress has elected a new leadership made up of 25 members and a five-person executive committee whose secretary is Muhammad Ahmad al-

Ghassany. The others are Ahmad Abdel Samad, Abdel Aziz al-Qadi, Abdel Hafez Jumaan, and Hamdhan Saifulzhariani. The leadership includes only three from the old group. That led the group around Yusuf Alawi, Muslim Ibn Nofel, and a number of the tribal sheikhs to break away, accusing the congress of a coup led by a nucleus doing China's bidding in getting rid of the devout Muslims.

Yaarib attacked the declarations, saying he will continue the struggle alongside Muslim Ibn Nofel's group. He has urged me to join them. A comrade commented that he is probably angry that he was not elected to the executive committee.

I ended up talking to one of their group for a long time. He asked me, "Are you a Muslim?"

I answered, "How would it change things if I were Christian, Jew, or even an atheist?"

Another broke in abruptly: "Don't you believe in God?"

I wanted to toy with him a bit, so I said: "Which one? There are so many Gods . . . and every religion has its own projection of what god is."

He shouted back: "Enough of your dodging the question! Do you believe in the God of the Muslims? Aren't you a Muslim woman?"

I answered: "I believe that I am a true Muslim woman because I believe in the God of justice and rights. Maybe I can help you understand me by looking at it this way: You picture God as a male, up above. Really, though, God is everywhere and can't be assigned a specific gender because the matter that made God is not the same as the matter that makes us and everything around us. The Quran itself says this."

Clearly, he didn't get what I was saying. The first one tried asking if I prayed. I answered that the Quran exempted us from the obligation to pray when we are traveling, and that that should apply to us here. Better for us to focus on what's useful. Better to ask me, for example, if I believe in the rights of the people or revolution or victory over our enemies.

They both fell silent for a moment, so I went on as sweet as could be: "We are not against religion — only against those who try to exploit religion to repress the masses and to justify their repression. Islam is the first system on earth to call for the abolition of slavery. Still, the institution of slavery endured throughout the period of Islamic civilization. Why? Because it was the property owners who made the decisions. The principles of religion are one thing. The ones applying them are something else completely."

Chapter Eight

At a complex fork in the main highway, Zayed drove harrowingly through complicated turns while shifting his attention constantly from the sideview mirror to the rearview mirror. Through it all, he stayed focused on the few cars that came up behind him. Then we entered the narrow streets of the old city. He pointed out the landmarks along the way: Kabrita fortress, House of Nadir museum, the walls of the old city, the US embassy. He slowed a bit as we drew near the British embassy, pointing out the flagpole fixed in the center of the open court behind the entrance: "In the past, slaves could come to this flagpole and touch it. Then they'd be granted total freedom and offered a certificate from the embassy to certify that they were free and that no one could claim them."

I liked this idea. I imagined a similar flagpole in every Arab capital.

He nodded at the ancient Al-Jalali fortress, which overlooked the area from the summit of a rocky hilltop that jutted out into the sea: "The Portuguese built this fortress four centuries ago, but the redoubts are still there. You can see the circular towers too. They were made into fortified prisons with iron grates over their windows looking out onto the sea. You climb fifty-two steps to get to the main entrance, then there's another forty-eight up to the next one. There, the chains you were transported in were exchanged for your prison chains — steel fetters that have special names: the *sanjour*, a foot and a half long, weighing twelve pounds, or the *younis*, which looks like a cannonball and weighs at least ten pounds. The prison cells have their own shapes and sizes too. On the ground floor, there's a holding cell wide enough for 120 people. Then there is cell number seven. Even though it's only about twelve meters wide, as many as sixty prisoners might be consigned to it. They had to take turns standing, sitting, and lying down to sleep."

Curious, I looked at him and said, "It's like you speak from experience."

He turned the car around and replied, "Of course. I'm a regular customer here."

It was the first time he had said anything about himself. "When?" I asked.

"I was about eighteen. When Sultan Said was still in power, they threw my big brother and me in jail after the defeat of '67. We never saw the light, and our only food was a couple of dates with bread in the morning and beans at night. The guards acted like wild beasts. None were Omani. It was just Baluch and other mercenaries. We wore cuffs that cut into our wrists and ankles, and we wrote on the walls with the blood that oozed out of the cuts. We just drew a sun or flowers . . . red flowers."

"Did you stay long?"

"In '69 we managed to escape with two comrades through an opening we made in the iron grating covering the window. We stole a British consular motor-boat parked outside and made it up to where Mina al-Fahl port is today. There, we ran out of gas and were surrounded. My brother got away, but I didn't. I was finally released with everyone else when Qaboos came to power in '70."

"And your brother?"

"He left the country after the revolution was finally put down in '75."

"And he never came back?"

"No."

"Why not? Didn't Qaboos grant a blanket amnesty?"

"You believe this blanket amnesty stuff? People who took the offer were held in custody for weeks while they were interrogated about their activities. Then they were forced to sign a condemnation of all their previous activity, alongside a pledge not to participate in politics."

"Do you know Salem?"

"The one at the Center for Music? We call him Salem Mutia. I don't know him personally."

"He was studying in Bulgaria. He told me the Front had sent him there. Did they do all that to him when he came back?"

"Everyone had to sign."

I changed the topic. "I get the idea you're still in the opposition."

He gave a laugh that showed off the polished white of his teeth. "You could say that."

"Well, what I can see is that a real modernization effort has taken place. If the Front had taken over, they would have had to do these same things. The infra-structure, for example."

"What kind of modernization are we getting here, all supervised by for-eigners? There's a British counselor in every ministry. American air and naval bases are scattered around the country. On Musandam Peninsula, in Thumrait. There's an old British base on Masirah Island; in 1975, the Americans turned it into a supply station for aircraft on their way to the Philippines. It was reno-vated in 1980, and it played a key role in the failed attempt to rescue hostages in

Iran using US helicopters that year. There's even an air base in Seeb, right next to Muscat. Then there's Israel. Not just the diplomatic and cultural ties, but the spies as well, having a romp all over the countryside."

"In Egypt," I said, "we also have American airbases, joint operations, and official relations with Israel. But we don't have any revolutionaries working inside the heart of the regime and thinking they can influence it. We are settling for the art of the possible."

He gave a scornful snort. "I never said Egypt was an example of revolution. Listen: this alleged modernization that's going on has stopped. It's over. The last mall was finished this year and there are no new projects."

"Mall?"

"You know—these big, enclosed shopping centers. The state has given what it can already. Now all its money from oil profits is going to buying expensive weapons and into projects demanded by foreign profiteers who come in and bring along high-paid management teams. Then they turn around and talk about 'Omanization.'"

"But it seems to me like the private sector is very active."

"Omani businessmen invest in projects that return to them the biggest short-term gain—mostly building and construction. They take loans from commercial lenders, then demand high rents to earn back the cost of the project in just two or three years. When the profits start coming in, they invest them in foreign banks."

"I wasn't thinking about building projects. There's also . . ."

He cut me off. "Take the university. It cost a billion, most of which passed through the hands of Margaret Thatcher's son and several ministers. See how smooth this road we're going down is? It gets resurfaced every so often by private contractors who are also the government. The system is set up to service the comprador businessmen from the ruling family, the ministers, the tribal sheikhs, and the notables. Anyone who becomes a minister or the head of a bureau becomes an instant millionaire. There's even a government policy to encourage it. When a bank director who stole a few million was exposed, he was given a two-year suspended sentence. A ministry official in charge of municipalities took a three-million-riyal bribe from a foreign company but was caught when his co-worker gave him up; he was given a *three*-year suspended sentence. A ministry official in the communications sector also got away with a two-year suspended sentence and a fine. Later, they were all pardoned. In fact, that last one was paid partial restitution!"

"This stuff is normal these days," I said. "In Egypt, we have so many such cases. And then—"

He stopped me. "I know what you're going to say. These mechanisms get money to circulate and create a type of business activity. The problem is that our bourgeois capitalists are backward compared to a nationalist bourgeoisie; they lack its ambition, its values, and its principles. This system is built on short-term policies. Oil revenue makes up about 85% of the state's budget, and 70% of GDP. You can imagine the dark future waiting for us in the coming decades when the oil runs out. The state doesn't think about that, nor does it care. Its main concern is getting along with Israel in order to curry favor with international institutions."

Is that not true of all of them?

The sun was going down and headlights began to flash on in the traffic. We made it back to the main road to the capital, which was completely empty of pedestrian traffic, and headed in the direction of the Corniche.

"Did you read it?" he asked.

I opened my briefcase, took out the bag with the diary, and nodded.

He grabbed the bag and put it under his seat. By the time he brought his hand back out, it held another bag, which he gave to me.

"Another notebook?"

He said nothing, his eyes remaining fixed on the rearview mirror. A cruiser behind us with those telltale siren lights mounted on its roof was flashing its headlights at us.

He quickly stuck the bag back under the seat. "Police."

He turned onto a side road and stopped the car. The cruiser pulled up behind us, and a policeman stepped out wearing a short-sleeved shirt and khaki-colored pants. He had on a helmet with some sort of decorative stripe across it. He ambled slowly up to the driver-side window, saluted, and asked for license and registration in a polite, deferential tone of voice. After shining a flashlight over the papers, he handed them back to Zayed, then he looked over at me and said: "Please fasten your seat belt."

Realizing I'd completely forgotten, I reflexively pulled the belt across me. He saluted again and headed back to his car.

I asked Zayed if he had a cigarette.

"Smoking is bad for your health," he said, turning the car around and shooting off toward the roundabout that Qaboos Street branches off from. He added, as though talking to himself: "He must have noticed us and seen that your belt wasn't fastened. They hang around in dark corners and then appear all of a sudden." He looked hesitant for a moment, then said as though coming to a decision: "You won't be able to contact your friends here in the capital. You're going to have to go to Salalah."

"In the south?" I asked, surprised.

He nodded. "Yes. It's more than a thousand kilometers, but the flight only takes an hour and a half. You could go by car, if you want, but that will take ten or twelve hours."

"What am I going to do there?"

"Friends of mine will help you."

"But wouldn't you find this strange if you were me? You ask me to go to the end of the earth without even mentioning who I am going to meet there or how I'll find them? You haven't even told me your name. What makes you think that I'm willing to take a trip like this in order to search for someone that—as you yourself say—I haven't seen in thirty years?"

He shrugged. "You won't regret going. It's an incredibly beautiful area. At the very least, you'll get to visit the tomb of the prophet Job." He laughed.

"But why do you care? What are you getting out of this?"

"Okay, let me tell you. It's just as well that you know a few things after all this fuss."

"Yeah, just as well."

"My comrades and I are currently in a bitter struggle on several fronts, including against a group of opportunists. They are the ones who organized a fake congress, declared themselves the new Front, raised the white flag to the regime, and started making all kinds of concessions. They're dreaming of sharing power with the authorities, but all they will ever get are posts as shoe shiners."

How many times have I heard these same expressions.

"They've been making claims that this friend of yours, Warda, had called for negotiating with the authorities and giving up the armed struggle. You know she's a mythical figure around here. Her disappearance is still a mystery. No one knows exactly what happened. Personally, I believe her comrades executed her. There are some who think she's still alive and will reappear when the moment is right. She's like the Mahdi. So you see, that's why the search for the truth about her is essential for this ongoing struggle against the opportunists."

"And how is that going to come out?"

"You've read part of her journal. The part I'm going to give you is the last bit that we have. There are other parts though . . . and they have the answers to all these mysteries."

"So where are these other parts?"

"In Salalah."

"So that's the reason you want me to go there?"

He turned to me smiling. "Exactly. You're the only one who can get to them."

"Me? Why?"

"Because she mentioned you by name and asked they be passed on to you."

I could not speak. This new information roiled around in my head. Finally I managed to say, "There's something I don't understand. You don't know what's in the remaining journals, but still you're saying that she asked they be given over to me?"

"That's what her daughter says."

"Daughter?"

He seemed slightly embarrassed when he looked at me. "Didn't you know she had a daughter?"

"No. How old is she? . . . Who's the father?"

"She's maybe seventeen or eighteen. As for the father, it's a fellow from a well-known tribe who was one of the leaders in the Front before he disappeared with her and her brother. The daughter, meanwhile, is in her paternal uncle's custody and no one can go near her. She has the last of the journals, but she refuses to give them to anyone besides you or another Lebanese fellow. So now you see, we were delighted when we heard about your visit."

"How am I supposed to find her?"

"She's the head of the Women's Center of Mirbat, near Salalah."

"What's her name?"

"Waad. Waad al-Ghimeiry."

I shook my head in disbelief. "Suppose I had never come in the first place."

"We were bound to find a way, but in any case, you're here now, so . . ."

"If I go, how do I contact your friends? For that matter, how do I get back in touch with you?"

"Oh, that's not necessary. They'll know when you get there. They'll be able to recognize you easily. Salalah is a small town. Its population probably doesn't equal two blocks in Cairo."

I looked at the landmarks flashing by us. I said, "I don't actually think that I want to learn her fate so badly that I would put myself through all these adventures. I'm just a visitor passing through. I've got nothing to do with your problems and your mysteries."

He took out the bag that he had hidden again under his seat. "Have a read first. You might just change your mind. I'll contact you again in two days."

I took the bag and flipped it over. There was printed the name Lacoste and the famous crocodile logo. It felt light, as though there were only a few pages inside. I stuck it in my briefcase, which I slung over my shoulder. We had made it back to the Rawi roundabout and I noticed the billboard for Kentucky Fried

Chicken nearby, so I asked him to stop the car. I opened the door to get out, but then paused. "Why are you so interested in her notes and journals right now?"

"Because we only just found out these last parts exist."

"You suppose these last parts will reinforce your side's position in the struggle. But what if it's the opposite?"

His smile broadened. "Don't you remember the story of Lenin's Testament?"

Chapter Nine

DHOFAR MOUNTAINS, 1968-1970

October 31, 1968

We formed an organization, the Council for the Resolution of the People's Problems. Five members: Rafie, Amar, Ghazal, Jedad, and myself. We will circle through the western region trying to solve tribal disputes, struggles over land and water, and personal differences. We should meet on a regular basis. Fahd opposed my election to the committee. Comrade Awad has taken my place as leader of our platoon. He's from Salalah — of African origin. Clear vitality. Also, an ability to mediate all kinds of disputes. His understanding of theory is still a bit lacking, though.

Jedad is 26. He was born in the northern part of the central region. He moved to Abu Dhabi in the early '60s and joined the police. There, he was able to take primary school classes and joined the Front's secret organization. In early 1965 he went back to Muscat on vacation and ended up joining the revolution.

November 1

The camp had a going-away party for me. I made fried *luqmat al-qadi* donuts, and we chanted revolutionary slogans. Comrade Awad asked me if I knew how to dance. I said, "Of course." I thought he meant Western dancing. When they brought me a belly dancing belt, I gave him a dirty look and told him that belly dancing is a symbol of women's exploitation from the era of feudalism and enslavement. I proposed we do a traditional Dhofari line dance instead.

Awad's wife is also Black. Full of charm. Tall, skinny, and flat-chested.

Contradictory feelings. I devoted three years of my life to these guerrillas. I wouldn't be surprised if Fahd played a role in my being taken from the military theater, since he doesn't hide his ambition to move up in the ranks. At the same time, I have to admit that I am happy. No question about it: warfare is inhuman.

November 2

We gathered to get to know each other, put together a plan of action, and form a set of guiding principles. Our main goal is to educate the masses regarding the new spirit of work, cooperation, coordination, tolerance, and resistance to oppression.

The first task is to overcome the challenges in getting supplies to the central region. Camels have to stumble slowly through rocks and crags to get there. I suggested using mules instead. They seemed resistant, even disdainful. Highlanders despise all pack animals except camels.

November 3

Dhalkut is a coastal town with beautiful buildings about 80 km up the coast from Salalah. Its population is mostly peasants who herd cattle in the surrounding hills and sow corn to harvest in the autumn. Tobacco grows wild there on the cliffs. We visited a mountain village to get a sense of opinions about the cause. The tribal sheikh attacked a woman because she dared to give her cattle water before his had drunk. We traveled most of the way on camels, then continued the last section on foot. We were greeted by revolutionary graffiti plastered on the walls: "Unite, O people of the Gulf!" "The hour for liberation has arrived." "Imperialism fears the people's brute strength." "Confront reactionary violence with organized revolutionary force!" "The people's liberation force serves the will of the people." "We spill our hot blood in the fight for greater good!" "The people's will is stronger than advanced weapons."

Thatched huts with roofs of palm branches, some a conical shape, like African huts. Some fly the Front's red, white, and black flag. The political commissar for regional unity and his wife welcomed us. She wore a nose ring and sandals. She offered us water from a hollowed-out coconut shell that she had ladled the water into with a bowl. She made tea in a small can that might have held cheese, olives, or shortening, boiling the water over one of their traditional Primus stoves. Nearby, a guerrilla crouched on a mound with a pair of binoculars. He had on a pair of shorts and a vest, and several ammunition belts hung across his chest. Next to him, a comrade wore a strange combination of red socks and rubber boots.

An old man rushed over to us. He asked us to treat his son. I said, "We aren't doctors." The commissar broke in and told him that we were with the revolution. I couldn't tell whether the old man understood or not. In any case, he persisted. The commissar then tried telling him that we were "representers," their local way of saying photographers, but he still showed no sign of understanding and insisted that we look at his son. We went with him to a hut at the edge of the village. There we found a young boy with a pus-swollen abscess on his leg. I told the officer to organize a transfer to Hawf, another hour down the coast, so we could use 14 *October*, our launch that's docked nearby, and get him to Ghaydah. Then from there to Al-Riyan airport and on to Aden.

We drank tea together and watched a group of women reinforcing stones that had fallen from a rim built up around a water hole. Before the revolution, every tribe had its own water source. Now, each one is open to all. We saw a young man lift a small bucket that we had sipped water out of and set it down in front of two camels. The commissar proudly showed off to us the first water pump in the liberated zone. It had long white pipes that fed into an iron tank resting on two rocks, with a pit to light a fire underneath. "We purify our own water," he boasted.

I noticed an unarmed man with a shiny pendant hanging on his chest. It had little medallions the size of large coins with colored pictures of Mao. I pointed at one of them and asked him, "Who's that?" He answered, "Leader of the Muslims." I asked, "Who told you that?" And he pointed to the commissar. The commissar explained, a little embarrassed: "We tell them this so that they'll stand with us." I told him this kind of deception was not acceptable, either by our revolution or even by Mao himself. If he wanted to win over the people, he needed to be their servant, solve their problems, and nurture their consciousness. At that point, there would be no need for lying.

November 4

We listened to the details of a rape case, and then we held a closed meeting to discuss our plan of action. Comrade Amar believed we should be stern in order to teach a lesson to the forces of reaction and at the same time inspire the public to stand against them. His speech was good. He has a persuasive speaking style, deliberate and wise, and he just sounds convincing. He can recite the Quran from memory, and when he is ready to make his point, he puts his hand behind his ear the way the reciters do as they chant. Because of this, we gave him the nickname "the Sheikh." Moajib, who worked before as a herder in the eastern region, supported him. The opposing view came from the other two comrades. Ghazal argued that we need to show a human face and try not to provoke enmity. He suggested light punishment. Comrade Rafie's agreement with this position surprised me. He was an outcast descended from slaves, who had suffered at the hands of the tribal leaders. When my turn came, I intended to support the first position. But Rafie gave me this heartfelt, paternal stare that stopped me. Then he took the pressure off me by suggesting that we let our people choose for themselves the proper judgment.

The local unit of the popular army had imprisoned the man. We ordered that he be transferred back to the scene of the crime, where the woman narrated in front of everyone else what had happened. Then I spoke on behalf of the committee. I made clear that all citizens possessed equal rights on land and at sea, and I asked those present to specify a just punishment for the perpetrator. In the end, they decided to forgive him because it was a first offense. We settled for having him apologize to the woman.

November 5

In the morning, I felt for a moment that I was back in Sana. The spirit of our old house, the lowing of the cattle, the cries of the people, the laughter of the children. I dreamed mistily. I snapped out of it when it became clear what they were doing. They were playing a game where they used tree branches as rifles and machine guns to attack the goats, which they pretended to be British and Pakistani soldiers.

Suddenly, I heard a faint, familiar buzz. In the distance, attack helicopters were flying toward us. I shouted a warning and ran to the hut where I had left my weapon. Watched as one chopper drew near and then hovered above us. Probably a reconnaissance mission. I crouched behind a stone wall, pointed my weapon up, and fired at it. Fire came on it from other directions, so it rose quickly and escaped. Soon after, there was a deafening explosion. It had struck the well the people use for their water, hitting two cows and a camel in the process. The comrades committed immediately to use funds from the Front's treasury to reimburse the villagers for the wounded animals. Then we slaughtered them and cut their meat into strips that we dried in the sun and made into jerky.

November 6

A young man escaped from his father's house on the English base and climbed up to our headquarters. He was carrying papers from an English officer. I was charged with reading through them and translating them into Arabic. The officer's name is Captain S. Hibbert. They seem like some sort of report or journalistic investigation. I wrote out a few paragraphs:

"I had the honour of being delegated to serve in the Sultan's army. It was fall and the hills were enveloped in fog and torrential rain, so we withdrew the company to the northern plains at the edge of the desert. It was two days' march before we could join with our next closest battalion in the region that we designated as the western region.

"Everything is quiet here for now. The rebels are taking advantage of the thick cover afforded them by the season to transport caravans of camels bearing weapons, ammunition, and landmines from their villages in southern Yemen. So I spent my first few weeks here undertaking a series of missions to cut off the supply routes they were using. I also took advantage of the chance to improve my command of Arabic and to get on a bit with the soldiers.

"The Sultan's army is made up of three divisions. There is also a small air force that consists of about a half dozen dodgy old Provosts with mounted guns and rocket launchers. There is a naval force as well, made up of two old wooden dhows, which is a kind of ship found commonly along the coast of the Arabian Peninsula. This small force is charged with controlling a region the size of the British Isles that lacks good roads and transport routes.

"Two-thirds of our force are mercenaries from Baluchistan who have crossed the Arabian Gulf to join the Sultan's army. The other third come out of the Omani tribes. The official language of the army is Arabic, but most Baluch do not speak more than a few words, so we end up relying on translators. Each company has two or three British officers and is equipped with No. 4 rifles, 3.3 mm revolvers, Vicker machine guns, and 81 mm grenade launchers. We have Bedford and Land Rover transport vehicles too, but we often resort to donkeys because there are so few areas that support large vehicles.

"During the first month of my stay, the area was quiet. Then one day I was returning in a Land Rover with a reconnaissance unit from an area called Jidreet on the Yemeni border when we were barraged with machine gun fire from an ambush carried out by about thirty rebels. I was wounded in the leg by the first round of fire, so I turned quickly and crashed into a bush. We were thrown from the vehicle. Unfortunately, the three soldiers riding in the back were hit. The ambush was well positioned in a covered spot less than 100 meters from us, but the thick fog and low visibility affected the aim of the rebels, who continued shooting at us for another ten minutes before retreating once we had gathered ourselves in fortified positions. We managed to get the vehicles running, even though two were struck in several places, and we worked our way back to camp with our four casualties.

"This operation gave us an important lesson. It was an important turn in the war, being the first time the rebels had used automatic rifles on us. The wasted shots scattered around us made it clear that most of them were armed with Soviet-made SKS 7.62 carbines. After that, we kept reinforcements close by and took the upper hand in most of our subsequent clashes. Not long after, the enemy started to use medium-range mortars for the first time, but they could not aim.

"As soon as the fall season ended, daily clashes started up with the rebels, who continuously attacked the handful of old fortresses made from mud brick that lined the coastal villages. They hit the camps with mortar fire almost every night, until it became impossible to control so unsettled an area. Water was scarce and our supplies ran low. We often had to transport our wounded on donkeys. Yes, we could contain the enemy; but we could not win the war.

"At that point, our leadership changed its strategy and we abandoned our fortifications along that arid plane in northern Dhofar. I had grown strangely attached to that region full of flies where we had organized successful raids in the thick forests of Jebel al-Qamar and killed a number of Shamas, an important clan within the Qarra tribe.

"Our new objective was to take control of water routes, starting by occupying a coastal village called Dhalkut located near Ras Dharbat Ali. From there, we could control the enemy's supply lines that originate in the village of Hawf on the other side of the border with South Yemen. We had a chance before we embarked on this new phase for two weeks of R&R near an abandoned Portuguese fort in Raysut, where members of our company learned to swim and we carried out ship launching drills. We had two dhows in our possession. The first belonged to the Sultan. The second belonged to an Omani sheikh and was piloted by one of his slaves. We could launch out of them with our three Gemini rubber dinghies.

"We made landing in Dhalkut without incident, but when we started to inspect the village it became clear to us that everyone old enough to carry a weapon had gone up into the mountains. We had just begun to unload when bursts of automatic weapons fire started to rain down on us, and then heavy mortar fire was launched from the thick tree cover on the slopes where a force of maybe fifty rebels hid. We stuck it out in our camp for all of three nights, but the succession of enemy attacks made clear to us the impossibility of occupying that spot, so we packed, destroyed the wells, abandoned the camp under cover of nightfall, and returned to Raysut.

"We had to change our strategic plan once again. We ended up spending the next four months on nocturnal disembarkation missions all up and down the coast of Dhofar, from Ras Darba in the west to the village of Sadah in the east. Some of these incursions succeeded brilliantly. We killed a number of rebels and managed to confiscate some of their automatic weapons. Likewise, we razed villages that were known to harbor rebels and shot dead the livestock of the villagers. Then there were the corpses of the dead rebels that we found: these we stacked in a corner of the Salalah Souk as a warning to anyone enticed by the thought of joining the guerrillas."

I was impressed by the captain's honesty. He called us rebels. In other reports, they just used the Arabic word for "enemy," written in Latin letters but never really spelled right.

November 7

The central committee of the Chinese Communist party issued a report two days ago on the crimes of Liu Shao Chi. It described him as seizing the reins of power and steering down the road of capitalism. He was called an apostate, a foreign agent, a traitor against the working class lurking inside the party, and an agent of imperialism and contemporary revisionism. The committee approved by acclamation a motion to expel him for life from the party and to strip him of all titles.

I ran into a comrade who had come from Hadhramaut. He said many Indonesians who traced their origins to the region had come back fleeing Suharto's massacres, and upon arrival here they filled the mosques with pictures of Mao and with slogans celebrating the cultural revolution and attacking "socialist imperialism," by which they mean the Soviet Union.

November 8

Four days of bloodshed in Jordan. The Palestinian resistance stood their ground. The Jordanian army used tanks and heavy weapons to crush the camps where the guerrillas and refugees were based. They arrested 200 resistance fighters. Should they call for the liberation of Jordan, so that it might become another North Vietnam?

The Front has issued the first declaration of its kind in the Arab world: polygyny declared illegal.

For the first time, a woman from the western region has joined: Tafoul Mutia, a 15-year-old-herder. Her family fears British vengeance.

November 13

The Front has sent a delegation of ten comrades for military training in China. I wanted to go. The comrades convinced me that the organizational work going on in the liberated areas needs me.

December

A great victory. Johnson has decided to stop the American bombing raids on Vietnam. The revolutionaries are advancing toward Saigon.

Israel has launched a raid on the Beirut airport, destroying ten planes.

Major differences have erupted inside the Sudanese Communist party. Ahmad Suleiman published some articles that described the armed resistance as the only hope for salvation. Abdelkhaliq Mahjoub wrote a strong response.

A fight broke out between Bakheet and Hamd that escalated quickly to the point that Bakheet shot Hamd and he died instantly. The men arrested Bakheet, but he managed to escape. I doubt that his tribe will give him shelter. The two men are from competing families within the same tribe. An old feud that goes back decades. A sheikh from the first family stole a hundred head of cattle from the second many years ago.

The men demanded that Bakheet be tried and sentenced to death. Some were saying it was premeditated murder, but others argued that it was just an accident. The defendant had been an exemplary soldier. Now what? Firing squad? We can't expel him from the Front or its military wing, because he could go over to the other side and take valuable reconnaissance with him. We have no prison to hold him in. We might be able to just put him aside, keeping him from important missions, relegating him to educational and cultural rounds.

January 1, 1969

We celebrated the new year at the camp on Jebel al-Qamar. The comrades reinforced the supply of tea and sugar and slaughtered a goat. We started singing. Comrade Ghazal came to me and said that he was organizing a small private party after the big party ended. I asked him who would attend and he said, "Just us committee members." He winked at me and told me that he was saving part of a bottle of arak for the occasion. I told him I had forbidden the comrades to drink and that it made no sense to allow for myself what I had forbidden to them. Then I threw in one more thing: "I promise you I'll drink with you until dawn after the victory." He couldn't even formulate an answer.

We launched a two-step mass-education initiative that starts with literacy classes, then moves to a combination of Arabic language and political principles. For the different levels, we offer literacy lessons at the same time that we teach political culture. As soon as the students master the letters of the alphabet, we add politically engaged spelling lessons: c-l-a-s-s, f-r-e-e, s-o-c-i-a-l, f-i-g-h-t, r-e-v-o-l-u-t-i-o-n, w-o-r-k-e-r, p-e-a-s-a-n-t, i-m-p-e-r-i-a-l-i-s-m. After that, the students move on to study simple texts extracted from the programs of the political commissars. These are 25 lessons that cover four main topics: characteristics of the revolutionary, principles of organization, the bases of Marxist-Leninist thought, and internationalism through national liberation and class struggle.

January 3

I visited the women's school. Without exception, every woman there was completely illiterate. Sisters, mothers, and wives of the men in the struggle. Four classes of 15 students each. A range of ages between 8 and 40. Refugee women from the eastern and central provinces whose homes were destroyed by the Sultan's bombing raids. We sat on the ground in a circle around a small table as they clutched their children. Two were pregnant. We studied together from 8 until 10, then they left to do their housework. In one year, 70 women will have learned to read and write.

I began to learn their stories. Tafoul from Kafkut told me how the mercenaries had burned and razed everything in her village, from livestock to homes. The same story from Mona, who came from the Nahiz Valley. Tafoul Salem sat and practiced assembly of an automatic weapon while she described how mercenaries attacked the village of Beit Zarbak, shooting randomly at a father of seven who had stepped outside unarmed and then burning down all one hundred huts in the village. Others as well.

January 4

The school has four teachers and a principal. When I was asked to speak to the class, I narrated to the girls a story from tribal folklore that warns against the wiles of women and even promotes female infanticide. It starts with a youth who saves his baby sister from the sword of his father, who is committed to murdering every baby girl. The brother escapes with her and takes charge of her upbringing. She grows, becomes a young woman, and falls in love with a handsome prince, but her brother opposes the match, and she in turn runs away with her lover after tricking her brother by promising to obey him. The original version describes how the brother reconciles with their father and comes to realize that it would have been better for the father to kill her from the start. I did not tell this part of the story. Instead, I changed it so that the brother and father reconcile and the father decides that he himself is the reason for everything that's happened because of the enmity he caused in the family when the girl was born. The girls already knew the original version; they liked the new ending I made up.

I studied their plain faces, marked by hunger, illness. I thought about their way of life. The words of Guevara sprang to mind: "They grow and mature without tutelage like weeds in the field, then too soon their lives are overrun by unrelenting and oppressive work." These moments only reinforce my certainty about the path I have chosen.

January 5

There is total ignorance around the topic of sex. Decided to give the group a class on the basics. Simple anatomy, for example, like the location of the clitoris and the female circumcisions they are exposed to and the way these reduce their pleasure and enjoyment of their own bodies. Also, how to compensate as best they can after it's been done, and the need to prevent the same tragedy from happening to their own girls. I discovered that the married women did not practice any form of birth control. I told them that, yes, we do want new citizens, but we also need to preserve the health of the citizens we already have. For that reason, they have to put some time between one child and the next, so their bodies can rest and their strength can come back. I pointed out skinny little Fatima, mother of two children and about to deliver a third. Laughter rumbled through the room, and one of them explained to me that she was possessed, a *mukhatila*. "She actually became pregnant two years ago when her husband went to work along the Gulf coast. The baby refused to come out at the natural time and has kept her under its spell until now." I didn't want to argue about the superstitions they all still believe in. I knew that they grew up around the traditional need to protect women whose husbands are away for long periods. Instead I persuaded them using real-life examples, explaining the need to rest a few months out of every year. I explained how to count out the days in their period. I promised them that the first priority of the revolution, once it liberated the country, would be to outlaw clitoridectomy and make widely available birth control measures and women's health supplies.

January 7

The husband of one of the women is one of our fighters. He says I am turning their morals upside down and putting decadent ideas in their heads. He has submitted a complaint to the council. Comrade Amar has taken his side. He, too, thinks I am corrupting them. I defended my position. I said it was impossible to distinguish social questions from national ones. This revolutionary husband is a skilled fighter. His woman, who is still nursing a child, refused to sleep with him out of fear that she would become pregnant again. She asked him to wait until the end of her cycle. Even some of the women have renounced me!

I argued with Amar, but he held his position that we have to respect traditions and customs. I shot back that the very essence of our struggle is rebellion against tradition, custom, and hypocrisy.

At night, Fatima began to go into labor. When I rushed to offer my help, she refused it. Womanhood is measured here in the act of childbirth. The pregnant woman leaves her family for an isolated place where she lies on a haystack or bed of straw and gives birth. Then she uses sharp rocks or a knife to cut the umbilical cord. The custom is that she walks on her own two feet back home carrying the child. The people feel that the woman who is assisted by another during childbirth is weak and lacks a maternal nature.

January 8

We participated in the opening of a major training center near the border called Camp Revolution. Run by a five-person leadership team made up of the supervisor Amr, a key member of the original group that engaged the armed struggle in June of '65; Amr's two assistants; and two political commissars, Abdel Aziz Abdel Rahman, who has studied in Egypt and Kuwait and is the son of a judge from Salalah, and Huda, who is in charge of political lessons for the women fighters. I expected to meet her at the opening of the camp, but she was in Aden dealing with organizational matters.

Forty young men and eight young women—a large number are Black. The girls stay in their own tents. Everyone sleeps on the ground. There are no bathrooms because not enough water . . . even for drinking. Comrade Amar caused a problem when he insisted on washing. He is so very focused on his personal hygiene. We get plenty of tea and rice from Yemen. Ghazal asked for lemon juice, then insisted, saying he had cramps. I'm always suspicious when these sudden illnesses pop up.

Everyone undergoes a four-month intensive training course. Young men and women train together. Revolutionary education has forged a new relationship between the sexes built on equality. Men no longer perceive women just as toys there to give them pleasure—as in, they give a command and their women submit. Women are now partners in life, and comrades. At times, relationships spring up between a young man and woman, but these lead not just to marriage but to continuation of the struggle too.

January 9

A withering day that starts at 5 A.M. Young men and women gather at the center to salute the flag, then everyone helps make breakfast—keeping their rifles at their side all along. Four hours' worth of military drills. Lunch and basic reading classes, then two more hours of military drills. Dinner at around 5 P.M., followed by four more hours of political education.

Political culture for those who already read Arabic is divided into two sections. The first includes the Front's writings: the charter; analysis of the social structure around the different regions of Dhofar, and of women and revolution in the Gulf; studies of Arab national liberation movements and labor movements, as well as Nasserism, Baathism, and the history of Arab communist parties.

The second section consists of the official set of texts adopted by the leadership at the second congress, including *The Communist Manifesto*, selections from Lenin, and the Little Red Book. Mao's call to sacrifice oneself resonates strongly with our guerrillas. There are also the lessons covering historical materialism and dialectical materialism from Stalin and a sampling of Arabic translations of the writings of Ho Chi Minh, Guevara, Castro, and Kim Il Sung. Then there are the books issued by the Democratic Popular Front for the Liberation of Palestine, and the Lebanese magazine *Al-Hurriya* that we rely on as a weekly sampling of culture.

January 10

I discovered by accident that Ghazal did not drink the lemon juice, in fact is still hanging on to it. Asked him about the cramps. He said they had gone away. He always tries to get things that are rare or unavailable to the others.

Aziza's husband came to the camp to ask that she be sent back home. She had gone through the brother of one of her girlfriends to contact the Front about a year ago. She started off gathering donations of food and supplies. Her husband tried to stop her, so she kept on in secret. When he found out, they argued and he beat her, so she left the house and joined the women's brigade. We decided to reject his request on the basis that she had volunteered for service of her own free will. In fact, if her opinion had been asked before she married, there never would have been a problem in the first place.

January 13

The Front has formed three new agricultural committees. It announced that it would abolish tribal ownership of land and the rents owed to the tribes. All lands and all wells under the Front's authority to become publicly owned. As a result, the Front is abolishing the monopoly of two tribes in the western region over the majority of lands and wells.

The land is now cultivated on a cooperative basis under the supervision of local agricultural councils. The cooperative as a unit of production does not differ a great deal from the previous unit of production that involved several families working together, in other words subsets of the whole tribe. The main difference is that we have abolished the rents and the accumulation of property by individuals or tribes. Since the Front is the biggest consumer of foodstuffs in the region, it usually buys the harvest from farmers with cash. In spite of the region's relative isolation, a cash economy has penetrated Dhofari society. We want to encourage this.

January 15

Our efforts have succeeded. Salem Hassan is now in Aden, will go to Bulgaria in a week for eye surgery.

January 18

A new victory for socialism: the Soyuz 5 Soviet spaceship lands back on earth after linking with Soyuz 4 in outer space. The operation established the first orbiting space station in human history.

Sati al-Husri, who focused in his writings on the nationalist cause, has died. His emphasis was on the creation of a common Pan-Arab political language, but he neglected other aspects of nationalism, most importantly the concept of economic cooperation. The Arab nation must enter together into the same phase of economic advancement. It won't work for one part to apply socialism, for example, while another still follows the principles of capitalism or feudalism.

For the first time, we ordered an execution. A tribal sheikh offered us strong assistance during a particularly tough period but then began to assert control over his personal account by skimming from the food sent to us by the Front's cell in Salalah. Then he killed his neighbor because he wanted his wife. Sometimes, they start off as innocent revolutionaries and end up concerned only with their own personal benefit.

Acts of murder before September 1968 were punished through payment of compensation by the family of the murderer to the family of the victim. Now they are punished by execution.

February

In order to break the economic embargo, construction began on a road connecting the sixth province in South Yemen to the liberated western region.

Members of the popular liberation army and the popular militia, chosen a few at a time from the various brigades, are carrying out the work. Citizens in the area, who will be able to use the road, are also helping out, and this is strengthening the connection between the Front and the people. The workers mostly lack the proper digging tools. They have no bulldozers, and they are subject to attacks from enemy air patrols.

The theater of operations has relocated out of the central and eastern regions to the western region that borders South Yemen. The army of the Sultanate has mobilized a large force to block the connections happening between the revolution in Dhofar and its rearguard in South Yemen. These forces are centered in remote villages. In Mazhub, Captain Clark has his headquarters, with satellites in Januk and Kharat.

The delegation is back from China. Members now in leadership roles in a number of units. They repeat the words of Mao every chance they get.

March

I met one of the Chinese—as we have come to call those just back from China. Asked him about his impressions. He spoke with wonder about their organization, the cleanliness, the discipline, the health, and all the advancements. I asked him about the political atmosphere and the cultural revolution. He looked hesitant, then said that China is still an enigma and its people have their own way of dealing with their problems. While we were talking, I sensed a rustling in the bushes and I jumped. He calmly said, "Don't be afraid, comrade. It's just a snake." He repeated a version of Mao's famous slogan "Imperialism is a paper tiger," which he paraphrased: "The snake is a paper tiger." That night, a young boy was bitten by what I believe was the same snake. We failed to save him. I told the Chinese comrade that snakes also have the power to kill.

A campaign to encourage settlements in the liberated zone is under way. The goal is to make farming the economic engine that drives the western region. Mobility is a basic feature of tribal life. Members of tribes tend not to settle down, and show a general distaste for the manual labor that farming demands.

The amassing of the popular militia goes on. Its mission has two components: it provides basic training for anyone who aspires to join the liberation army, and it embodies the concept of the "people's army"—that component of the masses that can take up arms without abandoning their role in the productive sector.

April 14

The Chinese Communist party has ratified a new charter: Maoist thought the most advanced stage of Marxist-Leninist thinking; Lin Biao its guardian. There are rumors of a split over whether to prioritize industrialization or agricultural development.

I have discovered that Sheikh Amar has been living a story of unrequited love. He's from the neighborhood around the fortress in Salalah where the Sultan's palace is, surrounded by the dwellings of servants, slaves, and soldiers. He fell in love with a young girl from the outskirts of town. Of course her family opposed the marriage, so he ran off to Kuwait, where he connected with the revolution.

April 24

The nationalist and progressive parties in Lebanon organized a protest against the government-implemented measures to interdict all guerrilla activity per the request of the Phalange party and others. When a soldier opened fire on the demonstrators, violent clashes broke out. Eighteen dead, 116 wounded.

Two new decrees issued in Baghdad: the outlawing of the miniskirt, and restriction of women in the workplace. I defended the first one to the other comrades, arguing that the miniskirt makes a woman into a toy and a sex object. Ghazal's mocking got to me, said that I must have an ugly pair of legs. I examined them carefully before I went to sleep.

May 3

The liberation army has taken on new responsibilities: digging irrigation ditches and wells, building dams, setting up warehouses. Progress is slow, and even the simplest tools and experience are in short supply.

May 15

The politburo of the Sudanese Communist party has turned down an offer from a group of officers to carry out a military coup d'état on its behalf.

May 25

Revolution in Sudan. A military takeover led by General Jaafar Nimeiry and Hashem al-Atta.

The embargo being imposed on the countryside here has cut the highlanders off from their traditional markets in the villages along the coast. We are facing a bona fide starvation campaign.

May 31

The wide fields with a large yield during the rainy season have been divided up along the eastern portion of the Jebel Qarra region. A portion goes to the residents, and the rest is for the Front to cultivate. Small dams have been built as well in an effort to save some water for the dry season. Farmers are being encouraged to cultivate maize, cucumber, and beans.

June 1

New information about the situation in Sudan. Babiker Al Nour and Hashem al-Atta—known for their close ties to the Communist party—have been appointed to the revolutionary council, although they were not directly involved in the handover of power. The coup leaders also appointed four leaders from the Communist party to ministerial posts without even talking to the party. The party turned around and issued a declaration saying that a military coup was no solution to the nation's political crisis. Abdelkhaliq Mahjoub suggested to his colleagues that they refuse participation in any ministries, but most members of the central council opposed him—most forcefully, Ahmad Suleiman and the group appointed to the ministries.

June 9

The fourth anniversary of the revolution. We put together a study circle to discuss an article in the French magazine *La Pensée* about the Asiatic mode of production. Marx designated four modes of production that have defined human history, namely primitive communism, antique or ancient production, feudalism, and capitalism. He predicted that the contradictions within the capitalist mode of production would result in a socialist mode of production that would resolve its contradictions. Stalin considered these categories definitive, but he ignored the earlier discussions of an alternative that could be called the Asiatic mode of production. This mode is characteristic of the development of the primitive mode in many Eastern societies, particularly in the large agricultural civilizations of China, India, Egypt, and the Fertile Crescent. These civilizations are distinguished by their foundation of industrial irrigation, lack of private land ownership (in contrast to the Romans and the Greeks), establishment of a strong centralized state, abundance of manual labor, and the use of landed peasants bonded through taxation of their land paid to an absolute ruler—the one true proprietor of all land—in the place of systems of slavery. In these societies, the state took upon itself the indispensable role of establishing an agricultural infrastructure by building irrigation networks and supervising the distribution of water. The state was markedly centralized. (The Egyptian Pharaoh, for example, was originally known as the "master irrigation engineer.") These characteristics differ completely from those of the ancient mode of production or the traditional feudal one. European feudalism, for example, did not depend on a total centralization, and even the monarch was not much more than a feudal lord picked out from among his peers and with powers that didn't extend very far outside his own fiefdom, except that he could impose his will on the weakest of the other lords. Here we see the clear difference between a scarcity of manual labor and the abundance of it found in Eastern societies and resulting in grand public works, like the Pyramids of Giza or the Great Wall of China.

June 14

Farmers are preparing for the rainy season. Tilling the land and planting seeds.

Incendiary bombs are everywhere, increasing in use during the planting season. It's a hellish invention that has become widespread, it seems, in Vietnam. Much cheaper than traditional bombs that must be launched from a Strikemaster. A 40-gallon barrel is filled with flammable liquid and rigged up with a fuse to ignite its contents. They can be loaded in the back of a Skyvan. Once the safety trigger is released, they can be dumped from the plane, the fuse already lit. The moment they hit the ground they become a huge fireball, emitting thick black clouds of smoke around the entire area. Just two barrels can devastate an area the size of a football pitch.

June 18

I had my 29th birthday a few days ago. So strange. Time has passed quickly. I never imagined I would still be here. I feel I have grown old. I noticed a gray hair.

President Qahtan al-Shaaby has let Muhammad Ali Haitham go from his post as minister of the interior.

June 22

The Egyptian armed forces continue to press their war of attrition against the enemy, firing their cannon across the Suez Canal. Moshe Dayan declares: "The Suez Canal has become a new front in our war." Palestinian guerrilla operations on every front: mines, ambushes, car bombs, Molotov cocktails.

June 23, dawn

Radio Aden has announced that President Qahtan al-Shaaby has submitted his resignation and the leadership council of the National Front has accepted it. The broadcast mentioned jockeying for position at all levels. The presidential council is made up of five members: Interior Minister Muhammad Ali Haitham; Culture Minister Abdelfattah Ismail, who was also leader of the movement before it took power; Defense Minister Muhammad Salih al-Awlaki; the leader of the Dhale militia, Ali Antar; and the leader of the Fadhli militia, Salim Rubai, who was also elected president of the council. Muhammad Ali Haitham has been named prime minister, and Abdelfattah Ismail general secretary of the National Front's organizing committee.

We have been given access to Democratic Yemen's broadcast facilities.

The liberation army has moved in to surround the British headquarters for the western region near Madhub.

June 25

The British have completely cleared out of Madhub. We found a huge Russian cannon, dozens of abandoned bunkers, and hundreds of empty boxes of ammunition with the Muscat Defense Ministry's insignia. An inspection of one of the bunkers found thick walls, a smooth floor, Yardley shaving cream, cases of beer, the full-color Sunday supplement for the *Times* of London, and sheets of carbon paper for reading code. All that's left of the enemy army is the companies stationed in Dhalkut and Rakhiut on the coast.

An old man came to us asking that we issue a letter ordering that his young wife return to his home and submit to him. If she won't agree, he says, he will be satisfied getting some oils or medicines that traveling salesmen bring from the city to treat human and animal ailments instead.

June 27

Tafoul took part in the defense of Shaabut, a battle that lasted 24 hours. She carried water, filled jugs for the fighters, and even fired a few shots herself.

We now control almost all the highlands, including the road from Thumrait to Salalah.

July 12

The comrades found in one of the stations that they occupied some barrels of fuel, a Pakistani ID with the name Said on it, and a note with these words written in English: "We are hitting them 24 hours a day and they keep firing back."

August

Our comrades have now occupied the coastal town of Rakhiut and taken its commissioner, Hamid Bin Said, into custody. With that, the western region of Dhofar is now liberated, and British Petroleum's operations brought to a halt. The government controls only Salalah and its immediate suburbs. The rest of the coastline is at our disposal. I went to Rakhiut for the trial of the commissioner. It's located between two mountains 48 km from the border with Yemen. Made up of 300 stone houses. The revolutionary court issued an execution order pursuant to the guilty verdict for treason to the nation and spying for the British.

Saddam Hussein has been named vice president of Iraq.

Agence France Presse: "The Palestinian resistance is headed down the path toward a war for national liberation."

September 1

A group of young officers, led by Colonel Muammar Gaddafi, have deposed the king in Libya and declared a republic. The American military base called Wheelus has come under Libyan sovereignty. Plan in place to cleanse the other British and American bases.

I went to a meeting where we talked about the new situation now that the western zone is totally liberated. The agenda included events in China and Aden as well as the latest news of the struggle. Comrade Rafie said that our latest victories raise two important questions: First, how to implant an allegiance to proletarian rule in a rural, precapitalist region made up of herders, fishermen, porters, slaves, and farmers—all completely ignorant of Marxist principles. Second, how to dismantle tribalism and wage war against tribal values and traditions while at the same time building a new foundation for society.

The liberated zone is almost a third of Dhofar's land area, stretching from Ras Dharbat Ali at the Yemeni border to Raysut. It's the least densely populated region of Dhofar, only 10,000 inhabitants. The people live off their livestock, seasonal farming, and some fishing along the coast. They are made up of 20 tribes, the two biggest and richest being the Aissa family and the Mashaikh. Both are from Qarra, and between them they control most of the arable land and fresh water.

About a hundred fighters have collected back at the central headquarters of the free western zone. They carry out various duties. They might be sent down the road leading to the edge of the desert that is marked by the wreckage of the Provost jet fighter we shot down in the summer, or they might head to the coast for surveillance of infiltrators and protection of supply and weapons shipments.

The flowers on the frankincense have bloomed. Yellow petals, a scarlet center.

September 5

I listened to the Friday sermon at high prayer in Rakhiut Mosque. Sheikh Ali had been its imam from 1960 until 1966, when he clashed with the commissioner of Rakhiut and was forced to leave. He's back now living with his wife, his mother, and his son. They support themselves with the money he is paid for officiating over religious ceremonies and from their goats. He used his sermon to attack imperialism and support the armed struggle. He spoke of socialism, arguing that Islamic law respects the principle that work is the sole foundation for ownership. He insisted that foundational for Islam is the notion that land ownership should be the purview of the one who exerts effort over the land and cultivates it. He said the Prophet forbade the renting of land, saying: "Whosoever has land, let him cultivate it, or allow his brother to do so. And let him not lease even a portion of it, not even for a share of the harvest." He also said that Islam forbids usury, commerce in currency, speculation, and monopoly, and he called for natural resources to be liberated, as well as privately owned production facilities, and urged support of the indigent and a guaranty of human dignity for everyone. He proclaimed that Islam is against the rich, backing this up with two verses from the Quran: "We never sent an admonisher to a habitation but its well-to-do people said, 'We do not believe in what you have brought'"; and also, "Corruption has spread over the land and sea from what men have done themselves." He also quoted Omar Ibn al-Khatab—or Ali Ben Abi Talib, I don't remember which: "The rich are never satisfied unless the poor are hungry." And another quote from Omar: "If I ask one thing of you, it would be to take the surplus wealth of the rich and distribute it to the poor."

September 11

Amina and her brother have joined us. She is 14 years old. Black, with a nose ring and a full, round face with a scarf wrapped around it. She comes from the community of African outcasts in Salalah. Her father takes itinerant work in the fields or carries rocks in construction for four or five rupees a day. He usually does not find work, though, so he makes string to sell from the shells of *narjeel*, which is their name for coconuts here. His wife does baking in a kiln for the neighbors, who pay her next to nothing. Amina ran away with her older brother, who is 21 and was working as a coolie on construction sites.

She told me, "The people were picking up pamphlets that attacked the Sultan, and it made them happy. We started to realize that we do have rights, so we decided to come up into the hills. But how could we get here when we were surrounded by barbed wire in every direction? Our only chance was by sea. My brother bought an old inner tube. We gathered some coconuts and stuck them together in pairs to make buoys, and put a pair on each end. Then we made another float. We worked at night by kerosene lamps. When we were ready, we went without any noise through the alleys and around the huts until we made it to the thick, high coconut trees between the city and the sea. It was midnight, and we hoped we could make it as far as the walls around Awqad to our west before dawn. We swam together in the sea for eight hours. I don't swim well and I was very hungry, cold, and thirsty, but I would rather have died than been captured by the English. When I was very tired, my brother lifted me up onto the inner tube and pushed me forward. We made it to Awqad and stayed with some people we knew there until it was night again. Then we climbed up into the hills and asked villagers where we could find the rebel camps, and they led us."

October 12

Lebanon's foreign minister has welcomed official American commitments to protect Lebanon.

Egyptian commando units cross the Suez Canal at multiple points, inflict heavy losses on the Israelis, and make it back to their base safely.

October 21

Explosion at the headquarters of the Palestine Liberation Organization in Beirut. The Lebanese army has been attacking guerrilla bases and has killed or wounded 39 guerrilla fighters so far.

November

An interview with Nayef Hawatmeh, now on the central committee of the Democratic Front for the Liberation of Palestine, in the magazine *Al-Talia* published by the Egyptian Socialist Union party. He explained why the DFLP broke with the other main left-wing Palestinian party, the PFLP. The issue between them, he said, was basically an ideological and political dispute that could be traced back to differences within the Movement for Arab Nationalism in 1961, when Egypt began to nationalize companies, which in turn sparked new trends in the region's political thought. The June War settled these disputes by exposing the petit bourgeois program of the Arab governments. The war showed their inability to deal with the issue of national liberation and overcome the challenges to a national-popular revolution in countries throughout the region. In this era of imperialism, the Arab regime has proved impotent—unable to achieve complete and total independence, much less to shepherd independent states into the era of heavy industrialization and mass agricultural production. Their program had no tools for delinking from the oppressive markets of the global capitalist system and for furthering development independent from them. Nor was it prepared to confront the new imperialism being led by the United States. So the progressive wing of the movement shifted toward a Marxist-Leninist revolutionary position, which it laid out during a meeting of the MAN central committee. The party's mainstream accepted the proposal without ever really being ready to make the essential organizational changes that the new thinking required. So responsibility to make those changes fell instead to the left wing of the movement. It soon became clear that it was impossible to transform a petit bourgeois organization into a truly Marxist-Leninist one. To do so basically required that one class standing be transformed into a new class standing that was against its own interests.

The interviewer tried to trap Hawatmeh by asking what alternative there might be to the petit bourgeois leadership given the lack of a critical mass or a political consciousness among working-class people, who remained a meager force in a region with low levels of industrialization and sustained persecution of those who organized workers. Hawatmeh answered: "There has to be an organized avant-garde committed to an ideological and class-conscious vision that can lead all the progressive forces and the classes that want progress and revolution in confederation with this petite bourgeoisie."

November 11

Rafie wants to marry Amina. Expressed my opposition because of the difference in their ages. Is that my only reason?

November 16

Nimeiry has announced the removal of the three members of the Sudanese revolutionary council who formed a bridge to the Communist party. They are Farouk Othman Hamdullah, Babiker Al Nour, and Hashem al-Atta. The situation looks very tense—especially between Nimeiry and the communists. Nimeiry is working on forming a mass organization like the Socialist Union in Egypt. He is copying Abdel Nasser in asking the Sudanese Communist party to dissolve and attach to his organization. But Abdelkhaliq Mahjoub said no, and he accused Nimeiry of being petit bourgeois. Ahmad Suleiman published an article posing the question: What makes Abdel Nasser a democratic revolutionary but Nimeiry a petit bourgeois? It explained Egypt's path to socialism without having a communist party and asked what was different about Sudan, besides that it was less economically developed. It asked why Abdelkhaliq Mahjoub had supported the dissolution of one communist party but not the other.

November 18

The Lebanese press is now saying that 11 members of the central committee of the Sudanese Communist party have been expelled from the party for taking the side of Nimeiry in the dispute. The most important of the 11 are Ahmad Suleiman, Mauia, and Abu Aisa.

November 19

A huge march in Washington. Half a million Americans who oppose the war in Vietnam.

Investigation into the details of the massacre at My Lai last year. On the morning of March 16, a company of American soldiers attacked the village of My Lai, firing at will on its inhabitants, including women, children, and the elderly. When the villagers sought shelter in their huts and storehouses, the soldiers threw hand grenades into them. Then they gathered the 400 surviving villagers in an open area, lined them up at the edge of a ditch, and fired on them under the orders of officer William Calley. During the killing, a child barely two years old tried to run away. Calley chased him down, grabbed him, and threw him into the ditch. How could the barbarity of humans go so far?

The Libyan revolution continues to hit back at imperialist control over various parts of the Libyan economy. The petroleum monopolies operating in the area are panicking. A joint defense declaration between Libya, Sudan, and Egypt is expected to be announced soon.

November 27

Decision in Aden to nationalize banks, navigation, petroleum distribution, insurance companies, and commercial firms.

December 1

Even though the Sultan has imposed a blockade on major sea routes, the coastline and the airport of Salalah are now exposed to our mortar fire. Our attacks still can't reach the city itself, though, just as the Sultan's forces are unable to enter the mountain area, unless it's as part of the most heavily armed convoy possible.

A former slave named Amar escaped by sea and came to us. Reads and writes well. Six other slaves followed after him. Also a young man named Nazr who is the son of the director of the local intelligence office for the Sultanate. Amar had a job in one of the Sultan's palaces giving instructions to the slaves, who were forbidden to leave their dwellings, to marry, or even to learn reading and writing without getting permission first. He's given us a wealth of information about life inside the Sultan's palace. It is filled with two-way mirrors and large telescopes for surveillance and has a fortified wing where 150 women are kept.

We opened up a school to teach basic literacy. Having to use some of our revolutionary pamphlets for textbooks because we don't really have books to teach reading. The students vary in age from a 9-year-old child to a woman in her twenties and a man in his thirties. The teacher is only 14, but the students treat him with great respect. They sit together during the afternoon break right after lunch to study together inside one of the caves.

In the evening, I attended an open meeting run by the top political commissar.

December 8

Front leadership in Aden decided to limit the membership of the presidential council to three: Salim Rubai, Abdelfattah Ismail, and Muhammad Ali Haitham.

A victory for women: Aida al-Yafai has been elected to the membership on the Front's national leadership board in Aden.

December 20

I went to Shairus, north of Rakhiut, to participate in the political circle for the advanced students in the school set up by the literacy campaign. They are graduating and moving up to positions inside the Front organization. The course is three months long and meets three or four times a week. The sessions can run long—up to five or even seven hours. They are conducted by the political commissar from the Shaabut unit along with his assistant. One session per week is devoted to political and organizational topics. Military training is ongoing. Both the male and female students are divided into detachments that take turns helping with food preparation, cleanup, and night watch. I stayed with the women in their own large tent.

December 25

Mariam has joined the circle. She is 16. Her family grows corn for three months and then herds sheep the rest of the year. They wanted to marry her to an old man. She heard about the Front and ran away. She has dark skin and she's skinny. Her hair is dark, smooth, and very shiny. It hangs down in thick waves. She walks with her head high and her posture erect, but she can also be shy. She's smiling all the time. I asked her if she missed her family. She said she doesn't think about them, only about the revolution. She wants to learn to read and write, then study politics. The Front school has taught her Arabic but she still has a way to go. When I said to her, "The life of a fighter can be hard," her answer was tough: "I can do anything as well as any man."

January 1, 1970

I am helping Mariam with her Arabic lessons while she teaches me new vocabulary from highlander language. Today, she asked me to tell her the story of Abu Zayed al-Hilali, who is considered here to be an archetype of chivalry and courage. He is always depicted wearing a mask that covers his beauty and protects women from being seduced.

January 5

The mercenary army has fallen back to defensive positions. Its theater of operations has withdrawn to the central and the eastern zones. There is a running battle for positions along the Hamrein road which we've started to call the red line. We surrounded them at several sensitive sites and forced them to retreat to fortified positions.

January 10

The number of civilians escaping from Salalah and the coast is rising. Said Masaud, who spent five years in Al-Hisn prison, is among those who have come up to us. A hundred prisoners bound together in a dark room. A two-day stay in the stocks is the common punishment. The guards are all Baluch being supervised by British officers.

January 18

Last night was Mariam's shift for guard duty. I stayed up with her for part of the time. She told me the story of the death of a brother of hers and how he was buried. Her father just stood next to the grave and cried until the spirits lurking there became angry. They told him his son had not died; he was simply put under a spell by a sorceress, who transported him to a village in India and turned him into a goat. When I laughed, she sulked for a while. Then she continued, saying the spirits described to her father how he could seize the sorceress and force her son back to his original form as a human being.

I couldn't suppress my laughter. I asked, "Did he come back?"

She lowered her head and went quiet, biting her lip. I knew she was angry, so I reached out, put my arm around her, and patted her on the back. But she just shot me a look and said, "You always make fun of me."

"Never," I said. "You will find here things that you don't know all about," she told me.

"Like, did you know that we have scorpions here that fly around like birds?" I was about to answer, but she put her finger on my lips and said, "One of my uncles caught a fish this big—" and she stretched her arms as far as she could before going on: "The people gathered around it. They could put their hands all the way inside its gills. It was big enough to mount a camel."

I burst out laughing, and she broke into a timid smile. "What would you think," she said, "if I told you that the Emir of Oman gave Haroun al-Rashid a black ant in an iron cage as a gift?"

This surprised me. "An ant in a cage?" I said.

She was clearly pleased that she had managed to get to me. "Yes," she said. "It was chained to the bars of the cage." I raised my eyebrows, and she explained, "It was as big as a cat. They fed it slices of meat every day."

"Don't be silly," I said. "That was not an ant. It had to be a bobcat or a leopard."

January 22

Found a pond nearby. Enjoy swimming there in the evening.

The prime minister Tarek Ibn Taymur has acknowledged publicly that the rebels control three-fourths of Dhofar.

Her voice is beautiful. She has memorized songs by Abdel Halim Hafez and Nagat al-Saghaira. She sang some songs for me—"In a Day in a Month in a Year," "Your Love Is Fire," "He Lives across from Me."

January 28

I was tending to the tin pail used to boil water over the fire when I heard the distant sound of explosions, like huge bottle rockets: *buk! buk! buk!* I was by myself in the tent, waiting for the girls to get back from their evening training session on the mortar launcher. But this was different from the sound of mortar rockets. I rushed to the door of the tent. I saw a beautiful green ray of light heading toward me very slowly. Seemed to be getting faster the closer it came. Finally, it was clear that it was headed toward the training area and I instantly realized what it was. I cried out and began running madly. It's the latest technology in British ballistics: a missile that can trace the chemical remains of mortar fire to aim toward the point of origin of the shots. I watched the beautiful rays of light splashing around the training area and the dazzling white plumes pouring out of the explosions. The Browning 50, I thought, which can fire all types of ammunition, including those with green tracers. I ran without thinking, begging God that Mariam not be hit. The firing stopped, and I could see the students gathered around something smoldering. I pulled them back. My eyes fell on two outstretched bodies ripped apart by shrapnel. A breast nearly cut off, hanging from a slashed torso. Then I heard Mariam's shocked voice next to me repeating: "God, turn it into *riwan*." I hugged her viciously and cried.

January 28

We circled the station carrying the bodies of the two martyrs and singing revolutionary songs. In the evening, we held a memorial.

The Baathists have executed 41 Iraqis in Baghdad on the charge of conspiring with Iran.

February 2

Bakheet has fallen into the hands of one of the units in the central region. He had been hiding, as I suspected, among his tribe in the eastern zone. I recused myself from participating in his trial. He was sentenced to death. We explained the reasons in a communiqué that we distributed throughout the region.

Rafie told me about his life. His father had been kidnapped by Arab traders in Tanganyika. They brought him to Aden and sold him to a trader in northern Oman, but he managed to escape across the desert to Dhofar, where he worked as a herder and gained his freedom. Many freed slaves choose to give their children high-born names, like Khamis, Said, Nabil, or Rafie.

The Saudis have offered military aid to the Sultan, but he has refused. Likewise, he rejected the advice of the British, who have recommended the use of psychological operations and want him to provide new social services. He just seems content with this stalemate while he stockpiles weapons in his palace.

February 10

I asked her what she'd meant by that expression she used — God, turn it into *riwan*. She smiled sadly and said, "It means may God turn it into a dream." She explained the origin of the phrase. A salesman carried all of his clay pots on his back to the souk instead of bringing a few at a time. As he was climbing a hill, his foot slipped and his sack of pots crashed down, cracking and shattering one after the other . . . so he called out: "Make it a dream." A morose silence overcame us as we thought again about the two martyrs. Then she turned to me suddenly and asked about the future. I remembered what Lenin had said before the revolution. He was sure that establishing a socialist society would not mean that everything would change at once. For example, the proletariat would not suddenly all turn into saints, as he put it. There are going to be negatives and problems still. It will be important to continue to struggle for the sake of full democracy, total equality, and a collective spirit.

February 21

I noticed Mariam combing her hair and then looking at the comb. I took it from her and said, "Here, let me." I sat behind her and wrapped my legs around her. I combed while looking carefully for any sign of lice. She told me that one nice thing about leaving her family was escaping from their way of combing hair. There, they shave everything off the back of the head except for three or four thin braids. That protects them against lice or scabies, but it also causes terrible pain — even death! The only salvation from this torture for young girls is to marry so that they can fix their hair however they want.

I asked her if she had ever been in love and her face turned red. She said she thinks only of the revolution. We talked about conditions around marriage, like the corrupt dowries that are paid. She said, "If I decided to marry, it would have to be because I wanted a life with a particular man, whether or not he could pay a particular amount of money to me or my family. Before the revolution, women were being bought and sold and passed around like cattle. Now, though, a woman must know her rights, and by doing so, she supports the revolution. Anyway, marriage has to come after the revolution to make sure it does not hold back our struggle." My heart went out to her, I was so touched. I embraced her. She raised up her face to me innocently and kissed me on my mouth.

February 22

I did not sleep well yesterday. I kept hearing the sound of her breathing, and smelling her.

The topic of beautifying yourself came up between Nabila and some others. Nabila said, "In the past, we had to trap our men, so we made ourselves pretty for their sake. Now, a woman should attract with her personality and not with fancy powder. The true beauty of a woman is in her nationalist spirit and her skill as a fighter."

February 23

I suggested to Mariam that we go for a swim in a pond nearby. We chose a secluded spot covered by a rocky ledge. Laughing like a child, she threw off her clothes before I had a chance to do the same. I looked over her body. It was lean like a boy's, except for her chest. I felt my mouth go dry and my palms turn sweaty. Suddenly, I left her and went back to the tent. I have to stay in control of my feelings. The issue is clear: I have forbidden myself my natural urges for a long time. My maternal instincts are now mixed up with another kind of feeling. A natural thing. It goes on around me all the time. Only now am I seeing clearly. Selma and Khula, for example. Not just here, either. Before in our house in Sana—and in other houses around us. Mai, back in Beirut. Our circumstances, the dangers we face—they bring us closer together. But it's not within my power to just give in. I am a leader and my consciousness is higher. Guevara said that we have to be ascetics. Again I asked myself: is he talking about the times we spend in the city getting ready to wage war, or is he talking about the war itself? What if the war goes on for several years? I gave a bitter laugh. I must find a comrade to marry. The problem is that I have not had the slightest feeling for any I have met so far.

February 24

I left camp and headed to Rakhiut on the pretext of an urgent matter just as the course was ending. I avoided saying goodbye to Mariam.

March

Armed platoons of right-wing Phalangists led by Minister of Public Works Pierre Gemayel are attacking the Palestinian guerrilla camps in Beirut and in the mountains. Interior Minister Kamal Junblatt has accused his colleague of secretly collaborating with the American CIA.

March 11

Pact between Iraqi Kurds and the government agreeing to Kurdish self-rule. All are optimistic about closing the open wound that is Kurdish history in the region and uniting behind the forces of revolution.

March 25

The body of a Kurdish communist leader has been found on a street in Baghdad. Accusing fingers are pointing at Saddam Hussein.

Qahtan al-Shaaby imprisoned in Aden on suspicion of conspiracy.

April 1

We participated in the opening ceremonies for the new people's school, the first school to be established by the revolution. There's a wide circle of medium-sized tents. Forty students—both boys and girls—coming out of the schools to combat illiteracy. There are two grades, but the second grade is equal to fourth grade in the Arab system. The students also learn technical skills like planting, farming, needlework, and general life skills.

I move about lackadaisically. Whenever I turn around, I see her face.

Groups of boys and girls work together to do everything—food preparation, cooking, cleaning—without the divisions of labor imposed by society's reactionary traditions. In a big pan, the contents of two jars are emptied. A boy makes the dough in another pan. Then they make it into balls and put them on a baking sheet. After that, the balls are rolled out on a sheet set over a fire. There's a row of large round pots that the rice is cooked in.

In spite of a lack of resources, the schools use cutting-edge teaching techniques. The history and geography lessons start with the Arabian Gulf. The teacher asks each student to represent a different Gulf country.

The instructor is a young man, with a copy of Mao's Little Red Book sticking from his pocket. They all sit cross-legged on wool rugs, organized, quiet, and attentive. (Could this be because I am here?) Their notepads on their knees and their pencils in hand. The teacher addresses them, saying: "In the name of the revolution, let us now start our politics class." The relationship between teacher and student is based on mutual respect, and the student bears a sense of personal responsibility toward assignments and projects. Beatings and verbal abuse are forbidden.

Monthly evaluations take place in meetings that students and teachers participate in to go over problems and errors, as well as to experiment with new techniques that could be instructive. I went to one of them.

A student asked to speak. He said, "Some of our comrades had to sleep yesterday in the open air. The student council requests that we be given some new tents." Another student criticized the council for letting the kitchen become dirty. He asked that it be moved away from the tents so that the trash could be thrown into the valley. A representative of the council answered that as long as the water pump was broken, it would be impossible to get water to the kitchen if it were moved far away.

Someone else summarized the final compromise: "The council agrees to revisit this issue after the water pump is fixed."

A majority voted in favor of the motion. A very young student raised his hand and said, "I want to offer a self-critique. Yesterday, after the demonstration ended, I never went back to studying."

A member of the council responded, "At that time, the teachers' council permitted us to sleep because everyone was tired."

I broke in and said, "Critique and self-criticism should not be a game. They should only be used in important cases."

At the end of the session, a representative of the students declared, "In the name of the revolution, this session is adjourned," and everyone shouted, "In our struggle for total liberation, we will spill our blood for the revolution!"

I was drawn to a handsome 6-year-old boy. He carried a rifle and wore a checkered kilt and an army helmet. I gave him a hug, then asked what he was doing with the rifle. He answered, full of confidence: "I'm protecting my comrades from the counterrevolutionaries." I nodded, trying to be as grave as possible so I didn't burst out laughing.

In the afternoon we played football, and then there was a party at night. We sang revolutionary songs: "O Martyr, We Won't Forget Your Grave," "Warm Greetings, Our Dear Popular Front," "O People of the Gulf, Unite!" The students presented a dance theater about superstitious practices used to treat the sick before the liberation, in the days when medicine was outlawed by the Sultan.

April

Egypt celebrates the 100th birthday of Vladimir Lenin.

The Sheikh of Bahrain and the Shah of Iran both call for the Sultan to be replaced.

The defense minister, Major Waterfield, and the head of the Sultan's army have both been replaced by two other Brits.

The Beirut papers are confirming that Britain's ambassador to Bahrain has offered the Sultan safe passage to India if he will step down from the throne. He has refused.

An Israeli Phantom jet has bombed a primary school in the Nile Delta. Forty-six children were killed and 36 injured.

There are reports that Abdelkhaliq Mahjoub has been taken into custody in Sudan and sent into exile in Egypt.

May

The women's platoon has petitioned to have the bride-price abolished.

The Popular Front for the Liberation of Palestine has called for the establishment of an Arab workers' party.

The first crew of medical assistants that can man our mobile medical service stations has arrived.

May 25

Revolutionary changes in Sudan: five foreign banks and one local bank nationalized. The reign of foreign companies on commerce there has ended. Foreign insurance companies and the cotton market have also been nationalized. Nimeiry announces plans to unite the revolutionary forces, saying that scientific socialism is the only way to come to grips with the challenges facing the masses.

June 1

We held a special session to study the tribal situation and the problem of agriculture. Ali Mohsen, a member of the Front's leadership, was in attendance. He studied in an Egyptian law school for three years. A very tense, anxious person. The settlement of some tribes in the western provinces still faces resistance in spite of the clear advantages.

Awad joined the meeting. I was surprised by the strange way he acted toward me. I wanted to show him some numbers, and held a sheet of paper in front of me and said: "Take a good look at this." His eyes settled on my breasts. Blood rushed to my face. I reproached myself for getting flustered.

We listened to recommendations for promoting farming by bringing in pumps, digging new wells, building irrigation systems, improving distribution, and making equipment available.

June 5

Some small groups in the north of Oman have united to form the National Democratic Front for the Liberation of Oman and the Gulf. Seems that the Iraqi secret police have a hand in it. Yaarib has joined the leadership. They have issued a communiqué declaring their struggle an extension of the Dhofar Front's uprising and promised coordination between the two movements.

Their first act has been to flood Muscat with Mao's writings. One of them left a briefcase full of his booklets at a sweets shop. When the shop owner realized what was in the bag, he became scared and threw the booklets into the street, and they flew all over.

June 9

We put out a new, expanded monthly called *June 9*.

Newspapers have arrived with articles written by Abdelkhaliq Mahjoub in which he opposes the nationalizations happening in Sudan, calling them haphazard and poorly thought out. He says that the confiscations that have been carried out during this time amount to economic punishment inflicted on the moneyed class, targeting many who want to invest in the national development plan and profit from it.

June 12

Attacks by the Front for the Liberation of Oman on the Sultan's military centers and those of the British have failed in Nizwa and Izki, not far from the big oil pipelines.

June 15

In one of the attacks on Nizwa, nine rebels were taken captive, including four members of the leadership. Yaarib is one of those.

June 16

A wide-ranging campaign of arrests around Mattrah has ensnared many of our comrades. No news of Yaarib.

One thousand dead and wounded in Jordan. Over the past three weeks, special forces under the direction of Sharif Nasser, head of the army and the king's uncle, have gone out into the streets. They have been carrying out ambushes and assassinations of rebel fighters. They have launched attacks using tanks and heavy weaponry on Palestinian neighborhoods, PLO offices, and aid organizations. At first, the resistance tried to fight back. Then their leadership demanded the resignation of Sharif, and the king accepted the demand. A cease-fire agreement has been signed.

June 20

Could these arrests in Mattrah be happening because someone arrested in Nizwa informed on us?

June 25

In the middle of the night, we happened upon one of our comrades who had been in the east, as she tried to find her way back to the rebel camp to go on with training. She joined 16 new soldiers who had been militia members for the past two years and were just promoted to full membership in the liberation army last month. The unit's leader told us about two ambushes that they participated in. In one, they surprised a unit of the Sultan's forces that tried to slip into the liberated zone. In the second, they attacked an enemy patrol on its way from Um Jawarif to Bi'r Sahlamut.

July

Yaarib is free again. He's the only one that has been released so far.

The Front has put together a model farm. Courses will be taught there on agricultural techniques to groups of 20 comrades at a time. Each course will last three months.

The Egyptian air defense forces shot down 6 Phantoms and a Skyhawk. America's Rogers immediately proposed going back to a cease-fire.

Abdel Nasser has announced his acceptance of the Rogers plan. A heated discussion broke out among us about his decision. I was with the majority who argued that this was a compromise of principles and capitulation to the Americans. But Rafie said that the cease-fire gives an opportunity to reinforce the guerrilla resistance, which, in turn, sets the stage for a total Israeli withdrawal and reinstatement of the rights of the Palestinian people.

The Economist for July 18: Omani Sultan Said Bin Taymur represents a danger to the region's security and stability.

The Iranian press is also discussing an imminent military coup in Oman led by the head of the army.

July 14

I had a meeting with comrade Ali, a 19-year-old fighting with the Rakhiut unit. He wants to leave us. Whoever abandons the fight faces capital punishment. We simply can't allow the chance that he will have contact with the enemy. He told me he wants to go abroad to make money. I answered that we are all fighting together for a complete change to the system so that all will have the opportunity to do better — "And you want to leave us to go and gather up some money for yourself?" He cried. He explained that he loved a woman from his same tribe who had married a man she didn't love. Then the man agreed to divorce her, but on the condition that her father return the bride-price of 400 riyals that he had paid. In the end, the father and the husband agreed that the father would return half of the 400 in cash. But then when comrade Ali asked for his daughter's hand, the father asked for 400 riyals, half a camel, and 20 goats. He piled onto that about 1,300 riyals to cover the cost of slaughtering a calf and offering rice and tea to invited guests for the wedding banquet and the whole week following. To top it all off, he wanted gifts for the bride and her relatives, including clothes, perfumes, makeup, and robes. Ali said he thought he could just barely raise the money needed to pull off the marriage, but then he would have no choice but to go abroad so he could pay back his debts.

The bride-price law must be repealed.

July 23

Conflicting reports from Salalah.

July 26

The tyrant has fallen.

Qaboos announced today that he would take power from his father. His exact words were: "I have realized lately with increasing alarm my father's inability to oversee the affairs of the realm. Now my royal family and my armed forces have bestowed power upon me. The former Sultan has left the country, and I will dedicate myself with alacrity to establishing a modernized government."

Chapter Ten

MUSCAT, DECEMBER 1992

Fathy put on a light jacket, while I maintained the status quo of shirt and slacks. Shafiqa stayed behind, worried as always about getting in all of her required prayers.

While exiting the parking spot, he asked, "Did you hear about what happened to Sarah?"

"Who is Sarah?" I asked as I fastened my seat belt.

"That sixteen-year-old Filipina maid that one of the labor contractors assigned to work for an old man. When he tried to rape her, she killed him. Fired thirty-four bullets. The medical examiner confirmed the vicious rape attempt. So the court sentenced her to a prison term of seven years and payment of forty thousand dollars to the dead man's family. But it convicted him at the same time and charged his family with paying twenty-seven thousand in compensation to the girl, to be deducted from the forty thousand that she owes them."

"It wasn't mentioned in the papers," I said.

We turned onto the Corniche heading in the direction of Muscat as he answered, "The papers don't publish these things. Every day, hundreds of Filipina women sneak out of their workplace and take refuge in their embassy, which helps smuggle them out of the country. They're pushed here by poverty, wanting to escape the sex trade. But they find themselves in slavery instead. Like that thing about Scylla and Charybdis. Where is that from, anyway?"

I made a lackadaisical attempt to remember. We came to an isolated stretch directly overlooking the sea and stopped at a hotel that looked like a fortress. We left the car and climbed up a flight of steps that forked in two directions. Taking the right fork, we climbed up to a door at the top. A wood-framed entranceway opened onto a long ballroom with rows of tables, and an Indian waiter led us to a table at the end of the room with a bottle of whiskey in the middle. At the head of the table, a wide-bodied man of medium height wearing traditional clothes sat with Salem at his side. They both stood up to greet us, and our host, Fendy, offered his hand. He had a light complexion and a thin beard with some gray mixed in. He shook my hand animatedly. "Welcome. Oman is honored by your presence."

I shook hands with Salem and sat down next to our host, with Fathy across from me. East Asian women wearing businesslike European clothes scurried around, offering attentive, anxious service. I noted that the restaurant was almost empty; other than us, there was just a group of three young Omani men sipping beer and a European couple sitting together in a far corner.

Fendy addressed me with an inscrutable smile. "I hope you weren't too upset about that accident in Nizwa? Fathy reassured me that you weren't injured."

Without waiting for me to answer, he waved at the waiter to pour us some whiskey. Fathy declined to have a glass since he was driving, settling instead for Perrier water. We all clinked glasses, then Fendy set down his whiskey and addressed me with that old familiar question: "How are things going in Egypt?"

I gave my usual answer: "They're going."

He asked, "Is Laila Alwy really getting married? How will that affect her movie career?"

I laughed, "No idea. I'm not following it."

"Here, we know everything about you Egyptians," he said. "Those who read our newspapers are up to date on all the Egyptian starlets. Did you hear about what happened in our Shura Council meeting a few months ago? Some of the really old-fashioned members complained to the minister of information about the papers publishing photos of actresses and singers next to their own pictures. Do you know how the minister answered them? He told them that starting the next day, the papers would stop publishing the pictures of their excellencies, per their request."

He exploded in laughter, and we all joined in, before he went on: "Have you looked at our newspapers? You still don't have colored pictures in your papers there in Egypt. Here we've had them for a while now. Did you notice something that happens when you read them? Let me show you."

He picked up a paper set to the side on the table and handed it to me. I took the paper and unfolded it, then started dutifully to flip through the brightly colored pages while he studied me with a big smile.

"Now look at your fingers," he said.

I raised my hands and turned them around while having a good look at the fingers.

"See how clean they are?" he asked. I realized it was true; my fingers were not stained in ink as they so often would be after reading newspapers and magazines.

"Our master complained about the ink on his hands after reading the paper," he explained, "so the ministry invested in a special high-priced printer—which has justified its cost, as you can see."

As soon as I realized who this master was, I offered praise for this civilizational advance.

The Indian waiter came by and gave us each a thick, bound menu, fancier than most books. I flipped through the pages aimlessly, distracted by two young men who had come and joined the three sitting at the other table. They were all wearing traditional robes in slight variations of white, beige, or gray. The cocktail waitress brought them two more bottles of wine.

Our waiter returned, and I decided to start with a shrimp cocktail and French onion soup. I was about to order grilled shrimp as a main course, but Fendy decided to order lobster for the whole table.

"How do you find Oman?" he asked me.

I chose my words carefully, mentioning my admiration of Muscat's cleanliness compared to Cairo and the orderly progress of vehicular traffic.

He nodded his approval, then added, "We have our problems. The biggest is that the modernization process that our benevolent Sultan has undertaken is moving faster than this society can take. It's still clinging to its old-fashioned beliefs and customs. Have you seen all the beards around? That's your typical response."

I looked up at the wall hangings decorating the area around us: copies of old maps showing the Omani coast, mounted in large wooden frames.

He continued, "We're a modern state by any measure. But did you know that we don't yet have any type of retirement system in place?"

He stared at me, waiting for me to ask for an explanation, so I obliged. He folded his arms with the look of a man who had all the answers and said: "Because our bureaucrats are so youthful, none have made it to retirement age yet." He lifted his glass, but then put it back down. "Our problem is that we have a small population with limited skills."

"We could just send over a million Egyptians," I said.

He scowled, then lifted his glass all the way to his lips and took a sip. Salem jumped in: "We're setting up university programs. Last year, the first graduating class finished at Qaboos U. And we did this even before we have enough of our people finishing middle school."

Fendy cut him off. "Omanis can't stand doing manual labor, so the youth dream of nothing more than getting university degrees that they can use to land jobs with the government."

At the young men's table, the voices rose and the discussion became animated, causing Fendy to purse his lips in disapproval. Then he said, "They're poets." He lowered his voice before continuing. "The one sitting facing us has never worked, but he publishes some stories or articles every now and then and considers himself an important literary figure. The young one next to him writes poetry. The guy with the beard is also a poet. Next to him is a Jordanian literature professor at the university, and the one at the end fell for the communists. He ended up going to one of their countries for a doctorate. He's a poet too. Every Omani seems to be a poet until proven otherwise."

I couldn't keep myself from looking at Salem, but he remained as stone-faced as always.

Fendy called the waiter over to pour us another round of whiskey, then went on: "You find them here every night. It's not enough for them just to drink and talk poetry. They cry and complain and wail. Pleasure itself can't please them."

To prove our host's point—or just because he'd had too much to drink—the bearded poet suddenly stood and subjected the important literary figure who had never worked to a loud, harsh critique, as he gestured grandly toward a plate of sliced cucumbers. The others intervened to calm him down, but he waved them off and announced that he was leaving. Before stepping out, however, he made a circle with his hand as if to encompass them all and shouted, "You are all just big talkers and backstabbers . . . all of you! . . . . *all* of you!"

A silence fell over the restaurant as the Europeans turned for a moment to see what was happening before going back to their conversation. I noticed the Indian waiter standing at a distance, his face frozen. Of course, Salem's face gave away nothing. Fendy, meanwhile, wore a broad, sarcastic smile. "I don't know what they want," he said. "We are taking big steps forward. We're democratizing. Just last month, the Sultan granted the Shura Council some big reforms that allow them to pass laws and conduct investigations. They turned around right away and sent queries to the information minister about why television signals from the other Gulf countries are being blocked."

"What was his answer?" I asked.

"He told them that his charge was to reinforce Omani television and that the other channels are not in his purview." He burst out laughing, then added: "Now that's a real diplomatic minister."

The young poet left and the others resumed their conversation quietly. Fendy went back to asking me questions: "Have you visited anywhere other than Nizwa and Hamra?" When I said I hadn't, he went on: "You have to visit the south. Dhofar. It's a piece of heaven on earth. Amazing hills covered with forests, natural springs, and moderate temperatures all year round. Can any such place be found on the face of the earth? You just have to see it. It's the place of the Ahqaf, which the Quran tells of. The tombs of several prophets are there:

Job, Houd, and Salih. It's also where the ancient peoples of Ad and Thamud walked the earth. I know you could care less about these things"—he smiled mischievously—"but it's still important to know about them."

I maintained a neutral tone: "Wasn't there a revolution there some years ago?"

His expression changed, and he waved dismissively. "That was just some childish silliness stirred up by commie agents. Security there is under control, as you'll see. Listen. I'll arrange a trip for you. Salem or Zakariya can take you."

"Oh, there's no need. I can go myself."

"But you have to get a permit to go, whether you travel by land or fly," he said.

The waiter set two more bottles of wine on the table of the poets, and I noticed the important literary figure wrapping his arm around the young man's shoulder, then brushing something off his cheek with his fingers. The youth repelled the gesture by removing his companion's arm. Then he took one of the bottles and furtively poured its contents into an empty beer bottle stashed in the pocket of his robe.

"What's the latest joke there in Egypt?" Fendy was asking me.

I told the one about the distribution of the budget and he gave a hearty laugh, then he said, "Listen to this one about the Iraqis. Their soldiers broke into a house during the occupation of Kuwait and stole everything of value. Then as they were taking off, the mistress of the house stopped them and said, 'Is that all? You just pillaged. What about the rape?'"

We laughed, and he kept going: "During their training, an Iraqi officer asked a soldier, 'If the enemy attacks you from the front, what do you do?' 'I shoot him with my rifle,' he said. 'And if he comes from the flank?' 'I shoot him with my rifle,' he said. 'And if he comes from the rear?' He answered, 'That's no enemy. That's my friend.'"

The plate of lobster was placed in front of me and I gave it a long stare. I had no idea how to deal with it. I waited until I saw Fendy go after it with a spoon, and I tried to copy him.

I realized another bottle of wine had been polished off, along with a bottle of beer, at the poets' table. It looked like they hadn't eaten anything. As we started drinking our coffee, I heard the Indian waiter tell them that it was closing time, and they all got up laboriously. The young man who had put the wine in his pocket had a huge red stain on his robe. We left not long after them, and I noted that our host had not seemed to ask for a bill or pay anything to anyone. Once outside, we found the poets sitting together near the rocks that overlooked the sea, having been joined by their same bearded friend who had stormed away in revolt earlier. He was still chattering with fervor, and when we came close to them he turned in my direction and spat on the ground.

We all acted like we hadn't noticed. Fendy shook my hand goodbye and said, "You know where to find me, if you decide to travel to the south." He headed off to his car with Salem at his side, while I followed Fathy to ours.

As he fastened his seat belt he said, "You have to go. This is your chance."

It suddenly occurred to me that everyone I met here made it clear they wanted me to head south. Shafiqa was the only one who hadn't, but I was sure she would be in favor of getting rid of me for a while.

Chapter Eleven

SALALAH, DECEMBER 1992

1.

We made it to the airport only after everyone had boarded the flight. One of the guards told us, "The plane's doors have closed. It takes off in thirty minutes." Zakariya protested that we needed to get to important meetings in Salalah.

He spoke firmly: "Come back at thirteen hundred for the afternoon flight."

Zakariya started in with every means of cajoling, the kind of thing we Egyptians are usually experts in. He let the guard know that I was an honorable delegate from the official Egyptian news agency and a personal friend of the minister, and . . . and . . . and . . . He even dared him to call the Information Ministry to check on our story. With this last statement, I saw some hesitation in the official's expression and I knew we would win the hand.

He invited us to wait in the VIP lounge while he looked for a way to help. At the entrance, we were met by a military officer and a soldier in a gray army shirt, black kilt, and helmet. The officer asked us to wait in the adjoining lounge, and we followed a red carpet in the direction he pointed. After a while, a couple wearing European clothes joined us. They seemed to be Arabs. The officer reappeared after a moment to explain that he had to break them up because she needed to proceed to the lounge designated for female VIPs.

The man protested that this woman was his wife, giving away a Lebanese accent in the process. The officer replied uncomfortably, "Even so, these are our orders."

Zakariya seemed disapproving of the husband's insistence that his wife stay with us, whispering to me while staring at his carry-on: "These Lebanese have no pride."

The couple separated and we all sat in silence for a few minutes before the officer reappeared and waved at us to follow. We walked out of the building and onto the tarmac, passing in front of a DC-10. Next to it a black Mercedes was parked. An impressive gentleman stepped out of the back seat wearing a white dishdasha with a dagger around his waist, a turban on his head, and traditional sandals on his feet. He greeted the Lebanese couple and waited until the two of them had boarded the plane, with Zakariya and myself on their heels. Then he left.

The doors of the airplane closed the moment we entered, and the Asian flight attendants sat us down in a row of seats just behind the flight deck. I looked back through the cabin at the passengers packed on top of each other in rows. Several wore suit jackets over their traditional robes. Most were weighed down with baskets and duffel bags.

Zakariya wiped away a tear as we fastened our seat belts, then he said, "Before the revolution the trip from Muscat to Dhofar was done by camel and could take about eighteen days."

I played dumb. "Which revolution?"

He smiled that strange smile of his and said, "The revolution of our master, Qaboos, of course."

As the plane turned onto its runway, shot forward, and took off, he started to move his lips very quickly. Then he pulled out of the pocket of his dishdasha a tiny copy of the Quran and flipped through it until he settled on a particular page and started to read in a low voice. I figured that he was reading *Sura Yasin*, which my father always recommended to ward off disaster. The plane continued its ascent until it had settled into its flight path, and only then did he close the book and put it back into his pocket.

I made an effort to connect. "I still can't believe I'm wearing summer clothes at the end of December."

"Have you noticed the way our seasons are so different from yours over there?" he said. "Here, our spring is just ending. Winter is on the way and will continue until March. At that point, summer starts right away, and fall comes after that."

I asked him about his hometown, and he said he was from Suhar, just north of Muscat.

"And where did you study?"

"In Bahrain. Then Pakistan."

He seemed uninterested in conversation; instead he pulled out his book, flipped to a page that had been dog-eared, and engrossed himself in reading in a soft whisper that suddenly grew loud from time to time.

We made it to Salalah in an hour and a half, where we found a government Land Rover waiting. It took us out into a sparse landscape dotted with distant walled fortresses. For a while we drove next to a high wall that blocked the view. Its top was adorned with a series of tiny, identical pyramids that came to a sharp point. Zakariya asked the driver what was on the other side, and he said it was the palace of one of the government ministers. He waited for us to ask him more, but when we stayed quiet he continued anyway. We learned that it was a marvel of interior design put together from more than sixty blocks of marble and stone. It had chandeliers imported from Egypt, English bathrooms, and a central air-conditioning system. Each of its doorframes was ornately decorated by craftsmen flown in from India.

At the main roundabout we headed left, passing by the Sultan's palace and several classic houses made from whitewashed bricks and rising up several stories. They had arched window frames with shutters adorned in the *mashrabiyya* style. One could detect some Indian influence in the ornate engravings at the bottoms and sides of the wooden shutters, as well as African influence in the shiny lines of red and yellow that stood out on others. Rows of coconut trees accompanied us all the way to the Holiday Inn hotel, on the coast overlooking the Indian Ocean.

Zakariya commented on the large, oblong balls that lined the hotel entrance: "These are boulders from the mountains that have been sculpted by the winds."

A young Indian carried our bags, but I held on to my briefcase. At the entrance, we sipped the cups of coffee that were waiting to welcome us, then headed toward the reception desk. I started to wonder if we were the only guests, since the silence in the place was total and the board behind the reception was full of keys. I pulled my passport out of my briefcase and we began the routine of signing in.

Zakariya smiled that strange smile of his and said, "Telephone calls here are 5 riyals per call."

Is this a warning against using the phone, or is it some kind of insult?

We gathered our room keys from the Indian receptionist. I took my larger bag and Zakariya reached over to help me with the briefcase, but I grabbed it and pulled it away. At that, the porter rushed over and grabbed the large bag; we headed to the elevator and took it up to my second-floor room.

Once the porter had gone, I threw my briefcase onto the bed and took a look around. I found myself in a comfortable room with a large picture window looking out onto the garden of the hotel. The big bed took up the middle of the room. To the side, there was a heavy armchair and a writing desk. I checked out the bathroom, then came back and had another look at the room, studying the telephone for a moment. I moved the heavy chair to the side, took Warda's diaries out of my briefcase, and tucked them under the edge of the rug before moving the chair back into place.

It seemed a pretty silly solution that wouldn't have hindered any professionally trained spy, but it just might do the trick in the case of a curious maid or waiter.

I washed up and changed clothes. Then I went downstairs, along the quiet hallway past the restaurant, and headed to the reception area, where Zakariya was waiting.

Before I could utter a word he said, "You must be thirsty." I noticed a sign over a door that read Kharif Cocktail Lounge, and started to dream of a cold bottle of beer, but he led me instead to another room with a sign over it that read Kharif Coffee Shop. The Indian waiter there brought us each a coconut shell. The top parts had been slashed with a big knife and they had fancy colored straws sticking out of them that channeled their cold, tasty inner liquid.

"The Dhofaris say anyone who drinks fresh coconut here must return to Salalah again and again," he said. I told him we said the same thing about the Nile waters in Egypt.

I finished off the liquid, held the shell in my hand, and looked down at the shiny white insides. When I asked what to do with the rest, he said, "Nothing. Just toss it." So I set it back on the tray, still mesmerized by its whiteness and the memory of its refreshing taste.

When we left the hotel, our driver took off down a thoroughfare that ran by the sea called Sultan Qaboos Road, which took us all the way to the Salalah town hall. Inside we found the public relations bureau, which was staffed by two young men wearing traditional clothes. One was dark-skinned, the other tall, skinny, and frowning. They both greeted my companion, whom they seemed to have met before.

The skinny one, who was called Khalaf, took us on a tour of the city by car. We observed a complete metropolis spread along the coast, with houses several stories high, car dealerships, restaurants, three cinemas, a hospital named after Qaboos, and a primary school with the same name.

"This school was consecrated for the children of the martyrs," Khalaf explained, "and its students receive monthly stipends during the time that they are studying."

I perked up. "What martyrs?"

"Who died in the battles that were fought here in Dhofar," he answered.

I realized it was easy to tell which side's martyrs the school benefited.

We passed by the radio and television broadcast center, a canning factory, and a cement plant. Khalaf told us that they also had factories that distributed bananas, milk, Pepsi, and 7 Up. The driver filled up at a Shell station, then took us down to the central market. We got out of the car and walked all through it. There was an area with coconuts and other products that was run by the hill people. They walked around wearing almost nothing, exposing tanned, muscular frames. Their hair was thick and jet black.

Zakariya asked to see the marks of the prophet Salih's camel, so we left the market and the driver led us to a large boulder clearly marked by the hooves of a camel.

"This boulder was the roof of a cave," Khalaf told us, "and it fell in when the camel walked over it."

"When was that?" I asked.

"In the time of the prophets," Zakariya answered.

I tried to remember what was special about the prophet Salih, but in the end I had to ask. "He's the one who was not allowed to lead his people," Zakariya told me. Then he pulled me by the arm until we were off a ways and he added under his breath: "Khalaf is from the Shahra. They are descendants of the same tribe that killed the prophet Salih's camel. She gave them milk and carried their honey and wine. Then when they killed her, God punished them by sending an army of bees that devoured their land."

We rejoined Khalaf and, back in the car, headed toward the west. Green fields appeared along the road with thick trees scattered around them. Here and there I saw a camel or sheep wandering alone. We came to a long incline in the road, and the car swerved toward a verdant thicket. It parked next to a tree whose branches stretched out nearly touching the ground here, and rising up three meters high there, full of dark green leaves like those on an olive branch. The driver shaved off some of bark with his pocket knife. Right away, a milky sap oozed from the shaved spot.

"Just leaving it like this," he said, "it would keep yielding until in a week we'd have a small pail of its sap—frankincense." Then all three of them started a competition to educate me about the role of frankincense in human civilization. I learned that the ancient Egyptians used it in mummification, that it was traded by land all the way to the Mediterranean and by sea as far as East Asia, that it was burnt like sacred incense in temples and churches, and that it is still used in homes today to ward off evil spirits and poisonous insects.

Khalaf led us to a big tent nearby. A dark-skinned man in his fifties with a scraggly beard and lightly sparkling eyes sat at the entrance. As soon as he saw Khalaf, he welcomed us, though it wasn't completely clear that he knew him. Khalaf signaled for us to sit on a brightly colored Taiwanese mat next to where the man was sitting, clutching a transistor radio. He was watching me with interest, and his dark eyes lit up when Khalaf mentioned that I was from Egypt. He went over to a camel that was kneeling nearby, filled an iron bowl with fresh milk, and handed it to me. I took a hard, hesitant look at the bowl topped with froth, but Khalaf encouraged me to go ahead and drink, so I did.

The man said to me, "Drink. Long live the Arab nation."

The phrase was strange; no one had heard such a call to arms in a long time. The man gave Khalaf a quick look, then turned back around to address me and, grinning broadly, said in the tone of a radio broadcast: "The Voice of the Arabs— from the Atlantic to the Gulf—calls upon you."

Seeing my surprise, he went on: "Oh yes. We know everything. Johnson was an ass, Nixon a big imperialist, and Nasser the hero of the Arab people." I was taken aback by his audacity, given that these slogans, coined in the 1960s, pretty much guaranteed today that anywhere from the Atlantic to the Gulf, their speaker would be thrown in jail.

After we had left the man, neither Khalaf nor Zakariya said anything. I noted that his tent was at the start of the road up the mountain. Maybe he had been deliberately planted here to show the regime's leniency to visitors, or maybe he was just backward and living on old memories, not even having heard of anyone named Carter or Bush.

We went back to the car and continued our ascent up the bumpy road. Colors among the tree branches around us formed a kaleidoscope from bottom to top. The leaves were green closer to the trunk, yellow a little higher, orange in the middle, and dark brown near the top. The highest branches were bare, and dry leaves were scattered underneath. It was as if the trees had all four seasons of the year gathered in their branches.

We made it to a plateau that had been cleared, in the middle of which stood a modern building with a tourist restaurant named after the prophet Job. We had lunch there, paying no attention to the exorbitant prices, knowing that the Center for Music Heritage was covering us. Khalaf, the driver, and I zeroed in on the smoked Scottish salmon, the grilled prawns, and the prawn cocktail. Zakariya, meanwhile, ordered a strange chicken dish with pineapple and rice.

After lunch we walked over to the shrine of the prophet Job, a rectangular structure with white and green walls. We took off our shoes and stepped onto the rugs. Quranic verses covered the walls. In repose in the middle was a huge body covered by a green shroud. Nearly six meters long, it almost filled the building. Small shelves around the sides held books, oriental pillows, and intricately carved shelves.

I scanned the mythical shrouded body with curiosity. As though reading my suspicious thoughts, Khalaf said, "There were giants back in ancient times."

"This big?"

"Wait till I show you the prophet Emran's tomb. All in all, the corpse stretches over nearly thirty meters. Of course, you know the story of the prophet Job already, right?"

Of course I knew the story, it having been drummed into all of us as children, but the details were now lost in a sea of many such old stories. I bought myself enough time to grasp at a few of its threads. It had started with a lightning bolt that lit a fire that tore through trees, vineyards, and storehouses of grain. An earthquake came next, then a dry wind started a plague that wiped out the livestock. Finally, the prophet himself was stricken. Boils covered his body and festered, and his body was infested. His wife, his family, and his friends gathered around to mourn him, but he remained steadfast and never lost his faith, not even for a moment.

I had never given the story much thought nor tried to interpret it, but I was still fascinated, wondering if this could really be the corpse of the prophet in front of me. Had he indeed endured all that the story taught us? Did he really have that much faith? If so, did it make him a better person than the rest of us?

As we turned toward the door, Khalaf remarked, "Newlyweds like to visit here."

Just the place to start off on that journey.

When I bent down to put on my shoes, I noticed in the front of the mosque a dark-skinned man sitting with his head bowed. His bare chest was covered in cuts and scars.

We got back in the car and started back up the paved road. Endless green stretched before us in profound silence. In the distance I saw a cluster of houses with cattle wandering nearby. Tents of various colors dotted the landscape.

Khalaf, his voice a lifeless monotone, said: "As recently as the 1980s this land was cultivated by the fellahin. Then, as the government started to offer better salaries for work in the city, they left the valley, allowing it to be taken over by wild orchards and herds of livestock. Those who could afford it hired Indians to come work their land and herd their animals."

We approached a sharp uphill, but the driver didn't slow down. Suddenly, he was slamming on the brakes and screaming as a long pickup appeared before us, crawling along behind a herd of camels that paced slowly across the road. We slowed down and followed until the camels loped off onto a side road and disappeared into the greenery, followed by the truck.

Our driver revived himself, pressed on the accelerator, and began to speed back up the ascent. I expressed surprise that a bunch of camels and a truck could take over the road that way. Khalaf answered, "It's not easy to coexist with the highlander lifestyle."

"But where are the highlanders?" I asked.

He smiled for the first time. "I see. You expected a herdsman walking along-side the camels with a stick? That approach has gone out of style. Today's herds-man uses a Chevrolet or Toyota instead."

Soon we arrived at a large tent on the summit of one of the hills. Inside, there were stacks of bagged rice, flour, and sugar, boxes of tea and soap, cans of shortening, and other supplies. I learned from the Pakistani owner that government helicopters brought him supplies from Salalah, which he then sold to the highlanders at market rates.

I snuck outside and lost myself staring at the natural beauty that surrounded us. As I surveyed the landscape, I noticed a modern wall on the next hill over, and behind it men in green military uniforms. When I asked Khalaf about it, he looked over at the wall, then said: "That's one of the administrative centers the government built out here. Each one has a mosque, a school, a post office, a medical clinic, and a general store."

What I was looking at seemed more like a military barracks. I kept looking at Khalaf from the corner of my eye, noting a touch of fear in his fastidious expression.

"Could we climb up and have a look?" I asked.

He turned back toward the car. "I doubt they would welcome visitors."

As we made our way to the car, he offered by way of clarification: "This area was once on fire with fighting and rebellion."

2.

I slept soundly for the first time in a while and woke up early. I luxuriated in the warm water from the shower spraying my sore neck and back.

The idea of sitting at breakfast with Zakariya just then convinced me to order room service instead. When no one answered, I started to go back and forth between the number for reception and the one for room service until finally someone answered, speaking English with an Indian accent. I managed to figure out that he was asking me what kind of breakfast I wanted after he repeated himself a few times. There was continental, American, or Arab breakfast, and I ended up choosing the latter, made up of white cheese, fava beans, and *labneh*.

"Coffee or tea?" he asked.

Normally I have a cup of tea with my breakfast and then follow it up with a coffee after I've eaten. To save time, I asked for both.

"Coffee or tea?" he repeated.

"Coffee *and* tea," I said.

He repeated again with tenacious patience: "Tea or coffee, sir?"

"Tea *and* coffee," I told him.

He was quiet for a moment, then said, "Thank you, sir."

Fifteen minutes later there was a knock at the door. I opened up to a young

Indian carrying a tray that bore grapefruit juice, a croissant, some jam, and a canister of coffee. Polishing off my English again, I said, "This is not my order."

"Yes sir," he said.

"So take it back and bring me an Arab breakfast," I said.

As he placed the tray on the desk, he said, "Yes sir." He passed me the bill for my signature, as though I hadn't said anything. Worn down by the back and forth, I gave up and signed.

After finishing, I went down to the lobby and handed the key to the Indian at the reception desk. The box under my room number was empty—no messages. When I asked the receptionist about Zakariya, he said, "Your comrade is in the car, sir." Thusly, the holy man was transformed into a comrade by the Indian receptionist after the collapse of the Soviet Union.

I found Zakariya waiting outside in a Datsun. He said, while wiping away his habitual tears, "We will go by the office first to get the Land Rover. We have a long trip ahead to get to Shisr, where they discovered an ancient city just a few months ago. It has a fortress with seven towers that goes back to 2000 BCE. They believe it's the city of Iram of the Pillars, mentioned in the Quran, the one that God buried under sand when its prosperity pushed the inhabitants into rapaciousness and greed."

"Who discovered it?" I asked.

"The famous British archeologist Sir Fiennes. He served in the British forces here during the Dhofar revolt."

"Strange," I said.

"Isn't it?" he agreed.

"No, I mean this Sir Fiennes. There's also Moshe Dayan in Israel. Why do these army generals switch over to working with ruins?"

Khalaf met us wearing a suit coat over a dishdasha. He let us know we were headed somewhere else because the ancient city at Shisr had been closed off. He said as he handed me the morning paper: "You can't take a step these days without discovering new ruins. Last year in southern Dhofar we discovered ruins that were thirty-five million years old: teeth, elephant droppings, a monkey, a crocodile, fish, turtles, and rodents."

"Really? That would make it older than our ruins in Fayoum back in Egypt, which are considered the oldest ruins in the world."

"That's right," he smiled. "You've been left behind."

I cast a glance over the paper and found that the top half of the front page was taken up by news of a summit of the Gulf Cooperation Council. The headlines declared that the GCC welcomed the new American administration and thanked the outgoing president Bush for his role in the liberation of Kuwait.

There was a full-color photograph of the Sultan with his signature white beard sitting on a big gold chair. The white, green, and red Omani flag flew in front of him. He appeared in another photo wearing a blue robe with gold embroidery and a silver dagger sparkling on the right side of his belt. Next to him was an emir with a serpentine face, and another who was short and wore a gold dagger in the middle of his stomach, just below his navel.

I studied the Sultan's gaze—serious, stern. Flipping through the pages, I came to a third photo of him, this time with a fat man in a cloak that showed off his dagger and with big dark glasses perched between broad snow-white eyebrows, and a mustache of the same color. The face seemed familiar, although I had no idea where I'd seen it before. The caption gave his name as "Harith Bin Ayesha."

I recalled a reference in the *Sultan Qaboos Encyclopedia of Names* to names drawn from the matrilineal line. Khalaf clarified that this phenomenon existed exclusively among the desert Bedouins.

"Maybe it's a last vestige of the days of matriarchal rule," I suggested, then I seized the chance to ask: "Is the women's movement active here? I thought I heard they have an organization."

Khalaf answered in his typical deadpan: "In Mirbat, there's a women's center that was founded by Her Highness the mother of the Sultan. I could take you for a visit if you like."

Bilal, Khalaf's dark-complexioned friend, joined us, and the car took off down Qaboos Street, then turned right toward the ocean. After a while we came to a rocky bay; it was covered in a fading mist that extended out some 500 meters, allowing just enough visibility to see the timeworn darkness of the stones.

"This area is called 'the *bileed*,'" Bilal explained. "That's how they say 'the town' in highlander language. It was once a port, and Marco Polo visited it in 1295, then Ibn Battuta thirty years later. God bless his soul. He called it the dirtiest place in the world, and said that fleas were swallowing the place. He was so surprised that people fed their animals sardines."

The eastern part of the area was built as a square that included a big mosque with round and pentagonal columns whose bases and crowns were adorned with inscriptions from Quranic verses.

As Bilal showed us the foundations of the ancient customs house, he said, "The winds that blow in from the northeast this time of year carried ships filled with palm dates and frankincense to the coast of Africa. In April, when the winds turned around and came from the southwest, they returned loaded with African ivory, honey, and tortoise shell used to make dagger handles."

Would it have brought some of his ancestors in shackles?

The blazing sun had worn me out and I asked if we could go back. I was dropped off at the hotel so that Zakariya could go on to town. I checked to see if I had any messages, then went up to my room. I washed and came back down to the nearly empty restaurant where one European family ate. I ordered a mix of small salads, kebab, and a bottle of beer. The Indian waiter shook his head and said that beer would not be available.

I waited until he left, then walked back up to my room, took two bottles of beer out of the minibar, and returned with them to the restaurant. The moment I put them down on the table, the Indian restaurant manager rushed over and agitatedly cried, "No! No!"

It took some time before I figured out he was saying that consumption of alcohol was prohibited except in the rooms and the bar. I decided to take my two bottles back up to my room. I replaced them where I had taken them from and went back down to the restaurant.

I ate quickly and indifferently, then went back to the lobby to glance at my empty message box. Hearing someone call my name, I turned to find Salem and Fendy, the bellhop carrying their luggage behind them.

"We didn't want to leave you here communing with Dhofar's natural beauty by yourself," Fendy said.

I stood speechless as Salem absorbed himself in registration. Fendy looked over at the restaurant and asked, "Did you eat? I'm dying of hunger."

I told him that I'd just finished and was on my way to take a nap.

"Finish your nap, then come by for a drink," he said.

Salem joined us. "After that, we can head over to my sister's house for dinner. I will show you how Dhofaris live."

I went up to my room, stretched across the bed fully clothed, and fell asleep instantly. When I woke up, I tried to call Zakariya but with no luck. I felt like having a coffee but didn't want to go through the ordeal of this morning again, so I headed down to the lobby.

I found Salem there waiting for me. When I asked about Zakariya, he said, "I've been looking for him too. Anyway, I doubt he would come with us. He doesn't like to drink."

We walked out into the hotel's garden toward a row of two-story villas. Then, with a completely expressionless face, Salem said, "Fendy has a chalet here booked for him all year round, but he only ever comes for a few days."

We arrived at the chalet in question and he knocked. The Filipino servant who answered had a ring hanging from one of his ears and moved with feminine elegance. We sat in the living room next to a table that held a large platter of fruit and a bottle of whiskey wrapped in a gift bag that bore the compliments of the hotel management.

Soon Fendy came down from the upper floor. He wore a gray dishdasha, a gold-trimmed shawl over his shoulders. He glanced over at the fruit platter and the whiskey as the servant set up a smaller table on which he arranged bottles of wine and liquor.

The servant poured me a gin and tonic, while Fendy and Salem had whiskey.

"Too bad you weren't here last month," Fendy said. "We were here filming the *rabuba*, a folkloric dance that the Dhofaris are known for—something like an Arabian waltz. There's a famous troupe here called the Ibn Tawfiq troupe. By the way, the name has the same origin as the musical instrument that Egyptians play."

"The traditional dance I saw in Nizwa was enough for me," I said.

He laughed, took a sip of whiskey, then said, "They are all different, and the Dhofari dance is really unique. It's one of the only ones where women dance with men. It's a progressive dance—isn't it, Salem?"

He winked at me, then laughed again.

"Maybe that explains why it's hard to perform," Salem said.

Fendy turned to me. "You'll have a chance to see it someday. No doubt you'll be visiting Oman and coming to Dhofar again. He who sees Dhofar . . ."

I completed the sentence for him: ". . . just once, comes back again and again."

He burst out laughing and filled his glass with whiskey again. "We have set off on a huge modernization project, requiring experts from all fields."

"There are many here already," I said.

He puckered his lips in disdain. "Are you talking about Omanis? They are good for nothing."

Salem stood up and said, "Time to go for our dinner date."

"That's fine, because I need to take care of a few things," said Fendy. "You can take the car. I won't need it."

We stepped out of the chalet and headed out to the road, where a Buick sedan and a Pakistani driver sat waiting for us. I fell back into the plush back seat, then turned to Salem: "I didn't know you were from this region."

"Actually, I'm not," he answered. "I'm from the Omani interior. My father was a wholesale trader. He would go down to Muscat with dates and lemons and come back with rice and coffee. As a boy I learned to recite the Quran in the Quranic schools. I memorized the whole thing, then moved on to the *Alfiyya* of Ibn Malik. Then I started to go along with my father on his trips. I saw the youth of the capital walking around in school uniforms and I wanted to be like them, but only the most privileged families could get their children admitted to school back then. My father pulled strings and found a way to get me in. I took my primary school diploma and wanted to keep going. The only way I could do that was with the help of the Front."

"So what is it that brought your sister here?"

"Her husband is from here. They met in London."

The car brought us to the city center. We entered a narrow street with old houses, one of which had a group of Indians crowded around a television near its entrance. We parked in front of a one-story building whose windows were adorned with color-coordinated blue and red frames.

A young man around ten years old opened the door. Salem went in ahead of me. When I hesitated at the doorway, he rushed back and waved me in. I found myself inside an average-sized hallway at street level with rugs and mats covering the floor. Salem slipped his shoes off before going through, so I followed his lead. We were met by a smiling woman with a dark complexion in her twenties who was clearly his sister. She was full-figured and wore a colorful silk robe that covered her whole body, and an equally colorful shawl that covered her head. She welcomed me bashfully. I noticed she wore rouge and her hands and feet were hennaed. We sat on some cushions as several boys and girls of various ages circled, studying us with intense interest. I realized I was a big event in their routine existence.

The sister's husband, a young man around her age called Fatum, joined us wearing eyeglasses and an unremarkable dishdasha. At this point, the sister stood up and became absorbed in bringing the dinner, with the help of an older woman. They set a large platter on the ground in front of us containing a real buffet: bisque, harissa, rice, grilled meat, fish, Lebanese kibbe, Egyptian-style falafel, salads, and fresh orange juice.

Salem explained, "They were going to make you authentic Dhofari dishes, but we were afraid you wouldn't like them."

As we gathered around the food, the other woman joined us and the boys and girls converged. A complicated discussion opened up about a piece of land that someone wanted to appropriate. The talk then turned to cloth that the sister had purchased at one riyal per meter and wanted to sell for three. I was sitting next to her husband, who mentioned that he was getting ready to travel to England to study for a PhD in economics. That moved us on to a new topic as I noted the potential for coordination among the countries of the Gulf Cooperation Council, which were beginning to organize production to reduce dependence on imports.

He rebutted this idea. "The market here is too weak," he said. "Abu Dhabi has a population of a quarter million, and all of Qatar only two hundred thousand. It's impossible to rely on a regional Arab market when the cost of production will be forced up by the lack of a local labor force and the increasingly affluent lifestyle. The solution might lie in putting factories someplace like Egypt."

Naturally, I welcomed this solution. "If all the money thrown around here were invested in building factories and farms in Egypt or Syria or Sudan . . . ," I suggested.

He contented himself with tacit agreement.

I washed up at a tap mounted on the wall near the door and came back for local papaya that his wife had sliced for us. It tasted like a cross between a mango and a watermelon.

Then I said, trying to sound natural: "I think there was a revolution here about twenty years ago, wasn't there?"

He answered evenly. "Yes, the Front was active back then."

"Are they still around?"

He glanced at Salem before answering. "No. That all ended a while ago."

Everyone else seemed absorbed in family conversation, so I lowered my voice a bit and asked, "Do you think they left their mark here?"

"The Front took control of the mountains," he said. "They sent children to South Yemen to study, and many went on to Iraq, Libya, and Eastern Europe. By now, these have come back as doctors and teachers. The idea was to open up the country, as it had been closed down with an iron fist by Sultan Said, who feared the world outside."

"Well, they got rid of him, then opened up wide," I remarked cautiously.

He ignored my remark and went on, "The old Sultan was a bold, brave, and charismatic gentleman, but he was very stubborn. The British asked him to step down, and he refused. Qaboos had been pent up here in his palace for six years, so they went to him and made a deal." He grabbed a slice of papaya and went on. "It was the British who installed Said in the first place back in 1932, when they deposed his father and sent him into exile in India."

Salem, who had been listening to us with interest, cut in to say someone was at the door. We heard a knock. One of the children stood up to answer, but Fatum stopped him with a gesture of his hand. A silence fell over us as the knocking started again, then stopped. After another pause, Fatum said anticlimactically, "It's my uncle." He noticed my surprise and explained, "If we let him in, he would have seen you. This scene is unacceptable to his generation. They could never imagine a stranger sitting with us like this. If my dear mother was still with us, she never would have let you in to begin with."

"In the mountains," Salem remarked, "there are places where you are not allowed to knock. You are supposed to just walk straight into the house."

"In the days of the Front, women were better off," Fatum said. "Here, one never sees the wife of his friend, but if he meets her in London, he can party with her all night."

A young man named Amin, who couldn't have been more than fifteen, broke in: "I agree that women's status here should be improved. Still, women's faces should be covered."

I asked why.

"Because of man's lust, which is out of control compared to a woman's."

We were drinking green tea when Salem announced that he was worn out from the trip. His sister suggested that he stay there and the driver take me back, but Salem declined, explaining that his hotel room was being paid for by the government. We excused ourselves and went out to the car.

As we got in, he remarked, "You have a lot of questions. People around here don't always like that."

I looked him over, unsure what he was getting at. After a moment he added, "Have you asked about your two friends yet?"

That, I hadn't expected. "Here? No."

When we arrived at the hotel, Salem walked with me to the reception desk. I found a letter waiting for me. It was signed by someone called Abu Abdullah who invited me to lunch the next day at his private tent. He offered to send a car to pick me up at midday.

I showed the letter to Salem, who said, "This is a big honor. Abu Abdullah is one of the most powerful sheikhs in the Kathir clan. He is an enlightened figure—although it's true that he refuses to educate his daughters."

"But why would he invite me? I don't know him."

"He considers any visitor to the region his guest. You have to go. But be careful about all your questions."

I asked the receptionist about Zakariya and merely received a bewildered look. I noted that the key to his room was hanging there under his room number. Salem took the elevator up to his room, and I headed for the lobby. An employee of the hotel was sitting at a desk near the entrance. He had a dark complexion and South Asian features. I walked over and addressed him in English. He laughed. I mentioned Zakariya, and he laughed some more, then suddenly said to me in a salty Cairo accent: "Speak Arabic, my friend."

"You're Egyptian?" I asked.

"Sure. From Gamaliya. My name is Metwaly."

Confused, I blurted, "One of the great names! Pardon me. Everything here is all mixed up."

I described Zakariya to him, and he stopped laughing. He looked around furtively, then whispered, "They took him this morning."

"Who the hell?"

"Who do you think?"

"But why?"

"It seems he's a member of the group."

"What group?"

"The beards. The Brotherhood. Here, they call them 'the volunteers.'"

3.

The car that Sheikh Abu Abdullah sent for me was a Jeep Cherokee. Khalaf was in the driver's seat. As I fastened my safety belt I said, "I had no idea Abu Abdullah was such an important figure."

He maneuvered the steering wheel without answering, then drove out onto the roadway that led toward the grave of the prophet Ayub. We then turned onto a mountain road that plunged us into lush greenery.

Wishing to break his silence, I asked him about his education. He said he had studied in Salalah through primary school but then stopped for a while. In 1970, he received a grant that allowed him to finish up middle and secondary school in Qatar, followed by university in Egypt.

"I bet you go through the same routine with every visitor—especially since all your visitors here are men," I said.

"Not necessarily. Next week we have a Danish woman interested in archeology coming."

"Is her name Julia?"

"Yes," he said. "Do you know her?"

"I met her in Muscat."

We passed by a family that had pitched a big tent next to a Land Rover and spread a large plastic tablecloth in front of it. They were obviously out for recreation. Khalaf used the English word *picnic*. He slowed down a bit when we came to some stables made of rock, and said in a weary voice: "Those stables are for plants, not animals." He explained that the highlanders cultivated barley, corn, and other crops in these closed pens to keep them from being trampled by livestock and camels.

We passed by several round houses that had cooking smoke rising out of them, their roofs made of straw covered with black tarpaulins. We came to a stop in front of a fenced-in plot. Khalaf pulled a big Coleman cooler out of the trunk of the car. A group of young men, mostly Filipinos and Africans, came running out to help unload boxes of mineral water, rugs, and a case of 7 Up.

I spotted Bilal kneeling in front of a stone pile, stoking flames and adding large chunks of glowing coals. Nearby, flames flew out of a pit that was attended by a woman wearing bright African colors—a pattern of big red flowers on a blue and green background. She was sprinkling flour from a plastic cup in her right hand over a wooden platter that she held in her left. Her fingernails were brightly painted. She had her back to me, so I stepped to the side to see her face, but it was covered with a mask framed with brass engraving that extended from her nose to below her chin. The only visible parts of her face were two triangles extending from the tops of her eyes to the sides of her nose.

Khalaf and I were led across an empty field that had rows of lush coconut trees at the far end, then down toward a one-story rectangular building made up of connected rooms, like a prison barracks or hospital. A thin man with a muscular build, though he was probably in his late sixties, came out of the first of the rooms. He was wearing a simple gray dishdasha and the traditional Dhofari headdress, which resembles the Palestinian one except for the shade of red and the placement of the knot.

Khalaf whispered to me: "Abu Abdullah."

He welcomed me, then spoke to Khalaf: "Show him how we make the *medhabby*."

One of the servants came by carrying a large platter filled with chunks of raw meat, which, with us following, he took out to where Bilal was standing. Khalaf helped him set the meat on top of rocks that, having been stripped and cleaned, glowed now like fiery coals. I squatted next to the two of them, staring into the flames as I listened to them gossip about a friend who had just had the great luck of receiving a 120,000-riyal payment—the equivalent of a million Egyptian pounds, or nearly one-third of one million US dollars—as compensation for land confiscated for a government project.

I asked them to explain, and Bilal spoke up: "Everyone turning seventeen has the right to take ownership of a plot of land anywhere between six hundred and nine hundred square meters for free. The land is distributed through a lottery, and the owner has to raise his own funds to build on it. The stroke of luck comes when your land becomes part of a government project."

The servant who had carried the platter of meat now turned his attention to carrying carpets, rugs, ice chests, water bottles, thermoses full of tea, Kleenex boxes, and ceramic plates inside. Bilal flipped the meat and set the cooked pieces on a platter.

I noticed that some of the pieces on the platter seemed underdone and asked him about it. He said simply, "Sidi Abu Abdullah prefers it that way."

Abu Abdullah called us to come back in. We found the carpets laid out in his room, which had filled up with maybe a dozen men, including Fendy. A high table was set up next to the wall, where Abu Abdullah oversaw a rice platter. The servant spread out plates and glasses of mineral water, then Bilal appeared in the doorway carrying the platter of grilled meat, which he set down before Abu Abdullah, who served a portion on each plate with his hands. He kept this up until the platter was completely empty, though he hadn't served himself. The servant took it and replaced it with another tray full of fruit.

After our meal, we had tea, and some of the guests started to leave. Abu Abdullah stood up to see them off. Fendy came over to me accompanied by a frightening-looking man in a white dishdasha and elaborate headdress. Fendy introduced him: "This is Abu Ammar. He was one of the leaders of the revolution."

I took a good look at his clean-shaven, plump cheeks and his piercing eyes, like a hawk's. "It's nice to meet you," I said. "I'd love to have a chance to hear stories of what happened."

"Telephone me any time, or come by for a visit," he said.

I agreed that I would, then went off looking for Khalaf and Bilal, whom I found eating beside the woman who'd been baking bread. When Fendy saw me with them, he appeared quite perplexed and offered to take me back to the hotel. He drove us back himself, not saying a word, and when we arrived he invited me to the chalet for a nightcap.

First, though, I went back to my room, took off my shirt, which was flecked with grains of rice and grease spots, and had a quick shower, then stretched out on the bed for a moment. After a while I went back downstairs.

The Filipino servant opened the door of the chalet and led me to the downstairs living room. There, I found Fendy sitting with a prominent Lebanese journalist who edits an Arabic magazine published in London. He was tall, with a light complexion, elegantly dressed, and spoke in a sonorous voice, no doubt honed by speaking with rich publishers. He was showing Fendy a colorful magazine with the name of the famous Sotheby's auction house on the cover.

As I entered, Fendy set the magazine down and asked what I wanted to drink. The fruit platter and bottle of whiskey that had been gifted by the hotel were in their place on the side table, but when I looked again I realized this was a new bottle of a different brand of whiskey. Even so, it was left aside and we drank from bottles collected on a movable cart.

I poured myself some gin, and the Filipino servant handed me a bottle of tonic water. I asked the Lebanese journalist if this was his first visit to Oman. He laughed. Fendy explained that he had had a room reserved under his name at the Muscat Sheraton for over a year. The journalist had been telling Fendy about his travels in the Islamic former Soviet republics. He now spoke of the positive economic conditions and possibilities for investment.

I sipped a second cocktail as the conversation turned to conditions in the Arab world. Fendy asked me if I thought the Arabs had a future, but before I could answer he went on: "Arab nationalism is a mere fantasy. In fact, Arabic itself is the cause of our decline. It's the language of the past and of dreaming about the past. The new reality is the Middle East, not the Arab world." When I didn't say anything, he pursed his lips and started back in: "I know what they say about us—that we fell for American tricks in letting them build a base here. The reality is that we went ourselves and begged them to build it. Listen. Abdel Nasser had the perfect setup to be able to confront the foreign powers, but what did he get from his policy of confrontation?"

The third drink made me gloomy. With the fourth one my head started to spin, so I excused myself. Fendy walked me to the door of the chalet and I headed down the dimly lit walkway. I worked my way through the dark villas toward the beach until I was walking on sand, stepping around the small dunes built up by crabs. The darkness was almost absolute except for an obscure light coming from out in the ocean. I found myself tripping and would have fallen if not for a hand that grabbed me and pulled me up.

It was Salem. "What are you doing here?" I asked him.

"I'm out for a walk," he said. "You must have been drinking with Fendy."

Silently, we moved down the beach in the direction of the hotel. Our way was blocked, though, by the fence surrounding the tennis court behind the restaurant. It was padlocked, and the only way around it seemed to be to circle back to where we'd come from. We stumbled into each other in the dark as we searched for a path to the main road. Finally, Salem pulled me by my arm and said, "Come this way. It's easier."

He led me through some trees with thorns that broke the light into slivers, until we came out onto the main road about two hundred meters from the hotel entrance. The road was deserted, as might be expected at that hour. There was nothing there but the hotel and some walled-off gardens owned by the Sultan. We started toward the hotel, but we had only taken a few steps when a car's headlights came toward us from the opposite direction and we stepped up on the sidewalk. Another car appeared behind the first one. Suddenly, the headlights began to bounce back and forth as though the drivers were struggling to control their steering wheels. They kept coming toward us, dancing around recklessly.

Salem grabbed my arm and pulled me quickly to the side, shouting, "Hurry up. Grab onto the pole." I had no idea what he meant until I saw him grab onto a streetlight and wave at me to do as he was doing. I ran to the next pole down and started to hug it. The first car came slowly toward us, still bouncing back and forth. I could see several men inside it wearing white dishdashas. The second car came up behind them.

They passed us slowly, and I relaxed a bit, loosening my grip. Then I realized both cars had stopped. It was as though the passengers were discussing something. Salem took off running and shouted, "Hurry!"

As he headed toward the hotel, I realized the first car was turning and coming back toward us. The second car followed. I looked around for a place to run and hide, but the street was completely empty and I was totally exposed. We were two sitting ducks.

Salem grabbed onto the next pole, and I ran until I made it to the one after that. The first car came closer. The light made us very plain to see as the car pulled up beside us and came to stop. The back door opened and a leg emerged as though someone were getting out of the car. But then the driver kept going and thunderous laughter echoed from inside.

The car drove past us as the second one stopped and turned its headlights on us. We were trapped between the two of them. The Palestinian resistance suddenly came into my head and I bent over to collect scattered rocks.

"Run," Salem called out.

We ran up to the next two light poles, each hugging one of them. The first car continued all the way past the hotel, while the second stayed in place. I counted the light poles between us and the hotel. Four in all.

We kept scrambling from one to the next as the car made it to the end of the road and turned around. The winds blew toward us the voices of the passengers arguing. There was only one pole between us and the hotel now, but the first car could reach us before we could get to it. As we sped up, though, it slowed, and we managed to make it to the outer door of the hotel.

There was no sign of the three taxis that were always parked outside. In fact, there was no human life around at all.

We walked down the hall to the open reception lounge without meeting anyone. The desk where my fellow Egyptian countryman had sat was also empty.

The only one there was the Indian receptionist with his frozen expression and the tic in his neck. Salem took his key and walked toward the elevator, saying, "Those were young drinkers leaving the hotel bar. Good night."

I threw a look back toward the entrance and grabbed my key, checking my mailbox before heading up to my room. Once inside, I hooked the metal chain to secure the door and went over to the window to look out onto the hotel's gardens. The curtains were open a crack. I stood there for a second, frozen; there was no sound or movement outside. I pulled the curtain all the way closed, turned on the side-table lamp, and sat in front of the television.

A young man appeared on the screen in a military uniform. He turned out to be a brigadier general leading the Sultan's air force. He was speaking on the occasion of the national day in celebration of the Royal Omani Armed Forces. The sultanate was celebrating the occasion by completing an arms deal for military planes with the United Kingdom.

I watched the screen until sleep overcame me.

4.

The next day, we headed toward the east over a paved highway. To the left loomed barren mountains pockmarked with wide-mouthed caves, which, I was told, quickly filled up with people and their livestock once the rain came down. The road was broad and smooth; still, a small cart rode along the shoulder, driven by an Indian wearing fluorescent yellow overalls, who—at the moment our car passed—bent over as though picking up imaginary garbage.

On the sides of the mountains, unpaved roads twisted up toward the hilltops, and every so often to our right the ocean would appear. Along the beach there were schools of sardines swimming, with seagulls circling overhead.

"The sardines show the fall season is coming to an end," Khalaf said. "We call the new season *Serb*. Pretty soon, the air will be full of butterflies, the dairy cows will give more milk, the beehives will fill with honey, and the trees with coconuts."

After twenty minutes we made it to the entrance to Taqa, where a barefoot Bedouin stood with a rifle over his shoulder. Khalaf spoke with him in a highlander language. The man's eyes were lined with kohl and he had shiny black hair. A leather buckle secured a rubber belt around his waist, holding up his colorful mauz.

Khalaf waved at him to get in, and as the man stepped into the back seat Khalaf whispered to me that he was a soldier in the royal army that patrols the mountains. We skirted the town and twenty minutes later came to the next one,

Mirbat, where the soldier jumped out. The town, shaped like a crescent and filled with low-rise houses, nestled at the foot of a mountain range that loomed a few thousand meters above it. It overlooked the Gulf's fine sands and clear waters dotted with fishing vessels.

I asked Khalaf if there was any connection between the name Mirbat and the Moroccan capital Rabat. He said there was—that the original meaning of the word *rabat* was a camp where cavalry gathered, and that Saif Ben Thi Yezn named this place for the cavalry that had protected the area from Persian invaders. I thought to myself that the story is always the same: A call for help to a foreign army for protection from another foreign army. Then a third foreign army. And so on.

We passed by an ancient fortress that still had three cannon and a mosque with a green cupola, then entered a wide, unpaved street lined with villas leading to a big yellow telephone booth.

I was surprised. "Is that a public telephone?"

He answered proudly: "It's for international calls."

"How do you use it?"

"With a card that you can get from any shop."

We stopped in front of a modern building with a placard in front announcing: Center for Women's Advancement. A full-bodied woman in her thirties, or a bit older, met us. She was short and dressed in bright colors. Her face was uncovered. She led us to a long room with one desk next to the door and another at the other end surrounded by armchairs, a leather couch, and a safe. She told us the center offers various services to women of the region, including education on the harmful effects of manufactured baby formula, distribution of a variety of means of birth control, and guidance on childrearing methods. Also, women can take courses in sewing and ceramics to allow them their own income stream.

She invited me to take a tour of the building. Khalaf excused himself, saying he would wait in the car, having already taken the tour many times.

She led me down a long hallway toward a closed door with a loud racket coming from behind it. Stepping ahead of me, she opened the door and went in by herself, throwing me an embarrassed smile, then came back out and explained, "They remove their head coverings while they work, so I'm reticent to take you in."

She closed the door and led me to a room across the hall with a display of craftwork produced by the members of the center: incense trays, water jugs, leather canteens and milk jugs, cradleboards for babies. There was a special display for brides, a raised bed with columns from which hung colorful cloth curtains to protect the privacy of the newlyweds.

I asked where the center gets its financial support and she said, "Her Highness the Sultan's mother and the ministry of social affairs."

"Who hires the center's employees?"

"No one. There's an elected supervisory council. All the members are volunteers . . . even the director."

We went back to the room we'd started in. Leaving the door open, she sat behind her desk. I plopped down in the chair next to her and said, "Is it possible to meet the director?"

A fresh, perfumed scent wafted through the room as a young woman appeared at the door; of medium height, she wore a black abaya and a thick face veil that covered everything, including her eyes. My guide turned to her and said, "We have a guest from Egypt." She told her my name and, turning to me, said, "This is the director."

I stood up. The director didn't say a thing. I've always hated this kind of conversation with people wearing dark glasses that mask the eyes. What good are face veils that cover the whole face and don't give away a thing? I felt flummoxed, but managed to say, "In my country, we don't see very many women fully masked like yourself. Even the few *niqabs* that women wear usually show the eyes at least."

She floated toward the other side of the room and I followed her hesitantly, while the other woman stayed in her chair observing us. The director headed toward the other desk and invited me to sit in one of the armchairs next to it, while she remained standing. Suddenly, I lost my composure.

"Have you ever tried talking to a wall?" I asked her.

For a moment, we faced each other in silence. Then she raised her hand and slowly lifted the veil.

I traveled back thirty-five years. The same wide eyes, delicate lips, bronze skin, and piercing stare. "Warda," I whispered.

She answered drily: "Her daughter."

"I knew her, you know."

She didn't answer.

"Is she . . ."

She cut me off. "I don't know."

I collected myself and said, "I read part of her diaries in Muscat and was told that you have the rest of them."

She didn't ask who had said she had them or who had given me the other parts. It was as though she was indifferent—or already knew.

"May I see your identification?" she asked. I was expecting something along these lines and had come prepared. I pulled my passport out of my pocket and handed it to her. She flipped through the pages in silence, read the name carefully, compared my appearance in the photo to the face before her, then handed it back to me.

"How long are you staying in Salalah?"

"Another day or two," I said.

"I will bring them to you here tomorrow. Or . . . tomorrow's Friday. Make it Saturday. No, Sunday. I won't be here Saturday."

"That's a long way off," I said.

She thought for a moment, then said, "Listen, I have a dentist appointment in Salalah this afternoon. Meet me at his office."

"I don't know the town at all," I said. "My movements are all controlled, and I don't really want anyone else to know about this."

"No one will know anything," she said. "Just say your tooth hurts or you lost a filling, and ask the hotel to direct you to the dentist. Don't ask for help from Center for Music Heritage people. They are all with the secret police."

"Well, how can I be sure that the hotel will take me to the same dentist that you have an appointment with?"

The expression on her face conveyed disbelief at my stupidity. "Most of the dentists here are Indian. Just make any excuse to say that you need an Arab dentist. There's only one in town. He's a crazy Syrian married to a Frenchwoman. He's the one that I have an appointment with. You'll find me at his office at six o'clock." She was quiet for a moment, then added as she pulled the veil back over her face: "If it happens that you meet my uncle, don't mention any of this. He wanted to invite you to our house today, but he was called away on an important matter and won't get back until late tonight."

"Who are you talking about?"

"Abu Ammar."

Coincidence or a planned event?

5.

I headed down to the hotel lobby at five o'clock, begging God to save me from running into anyone like Salem or Khalaf. The lobby was empty, except for the Indian receptionist in his immutable position. The desk where my Egyptian compatriot sat was empty again.

I asked the receptionist about a dentist. He offered me a telephone book and remarked drily, "You can just look one up."

I flipped through the pages, pretending to be studying the various names. I said, "But these are all Indian." He gave me a challenging look, but I forged ahead. "Aren't there any Arab dentists?"

He gave his head a mechanical shake. Just then, though, I saw Metwaly headed off to take his position at his desk. I took the phonebook to him, told him I had a toothache, and asked if I could find an Arab dentist.

He smiled. "We have one who's Syrian. Will that do?"

"Sure. Fine. At least we will understand each other."

He wrote the doctor's name and address on a piece of paper and handed it to me. "He's on Nahda Street. The taxi can get you there in twenty minutes."

"How much should I pay him?" I asked.

"The driver will tell you. Probably about three riyals."

It was only five-thirty, but I wanted to get going right away, before I ran into anyone.

A Pakistani driver drove me. We went down Qaboos Street, then turned left and crossed through the historic Al-Baleed district, making it in ten minutes to Nahda Street, an area full of carts, people, and activity.

I got out in front of a movie theater showing an Indian movie whose poster depicted a fierce battle. The dentist's clinic was in a two-story modern building with a complex structure. I passed through an entrance behind a high fence and walked down a winding corridor until I came to a dark stairwell. On the second floor I found a door with a lit sign displaying the dentist's name. I pushed it open and entered an empty waiting area illuminated up by neon, with a desk and a television. I waited awhile, then looked at my watch. The hour was rushing toward six o'clock.

A brown door made of glass and steel creaked open and a man in his fifties with a pale, anxious face appeared, wearing a white coat over his shirt and slacks. Clutching the edge of the door, he bent his head toward me: "Are you the Egyptian gentleman?"

So he expected me. I nodded.

"The nurse has stepped out for some videotapes," he said. "Please come in."

I walked into a pretty normal exam room with all the customary equipment, though perhaps on the older side. He motioned for me to sit, so I did.

He pressed his foot on the chair pedal and with his hand adjusted the headrest behind my neck, saying, "I heard you are having pain in one of your molars."

I laid my head back, opened my mouth, and pointed at a molar that actually was starting to hurt.

He said while pushing a cold metal tongue depressor in my mouth, "Everyone here complains of tooth infection because of the calcium deficiency."

He set the tongue depressor to the side and picked up a long needle. "I'm from Aleppo," he offered. "I've been here a few years. Abu Ammar opened this clinic for me in exchange for 50% of profits. I do the work, and he collects his share. Sometimes it comes to twelve hundred riyals, other times as much as fifteen hundred."

One hundred twenty thousand Egyptian pounds per month. "That's a nice sum," I said.

"It doesn't go as far as you would think," he said. "Anyway, I'm thinking of moving on. Competition is stiff now from Indians and other dentists. There are even Omani women doctors now."

He started to probe in my mouth with the needle. I acted like I was in pain.

"You have some gingivitis and one of your molars needs a filling."

I told him I could have the work done in Egypt, that for now I only wanted something for the pain. He smeared an analgesic on my gums and wrote a prescription for a painkiller. Then he picked up a yellow envelope from the desk and handed it to me.

"This is for you."

I hesitated, then asked, "Did she come?"

"An hour ago."

I took the envelope and asked what I owed.

"Nothing," he said.

"How?"

"I didn't do anything. Besides, you are from the land of Gamal Abdel Nasser. That's enough."

I thanked my good luck and left. Outside, I stood and thought. I tore open the yellow envelope and took out two notebooks. They were a little smaller and thinner than the others and gave off a humid scent. Before I put them back in the envelope, it occurred to me: They must have been buried somewhere.

Chapter Twelve

DHOFAR MOUNTAINS, 1970–1972

July 28, 1970

Our first communiqué described the coup as a "predictable farce."

The second was even harsher. Rafie criticized its tone, calling it hysterical. Examples of the expressions it used: "the pampered boy who has lived a life of luxury"; "this pitiful figure who has nothing to offer the country"; "the revolution rejects such grotesque figures."

The new sultan is the son of the old sultan's Dhofari wife. He grew up in Salalah and studied in England—a graduate of the Sandhurst Military Academy. He was stationed in Germany with the British army and then returned to England to work in administration. His father assigned him to undertake an intensive course in Islamic law upon his return to Salalah, and also arranged a trip around the world. After that, the father refused to give Qaboos any governing responsibilities and only deigned to see him once or twice every year. He remained cooped up in his house in Salalah for almost six years.

August 3

The British press has published photographs of slaves of the old sultan. Some of them had maintained silence for so long that they became mute. They stood with heads bowed and eyes fixed on the floor.

July 29 edition of the *Financial Times:* Shell Oil—which owns 80 % of the Omani national petroleum company PDO—asked the British government to overthrow Said.

A secret military council chaired by Hugh Oldman and made up of the leader of the Sultan's forces, John Graham; director of development, David O'Gorman; two other Englishmen from the office of development and planning; Thuwainy Ben Shehab; and Qais al-Zawawi.

August 10

We have learned some details of the coup. It was engineered by a group led by the son of Bayraq Ibn Hamud al-Jafiri, son of the governor of Dhofar. It also included an English intelligence officer from the Sultan's air force who studied with Qaboos at Sandhurst. They contacted supporters in Muscat through a PDO official who came to Salalah regularly for meetings. Britain's general consul in Muscat collaborated with them. They paid off the palace guards. Then Bayraq Ibn Hamud sent in a group of his followers from the northern Hawasinah tribe. They broke into the Sultan's wing during his afternoon nap. When he picked up his pistol and aimed it at them, Bayraq spoke up, saying: "I demand this throne on behalf of our leader, Qaboos." Shots were fired. Said was struck in the leg. Finally, he gave up and signed an abdication statement. He was transferred first to a British air base, from there to Bahrain, and on to a private hospital in England.

A British platoon deployed to protect Qaboos arrived in Salalah under the command of Sergeant Major Bob Slaughter, and they now stick by the new sultan constantly, even taking turns sleeping in front of his bedroom.

August 16

Qaboos proclaims to a Kuwaiti newspaper that he does not believe the revolutionaries to be actual communists and he is confident that he can win them over to his side.

A strange news item from Aden: Muhammad Ali Haitham has resigned from all his official positions and Ali Nasir Muhammad has replaced him.

The Front has passed a law—the first of its kind in an Arab country—reducing the official bride-price to a token payment of 12.5 riyals. Another new law makes incompatible political beliefs between a husband and wife legal grounds for divorce. Now I can get married!

Qaboos has announced the lifting of travel restrictions and certain other limits on personal liberties, like wearing eyeglasses and owning a radio. He has called on Omanis living abroad to return and help rebuild the country. We discussed Qaboos's call during a wide-ranging meeting of the central committee and the leadership of the military wing. The majority felt it was a trick. Rafie, on the other hand, saw a substantive change and said we needed to wait and watch for a while. He said that popular revolution is tactical, and that whenever it is possible to achieve the same objectives without bloodshed, that is preferable. Our ultimate goal, he reminded, is to improve the lives of the masses. Fahd came back at him with a staunch counterattack, accusing him of defeatism.

There were one or two comrades who agreed with Rafie. When I spoke, I said that what happened had been a coup engineered by the imperialists. While we were still in the meeting, a piece of news came in that settled it: the authorities had boosted their siege on the rural areas, including the policy of bombing the highlanders' livestock. We agreed by acclamation to carry forward the struggle. And to intensify it.

August 25

Pamphlets distributed by the Sultanate over the liberated zone urge the people to surrender. One includes a rudimentary drawing of trees and houses with this caption: "You, fighters of the Front, is not this life better than life among caves, rocks, and graveyards?"

A new radio station has been established in Salalah, launched with the announcement of the liberation of the slaves we set free.

The government has introduced a development package for Dhofar worth six million pounds sterling. They have set up a model village along the coast next to Salalah and invested in irrigation pumps. British construction companies have expanded Raysut harbor. The British Middle Eastern Bank has opened a branch in Salalah. Yet another British investment project in the city is costing eight million sterling. All of this is designed to encourage the highlanders to leave the hills and come settle on the coast.

alternative form of colonialism

August 30

A strange pamphlet is being circulated by the government: "You sons of Dhofar, the Sultan has purchased an atomic bomb—but he won't use the entire thing. He'll only drop a fourth of it on you. It will destroy you, you communists! You are agents of Moscow, Peking, Tel Aviv, and Washington! Agents of Asians, Africans, and Latin Americans!"

nationalism vs internationalism

Some have accepted the offer of a general amnesty that Qaboos has announced and have fled to the side of the government. We have announced our rejection of the amnesty offer via Radio Aden and warned all enemies of the Front and the Liberation Army to stay out of Salalah. We have let all groups know that anyone trying to benefit from this amnesty will be subject to severe punishment—even execution.

September 5

Many coming back from the Gulf are accepting Qaboos's offer.

September 12

Several tribal leaders in the eastern region of Dhofar have staged a counter-revolt. They have captured as many as 40 of our cadres, aiming to give them up to the government. They are confiscating money and property that belongs to the Front. The east is the most populated of the provincial areas, but it has seen the least fighting. It is distinguished by a strong tribal system and by proimperialist social forces. Also, the mother of the new sultan comes from one of its tribes.

September 15

We have moved large units of our fighters from the central zone to the east. Fahd has taken over their leadership.

Pamphlets from the Sultanate are accusing us of being atheists and communists: "Their women and girls have become sluts and prostitutes. They do not believe in God, Islam, or any other basic traditions or national or religious values." It's not surprising. Their property and possessions are threatened and they suddenly become defenders of traditional values.

Fear of losing traditions

September 20

Another plot has been hatched: Saudi Arabia has taken advantage of the turmoil by annexing the northern region of Dhofar. Members of the Rawashid tribe have been paid to invade and occupy strategic posts in the north and center of the province. They carry Saudi nationality and their sheikhs receive direct payments from the kingdom.

September 25

We have succeeded in pushing back the Saudi conspiracy.

Slaughter in Jordan. A total of 20,000 dead and wounded. Amman has been bombarded with 120,000 tons of explosives.

September 27

A heroic stance by Nimeiry. He managed to save Arafat's life by getting him evacuated from Jordan.

Cairo agreement between the Jordanian government and the Palestinian resistance is signed in the presence of King Hussein, Yasser Arafat, and other Arab kings and presidents. Includes a cease-fire and withdrawal from Amman of armed forces on both sides.

Allende, the Marxist candidate, has won victory in the Chilean elections.

Fierce battles in the eastern zone. Many sheikhs and tribal leaders have taken their arms and their information and gone over to the government side. They are being organized into military units that the government is calling "national platoons." The platoon could include anywhere between 30 and 100. They are being drilled by an English special forces unit made up of 70 men and going by the nom de guerre "Batmen." The first company they trained was given the name Saladin. They were issued military uniforms that they called "dress," but they kept their traditional tribal clothes anyway: a mauz around their waist dyed a blue-black color and held up with an ammunition belt. Always shirtless during the summer months.

September 28

Gamal Abdel Nasser has died. We spent hours sitting around the radio while the Quran was recited. Finally, the news came. Anwar Sadat announced it. In a daze. We all wept, one after another. Fahd made the comment that the leader of the petit bourgeois had left the stage. I turned and shouted in his face that he could never dream of giving the masses of the Arab world one hair of what Abdel Nasser had given them. I'll announce a period of mourning during which all units will listen to lectures on his contributions to the revolution.

September 30

A massive funeral for Abdel Nasser in Cairo. Throngs of followers chanted: "You, beloved of the millions!" Castro issued a statement that his death had struck a blow to revolution in the Arab world.

October 12

An important figure in the eastern-zone resistance called Muhammad Za-kheinan has been lost—gone over to the enemy. They have learned from him our weak points. They ended up sending a big force and besieging our base in the east that's overseen by our comrade Mubarak Hamd al-Kitani. Several of his commanders urged a retreat once they realized that the Sultan's army controlled the summits surrounding their valley. Some of the others thought they needed to defend their strategic position and their weapons cache, saying they could lose everything since there were too few of them to carry their stockpile of ordnance and weapons somewhere safer. Mubarak told them, "This enemy could never overwhelm us. Our lives and our weapons are too precious. We'll pull the rocket launcher back to the most secure spot and stay there with it. If enemy forces advance, we will resist." He then threw the rocket launcher over his shoulder and pushed his way through, followed by the comrades. In the end, the group managed to escape the siege and join nearby groups, who were then able to surround the enemy and force them to retreat. After that, the comrades all started to call Mubarak the "anti-deserter." He is 22 years old, born in Sur, to the north of Muscat. He moved to Kuwait in 1965, where he came in contact with the Omani resistance. He participated in actions by the PFLP inside the occupied territories.

October 15

We have put down the revolt in the eastern zone. Our cadres who were taken prisoner are free.

October 16

The national forces have now proven themselves to the enemy. They have carried out reconnaissance missions, ambushes, attacks, and intelligence gathering, and by now are a symbol of the state's foothold in the mountains. They are reinforced by tribe members who have been conscripted. The government has armed some of those rebels whom they convinced to leave the Front by saying they would end up on the losing side. Thousands of unemployed youth have also been absorbed. The families then benefit from the provisions given out to the soldiers in the units as supplement to their salaries. Most march with their troop for half the month and take the other half to be with their family and tend to their livestock.

October 18

A split in the Sudanese Communist party leading to the expulsion of 12 members.

November 5

Aden's new agricultural reform law a major leap forward: ownership limited to 25 feddan. Simple fellahin and the marginalized are to run councils in charge of issuing titles, distribution, and establishment of cooperatives.

November 8

A new chapter in the struggle for power in Syria. Al-Assad has taken complete control.

November 16

[margin handwritten note: Fall of communism]

The Sudanese revolutionary council has expelled three members known for their connections to the Communist party. They are Babiker Al Nour, Farouk Hamdullah, and Hashem al-Atta. Also, Abdelkhaliq Mahjoub has been jailed. They are bearing down on the whole party.

December

We had one big party to celebrate three marriages between comrades. One of the three couples was Rafie and Amina. The contract ceremonies were officiated by the local leader of the Front. Entertainment was provided by Abu Salasel, a famous musician specializing in local *dan* music who has recently joined the revolution.

I wrote an article for the magazine *June 9* about the role of women in the revolution in the Gulf. I began with Karl Marx's observation that one can gauge the degree of progress in any society by its treatment of women, and added that revolutions can be judged the same way. I wrote: "All forms of oppression and exploitation in class-based society are embodied in the woman, for woman exposes society's double oppression—she manifests the oppressiveness of feudalism at the same time that she suffers from the capitalist mode of production in its normative institution of marriage and the familial burdens it places upon her. Her oppression starts in the home and then spreads to the general society, which imposes upon her all sorts of traditions and ancient customs that undercut her power and steal her humanity. The Dhofari woman in particular is burdened under the authority of four sultans: the political sultan in Muscat, the sheikh who runs the tribe, the imam who uses religion to oppress her, and finally the father, brother, and husband who exploit her within the family. Forms of oppression of women vary according to the social system. For example, the Maria tribe near Atbara in Sudan includes Muslims, Christians, and animists. It is their custom to offer to guests the wife or daughter of the host. Meanwhile, in Kokaban, which is a Zaidi area near the border with Saudi Arabia, women are yoked to the cattle and made to plow the fields."

January 1971

We had a party to welcome Salih. He used to be a slave and worked in Kuwait. There he learned to read and write. He joined the Front and they sent him on to Baghdad for a course in politics and military training. In 1965, he came back to Oman. He was imprisoned the same year and sent to a castle fortress in the mountains. He was released during the general amnesty, but life in Salalah did not suit him, so he fled to the mountains. He has difficulty walking because of the lingering effects of iron shackles that bound his legs together for five years. He will travel to Aden for treatment.

Our revolution has started to attract the world's attention. For the first time, an international delegation has come to visit from the Soviet Union.

I could not participate in the meetings with the delegation. They visited our people's primary school in Jabilut, 25 km from the border with Yemen. We had to question the school principal after the visit. His students had welcomed the visitors with a demonstration, holding up signs that said, "Down with Soviet socialist imperialism!" He defended himself by saying that it wasn't his idea, just a spontaneous expression of the will of the people! He turns out to be one of the fighters who had visited China. Ghazal stood up for him. He cannot conceal his hostility toward "revisionists," as he calls the Soviets. Rafie said it was a minor incident and should be ignored. I argued that we are committed to not taking sides in the Sino-Soviet dispute. Fahd added that we should not be permitting anything that threatens our relationship with the Soviet Union, given all the aid we receive from them. Sheikh Amar stayed quiet, leaving us to wonder about his position. Finally, we took the unanimous decision to issue a warning to the principal against any other such activities being carried out without consulting the leadership.

The national army is consolidating its gains among the tribes. Every platoon includes representation from various tribes. Qaboos claims to be building a modern state.

February 5

The leadership of the Palestinian resistance has engaged in public self-critique for the first time. Abu Iyad, the number-two man in the Fatah organization, has announced that the resistance is determined to remain in Jordan, adding that they oppose establishing a Palestinian state in the West Bank and Gaza because it would end up a vulnerable entity at the mercy of Israel. He said that some of the slogans coined during the September events went beyond anything the resistance had the capacity to carry out. He gave as an example: "We will not stop the struggle until the throne falls." He admitted that by the fourth day of fighting the resistance was hoping for a cease-fire.

February 12

Jordanian heavy weapons have launched a new attack on the Palestinian resistance. Thirty-two dead and 100 wounded in the fighting on both sides.

Nimeiri has attacked the Communist party in Sudan and calls for it to be crushed.

March 1

Comrade Fahd has caused a big problem. He caught one of the fighters praying and started mocking him and calling him backward and reactionary. Comrade Amar stepped in to defend the soldier. When the council convened, Fahd criticized Amar's conduct, saying he should not have opposed him in front of the soldier, that it would have been better for him to hold his tongue until the council met. We have to appear united before the lower ranks and the masses, he argued. Amar answered in his typically quiet and logical tone, saying that this unity principle was a merely formal matter and what was really important in this particular instance was Fahd's mockery of the soldier and disregard for his feelings. Fahd went mad and started accusing Amar of backwardness and ignorance. Amar walked out of the meeting.

March 2

Comrade Amar has disappeared.

March 3

State of shock. We have evidence that Amar slipped into Salalah and joined the government's army! I confronted Fahd and told him that he bore responsibility. Ghazal said that Amar was soft, had not evolved, and was still clinging to traditional ideas. Rafie said he most probably had decided to desert some time ago. I suggested that we circulate a general publication declaring respect for and inviolability of religious belief. A committee was formed with myself at the head to take necessary measures to avoid any lasting harm resulting from Amar's defection.

March 7

For the first time, Salalah has electricity, supplied by a small station with two generators, each of which produces 550 kilowatts.

The number of defectors to the national army has reached 200.

Guerrilla fighters with the Popular Front for the Liberation of Palestine have attacked an Israeli fuel convoy on its way to Eilat. Are they trying to prove that they can be more revolutionary then Nayef Hawatmeh's group?

April 28

We have opened the 9th of June middle school in Ghaydah, Yemen, which is just 200 km from the border and about 75 km inland. It consists of 320 students divided into eight classes taught by nine teachers. The curriculum covers levels three to five, which is the equivalent of the second year of middle school in the national system. We all drank tea in a tent that housed the school administration. Benches and tables were made from ancient wood. Comrade Abdel Samad Ahmad, a member of the teachers council, spoke of the importance of the students' ideological formation, stating that critique and self-critique are the daily bread of the revolution. Each class has its own tent, and a full course contains 40 boys and girls. Preference is given to children of martyrs wishing to enroll. Textbooks like the *Arabic Reader* are shared by two or three students. When there are no texts, lessons are copied by stencil and distributed on paper. Notebooks and pens are donated by friendly states. There's no one uniform. They wash their own clothes. Long and short pants and mauzes. Most wear a khaki cap that they wash twice a week. Most of the teachers were recently university students in either Yemen, the Gulf, or Egypt, and have cut short their studies to answer the call of the Front. Some also had already graduated, like the Syrian volunteer. The school year goes for eight months, and the new year starts immediately after the old year ends.

[handwritten margin note: limited resources but valued education]

May

We have taken over Hajlit, the last center under government control along the red line. I met the unit that won this victory. Their morale seemed low in spite of their triumph. Then I learned that they had had to kill former comrades who had gone over to the government army.

Massive demonstrations in the United States against the Vietnam War, poverty, and repression.

May 13

Anwar Sadat has undertaken something he calls a corrective movement aimed at Abdel Nasser's allies.

June 9

The third general congress of the Front has convened in Rakhiut.

June 12

A report by Rafie. He is repeating his old defeatist notions, calling for acknowledgment of what he considers "steps toward modernization" taken by Qaboos. He argues that political work is most significant and that military action is not an end in itself, but rather an instrument to facilitate political progress. His bottom line is that the goal of taking power must be abandoned and that we should be satisfied with a place at the table.

June 13

We all criticized Rafie. We demanded that he reconsider his ideas. He offered a self-critique. He said that his petit bourgeois background clouded his view of the sound path forward and that he was ready to pursue the struggle all the way to victory.

June 19

The congress ended with a number of historic decisions: (1) declaration of common ownership of all lands in Dhofar; (2) formation of popular councils to administer liberated areas; (3) a call for unification with the Oman Popular Front; (4) establishment of a revolutionary party of the masses to direct the revolution as it applies a Marxist/Leninist vision.

With the decision to form the popular council, the committee that mediates problems brought by the people has been disbanded. The councils will also sponsor cultural programs.

June 29

There are reports that Abdelkhaliq Mahjoub, secretary of the Sudanese Communist party, has escaped from jail.

July 3

The Iraqi Baath party has launched a campaign against communists and Kurds.

Our forces currently control two-thirds of Dhofar. The Sultan's troops have only the coastal area.

July 13

Allende's government has announced the nationalization of some of the copper mines owned by US interests. Comrade Fahd remarked that Allende is a reformer and not a revolutionary. Ghazal backed him up, as did two other comrades. Rafie said that Allende is trying to prepare the way to implement a long-term socialist project by establishing a national popular government built on traditional constitutional foundations. Fahd says such a government could never be truly revolutionary because the traditional foundations are all in the hands of the reactionary classes. These elements, he argued, will never accept real change; they will counter any attempts at such with force. He is right.

The Jordanian forces have waged a wide-ranging attack on Palestinian resistance fighters using tanks and warplanes. There are hundreds of victims. Also 2,300 Palestinian guerrillas being held in Jordanian military prisons.

July 18

Discussion over the declaration establishing the United Arab Emirates.

July 19

At 6:30 in the evening, Radio Khartoum interrupted its programming for a special announcement from Major Hashem al-Atta announcing a new initiative by the Sudanese military to correct the path of the May 25 revolution. They have arrested Nimeiry.

The news from Sudan is on every channel. A revolutionary council has been set up consisting of seven officers including Abdelkhaliq Mahjoub's brother. The council is chaired by Lieutenant Colonel Babiker Al Nour, who has been in exile in London. They have announced the formation of the National Democratic Front, an alliance of workers, farmers, nationalist intellectuals, soldiers, free officers, and nationalist owners. The ban on activity that was imposed on the Communist party has been lifted.

July 20, morning

The central committee of the Sudanese Communist party has announced its support for the coup.

July 21

Sadat has decided to form a special revolutionary tribunal to try 100 loyalists of Gamal Abdel Nasser. The main ones are Ali Sabry, Shaarawi Gumaa, Sami Sharaf, Muhammad Faik, and Dia al-Din Daoud.

July 22

Nimeiry has been reinstated in Sudan with the help of the Egyptian, Libyan, and English intelligence services. Hashem al-Atta has been taken into custody. This morning, Libya intercepted a British Airways flight carrying the coup leader Babiker Al Nour and his colleague Farouk Othman Hamdullah. Two Libyan jets forced it to land in Benghazi while it was en route from London to Khartoum. The officers and their entourage disembarked and the plane returned to London.

Forty-five high-ranking officers in Iraq have been arrested and charged with conspiring against the regime of al-Bakr and Saddam.

July 23

A quick trial was held this morning in Khartoum for Major Hashem al-Atta and a number of his confederates. It ended with their being sentenced to death by firing squad. Nimeiry declared his gratitude to Sadat and Gaddafi for the assistance they gave in foiling the coup plot and apprehending its leaders. Babiker Al Nour and Farouk Othman arrived today in Khartoum on a specially chartered flight under armed guard.

July 24

Nimeiry has announced that a verdict in the trial of Al Nour and Othman will be announced tonight or tomorrow morning and carried out immediately.

July 25

The execution by firing squad of Major Farouk Othman Hamdullah was carried out this afternoon. Abdelkhaliq Mahjoub has been arrested.

July 26

Babiker Al Nour was executed by firing squad, and Shafie Ahmad al-Sheikh, the president of the worker's alliance and a prominent leader in the Communist party, hanged.

July 27

The Sudanese military council has issued a decree condemning Abdelkhaliq Mahjoub to death.

July 28

Abdelkhaliq Mahjoub was executed by hanging this morning.

July 30

Farouk Abu Aissa, the Sudanese foreign minister and a leader in the Communist party previously, has announced that all who were executed were given fair trials.

Ongoing bloody pursuit of members of the Communist party and their fellow travelers.

August 13

The delegation from the Arab Workers Alliance has completed its visit to Khartoum and issued a communiqué declaring that the Sudanese Workers Alliance and its leader, Shafie al-Sheikh, were innocent of the charge of having helped plot the coup.

The US magazine *Newsweek* has published a picture of Nimeiry in his car the night of the execution of Abdelkhaliq Mahjoub, reporting that he spent the night riding around without ever taking his hand off his bottle of whiskey.

September

Strikes in Muscat and Mattrah against the increase in the cost of living due to Qaboos's development projects. The building up of the port, roads, and the airport is relying on skilled foreign workers. That has caused the price of food and lodging to skyrocket. Local workers started to direct their protests against foreigners, but the movement stopped with the arrest of its leaders.

Sadat is talking about a decisive year.

Nabila Said (18 years old) has joined us. She's been placed in a platoon with

complications of industrialization

4 women and 20 men, and the company leader is a woman. The highest military position obtained by a woman in the movement to date is that of company commander overseeing three units.

October

Qaboos has attended ceremonies in Iran commemorating the 2,500th anniversary of the throne of Persepolis. Sadat was also there. The Shah managed to gather up all the birds of a feather.

A British campaign called "the Leopard" hopes to establish a chain of positions at the edge of the desert that will cut off the main routes to the eastern zone.

Tafoul has been martyred during a British air raid. Amina was also hit and has a deep wound on her back.

November 20

Tarek Bin Taymur, the Sultan's uncle, has resigned as prime minister. Qaboos has taken over the post himself. Rumor has it that Taymur wanted to set up a constitutional monarchy.

November 28

The Iraqi Baath party has embarked on a project to draft a charter for national action. There is a consensus that all the defeats and setbacks suffered by the revolutionary movement in Iraq and the Arab world go back to minor contradictions existing among the revolutionary movements. Such small matters push aside the big differences between the movements, on the one hand, and imperialist, Zionist, and reactionary forces on the other. The new charter will call for more revolutionary democracy in order to strengthen the masses and the revolutionary parties.

The trial of the American revolutionary communist Angela Davis has begun.

November 30

Iran has occupied three islands off the coast of the United Arab Emirates. There had been a preceding agreement over one of the islands between the Iranians and the ruler of the Emirate of Sharjah. Under British pressure, the emirate conceded half of one island to Iran for a period of nine years in exchange for 1.5 million British pounds.

December 2

Assassination of the Jordanian foreign minister, the traitor Wasfi al-Tal, in Cairo. A new Palestinian resistance organization that calls itself "Black September" has declared responsibility.

Revolutionary decree issued by Colonel Gaddafi nationalizing the British *Libya nationalizing* Petroleum company's Libyan operation. He has also withdrawn all Libyan reserves from British banks in protest of Britain's role in the Iranian seizure of the Emirati islands.

Operation Leopard, seeking to infiltrate the liberated area, has succeeded in establishing a new British operations center in Tafi Attar. We decided not to clash with these forces directly, but instead to carry out counterattacks until the government tries to establish permanent bases.

Latest figures: 290 have fallen in clashes during the past three months, going back to the first of October. Of these, 170 fell in clashes in the east, 41 in the central zone, 20 in the Ho Chi Minh area, and 59 in the west. Government forces lost 136 fighters in clashes that took 31 of our own. The imperialists lost two planes, a helicopter, and a number of armored vehicles. Some have guessed that these are overestimates.

In Ahlaish liberated zone, a congress has convened to establish the Popular Front for the Liberation of Oman and the Arabian Gulf. It was formed through unification of the Front and the National Democratic Front for the Liberation of the Occupied Arab Gulf. Some of the attendees walked for two weeks to get to the site of the conference. Yaarib was not able to attend. He was elected to the executive committee responsible for the Omani northern zone.

February 5, 1972

In Khartoum, Nimeiry has received George Bush, an emissary from the American foreign ministry, and a prominent figure in the CIA.

February 12

A fierce campaign fought by 2,000 mercenaries to overtake the province of Beihan in southern Yemen has failed. The leader of the mercenaries is Sheikh Ali Bin Naji, who fought against the Egyptian army in 1962 at the battles of Sarwah and Arqub where two Egyptian officers, Nabil al-Waqad and Abdel Minaam Sind, and the Yemeni Ali Abdelgheny were killed.

February 13

Decision for me to travel with a party delegation the 1,500 km to Aden to attend the fifth congress of the National Front. I can't sleep. I will finally get to see this tiny country of 1.5 million that has become the home base for revolution throughout the Arab world.

February 17

We spent three days between a Land Rover, a pickup, camels' backs, and walking. Ghazal and I and another comrade from the house of al-Ghassany. Sparse fields. Wells almost completely dry. The narrow mountain passes are clogged by the caravans of 20 or 30. Camels carrying supplies. Also some random bombings by the British. A large rock called Ras Darbat Ali that overlooks the Arabian Sea is the last point before the border. 3 m tall, it takes the form of a V. The legend is that Imam Ali split it in half with his sword when he found it blocking his way. I asked a fighter stationed next to a rocket launcher where the weapon came from. "We looted it from the British," he said. An inscription on it said "United Arab Republic." When I pointed to the words, he said, "The British took it from Egypt and we took it from them." We went down through one of the valleys and then climbed back up Jebel al-Qamar. That took up a whole night of walking. Then we went down to Hawf, the first village in the sixth province (Al-Mahra). We had a meal of boiled fish and dates at the office of the Front. By skiff with a 3 horsepower engine to Fatk, then by Land Rover to Ghaydah, the capital of province six. A rickety plane took us to the airport of Riyan in Mukalla. Its houses are connected, tucked between the mountains and the sea in a narrow strip. Some are up to six stories tall. From the plane, they looked like rows of sweets packed into a box.

We picked up a new broadcast in Arabic from Monte Carlo. A new trend, quick pace.

February 28

Another rickety plane, taking us to Aden, 500 km away. I thought of my childhood days, when my father took me with him on his business trips to the various corners of the British zone—its minisultanates and tribal sheikhdoms. There were the Awlaki warriors, for example, descendants of the Maan dynasty that had worshiped the moon. Their chests shining with dark blue body paint, their hair fastened behind, a curved dagger at their belt with a miniature pot of kohl in its handle. I think we visited Lahaj, where a local potentate surveyed his fiefdom with a lion that had been given to him as a gift by an Abyssinian ruler. There were also the rows of English armored vehicles with their long antennas. Stations guarded by soldiers in shorts. The valley of murders in al-Wahidi sultanate. Trenches stretched from the houses to the wells to allow women to collect water without exposure to the flying bullets. Long rows of withered palm trees, stripped for their oil. Hadhramaut, whose buildings are as tall as 80 feet. Sayoun's awe-inspiring palace of the sultan. I went up 100 steps to get to the floor of the harem while my father met with the sultan. Shebwa, which sits above one of the great cities of the kingdom of Sheba. Once we approached Aden, I remembered the thick fog and the choking humidity that engulfed the mornings. The camel races, and the clacking of the windmills that harvest salt from the seawater along the coast. The hubbub of the port. Fishermen repairing their nets spread out on the beach. Ships coming from the Mediterranean and headed for the Indian Ocean carrying coal or petroleum. And the passenger ships with Europeans wearing white suits or safari gear and filling up the souks.

Aden's airport is small. I was expecting it to be cleaner. It serves two airlines, one Ethiopian, the other Somali. Two comrades received us. One was from their National Front, and the other represents us in Yemen. We carried our own luggage from the plane to a dilapidated army jeep. After all these years in the wilderness, the city strikes me as confusing and agitated. Even the low buildings seem like towering skyscrapers. Cars race along at scary speeds. So many people. Barbed wire is everywhere. The Khormaksar neighborhood had British barracks and flats for their officers and civilians. Now it has an embassy row and housing for foreigners and officials. The Crescent Hotel. An old Edwardian building left over from the era of colonialism. Classic ceiling fans. A broken elevator. The lighting is feeble. The staff are mostly former resistance fighters.

Moussa, our director of media in the Aden office, took us to his house. His wife loaned me some shampoo and I took the most sublime hot bath of my life. I brushed my teeth so thoroughly using her toothbrush. We drank Seera beer, the local brand. It tastes like Stella, the Egyptian beer. We ate lobster for dinner. The state is now supervising the lobster traps. All fishing has been nationalized. The whole fleet of ships is probably only 30 or 40. They export to the GDR and Russia. Local television is nothing but news of the revolution and Egyptian shows. Electricity and water are cut off at ten at night, every day except Thursday and Friday.

February 29

We had a breakfast of navy beans and lentils. So many newspapers: *October 6, Al-Hurriya,* both the Lebanese and the Syrian Communist party papers. Not a single foreign newspaper, not even an Arab one.

The Front in Aden had set aside an allowance for each of us to cover personal expenses, but we refused it. Tour of the city in an open military jeep. Kiki House was a way station for children captured in Africa on their way to Saudi Arabia or the Gulf. Now it has been renamed the House of the Sultan. The Maala district. We took the main artery that connected it to the Arab section of the Kraytar district. The offices of our organization. A group of medical health trainees from Dhofar. We met comrade Saleh, who during his time in prison came down with paralysis in his foot. We made the decision to fly him to East Germany for treatment, but he refused to go, insisting that he wanted to rejoin the fight. Here, our comrades live at the same level as we do in Dhofar. They earn the same salary of 10 dinar. The Front covers most basic expenses. Lodging and electricity are paid for by the Yemeni government.

There are still villas left by the English, with ornate architectural features and gaudy colors. Squatters from the countryside have taken them over. The new city is next to the port: blocks of low-income housing built by the Germans. Open-air cinemas, casinos, and cafes. We sat in a cafe by the sea. Ghazal was going to order a beer, but I warned him that we were in a public place. He became angry and started calling me "Sheikha Warda." The port is devoid of ships—no movement at all. The Suez Canal closed and the imperialists fled the region, throwing tens of thousands of workers, technicians, and cadres out of work. We had lobster and seafood biryani for lunch. Women wrap up in a cloak that resembles the traditional feminine robe in Sudan. Some wear a skirt and blouse. Scent of sandalwood and fragrant oils. Inscriptions covering hands and feet. The grating cries of the grackles, which swarm everywhere. The British introduced them to clean the city. They forbade hunting or killing them. Our driver said that now, if you try to kill one, all its comrades will attack. Old government shops have been nearly emptied of any products. The whole city only has five taxis. Everything stops for a nap between one and six in the afternoon. The state is trying to wipe out addiction to qat, restricting its sale to Thursdays and Fridays. It comes in by plane from Ethiopia.

March 1

Had a checkup with a female specialist who graduated from Egypt. She examined me carefully but couldn't find the source of my painful and irregular periods. She advised me to marry and have children. I was stunned by her attitude. No matter how much education a woman receives, she cannot liberate her mind from the influence of patriarchal society. She still sees herself as having one main priority in life.

March 2

Shehab is here. There's a delegation attending a congress. I was elated to see him. He gave me a big hug. Hasn't changed much, though he's lost a good deal of hair. He's married now to a Lebanese painter. Says he thinks about me often. We had quite a long talk. He says Rushdy has published a series of studies on revolutionary movements in the Arab world and that he met him in Beirut.

March 3

I met the members of the Yemen Society of Women. People are chanting Salim Rubai Ali's nickname, "Salmin," in the streets. The leadership here, instead of sitting on high, refuses all forms of privilege. The lower salaries were only about 9% of top wages in the country before. Now they are up to 22%. Ministers make 75 dinar per month, and the lowest wage laborer makes 15. Even the chairman of the presidential council, the effective head of state, makes only 100.

Fervor among delegates during a session led by Salmin urging the congress to speed up the establishment of a vanguard party that will bring about dictatorship of the proletariat. Abdelfattah Ismail thinks that such a party cannot be established yet because of the current lack of class consciousness and ideological commitment.

We met with Salmin in the presidential palace, a round building once used as the headquarters of the British governor. We just walked in, without being stopped or questioned. The European clothing strikes me as odd. His eyes are constantly moving. A simple man—a man of the people.

We went to Abdelfattah Ismail's house at the top of a hill overlooking the port. Calm, quiet manner. A full head of thick, smooth hair. Keen intelligence. I asked him about his position vis-à-vis the communists. He said they are good comrades, then he smiled and added: "They are good talkers too." I thought of Guevara's writings about them.

March 6

The congress ended with the election of a central council made up of 31 members to replace the general leadership. The central council turned around and elected a seven-member political bureau with Abdelfattah Ismail as general secretary. Salim Rubai is the chair of the presidential council of the republic and assistant secretary general of the party.

A new leftist breakaway faction of the Popular Front for the Liberation of Palestine is defending airplane hijackings. It describes them as a tactical part of the struggle. It also argues that progressive Arab organizations are nothing more than petit bourgeois organizations setting the stage for transformation to reactionary regimes.

Qaboos has met with Saudi king Faisal in Riyadh. The British press said that the meeting was put together by the American treasury secretary Robert Anderson, who had seen Qaboos in London. The summit resulted in an agreement to halt Saudi assistance to Imam Ghalib and to strengthen Saudi support for Qaboos.

Signing of an agreement on naval cooperation between Bahrain and the United States that will allow three American naval carriers to be stationed in the port of Jufair.

March 7

We had a party last night in comrade Moussa's home to celebrate the end of the congress. The food was prepared by a Somali housemaid and paid for by the Front. Shehab attended. He flirted with me aggressively, even though I showed no interest. I realized that he wanted to assert his authority over me, and I resisted, but my resistance was not so strong. Maybe I was nostalgic for our old times. Or maybe the desire to feel a man's rough cheeks and strong legs overcame me. I might have wanted to test what kind of power I still have over him. When he was inside me, I was amused by the sudden memory of my doctor's exam. The strange thing is that I really enjoyed it. Maybe because of our old intimacy. But today it's clear: I have confirmed that I no longer have even one speck of deep feeling for him. *Finito!*

March 10

Land Rover from Ghaydah in the mountains. Songs and chants the whole way. Salih came along with us, insisting on returning before he is done with treatment. Views of ocean waters on one side and mountains on the other the whole trip. We made it to an abandoned village called Damqut. We searched long and hard before finding a shop that was open, though it sold only a few canned goods. We set out from there in a rickety *sanbuk* sailboat. We clung to its sides, singing, "People power! People power!" Something, either a big shark or a dolphin, rocked the waters around us until the boat nearly capsized. Salih started to scream, "I can't swim," so we struck up a sailing song to distract him. We made it back to shore at the border. There, we were met by comrade Said Ali, a member of the executive committee, and were shown around the almost completed building for the first hospital constructed by the Front. We rested after dinner on the rooftop patio of his house, where we inhaled fresh air for the first time since Ghaydah. The conversation turned to Muslim Bin Nuwaf, who has gone over to the government side. On the sea, searchlights flash from the Sultan's naval ships looking for skiffs delivering our weapons. Suddenly, rockets showered down on us from a British battleship off in the distance. Magnificent explosions. No one hurt.

March 11

We have moved on. By the end of the day we had come very close to the British, who are in Sarfait. Although they have a presence near the border, a liberated "bottleneck" about five miles wide keeps our supply route to Yemen open.

March 31

Sudan has obtained a $40 million loan from the International Monetary Fund to take care of a deficit in its balance of payments.

April 2

The government has set up heavily fortified centers near Sarfait. They have reinforced surveillance on all the routes leading from the coast up to the mountains. They call this initiative "Operation Simba," and it has included bombing raids inside Democratic Yemen, including hits on Hawf.

April 8

Staggering news: After Salih left me and headed back to his unit, he learned that the revolutionary court had executed his father on the charge of cooperating with the enemy. He went mad and had a breakdown. He ran away to join government forces and began to point them to our camps and our weapons.

The first congress of the Arab Socialist Union in Libya. 530 members, including 40 women. Gaddafi claims that the *"jamahiriya"* system combines nationalist capitalism, peasant movements, workers, intellectuals, and soldiers, all melded into one. He says he has built a theory of the third way based on three principles: socialism, religion, and nationalism. He claims that his socialism is different from both Marxism and capitalism.

April 15

I have reviewed the order issued by the revolutionary court against Salih's father. In accordance with local traditions of hospitality, he took some fresh milk to a government patrol. Dozens of similar judgments have been issued throughout the area. I wrote a report for the executive council asking that they block the carrying out of any death sentence until it is reviewed by the complete membership of the central committee. I also asked that a corrective be issued regarding the execution of Salih's father.

April 28

The Vietnamese offensive proceeds apace. The revolutionary forces have confounded the American military, managing to enter the cities.

May 7

Attempt to strike democratic Yemen. A massing of troops at its borders. The US and Israel are working together to take control of the entrance to the Red Sea. Provocations along the border between the two Yemens.

Palestinian revolutionaries have hijacked a plane filled with passengers from Belgium and forced it to land at Lod airport. They are demanding the release of a number of their comrades who are in Israeli prisons. The operation's immense symbolic value is its proof of Palestinian presence inside Israel proper.

May 24

The enemy has dropped 200 paratroopers into Khal-Arut, about 10 miles east of Hawf.

May 25

British bombers launched an attack on the Yemeni border. It lasted all day. Struck civilian targets: a school, a health clinic, the Center for Illiteracy Prevention, and family homes. They killed five of our fighters in addition to women and children. We shot down two Strikemaster bombers.

Gaddafi has offered the Sultanate assistance in fighting us.

Grand opening of the Hospital of the Martyr Habkouk in the border area. It has a total of 14 wards. 2 clinics, 3 caves, 3 tents, some tin sheds, and others of wood. A committee of health experts trained in Yemen attended the opening. The clinic is also a pharmacy. It serves between 60 and 80 patients—men, women, and children. A 70-year-old tubercular patient with a Kalashnikov slung over her shoulder offers us a hand with security. Patients spread sheets and rugs on the ground to sit on. A vegetable garden is being cultivated nearby. Medical assistants go into the residential neighborhoods to make house calls and teach about health. Ambulances bring the dire cases back to the hospital. The only doctor, Waleed, shows obvious signs of exhaustion. A Kalashnikov across his back at all times. He is barefoot like his patients. He was delegated by the Popular Front for the Liberation of Palestine. Palestinian, in his 30s. His face was disfigured during an operation in the occupied territory. I asked him if he didn't think Palestine needed his help even more than we do. He answered while rolling himself a cigarette: "The struggle is the same everywhere. The problem here is raising the level of consciousness." He has been here for a few months now and has managed to visit several villages. He relies heavily on basic analgesics because of a general lack of medicines. He examines the patients, leaves them some pills, telling them to take two, then leaves. Most of the patients don't understand that they are supposed to swallow the pills. Instead, they tie them in a cloth and place them over the spot suffering from pain. Strangely, they actually start to feel better.

Three Japanese attacked Lod airport to show solidarity with the international revolutionary movement.

June 1

The Sudanese minister of national guidance visited America and promised that diplomatic relations between the two countries will be restored. The Sudanese millionaire Khalil Othman says, "Foreign direct investment is now being welcomed in our country. A group of international businessmen from Japan, America, and Britain are headed here to take a look at all the great projects they can get involved in."

June 7

Twelve British soldiers were wounded when our forces opened fire on their mess hall in Salalah. The injured were evacuated to Cyprus by special charter.

June 28

Once the rainy season started, we seized the initiative and forced the enemy to pull out of Thaqeeb. They regrouped in Simba at 4,500 feet elevation. It's only 7 km from the Yemeni border and allows for control of the route between the two countries. They then tried to break through the mountains to the coast, but failed. They became captives there. They have just the one company and it's stuck there for the next five months. Our bombs repeatedly hit their airfield runways that the Skyvans and Caribous use. They are now completely dependent on supplies brought by helicopter.

During a battle that lasted 14 hours in Wadi Kohout near Sarfait, Qaboos's uncle Muhammad Ahmad Hasheet was killed.

Confusion in the ranks of the government: a committee for national defense has been formed which includes the foreign minister, the assistant to the minister of defense (the Sultan), the British leader of the Sultan's forces, the British director of the secret police, the British advisor for security, the economic advisor, and the chief of police, who is a Sri Lankan carrying a British passport.

July 4

As he received Qaboos at the Amman airport, King Hussein of Jordan announced that he will send a military delegation from the Jordanian army to the Sultanate to battle the rebels. The resemblance between the two is eerie: about the same age and height, both with degrees from England, both hate their father. And both love the West.

July 8

Sadat has decided to send home Soviet advisors and military experts based in Egypt. The move exposes his lack of commitment to waging the war of liberation.

A meeting to discuss Fahd's suggestion that we seize Mirbat. Results of a recent reconnaissance mission: 40 men stationed in the fortress. A few more are in the town, and eight officers from British special forces plus two Omani cannon holding down the trenches around the fortress. The British commander is named Captain Mike Kealy. He lives in a house protected by Browning rifles and rocket launchers and fortified with sandbags. I opposed the proposal on the basis of our previous decision not to get drawn into conventional warfare. Fahd screamed in my face, "What is conventional? We'll surprise them in their sleep." He argued for the political significance of the operation, since it would be carried out on the first anniversary of Qaboos's coup.

July 23

A wide-ranging attack on Mirbat carried out by a force of 100 led by Fahd. It began at 5:30 a.m.

July 24

Our forces held Mirbat for 14 hours.

July 25

We lost 70 fighters in the Mirbat disaster. I have heard the testimony of some of the survivors. A group of 20 men advanced toward the barbed wire that surrounds three-fourths of the town. Behind them, a group of 10 or 12 men filled in the plain. Forming rows and keeping a distance between each other, they advanced with their weapons over their shoulders. Short bursts of gunfire coming from the British commander's house surprised them. Our men made it to the barbed wire and began to cut through it, some of them using their bare hands. Others threw a blanket over the wires to cross. 7-mm shells exploded around them at rates of extreme rapid fire. The explosions knocked some of them away from the fence. Others fell across the wire and dangled there like dummies. Fahd yelled encouragement to the survivors and waved at them to advance. A new round of fire came. Some were able to cross over the fence and get to within 40 yards of the fortress, whereas others held back. A dead fighter hung from the wires like a scarecrow made of straw. Another hung upside down with his limbs outstretched, as though crucified. Two crossed the fence and went down immediately, the leg of one shaking uncontrollably. Two others tried to take out the cannon. They advanced 100 yards before running into a spray of bullets and collapsing to the ground. One managed to keep on, zigzagging toward the cannon well and even jumping up on its wall. The others ran toward the fortress firing heavy weapons. But then came the airplanes.

I imagined Fahd—khaki uniform, pointed hat, ammunition belt across his chest—felled over the fencing, screaming and waving his arms, his rifle just beyond his reach. Maybe he imagined himself a hero like on one of those Chinese posters.

Waleed and his assistants are working round the clock to treat the wounded.

July 27

A fighter has lost his leg. Two holes right below his knee as a result of an explosion. He told me the story of how his comrade Muslim was killed. He pulled back toward the beach as they had been ordered. Two groups of British soldiers caught up with him. He waded out into the water up to his waist. The soldiers yelled at him to throw down his weapon and surrender. He turned and fired on them and was killed.

The loyalist forces are distributing pamphlets with pictures of weapons they have confiscated. The text reads: "The communist leadership expected an easy victory in their recent Mirbat attack. Instead, communism was struck a mighty blow. The communists ran away, leaving in the hands of the Sultan's triumphant armed forces 29 dead, 12 wounded, and a large cache of weapons. These pictures are by no means everything that was confiscated, but they show some of the weaponry that the communists left behind." Their writing had improved a bit, although one still finds grammatical errors.

Another pamphlet, entitled "The Hand of God Crushes Communism," shows a crude fist with the flag of the Sultanate tattooed on it. It's squeezing a meager human frame, but all one can see of it is arms stretched out over the fist, a star underneath, and drops of blood dripping down.

Some of the prisoners were taken to Salalah, where British officers subjected them to public beatings and humiliation.

August

Without notifying the command structure, a group of renegade fighters attacked the town of Taqa. They managed to occupy it for four hours. Eventually they withdrew, but not before taking a large haul of food supplies from local merchants, leaving them money in compensation.

We have made a firm decision to put limits on all attack operations.

Chapter Thirteen

SALALAH, DECEMBER 1992

The telephone rang. I put aside Warda's diaries and picked up the receiver, recognizing the voice immediately: "Zayed!"

"Were you expecting me?" he laughed.

"Yes, where are you calling from?"

"I'm in Muscat. Listen, how much longer will you be in Salalah?"

"I leave the day after tomorrow."

"Could you wait an extra day? I want to see you there."

I hesitated. I had had enough and was dying to get back . . . at least to Muscat, if not Cairo.

"Can't you see me in Muscat?" I asked.

"No," he said. "It's better there. I'll call you the moment I arrive."

I set down the receiver feeling annoyed. I had just asked Khalaf to book my return flight, and now I would have to call back and ask him to postpone it. I turned back to Warda's journal, but before I started reading, the phone rang again.

I heard Salem's voice. "What are you doing?"

"Reading. Why?"

"I arranged a meeting," he said. "Can you come out?"

"Now? I haven't had dinner."

"Don't worry. You'll eat."

I dressed and put the journals back in their bag, then stuck the bag under the mattress.

I found Salem in the lobby. He led me straight out to where his brother-in-law was waiting in an old beat-up Mazda parked on the other side of the street, facing toward the center of town.

I crossed behind him, asking, "What's going on?"

He opened the door to the back seat and said, "Get in." I sat behind his relative and we took off.

"Did you know that your friend's sister has a daughter living here?" he asked.

I avoided answering by asking a question of my own: "Are we going to her?"

"Of course not," he said. "We are going to meet someone else—someone who was in the movement and went to prison." Then he turned in his seat and said, "But didn't you meet her when you were at the women's center?"

Nothing is hidden around here.

"I met a woman named Waad, but I didn't know about her connection to Warda," I said.

"That's her," he said. "What did you think of her?"

"I wasn't exactly expecting a religious fanatic."

"What do you mean?"

"She wears that thick, black face veil that covers everything, including her eyes."

"Oh, that's the veil worn by the sherif descendants who trace their lineage from the Prophet. It has nothing to do with fanatics."

Fatum took us along the beach down Qaboos Street. He turned the radio dial to the news and we listened to a bulletin about the assassination of one of the leaders of the Socialist party of Yemen in Aden. Salem remarked: "I think this is the fiftieth assassination of its kind since the unification of the two Yemens."

As we drove past a bird sanctuary, Fatum said, "Thank God the disease didn't spread to us."

Salem shot back at him: "Have you already forgotten about Suhayl?"

Curious, I asked: "Who's that?"

"He was one of the Front's first leaders," Salem said. "He died just yesterday, in a car accident in Nizwa. It was harrowing. He left behind a wife and seven children."

Fatum was nonchalant. "Just one accident."

I got the feeling Salem's answer was starting up an old argument: "What about the imprisonments? Like Abu Sikha, who graduated from Kiev National University, came back at the end of last summer, and has been sitting in prison ever since. Muslim Ibn Nofel, too, was brought back from the Emirates in handcuffs and had his passport taken away."

And how exactly did you escape just such a punishment, Salem, my friend?

Fatum objected: "Muslim was arrested because of his debts."

"How could he have debts?" Salem asked. "Since he joined the government in 1970, he's had this big salary, eight hundred thousand riyals, plus a plot of land, plus a director's bonus, plus another thousand a month from the Sultan's royal court, plus free food from the Dhofar government. Lately, he's even gone into oil and gas, signing an exploration agreement with the Yemenis as a representative of one of the big companies."

Fatum turned his attention to the semideserted dusty road. He came to a stop in front of an old two-story house surrounded by an unkempt garden. Its gate had been left ajar, and we pushed through it with the car.

We walked up a few worn steps and Salem gave a knock on the wooden door. A balding, nervous-looking man of medium height opened up. He waved us inside and led us to a cavernous room with stark walls. Mats covered the floor, and a couch and several armchairs crowded together in the middle.

We exchanged greetings and queries about family and friends. A tired-looking servant brought in a bottle of arak from southern Yemen and a plate of olives, followed by several more plates: liver with hot sauce, grilled fish, feta cheese.

"Masaud," Salem said finally, "our Egyptian friend here would like to ask you about Warda."

He turned, gave me a penetrating look, and said, "Warda died."

"When?" I asked.

His eyes grew earnest.

"She was martyred during the battle of Mirbat," he said.

"Mirbat, or Taqa?" I asked.

He seemed irritated. He glanced toward the door, then suddenly his expression changed, and he looked anxious.

Without shifting his eyes from the door, he asked, "Did you hear that?"

Salem and I exchanged looks.

"There's no one there," Fatum said. Masaud faced us again, but his mind still seemed focused on the door.

"Do you know her brother?" I asked.

He shook his head. "She didn't have one."

"Did you ever meet her?" I asked.

He turned back to the door and nodded for us to listen. We heard the sound of a dog barking, then his body stiffened and he whispered, "They have come."

I took a sip of my drink and picked at the olives. There was some more barking before it faded. Then he turned toward me and leaned forward. "The truth has two faces."

I had no idea what he meant, but he went on: "I am going to tell you a tale about Juha, the jokester. A man came to him and gave him a lamp and asked to be served dinner, so Juha obliged. The next day two men came, saying they were friends of the man with the lamp, and they had dinner with Juha as well. The third day, three men came saying they were friends of the two men who were friends of the man who gave him the lamp, and Juha gave them dinner too. The fourth day, four men came saying they were friends of the three who were friends of the two who were friends of the man who brought the lamp, and they asked for dinner. Juha gave them just some water—nothing else—and said,

'This water is friends of the water that I gave the three men who were friends of the two men who were friends of the man who gave me the lamp.' Do you get it?"

I admitted I didn't understand. "It's a fable about the generosity that the Arab tribes have always been famous for. At the same time, it shows you the greed and gluttony of others. The truth has two faces."

He filled himself a glass and went on. "Before the days of the Front, a man would not even leave his region until a temporary agreement was struck with the surrounding tribes whose sovereign space he would pass through. One man wanted to go bring his wife back from a visit to her family. He stayed there awhile, until the period of the agreement expired. He ran out of tobacco and had to risk his life to get into a rival's village, where he was recognized by a woman from his own tribe. Luckily, she kept quiet and he escaped with his life."

I looked up at him totally confused. He smiled, "It's a tale of fate. He lived to fight another day."

I realized after the two stories that I wasn't going to learn anything from him, so I sat back and let them go on trading stories among themselves.

Chapter Fourteen

DHOFAR MOUNTAINS, 1972-1975

August '72

Ongoing discussions around the Mirbat tragedy. Considerations around increasing the northern Front's activity to relieve some of the pressure on the south.

Sadat has claimed that a plan for an Israeli offensive in June of '67 was presented to President Johnson in the presence of his CIA director and that the plan was given his blessing at the time.

Eyeglasses with Fahd's prescription arrived. The comrades had encouraged him to make more of an effort to read and become educated, but he resisted, complaining about weak eyesight.

September 5

More Chinese reports of an attempt to assassinate Mao, carried out by Lin Biao, who tried to escape on a plane that crashed in Mongolia.

The Palestinian guerrilla group Black September took hostage seven Israeli athletes in Munich. Demanded the release of 100 Palestinian prisoners held in Israeli jails. The German authorities followed the instructions of Israeli intelligence services. Result: killing of all the guerrillas and all the hostages.

September 7

An intense conversation with Waleed. I expressed my discomfort with the Munich operation and the other hijackings. I didn't know how to explain what I thought. I just couldn't reconcile the bloodshed. I said we should not engage in operations that others considered extreme or we would lose the support of the international community. He blew up in my face: "Shit on the international community! It was completely content when the Palestinians faced slow death in the camps. Where was this support of the international community when King Hussein exterminated 30,000 Palestinians in a few weeks?" The debate was interrupted when one of the wounded started calling to him.

September 8

As soon as Waleed saw me this morning, we started up again. He said very calmly that the Palestinian operation had succeeded in grabbing the attention of the world for a full 24 hours. I told him I had followed foreign news broadcasts and they had all condemned the guerrilla operation, calling it terroristic and reckless.

He cut me off: "But they changed their tune once the hostages died. More than one European paper wrote that people forgot that the state of Israel itself used the most violent type of terrorism for 25 years to achieve its goals. Europe's conscience was coming to question what might motivate eight men in the bloom of youth to carry out such a suicide attack."

I hit on the hole in his argument. I said: "So you are, in fact, interested in world public opinion after all."

He thought about it silently for a moment, then said, "You're right." Then he went mad all over again: "The next day, the Israelis quietly killed 200 Palestinians, including women, children, and the elderly, and no one did anything."

We headed toward the hut he was staying in. I said: "Forget world opinion for a second. There's one key point. We who fight in wars of popular liberation must only attack those who can be considered the people's direct enemies."

This comment provoked his aggression, and he screamed at me: "Now, you listen. My father died in a tent worse than this hovel, although we owned a big house with a yard full of olive trees. There are 18,000 Palestinians in Israeli prisons. The world doesn't care. What are we supposed to do?"

I almost thought I saw tears well up in his eyes and found myself stretching my hand out to him. I touched the scar that spread across his face. After that, things progressed naturally as I took him in my arms and his tears began to flow. I was going to help him to enter me, but he came too soon and the moment was lost. It will never happen again.

September 15

Revenge bombings by Israel on civilian targets in Syria and Lebanon.

A Vietnamese delegation is visiting Hawf and western Dhofar. Hussein Musa from the Aden bureau is accompanying them. Amer Ali participated in discussions with them as a representative of the central council alongside two members of the local leadership, Talal Saad and Ali al-Haj.

Fahd wears his glasses all the time now, even though they are just for reading.

September 20

American-style justice: the US army has released officer Calley, the main figure in the My Lai massacre. In September 1969, he was sentenced to a life sentence in prison. His sentence has been suspended and he has found a job at a life insurance company!

September 26

Northern Yemen forces have attacked the south with the support of Saudi Arabia.

October 12

Southern forces have routed the attackers.

October 17

Sultan Said died yesterday at the Dorchester Hotel in London, where he has been staying since he was deposed.

October 18

Opening of the US embassy in Muscat.

October 21

Khiyar Massaoud has been killed in a battle along the Nasheb elevation just east of the red line. Fifteen dead and wounded from among the enemy forces.

October 28

Bombing raids have destroyed the Martyr Habkouk Hospital. We had just inaugurated it five months ago. It will become a mobile hospital unit.

Cairo: signing of unity agreement between the two Yemens. This ends the undeclared war they have been fighting for three weeks. Amazing!

November

Castro has received two members of the Front leadership who traveled to Havana with the Yemeni leader Abdelfattah Ismail. A joint communiqué, broadcast over Radio Havana, expresses support for our struggle.

Hanoi has published the text of an agreement with the US. It consecrates the triumph over the mightiest imperialist force in history. The US commits to respect the independence, sovereignty, and unity of Vietnam, and to fully withdraw from its territory.

Yasser Arafat announced that the Palestinian resistance has lost 71,000 followers in nine years. This includes 30,000 martyrs on the battlefield, 17,000 in Israeli prisons, 13,000 civilians who were mostly women and children in detention facilities, and 7,000 in Jordanian prisons.

December

We have lost some of our control over the areas to the east of the Sambari mountains.

The British authorities in Muscat have arrested our comrade Mubarak Hamd, the anti-deserter.

Campaign of arrests rounded up 90. Stashes of weapons confiscated. No news of Yaarib. Among those arrested are members of the official Omani Society for Women: Rahima al-Qasimi; Thebat Folaifel, who is prominent in the Kindi community; Mariam and Fatima al-Hishar; and others . . .

King Hussein has executed six guerrilla fighters from among the Palestinians rounded up after Black September.

Golda Meir has praised King Hussein for his courage and ferocity.

Khalil Abdel Daim, the former chairman of the Jordanian joint chiefs of staff, was named ambassador to Muscat.

January 1973

The government has published a leaflet featuring pictures of three comrades, with a number above each: 5,000 riyals over the first one, 3,000 over the second, and 5,000 again over the third. The leaflet says they are wanted for their connection to a clandestine cell and for importing weapons from South Yemen. These are the weapons confiscated by the "valiant army of the Sultan" on December 23. At the bottom, in broad script, is written: communism = oppression = barbarism = brutality = death.

Comrade Mubarak, Hamid Majid, Muhammad Talib, and others have been subjected to the most vile torture at the hands of Jordanian and British secret police. Torture of the women is ongoing. Also subjected to slander and brainwashing.

In Egypt, there's talk of change in the international situation as a way to justify reneging on old commitments. Shouldn't Vietnam's victory count as one of these international changes? Yet they are so quick to diminish its importance.

lack of solidarity

Golda Meir has addressed the new borders, saying Israel can never withdraw from Jerusalem or Egypt's Sharm al-Sheikh.

January 27

Signing of cease-fire agreement in Vietnam.

Establishment of a government-run telephone network in Salalah (250 lines).

Major Ray Parker-Scofield, director of the Dhofar gendarmerie, declared in a telephone interview with the press: "Oman is the last place on earth that an Englishman can still be called 'Sahib.'"

February 2

Liberated zones are taking heavy bombardment. Civilians are fleeing. Some of them have had to settle in remote caves, away from the lines of fire. Everyone I have met has lost livestock in the most recent fighting. A large group of refugees has gone over to the Yemeni side of the border. There's also an economic embargo now that has cut off imports and led to an acute food crisis, made worse by systematic burning of crops.

HaOlam haZeh, the Israeli weekly: "Iranian occupation of the Omani Islands in the Gulf will insure the continuous flow of Iranian oil to Israel through Eilat."

February 15

The Front's official newspaper, *June 9*, has arrived from Aden. Pictures of Omani prisoners on its front page: Yahya Muhammad al-Ghassany, Murshid al-Shahi, Ahmad Hamidan, Sayid Muhammad al-Selim.

Those comrades coming back from Cuba report that Guevara went to the Congo in November 1965 to train revolutionaries, but failed in his attempts to organize them, bumping up against their wild beliefs. They thought that they could keep the Belgian warplanes from harming them by rubbing their bodies with herbs soaked in water and painting the tribal insignia on their faces with coal. They also report accusations directed at Guevara by the communists that he was rash and reckless. Said to refuse to listen to the advice of the Bolivian Communist party, which foresaw that society lacked the political maturity necessary to begin an armed revolt. Guevara considered the party to be a weak organ that had lost its revolutionary spirit. At a certain point, the party decided to change its position and support his movement, expecting to be able to co-opt its leadership, but he insisted that their leadership remain autonomous.

tragiony in Congo w/ Guevra

March

We formed a commission to study the collapse at Mattrah. I recused myself because of my relationship to Yaarib. It came out that Muhammad Ibn Talib, one of the main leaders of the Front in Oman, was followed for weeks before the wave of arrests. He had been staying with Yaarib during this time.

April 5

Richard Helms, director of the American CIA, has been named the new US ambassador to Iran, effective immediately.

We have established that Yaarib was not arrested, but he has disappeared. Is he in hiding?

April 10

An Israeli team has assassinated three leaders of the Palestinian resistance in the heart of Beirut. The Israelis moved freely for a period of two and a half hours, then suddenly disappeared into the US embassy.

The Shah of Iran tells the American magazine *Newsweek* that he is responsible for protecting the region around the Arabian Gulf, which is home to 60% of the world's total oil reserves and the key to the West's economic security. He has borrowed $3 billion to purchase weapons.

Celebration of the first anniversary of the opening of the two schools. We held the ceremony inside the schools' tents, across the border with Democratic Yemen. There are now 1,000 students, and a quarter of them are girls. Comrade Said Askari spoke on behalf of the Yemeni National Front. Meanwhile, Sayyid, who is a member of Fatah's bureau in Aden, called for unity among the different Palestinian groups. Amina Mohsin spoke on behalf of the Union of Yemeni Women. Said Dablan, the Front's representative, affirmed the connection between our different struggles. In the evening, we sang songs together and watched two films — one on the revolutionary movement in the Gulf and the other on the Palestinian uprising. The girls sang a song in the Himyarite language, which was so delicate and sweet and had a sad rhythm to it. It told of the enemy's campaign to control the road from the western region to the interior: *our blood will hold our hills / and all lines of battles / we will cut our way through valleys, rocks, and craters / we will struggle to retake our lives from the traitors.* The people of the surrounding villages all gathered together in a sandy clearing. The flags of the Front and of Democratic Yemen flew at the entrance to the clearing and on surrounding hills. The guards stood at their stations through the whole celebration. We chanted to sacrifice our blood for the cause of the people of the Gulf and for the principles of the revolution. Everyone was barefoot except me.

A comrade brought a tape recorder with him and played "Nana," a popular song in Dhofar sung in Himyarite. An argument broke out between Salem al-Attar and Ahmad Jallal about what the song means. Salem said the lyrics say there is no escaping our struggle to the death with imperialism, but Ahmad insisted that it is a call for all classes and groups in the nation to join the fight. In the second verse, a fighter from the liberation army says to an enemy soldier: "What do you see every morning? Look up from the barricades. The liberation army is on the march."

I looked at the faces of the students and thought about them finishing secondary school by the end of next year. After that, most will either join the revolution or receive grants to complete their studies abroad.

April 25

NATO's leader in Iran.

A government pamphlet in crude handwriting with a star in the middle and a stick figure of a man raising his hands in surrender. Next to him, another stick man spread out on the ground. The caption reads: "The government of his Highness the Sultan offers reward money for assistance in apprehending dead or alive leaders of the communist terrorists."

May 1

We celebrated International Labor Day.

The new round of government pamphlets are like lottery tickets. Pay a riyal and you can win 5,000, the reward for a revolutionary. A military commander is worth 4,000, and a political commissar 2,500. I told the comrades I was thinking about going back to military operations so that I would be worth more.

May 3

Problems with supplies. The caravans coming from Aden have shrunk down to six camels a week.

Questions surrounding Yaarib's behavior in the time leading up to the campaign of arrests.

May 10

One of the Yemeni subofficers from the Sultan's air force has come over to our side. Sergeant Muhammad Amar, age 21. In 1968 he moved from Socotra to Saudi Arabia, where he worked in Dammam sweeping floors in an American restaurant that catered to Aramco employees. In 1970 he was conscripted into the Saudi army and sent along with 80 Socotrans to Al-Sharura air base near the border with Yemen. In early '71, this group was sent to Thumrait, northern Dhofar. They were earning Saudi salaries while wearing Omani uniforms. He showed his Omani passport, number 007797, which was issued to him so he could spend his breaks in Dubai and Bahrain. He also had a stack of orders written out in bad Arabic by an English officer called Michael.

May 17

The new mobile field hospital is made up of several trailers. There are 40 civilians from the western region and several military officers. Since there's a shortage of medicines, the policy is to give thorough treatment only in dire cases, instead of giving partial treatment to everyone.

May 21

Newsweek: The Shah is building the largest military base in the Indian Ocean in Baluchistan with the help of American contractors. Construction complete in two years.

Clashes between the Lebanese army and the Palestinian resistance.

May 22

Le Monde has published a statement by our official spokesman. He says: "If you exclude the desert, we now control one-sixth of the Sultanate. The size of the Sultanate is three times the combined area of Kuwait, Bahrain, Qatar, and the UAE, and its population is four times that of all of those countries put together. Once we control Oman, no one in the Gulf will be able to stand up to us."

June

The enemy is now setting up a series of stations from Makhsis to Wadi Qim in the north, connected by barbed wire, landmines, and electronic listening devices. This will allow them to pursue us during the rainy season, thus stealing our chance to resupply under the cover of fog and rain.

We decided to respond by bombing Salalah.

After the bombing, the enemy set up more stations—in Adami, Hattal, and Atibat al-Sheikh. Attacking Salalah has become more difficult.

June 28

British airplanes dropped leaflets with the word *Warning* written across the top. Underneath, a crude drawing of hills stretching from Wadi Taheez on the right to Wadi Tamreen on the left. The region is bordered by a rocket launcher above crudely drawn houses placed between two arrows directly above Salalah. The caption beneath the drawing reads: "The arrows in the drawing above point to the safe routes that citizens and their livestock can take if they want to make it to Salalah. It is important for citizens to stay away from the forbidden zone between the two arrows in the picture, which contains rocket launchers that are prepared to fire day or night. Remember this warning at all times, for your own safety and for that of your sheep, cattle, and camels."

Strange statements coming from China's foreign secretary on his visit to Tehran. He rejects any support of any subversive movement that might try to upset the peace and stability of the Gulf region!!

A global petroleum consortium led by Sunoco and Elf-Aquitaine has acquired drilling concessions for the Straits of Hormuz.

July

Gaddafi claims that the Libyan revolution represents the serious branch of the international left, standing against capitalism and against the reactionary communists who cling to concepts from the 18th and 19th centuries.

July 17

Iraqi president al-Bakr signs pact with Aziz Muhammad, general secretary of the Communist party, covering labor laws and workforce issues within the nationalist, progressive front. Where is this headed?

Yaarib has appeared in Beirut. We will try to get him to testify about the arrests surrounding Mattrah.

July 18

We have confirmed the death of the martyr Mubarak Hamd, the anti-deserter, at the age of 25 as a result of excessive torture. The authorities refused to surrender his corpse to the family. They buried him with other comrades in unmarked graves and forbade his family from receiving mourners.

August 5

Unlike last year, the enemy has managed to hold on to the centers that it has set up all along the border with the western region, except at Tawi Attar. They have also managed to capture several weapon and supply depots. More guerrillas are surrendering. I have begun to worry.

Meeting of the central committee to discuss problems in our current military formation. Divisions are now divided into detachments that cover a particular region, with the leadership divided among the different detachments. We decided on a new structure wherein all troops fall directly under a unified leadership. Fahd opposed the plan once he realized that he would not be the supreme leader in the new structure.

August 29

The tenth conference of the Chinese Communist party has condemned the Lin Biao anti-party junta. They described it as bourgeois avarice, conspiracy, hypocritical, antirevolutionary, renegade, and treacherous toward the party. It also expelled Mao's personal secretary, calling him a Kuomintang nationalist opposed to the Communist party, a Trotskyite, a traitor, an enemy agent, and revisionist.

September 11

Bloody coup in Chile. Allende dead.

October 6

The myth of the Israeli superman is dead. At two o'clock, the Egyptians crossed the Bar-Lev line. SAM rockets downed a Phantom. At first, we refused to believe they did anything, then presumed the Egyptian attack would fail as usual. After a few hours, we confirmed that the news was true. A serious tone to Egyptian broadcasts, completely different from the hysteria of '67. That gave us confidence.

October 7

Israel has lost 30 planes and 22 tanks.

October 8

Liberation of Qantara. In three days, the Israelis have lost 81 planes and 128 tanks, with 123 taken prisoner. Egypt is in total control of the eastern bank of the canal. Radio Israel says that the army has taken up defensive positions. Syrian forces are advancing within Golan.

October 9

Destruction of an Israeli armored brigade in Sinai. Surrender of its leader, capture of 120 tanks.

October 11

America has begun sending warplanes with bombs and rockets. The Israeli PM has announced that they have acquired 48 new Phantom jets.

October 12

150 new American Phantom planes have passed through Madrid airport on their way to Israel.

October 14

Egyptian forces launch a comprehensive attack on the frontlines. Armored battalions clash in a 12-hour long battle. 150 tanks destroyed. Dayan declares: "We are fighting with broken hearts and have no idea how long this will go on." Israel's ambassador to London calls for a cease-fire.

October 17

Arab OPEC ministers have committed to cutting oil production by at least 5% every month until Israel agrees to return all lands that it occupied in 1967.

October 19

Israeli forces under cover of night sneak across Egyptian lines.

October 22

Sadat has ordered a cease-fire in accordance with the Security Council resolution.

I will lead a delegation to Moscow to attend the anniversary celebrations for the Bolshevik revolution of November 7. Comrade Amin, in a speech before the executive council, said: "We must show them that we respect our own women as much as they do theirs." He has dangled the hope that we can stop in Beirut, where I would be able to see Yaarib and Amad.

November 7

We are still in Dhofar, travel logistics having delayed us.

The Front's radio station in Mukalla has started to broadcast. On air every night from 6 to 8 in the evening, Aden time. Its signal strength is 25 over 49 metric waves at a frequency of 11,770 kilocycles/second.

November 11

We took a Russian Ilyushin Il-76 from the airport in Aden. I am carrying a Yemeni passport. Traveling with two comrades from the executive council. They treated me with kind attention, then forgot me entirely the moment the blonde Russian flight attendants appeared. I have stocked up on heavy clothes—a wool overcoat, a cap of synthetic fur, a long scarf—borrowed from the wife of one of the diplomats. We stopped two hours in Cairo without leaving the plane. The Soviet comrades received us at the airport and took us to a hotel near Red Square. We have been assigned a handsome young handler named Boris. Speaks Syrian Arabic.

November 12

It's freezing. But I still haven't seen snow like I expected. Modern buildings along Kalinin Prospekt. Moscow University's 32 stories over Lenin Hill. Gorki Park. The mayor stood in front of the city's electrical grid and told us that Moscow's development plan is to make it the model modern city by 2000. Half a million new units of public housing will provide lodging for two million citizens. The current population is eight million. Another project commits about 300 million dollars for new buildings that will be used in the 1980 Olympic games. The subway system is mesmerizing, each individual station an artistic wonder. It connects all the outskirts of the capital across lines that run for 100 miles, and its reach will be doubled by 2000. We visited new subdivisions south of the city with 12-story apartment blocks. They are complete co-ops, with schools, markets, rec centers, and hotels. The next phase will have 16-story buildings. In the evening, we visited the Bolshoi, the finest theater in the world.

We saw a performance of Tchaikovsky's ballet *Swan Lake*. The most exquisite cultural exprerience!

Boris is fun. Stays with us in the same hotel.

November 13

Children live like kings in the Soviet Union. Everything is readily available: free healthcare, books, toys . . . more than 2,000 nursery schools in Moscow alone. It also has 1,000 primary and secondary schools, including dozens for specialties. The director of the school board told us that they had recently added new sports and contemporary physics to the curriculum. Still, the Marxist and Leninist portion of the curriculum has not changed. Schooling takes ten years. The more talented students are farmed out to schools that specialize in music, science, physical education, etc. At school number 1 of the 172 specializing in PE, we observed how they train the future world champions — 12- and 13-year-old girls. The director could see that I was enthralled and she came and explained to me: "Gymnastics is 50% athletics and 50% art. They must have a sense of beauty, so we never work out without piano accompaniment."

Lenin's picture is everywhere. He is in the libraries, schools, parks, and subway stations. Sometimes he seems like a benign uncle, at others, a stern parent. He rests in a red granite tomb in the middle of the Red Square, near the Kremlin walls. Long line of visitors. We came up to it slowly, passing by the monument to the unknown soldier. Guards with microphones keep the line in order. We stored our bags and cameras with a caretaker at the entrance and wiped our feet before entering. The Russians in front of us removed their hats. We went into the mausoleum and passed quickly, circling around the left side and then the right. Up a flight of steps, down a few more, then we were outside, trying to recapture the memory of the glass-encased body . . . That afternoon, the Pushkin Museum of Fine Arts. In the evening, a comic play that I didn't understand one bit of. As we headed back at night, we saw a crowd gathered in the street. It was a long line to get into a bookstore! They were getting ready for tomorrow's opening, so they could purchase the new edition of an old book. 3,560 magazines and 30 different newspapers are published in Moscow.

November 14

We spent the morning in the Museum of the Revolution on Gorki Street. We visited the headquarters of the central committee of the Soviet Communist party. An elderly official met us and gave us a history lecture, saying: "My generation knows what hunger is. There was the war and after that some very difficult times. Up until '58, I was living in one room together with my wife, her mother, and my son. Thirty of us had to share kitchen, toilet, and bath. Everyone was like that. Now things are different. The buildings are simple, but at least every family has their own apartment. Many own cars as well. We are even helping many other countries. Our problem now is labor productivity. We are lagging behind the United States in that area, and in the variety of what we produce."

He had spoken at length and was clearly tired. He left us with a younger co-worker. I explained the political and military situation in Oman and the rest of the region. I went into our strategy of hit-and-run attacks to bleed and exhaust the enemy. I said, "They find they're putting huge resources into holding areas that don't have much military value, so they withdraw." He smiled and asked, "Do you think you will drive them out completely?" I told him the Vietnamese were doing exactly that right now.

"That's a different situation," he said.

"Of course"—I seized on my chance—"They have access to modern weap-onry, especially shoulder-fired anti-aircraft missiles. That's the one variable that levels things between guerrilla fighters and an air force. That, and we also need a modern communication system."

November 15

Series of meetings with representatives from the alliance of labor unions, women's alliance, peace council, war veterans, Society for Afro-Asian Soli-darity, editors for Arab affairs at the newspapers *Pravda* and *Izvestiya*, journal-ists with *Moscow News*, Novosti news agency, and the Arabic department at Radio Moscow.

As we left the hotel in the morning, I saw a strange scene. A policeman was grabbing a young man with long hair and holding his arms behind his back viciously. I asked Boris what was happening and he waved it off, saying, "Oh it's just one of the hooligans." I learned from a Yemeni comrade there studying at Lumumba University that the term applies equally to homeless, to youth influ-enced by the West in dress and music, and to political dissidents.

November 16

Boris came along with me to the private hospital run by a suburban central council. Deluxe space with the latest equipment and a beautiful garden. Revo-lutionary fighters from around the world are treated for all types of problems. I got to know an elderly gentleman from Venezuela being treated for an eye disease. He became upset when I related what I had heard about the disputes between the communists and Guevara and went quiet. A complete troop of doctors gave me an exam. A bunch of tests and x-rays. After a wait, Boris came in to interpret the results. From among the doctors, an elderly woman with stern features returned and explained to me that I was in good general health and that the aches and pains I had been feeling were the result of my lifestyle. She said revolutionary work did not have to rule out having a family and recommended that I marry and have children, adding mournfully: "It might even compensate for life's setbacks." She may have lost someone special in a war or in one of Stalin's concentration camps.

In the evening, we dined in an Uzbek restaurant. I began to throw back drinks with Boris. I had to prove to him that I am liberated. When we got back to the hotel, he invited me to his room. The old watchwoman in her chair at the end of the hall gave us a soft, conspiratorial smile. He had her bring us some vodka, tomatoes, and cucumbers. He sliced the cucumbers lengthwise, quartered the tomatoes, and sprinkled salt around. I settled for just one glass, even though he was gulping straight from the bottle. His face became flushed and he started to slur his words. He told me a joke about Lenin rising from the dead, walking out of his tomb, having a look around, and then going back inside with the comment, "This isn't what I had in mind." I kept my eyes on his sensuous lips. He said he liked me and wanted to give me a kiss. I didn't try to stop him. In truth, I wanted him to hold me. He moved toward me and then collapsed on the ground. He was dead drunk. I left him there, stretched across the rug, hugging the empty bottle.

Tomorrow, I go for a visit to the Yemeni and Omani students studying at Lumumba U.

November 23

The moment I made it back to my base in Dhofar was like returning to my home. The strange thing is that here, at the end of the earth, I am more in touch with world events through my radio than I was in Moscow.

December 1st

Qais al-Zawawi, who owns Oman's Mercedes concession, has been appointed minister of foreign affairs. He's from Muscat, of Saudi origin, and educated in India.

The government has acquired 25% of Petroleum Development Oman. The war is consuming a big portion of Oman's budget—about 30 million riyals (80 million dollars) in the past year.

The past weeks have seen successful operations in many different regions. We hit an enemy base in Sarfait and destroyed its runway. Also, the runway and several watchtowers at the air base in Salalah. The last operation was led by a tough warrior named Dahmish.

December 13

In the central zone, we celebrated the return of several of our brothers to the revolution's side: Damis Salem Jaabub, Ahmad Suhail Salem, Ahmad Suhail Sharkh, Salem Ahmad Majhid, Muslim Ahmad Yatishut, Salem Ahmad Mikiaaf al-Birahmi. They were with the government troops. They escaped from the base at Al-Maamoura, confiscating along the way a Land Rover, four machine guns, and seven rifles.

The government has put a 7,000-riyal reward on my head!

December 21

Kissinger waves a victory sign as he arrives in Geneva for meetings about the Middle East conflict.

The enemy is working hard to finish constructing its defensive "Hornbeam line" west of Salalah. It stretches north for 85 km parallel to the red line. It's mostly an electric barbed wire fence with some landmines that's patrolled by night.

December 30

The arrival of Iranian troops continues. They have been put on the uninhabited island of Al-Halania and are forbidden to show themselves in the streets of Muscat or Salalah. The first group is estimated at 3,000, including both officers and rank and file. They have been charged with retaking the red line, the 72 km–long strategic track that runs from Salalah through Thumrait, connecting them to Muscat.

We have declared a high alert.

Their Hornbeam line has succeeded in stopping our attacks on Salalah and the regions surrounding it and in cutting off the flow of heavy weapons and ammunition to our eastern bases.

Formal investigation begun into charges traded by comrades around donations from international advocacy groups. Decision to convene a congress at the start of the new year.

January 1974

Voice of PFLOAG Radio from Aden for ten minutes every evening starting at 7:45 as part of the daily program for Oman and the Gulf, which starts at 6 and ends at 8.

A new issue of our bimonthly newsletter *June 9*. Included is a list of donations from advocacy groups in Europe and America and an Arabic translation of a poem by Brecht:

General, your tank is a powerful thing.
It can break down a forest and crush a hundred men.
But it has one defect:
It needs a driver.

General, your bomber is powerful.
It flies faster than the wind and carries more than an elephant.
But it has one defect:
It needs a mechanic.

General, a man can be turned to many uses.
He can fly and he can kill.
But he has one defect:
He can think.

February

Iranian forces succeeded in opening the road to Thumrait. They launched a simultaneous two-pronged attack from Salalah in the south and Thumrait in the north.

The government has built a new electric power station that can produce 8,497 kilowatts of power, distributed to Jibjat and Madinat al-Haq to support the water supply, clinics, schools, and communications.

Chou En Lai stated before the tenth congress of the Chinese Communist party last August that Lin Biao, the former defense minister, had been corrupted by the ideas of Confucius and, like the ex-president Liu Shao Chi, harbored hopes of a return to capitalism. Unlike Liu, however, Lin regularly quoted Mao. Chou also said that Lin had been pessimistic about the future of the revolution from the start. Before the ninth congress, Lin had co-authored a wide-ranging political report on ways to sustain the revolution in the aftermath of the dictatorship of the proletariat, emphasizing that the priority must remain industrial development. Thereby, the report betrayed its debt to the revisionist sophistry of Liu Shao Chi's reports for the eighth congress, claiming that the primary contradiction in China was not between the proletariat and the bourgeoisie but rather between advanced socialism and a backward production force. Chou accused Lin Biao of launching an attack on the excesses of the battle against revisionism, of criticizing the productive labor of party cadres working in cooperatives as a kind of camouflaged unemployment, and of denigrating the flight of youth and intellectuals to rural areas by calling it something like a sentence of hard labor.

March

The Sultan has visited Iran. Upon his return, he ordered the construction in Thumrait of a new airfield with a 4,000-meter landing strip to be completed by the end of the year no matter the cost. Estimates are running to 50 million riyals—145 million dollars.

It only took him a minute at the start of his cabinet meeting to authorize gigantic projects. Abdel Hafiz Salem Rajab, the minister of transportation, will oversee a desalination project involving the storage of electricity. The cost of the project is 57 million dollars. The minister slipped in that the project will expand the flow of water to Sultan's Park by a million gallons per day and that it is projected to open on the national holiday coinciding with the Sultan's birthday. The approval came before any study or review was completed. In the blink of an eye, the budget increased to 300 million dollars.

March 27

This popular commentator on Salalah Radio who calls himself Abu Nabil and who uses ridiculous language really gets on my nerves.

April

Sadat has decided to diversify who he trades with for weapons and military equipment. His problem with Soviet arms deals is that they don't offer a little something on the side, I guess?!

May

The Iranian troops are all in place after 3 months. They are here to improve the government's capacity to kill. They have no influence over the sentiments of the citizens because they are never seen. Their supplies, water, and 3 meals a day are flown in from Iran every day.

June

Iraqi bombers have hit 14 towns and 204 villages inside the Kurdish region. 1,500 dead. A group of communists in the military have been arrested. It's only a few months since the National Front signed a pact granting autonomy.

June 8

We are getting ready for the fourth congress.

Our courageous comrade Ahmad Muslim Qiay (26 years old) has given his life in the high country. The battle went on for an hour and a half. Nine enemy were killed or injured. The martyr was just back from the Soviet Union, where he had undergone training in firing SAM rockets. He was born in Dhofar to a father who was a herder. In '64 he emigrated in search of work. He settled in Kuwait for six years, where he joined the Popular Front. When he came back home in 1970, he immediately signed up with the revolution.

June 13

Military coup in northern Yemen. The lieutenant colonel Ibrahim al-Hamdi has taken power. It's a bourgeois military movement to overthrow tribalism, feudalism, and the medieval mentality that never changed after the republic was established. Al-Hamdi was connected for a while with the Movement of Arab Nationalists.

Nostalgia and melancholy have come down on us. We have withdrawn from the hill country and the surrounding valleys. We have left the deep forests. We have packed in those wide-open horizons. The pure air of the north fades in the distance. The troops have been sent to their homes for a respite before we regroup.

Dahmish, Awad, and I spent the downtime at the hut of an elderly man living alone. We lit a fire to warm up and dry our clothes. The old man brought us fresh milk in a leather sack, then handed me a metal pail and said, "Boil it. The fire is there." I poured the milk into the pail and put it over our fire. Did he do this because he believes that boiling purifies, or was he just humoring us? In either case, it was progress. He said he had just come from the city. We asked what it's like there now. "I'm an old man. I don't have news," he answered. Awad asked if he had any tobacco. He pointed to the corner where there was some raw tobacco stored. Awad took the jar and crushed some of the leaves. The old man packed it into a clay pipe, then set a piece of lit coal inside. They passed it back and forth in silence. Dahmish didn't smoke. He just watched quietly. Every now and then he would look at me. He blushed like a boy when our eyes met. Something in his eyes made me a touch shy. After a while the old man pointed to our weapons and said, "Hold on tight to these kalashins you have, children, and be careful if you go to the city. If you can't keep them with you for any reason, leave them with us here in the country. These things are not for those down there. I have seen those scum carrying them around down below." We pressed him on what else he'd seen in the city. "I am an old man and I don't play with politics. I have neither money nor family . . . My hearing is bad. But I can see, and I know everything that goes on, wherever it may be. I am telling you — don't cross paths with that scum. The people are with you. Be strong." When we were ready to leave, he bade us goodbye with these words: "God give you victory."

Dahmish is an intrepid Dhofari from Mirbat. From the Kathir clan. 5 years younger than me. He ran away to Kuwait when he was 18. He worked as an oilfield worker in Khafji. There was a big group of Omanis working there who spoke of nothing but changing the conditions in their homeland. Some of them started a reading group. Their reading material was whatever books and magazines they could lay their hands on. Then they learned about Dr. al-Khatib and his Movement of Arab Nationalists group. He would stop by from time to time, or they would go to him at his clinic. He told them that Dhofar had a historic mission to light the fire of armed revolution in the southern Arabian Peninsula, led by themselves and their sympathizers to the north. By the time they had several meetings, he had convinced them to join the armed struggle. Dahmish carried letters of introduction through Bahrain, Qatar, Dubai, and finally back to Dhofar, where he recruited his brother and some relatives. His brother had been fighting in the eastern zone, then came down to Salalah. I asked about details of his life in Kuwait, like did he have a lover. He laughed and shook his head, but I get the feeling he's not really so innocent.

A wide-ranging meeting was convened of central command and local leaders at the temporary camp of the 9th regiment. Comrade Rafie stated that the revolution currently possesses the technical skills to carry out its operations, as it also has a general knowledge of traditional warfare from the rank and file with experience in mercenary armies in the Gulf countries. A deeper knowledge of technique in traditional warfare, however, is limited, and this limited knowledge makes us unable to map out a proper military plan with which to confront the enemy. The only solution is to send a group of committed cadres to study at military academies abroad. Fahd argued that we had actually sent a number of comrades to the Soviet Union. Rafie answered that these groups had trained with weapons. What was needed was cadres who had studied in military school and graduated with the rank of officer. Dahmish spoke forcefully in support of this proposal.

July

A British television crew came to film the government's schools. It asked them to sing and they broke into one of the anthems of the Front: "The Time Has Come for Freedom!!"

Kuwait has given Democratic Yemen a 5-million-dollar grant. Qaboos responded by kicking out their chargé d'affaires.

The Kuwaiti parliament has criticized Iran's military assistance to Qaboos. A speaker called it a threat to the entire Arab world.

We have convened the fourth congress of the Front in Al-Houta, Yemen, about 70 km north of Aden. Some members of the central committee could not attend. Two disappeared completely and in all likelihood have gone over to the government. Three are in Muscat, either in hiding or in custody. Yaarib didn't attend. Maybe he is afraid that the issue of the Mattrah arrests will come up. We heard a report detailing the number of deserters who had gone over to the government and another on the lack of supplies and the breakdown in communication networks. Another report laid out the way the closures along the border with Democratic Yemen caused by bombings and landmines had led to suffering and shortages among the people. Bedouins cannot make it to the open grasslands across the border now. The supply of dried sardines, relied on as feed during the dry season, had been cut off and livestock have perished as a result. The highlanders rely on seeds that they now have to try to bring up from the coast.

The military briefing explained that the enemy has the advantage in the air, in heavy weaponry, in the ability to mobilize, and in open supply routes except in certain places during the rainy season. We, meanwhile, brought in troops a year ago that still need more training because our military leaders are competing instead of working together. The briefing touched on our deficiency in military planning and our lack of ammunition and materiel. It critiqued the style of warfare being waged, in that the general model was rocket fire that has little effect given the types of rocket launchers being used, the lack of expertise, and the limited amount of ammunition. It confirmed the contents of the 9th regiment's report and called for military strength to be concentrated in three regiments. These would mostly be based in the western region, west of the red line. The rest of the smaller forces would then wage a guerrilla war against the government centers. The immediate goal is to hold on to the western region and its central base in Rakhiut as the fixed home of the revolution and a no-go zone for the enemy.

Long arguments broke out around political strategy. Rafie asserted that a total military victory would be impossible. He called for emphasis on political work and said we should avoid direct military confrontation with government troops. Fahd fiercely opposed him and was backed up by the Dhofaris and by Ahmad Said Suleiman, the former general secretary. They feared that such an approach could leave some of our fighters stranded in the mountains. The two sides traded accusations. It went on to the point of exchanges of innuendos and suggestions of financial impropriety. The dispute escalated even more when the secretary general announced that Gaddafi had agreed to open an office for us in Libya once he was convinced that the Front was not a Marxist movement. He had announced his readiness to give financial backing as well. The secretary general made the point that we are in dire need of such assistance in light of Aden's economic difficulties and the external pressures weighing on it. (Abu Dhabi offered them assistance but on condition that they stop supporting our movement.) He suggested we drop the slogan "Liberation of the Arabian Gulf" from our name and from our charter. This proposal passed by a narrow majority. I was one of its supporters. Dahmish didn't speak, but he followed all the discussions closely. He waited until I raised my hand to vote, then he followed my lead. I think he is just supporting me, more than anything.

I asked comrade Awad about the men in his troop. Only a few had abandoned him, but six had died in various battles. He said he was nervous about Abdullah and Soweid, who are joined at the hip. Abdullah won't speak with anyone else. They even sleep next to each other. He spoke of what he called an "unnatural relationship" between them and talked about the risk of burnout in fighters, who become withdrawn and depressed. I thought about Abdullah's sedate and submissive expression and Soweid's forcefulness. Is this "burnout"? That the horror of death and defeat pushes each into the embrace of the other? Is desertion or surrender next? Or is it just a natural attraction seeking to fulfill itself in its most viable expression? Does what sustains us give us the ability to resist and endure? Does one lose one's revolutionary spirit at the very moment of yielding to one's most urgent and powerful of feelings? I compared in my mind the fierceness of Fahd, who claims no personal attachment to a woman — or man — with the serenity of Rafie, who's always accompanied by a Zanzibari woman, ever since Amina was struck down. Which of the two is more revolutionary? Which is more helpful to the revolution?

We threw an evening party at the end of the congress. Awad proposed a traditional Dhofari dance called the *rabuba*. We formed two groups facing each other, with a few to the side playing instruments. Each line moved toward the other, then everyone passed between the two facing them. We turned and did the same movements again. Awad's voice rose above us, singing:

You are far away from Souli,
Almost to Hamran.
I try to find the strength,
Willing myself to go on.
My heart pulls me back
To our homes in the east,
To my loved ones and my friends,
All together in one place.

We should have been happy, but we were sullen. The lyrics didn't seem quite right. Clearly our spirits have dampened.

August

Nimeiry has agreed to send Qaboos more advisors with experience in combating communism!

Baron Beswick, the head of British Aerospace, signed a contract during his visit to Muscat to sell Rapier weapon batteries for use in air defense rockets, 12 Jaguar warplanes (latest model), communication systems, and early warning radar systems.

September

Military coup in Ethiopia following a widespread national popular uprising. Emperor Haile Selassie sent into exile after 44 years in power.

October 1st

Decision to reopen the northern front. Yaarib is still in Aden.

At the celebration of Democratic Yemen's seventh anniversary of independence, President Salim Rubai Ali announced that he would seek diplomatic relations with the Emirates, Qatar, and Bahrain, saying: "How far do our material resources go? What has colonialism left us in terms of economic, agricultural, or industrial infrastructure that we can use to bring about economic development?"

October 29

A new blow on the northern front. A Land Rover was stopped at a checkpoint near the town of Al-Hazm. In an exchange of gunfire, Ahmad Ali Zaher al-Miyahi, a member of the executive committee, was killed. Two other comrades were gravely injured but managed to escape. The next day, the authorities found them unconscious. It seems the vehicle was carrying weapons and a large sum of money. Investigations revealed that the Front had managed to penetrate the government's security forces.

Our comrade Nabila Said (20 years old) was shot in the leg during an operation near the Yemeni border. She was transferred with her husband by militia forces.

November

During the National Day celebrations, the Sultan announced the importation of the first colored televisions.

The government has taken back the mountains. It's established a platoon called "Abu Bakr, the Companion" in Kaftaweet.

The ruling military council in Ethiopia has announced that it will build a socialist state.

Vietnamese liberation forces are approaching Saigon.

December

The government has managed to establish companies in Zeek, Ayum, Borj, Keshaat, Ashinhid.

The primary Iranian operations have been launched in the western zone. We have concentrated our troops in Rakhiut, and formed a leadership council for the town made up of Fahd, Awad, and myself. They immediately set about putting in place our cannon in the most strategic spots. I'm in charge of political affairs and public relations.

More than 700 fighters have gone over to the government side.

I was in the middle of a political study group in the town mosque when I heard Dahmish calling me in some distress. As I ran toward him, he took off and ran ahead, shouting for me to hurry. Fahd was ready to execute three comrades. Young men.

"Where is Awad?" I shouted.

He shouted over his shoulder, "In the hills."

I ran to our office, where I found Fahd standing in front of three adolescent boys, their hands tied behind their backs. He cursed at them and spit in their faces. In a complete rage. His eyes pierced through me, but I kept under control. I asked what had happened while I tried to catch my breath from running.

He shot me a contemptuous look, then said, "These bastards want to run away. I'll make them an example for every traitor and weakling."

I looked at them. They were shivering in terror. The oldest one was probably 16. The youngest was not yet old enough to grow a mustache. Surely, I had crossed paths with them in our revolutionary schools. I might even have chatted with them. I said that there is a standing order issued by the central committee that no executions be carried out before the committee itself has reviewed the case.

"But we're in an emergency," he said. "The homeland is on the verge of falling to the enemy, and you want to talk to me about the central committee? These bastards are selling us out for a handful of rotten sardines."

"The order is clear," I said. I could see by his face that he would not budge. "Let's at least wait for Awad and discuss the matter together with him," I tried.

"We don't know where he is, and we're running out of time," he said.

"We are fighters in a just cause," I said, "not butchers. These are guilty of nothing but giving in to their fear."

"I'll take the responsibility for it," he said.

"The matter does not rise to the level of life and death," I answered.

"No one will dare stop me," he said.

"I will dare," I answered.

My tone of voice surprised me—even more, what I did next. I grabbed the Kalashnikov from my shoulder and pulled it to my side. He looked at me incredulous. Then he looked at his weapon lying on the ground. We heard a noise and both turned toward the door. Dahmish had switched off the safety and was aiming his weapon. Fahd looked from one of us to the other, then picked up his weapon and left. I tried to catch my breath. I was shaking. I ordered Dahmish to untie the boys. They were thunderstruck.

I spoke to them softly: "The revolution isn't a picnic. There will be moments that test our mettle. We are passing through a challenging time, but our victory is certain. If you want to desert us, I won't stop you. Just promise me you won't join the enemy or try to contact them or pass them any reconnaissance."

The one who seemed oldest stepped forward: "We won't desert you, comrade. I criticize myself for my weakness."

His two friends joined in and voiced the sweetest self-critiques I had heard in my life. I embraced them, then ordered them to rejoin their company immediately.

To Dahmish I said, "Why do you think I'm standing up against execution?" He couldn't meet my eyes.

"Because you are Warda," he said. I'm not sure if it was his tone of voice, but for some reason blood rushed to my face like I was a young virgin enthralled by a flirtatious remark.

I spoke, a little embarrassed: "If you had not been here with me, I couldn't have done it." I stepped forward and kissed him on the mouth.

The three youth are from the Shahra tribe. Characteristically, they surrender to a foe or run away without fighting back. They don't even defend themselves. Awad says they have a problem with the sight of blood, to the point that they cannot shed the blood of any human. Must this brand them as cowards?

I decided to include them in the new year celebrations.

January 1, 1975

Our party was a success. We did a traditional Omani dance. We made a large circle, and a comrade with a strong singing voice stood in the middle. Our movements: a step back with the left foot, then a complete turn, then lean forward, then four rapid claps of the hands. We answered back to the singer's call: "Dear one, stay with me." Then the three young men had their turn. They entered the circle, and two of them took on the roles of a tiger and a rook. The singer accompanied them as they acted out the struggle, until it ended with the victory of good over evil, the human mind over the brutality of beasts.

Qaboos is in the United States. He hopes to buy rocket launchers worth 1.5 million dollars. The Americans want landing rights at Oman's British airfields in exchange.

Dahmish avoids being alone with me, and yet he showers me with his glances. These looks give me a warm feeling. He blushes like a youngster if our eyes accidentally meet.

January 3

Comrade Said al-Marzouqi managed to sneak his new poem out of prison:

You're a communist.
You're a heretic.
You're an atheist.
We will burn you.
We will kill you.
May you be over and done,

And the matter remains open
The fight will go on.

To the contrary—
The matter will never be closed.

January 5

At five o'clock this morning, we woke to the sound of DShK gunfire. Two Iranian fighter jets flew over and dropped their bombs about 2 km to our east. Shouting erupted, and we all took refuge in the caves. The population has become expert in recognizing the types of warplanes because bombings have become so common. This one is reconnaissance, that one freight, and the other a bomber. I ran to headquarters. Not a soul. Fahd and Awad went straight to our rocket launchers to move them and to engage the bombers. Dahmish was with them. I yelled at everyone around me that they had 10 seconds to grab a boulder and secure themselves between seeing the smoke from the bombers and the explosion of their bombs. The mounted rocket launchers on the planes began to fire. I yelled out again: 18 seconds between rocket launch and explosion. Bombs fell around us by the dozen. If Rakhiut falls, the free zone will be lost. Everything lost. Planes came in at low altitude. We stuck close to the walls. One of the walls collapsed on four fighters trying to hide behind it. A missile struck the flag outside the mobile hospital. I was running through the bombs as they fell. Cries of children and the wailing of women.

Someone shouted out: "Get down!"

I yelled to the gunners at the top of my voice: "Fire at anything you don't recognize."

The bombing stopped. Corpses beneath the rubble. A dead woman hanging from a tree. A 3-year-old child calling for his mother. The wounded crawled toward the hospital. I heard my name called. One of the young men I had saved from execution had a gaping wound in his stomach. Crying and screams. Waves of debris followed by waves of men followed by waves of smoke from rifle and machine gun fire. Then the piles of bodies.

We gave the order to abandon the town and retreat toward the border with Yemen.

Chapter Fifteen

SALALAH, 1992

There was something confusing in this new volume of Warda's diaries. I had no doubt that she had written them because the handwriting was the same as in the previous notebooks—big, clear letters full of daring and courage; punchy and precise prose relating sights and sounds; careful scrutiny of her innermost thoughts and feelings; sophisticated awareness of the latest developments in world events; and a persistent curiosity about everything. Still, a creeping feeling of something missing haunted me.

I closed the book and examined its worn cover, then flipped back through its pages. They didn't have numbers, but it seemed certain that nothing was lacking or added. The pages and the narrative connected smoothly, and the sequence of dates at the top of each entry was consistent. The staple that anchored the notebook was in place and didn't seem to have been tampered with or altered.

I reread a few of the entries, settling on the last few lines, then going back over in my head what had come before. Finally, I tucked the notebook back in its hiding place under the rug and went out.

I went searching for my fellow Egyptian and found him leading Friday prayers in one of the rooms on the second floor. I headed back down to the lobby to wait for him there until he was done. When he showed up, I headed over to him and asked, "Do you know Abu Ammar?"

He laughed: "Al-Ghimeiry? Who around here doesn't know him? He's a sheikh of one of the largest clans and he owns most of the grocery stores and pharmacies."

"Do you think you could get me his phone number?"

"For you, my friend, that's nothing." He went over to the reception desk and fished in one of the drawers; then he looked through a registry, and finally came back to me with the number. I remembered Zakariya's warning about the charge for telephone calls, but there was no getting around it.

A voice answered in a mysterious accent: "Ghimeiry house."

I said who I was, and the voice asked me to wait. A long time passed as I counted out the riyal it was costing. Finally, a decisive baritone came on the line: "This is Abu Ammar."

I reminded him that we had met at Abu Abdullah's and he had promised that we would get together. Right away he answered, "Yes, you're most welcome at any time. Are you free tonight?"

I could not suppress my excitement. "Yes!"

"I'll send over a car at seven o'clock. Is that a good time?"

"Great!" I said.

I knew that Salem was with his sister and that I was unlikely to run into Khalaf on his day off. Still, I avoided the restaurant, ordering spaghetti with sauce and a salad from the room service menu instead. I rested awhile after lunch, then I took a shower and tried my hand at ordering a coffee. I whiled away the remainder of the afternoon between the balcony and the television until the telephone rang at seven o'clock.

I found waiting for me downstairs a driver who could have been from India, Pakistan, or Bangladesh. I still couldn't distinguish between them — if indeed they are even different peoples. We took off for Mirbat this time, driving very slowly through the old quarter where the fishermen and veterans from the national platoons lived. We passed by some abandoned old houses whose owners had chaotically put up new modern structures, with gutters hanging everywhere as a testament to the ravages of the rainy season.

We stopped in front of an old two-story house surrounded by a high stone wall. Its gate was made of iron with Quranic inscriptions. An Indian appeared from a door to the side and led me in silence across an entryway tiled in ceramic to another door that led to an open-air hall. We crossed it and entered a wide room with a distinct clean smell. It was cluttered with massive armchairs on top of thick rugs, and at the end of it was a very large television sitting on a broad stand with a VCR player above it.

I sat in one of the armchairs, in front of a small table with gilt edges; on it rested a round brass tray holding two pitchers, one full of coconut milk, the other of orange juice, and several plates with assorted fruits, bananas, papayas, pistachios, cookies, and small cakes.

Abu Ammar joined me moments later, embracing me and kissing my right shoulder, then taking an armchair across from me. He leaned his left arm on the armrest and hung over me with his eagle eyes.

When I commented on the smell, he looked surprised. "You don't know about aloe? It's a precious fragrance. A little piece of it about the size of a key lime could cost you a hundred riyals if it's pure."

I shook my head in disbelief, doing the math in my head and equating the hundred riyals with three hundred dollars by the pre–Gulf War rate. That's about the same as the monthly salary of an Egyptian government employee of middle or higher rank. He made a dismissive wave and added, "It's nothing, though, really. In our leader the Sultan's palaces they burn large amounts every day."

The Indian who had let me in came back into the room and poured some coconut milk into my cup. I took a sip and put it aside.

"Try these pies," Abu Ammar said. As I responded that I wasn't hungry, my eyes caught a glimpse of a large gold ring on his left hand and a big gold watch around his left wrist.

I summoned my courage and said, "Yesterday I visited the Women's Center and met your niece."

As he gathered his robes up around his legs and settled into his chair, he answered: "I heard."

I fumbled over how best to ask if I could see her again. Luckily, he rescued me. Standing up, he said, "I will ask her to come and join us."

He left the room and I let my eyes roam. There was a window that looked out onto the hall at the center of the house, but there was no portal to the street outside. Noticing a set of books stored near the television, I walked over to take a look. I checked out the titles: *History of Bou Saidian* by Ibn Zuraiq, *The Beginning and the End* by Ibn al-Kathir, *Encyclopedia of Names and Manual for Naming Your Son*.

I went back to the chair and settled into it, letting my gaze wander to the high ceiling and the fan mounted in the middle. The edges of the ceiling had gold leaf with barely distinguishable Quranic inscriptions. I lowered my eyes until they rested on a portrait of the Sultan in the bloom of youth, his image differing markedly from the ubiquitous portraits of him as a ruler today. Here, he was a short, thin young man with a shy smile and a hint of uncertainty. Abu Ammar came back after a while and settled back into his seat, gathering his robes under his legs, which he folded under him, and then stretching his hand out to the toes of his bare feet.

"My niece begs your pardon. She's worn out," he said, then gave me a cunning look as I tried my best to hide my disappointment.

"You didn't drink the coconut milk," he said. "Maybe you want something else?" Without waiting for my answer, he got up and said, "Just let me pray first."

The Indian brought him a prayer rug and unfurled it in the corner facing toward Mecca. He stood at an angle that allowed him to see me from the corner of his eye as he prayed, and I stayed frozen in place as he completed his cycle of four *rakat* and finished up by saluting the angel on each shoulder. The Indian snatched up the rug and folded it, then walked out; when he came back, he was carrying a tray with a bottle of whiskey and a bowl of ice.

"Let's have a drink before dinner," Abu Ammar said.

"I don't want to put you to any trouble," I said.

As he poured the two glasses and handed me one, he said, "We don't have the chance to meet someone from the fraternal land of Egypt every day. Tell me about it. I visited it only once, thirty years ago."

"It's changed quite a bit," I said.

"We have also changed."

I wasn't sure whether he meant that the two of us had grown old or that his country had advanced, so I chose a diplomatic answer: "The changes are obvious in every respect."

"Tell me, have you ever tried hyena meat?"

This query surprised me, and my disgust must have been obvious because he started laughing and waving his finger at me, saying, "Oh, you're one of those."

"Of which?"

"Some of the highlanders here forbid their slaughter because they consider them mystical beings who enchant and punish anyone who kills them. A different camp believes that the Prophet rode a mare that he once punished by whipping her back legs, and it became a female hyena whose meat was made halal by his touch. Believe me, it's very tasty and it has all kinds of benefits. Like, if your back hurts, you just eat its back meat, and if your right arm hurts, eat some meat from its right arm, and so on."

"My father believed that," I said. "Not the hyena in particular, but he thought you could eat meat from a body part to cure a specific pain in your body. When he got to my age, he always ate sheep's testicles."

He laughed and poured me another glass. The Indian brought in a portable kiln with a fire lit underneath and set it on the ground near Abu Ammar's feet. He left the room and came back again carrying a small table bearing a tray with rolls in silver wrapping and a big glass jar containing a soft black substance. He put the table in front of Abu Ammar, then sat on the ground between him and the kiln.

"Don't worry. I won't make you eat hyena. We're going to eat respectable Dhofari cuisine." He rolled up his sleeves and undid one of the wrappers to reveal a bunch of banana leaves. The second one contained a piece of seasoned meat. He stuffed the meat and some onions into a banana leaf. Then he scooped some of the black substance out of the jar and slathered it over the banana leaf. He did this a few more times until the meat was wrapped inside a thick black case, which he gave to the Indian who put it on the fire.

He pointed to the black substance and said, "It's mud that hardens over the fire and stews the meat inside it."

He took another piece of meat and concentrated on getting it wrapped in another banana leaf, then he said: "This area was nothing back in the days of the last sultan. Our tribe owned a lot of land, but our lives were so challenging. My brother emigrated to Kuwait, joined the rebels as soon as he got back, and convinced me to join them at the same time."

He carefully finished wrapping the meat, then handed it to the Indian who set it on the fire.

"Our leader, Qaboos, came to power in the summer of '70 and started building infrastructure. Many young rebels came down from the hills to Salalah, and once the government confirmed their good intentions, it gave them positions in the new offices. We started to reap the fruits of the changes. The builders went to schools in the main centers up in the hills. They made water available for camels and cattle herds, so we no longer had to trek for miles just to get to it. They opened supply routes and began to distribute summer and winter clothing. In short, the demands we had been making were answered. What could we do?"

He finished wrapping the last piece of meat and gave it to the Indian, who set it in the kiln, which he covered with a lid made of clay. He then carried away the tray holding the leftover banana leaves and mud and, right away, returned with the standard pot of rice, two plates, and table accessories for two, which he set on the small table. He then sat at the feet of Abu Ammar and turned into a statue of stone with eyes fixed on the covered kiln.

Abu Ammar saw me staring at the Indian and said, "We call him Tagore after the famous poet because he has an air of wisdom about him. He never opens his mouth."

I went back to the earlier topic: "But the revolution went on for a while after Qaboos became Sultan."

He poured himself another glass and filled mine too. "That was just a few hardcore communists being propped up by South Yemen. They kept at it, calling for violent revolution, a classless society, and proletarian rule. People here are simple folk. They only understand what they can touch and feel." He went quiet for a moment as he studied me, then he placed his hand on his chest and said, "As for me, what's in my heart stays there."

I mulled this over as, swallowing the last of his drink, he turned to the Indian and nodded his head. The servant lifted the cover to reveal that the fire had expired and the embers gone cold. He reached out and quickly grabbed one of the packets, broke off the hard casing of dried mud, and tossed the meat onto the tray.

"In the late '50s," I said, "I met a group of Omani students in Cairo. One of them was Waad's mother—her and her brother. Her name was Shahla, and we called her brother Yaarib."

He focused intently on the contents of the kiln without speaking.

"What happened to them?" I asked.

He took one of the packets, tore off the banana leaf casing, set the meat on a plate, and handed it over without looking at me. I took the plate and grabbed the piece of meat with my hand, then tossed it right back down, blowing on my seared fingers.

He absorbed himself in carefully unwrapping the next piece, then he said: "So many fell in battle during the war, then disappeared without a trace. I don't really know what happened to Warda—that's the name we knew her by. Did you know her? Personally, I never met her. Then there's my brother. He was a true believer. He stayed with the Front until the end."

"Died in battle?"

"Probably. He disappeared with her."

"What about Waad's uncle Yaarib?"

"I don't know him."

"You haven't heard anything?"

He hesitated for a moment. "Warda was originally from the northern plain. Her family emigrated to Sanaa. When she came to Dhofar, she worked in a completely different area, so we didn't meet. I left the Front and broke with my brother. I never saw him after that."

He picked up his meat and bit off a piece. I followed his lead and found it tender and delicious. We devoted our attention to the food while he prattled on about his childhood and his life in the camps in the hills. The Indian brought us dessert, but I satisfied myself with a cup of green tea. I looked at my watch once I had finished and saw that it was almost eleven.

"It's late. I must go."

Without moving, he said, "You are going to spend the night here. It's indeed late and the driver has left for Salalah and won't be back until the morning. He'll take you back to the hotel then."

"It's not necessary. I can just get a taxi."

"Not at this time of night."

"Couldn't you order one over the telephone?"

"We don't have that system here yet."

A vague anxiety overcame me. I became determined to go. I stood up and said, "I don't want to put you to any kind of trouble."

He, in turn, stood. "We have plenty of extra rooms here and anything you could need."

He took me by the arm and led me out of the room, with the Indian follow-ing. As we crossed the courtyard he said, "Before the days of air conditioning and electric fans, we set mats out here to sleep at night."

He stopped at a locked door, opened it, and switched on the light. Then he turned to me and pointed at the next door. "That's the bathroom. If you need anything, just call Tagore. Good night."

He waited until I'd gone inside, then he left with the Indian following on his heels. I shut the door, set my briefcase down on the floor, and looked around. It was a medium-sized room with a bed at the far end like the one I'd seen at the Women's Center, a full meter or more above ground. It had a thick, brightly colored blanket for a cover, and sheets produced by the same handiwork. A white robe, carefully ironed and folded, rested on a table next to it. I took off my shoes and socks and put on a pair of the cloth sandals that I found in a fancy box next to the door. I stepped over to a leather armchair with wheels on the bottom — like the chairs found in the offices of foreign companies. I sat and rested my arms, then made a half turn, surveying the room. A brown rug covered the floor, and cushions were stacked in piles next to the wall. Clothes were arranged in the wall on something like built-in shelves. Above them was an indentation in the wall shaped like a lantern and holding a decorative vase. Another alcove over the bed held rows of drinking glasses with gilded rims. The rest of the wall was covered with over twenty pictures of animals and birds from Taiwan in tiny frames. A brown cloak hung from a hook directly above an air-conditioning unit.

I stood up, took off my shirt and pants, hung them on top of the cloak, and put on the white robe. Then I opened the door and stepped into the hallway that led to the courtyard.

Darkness enveloped the house. A weak light over the bathroom door struggled futilely against the utter blackness. When I looked up to the floor above, I could barely make out a wooden railing. I listened for any sign of life, but sheer silence reigned.

I pushed the bathroom door and went in. It was as though I had gone from one century to another. The bathroom boasted all the latest features, from ceramic flooring to a sunken tub to an electric water heater. I rinsed off, picked up a clean pink towel, and went back to my room. Its door resisted my attempts to firmly close it. There was a wooden bolt with a thick lever that had holes in its surface and a second bolt with wooden prongs. A stick leaning against it also had wooden prongs and seemed like some type of door key.

Since I couldn't figure out how to use the stick, I had to leave the door ajar. I swallowed the pills for stomach upset and blood pressure that I carry at all times, drank some water, then turned out the light and waited for my eyes to adjust to the dark. I climbed into the bed, but as I started to bend my knees I realized I had severe muscle strain. I stretched out again and closed my eyes, then opened them again. I was nervous about the unlocked door, and my eyes involuntarily fixed on the thin rays of light stealing in through the crack. Thinking I heard strange noises, I held my breath to detect them. Dogs barked in the distance. I heard wood creaking and some obscure rustling. I decided after a bit that these were the normal nighttime sounds of any old house. I must have dozed off because suddenly there was a light movement at the door, and I realized that it was swinging open very slowly. In the light from the hall, a shadow of a human frame appeared to be sliding in.

It might have been the scent that gave me a hint, but in any case, something instinctual clued me in to the intruder's identity, even before the electric lamp was switched on. I was struck by the ease with which Waad managed to close and lock the door. Without even using the key, she effortlessly fixed the prongs of the bolt inside the holes in the conjoining piece.

I pushed myself to a sitting position and swung my legs around, covering my thighs with the robe. She came within a few steps and faced me, a wild fire in her eyes. Her face and head were bare. Her hair spilled onto a silk gown with Chinese embroidery that extended to her bare feet.

Her tone was sharp. "What are you doing here?"

Struggling to find words, I came out with, "Looking for you."

"Why? Haven't you already taken the journals from the dentist?"

"I have them. But I want the rest."

She raised one hand to her waist in a pose of challenge. "What are you talking about?"

"There's still another volume."

She brought her hand to her collar and began to play with the buttons of her gown agitatedly. "Who says so?"

"It's obvious. What I've read so far leaves so many questions unanswered. And besides, you had no hesitation about giving me the last volume. Why? Because Warda recorded that this be done in her journals. But I haven't found a word calling for the notebooks to be given to me in what I've read so far. There has to be more."

She flicked the top button of her gown open while keeping her eyes fixed on my face. As her hand moved down to the next button, my eyes settled on her fingers. When the next button came undone, the gown slipped back to reveal her bare chest. She stood there arms akimbo, her breasts fully revealed in all their glory.

"Was she more beautiful than I am?" she asked.

"Who?"

"Warda," she said.

How could I answer, having seen no more than Warda's face?

"Don't you remember how she looked?"

She took a step toward me without looking away from my face or trying to cover those poised breasts with their erect nipples.

"I never saw her—neither her, nor my father . . . ," she continued.

As she came close enough for her cloak to brush my leg, she reached out, gripped my hands, and pulled them forcefully to her breasts.

". . . So you tell me."

I said nothing, not because I had nothing to say, but because there was no chance. Before I could gather myself, in a moment straight out of a dream, she dropped her cloak and planted herself before me in complete and glorious nudity. Then she pushed me onto my back and climbed on top of me. A sheer curtain over the bed had revealed the patterns in the ceiling, but now her bold visage blocked out everything beyond.

She encircled me with her arms, then brought me between her legs and started to take me. I pretended to be overpowered, surrendering myself to her as she rocked over me like a child, letting loose all the defenses I had devoted my life to building up. *To prove what exactly?* Transported millions of light-years away. I started to come, keenly conscious that I had never experienced this degree of pleasure but also understanding that I had to move her away at the crucial moment.

Am I making love now with Warda—or with myself?

She stayed on top of me, staring at me intently. I felt the pressure of her muscular hips on top of me as I gently moved her off me. I turned to the side to face her, trying to ignore the soreness in my neck.

"What is that perfume you're wearing?"

She gave a playful smile and answered in an accent imitating Egyptian film heroines: "Why what do you mean 'perfume,' sir? That's hair oil. Pricey. Sandalwood, musk, and saffron in rosewater."

In addition to a fragrant smell that no known perfume can compete with.

I passed my hands over her body, probing its curves. After a moment, I whispered in her ear: "How do you say this in highlander?"

She buried her face in my chest playfully. *"Hob."*

"Love." Is there any expression more exact and elegant?

I said I was surprised that she hadn't been circumcised, and she laughed and said, "Just lucky." My fingers continued to explore as she buried her head in my chest, her scent enveloping me and intoxicating me, until I gave one last shudder and let my hand drop.

"Are you going back to Egypt?"

"Yes."

"Tell me all about it. Can you see the crocodiles that swim in the Nile?"

"We ride them in the waves even."

"Take me back with you. I am dying every day I spend here."

"What do you mean? Your uncle is open-minded. He basically admitted to me that he still believes in the Front. He was even open to the idea that you come and sit with us."

She laughed bitterly. "You won't find anyone more reactionary. He doesn't even let his daughters leave the house. He blocked me from going to the new university in Muscat to continue my studies. I struggled to be allowed my two days a week of work at the Women's Center, and still, he only agreed to soften me up enough to give him the journals. If it weren't for them, I'd be spending all day every day in his house with his wife. On the top floor, there's a thirty-five-meter-long hall, covered with rugs and surrounded by cushions. Can you guess how many cushions? I've counted every last one during times I was up there, I was so bored. There's sixty-five. The window curtains are drawn and the lights switched on even in the middle of the day. His wife sits up there every day in a long, wide dress made from local plant fiber, decorated with little gold flowers and silver bulbs that she knitted herself over the course of a month."

I put my hand over her mouth, thinking I heard a sound outside. I listened for a moment and when I didn't hear anything other than the thumping of my own heart, I jumped up and went over to the door. I stood there and listened.

There was definitely some kind of rustling noise outside. I turned around only to find her hiding under the covers. The rustling stopped and the normal empty house noises started again. I reached and turned off the lamp, then peered out into the faint rays of light coming from outside. The beams shined straight without disruption.

I went back to the bed and tumbled down next to her, rolling onto my side and putting my hand under her head and wrapping my other arm around her. She crawled into my embrace, pressing her moist loins against my leg, and whispered: "It might be a cat."

"Or your uncle?"

She considered, then said, "I doubt it. He sleeps in a whole different wing of the house."

I pulled her to me and kissed her head.

As though taking my child into my arms.

"I was telling you about how we spend our days. My uncle's wife calls her daughters and they all come in wearing the same thing she does. They have to sit in place all day, acting polite and submissive. Should they start to move around, she shouts at them, 'Your clogs!' and so they have to go barefoot. That's an example. She just never leaves them alone: 'No. Don't do that!' They have to sit on the floor with their legs crossed. Have you looked at my feet? They're straight. Here, everyone's feet are curved from sitting cross-legged all day. At a certain point, she starts organizing the sitting, and we all bring her fruit, drinks, and nuts. But whenever we offer her something, she says she is fasting because it's the fourteenth or fifteenth of *Rajab* or *Shaaban*, or because it's Monday or because it's Thursday or whatever. Have you watched any television here? We never watch anything but Friday prayers and shows about religion. Any idea what the only entertainment is? When anyone becomes very sick and won't get better, they call the witch doctor. She's a big woman who throws her voice to her stomach. She pretends that she's been pregnant for years and that the fetus is speaking. She brings them all together in a dark room filled with smoke and the patient sits in the middle. Then they start rocking their heads back and forth and chanting until the poor thing gets dizzy and begins to babble nonsense. In the end, she collapses."

She sat up and pressed one of her legs between mine.

"Tell me about her."

I told her how I met Warda. She asked for a physical description, so I obliged. Before long, I realized I knew nothing very important about her.

"Did you love her?" she asked.

I hesitated, then said, "I think so."

It was her turn to hesitate: "Did . . . did you sleep with her?"

I answered no.

I felt her leg shiver. "Believe it or not, I actually hated her until I read the journals. I imagined her a woman without values or any sense of responsibility. I thought she had just . . . abandoned me."

I asked her then about Yaarib. "I've never seen him and he's never come here, even though I'm pretty sure that my uncle is in touch with him. I think he's in Muscat."

"And the journals?"

"They fell into my hands by accident. About a year ago. A Bedouin came and gave them to Tagore. He brought them to me. I hid them, after pulling out of him a promise not to tell my uncle. Still, he found out. Not sure if from the Bedouin or from Tagore. He asked me to give them to him, and at first I wouldn't admit I had them. I wanted to keep them for myself. When he pressed me, I ended up giving him some but kept the rest for myself. He was still suspicious and has watched me carefully ever since. He's always going through my things, but I've stayed a step ahead."

"And why did you keep the last part from me?"

"One reason is that there's stuff in them about when I was born. My parents never formally married. Many people at that time were marrying according to the Front's way of doing it—in front of a political official. But they didn't even do that. After the revolution was over, the Front marriages were formalized. My uncle used his influence and made me legitimate as part of that process. I still felt ashamed, though. Often I'm overcome by the sense that I am an abandoned bastard."

"Is there another reason?"

"The other reason is that I want to use the last volume to win my freedom. It includes some secret that they're dying to know, but I'm not sure exactly what it is. I want to try to force my uncle to send me off to study in Beirut, Egypt, or London."

"Who are 'they'?"

"I'm not sure. They have been trying to reach me in all kinds of ways. They've left not even a pebble unturned."

Paranoid fantasies? Hysteria?

"A person in Muscat told me that you refused to give this part to anyone but me. How did he know that?"

"One of my girlfriends has a brother who was in the Front. She was the one who told me that they had the first volumes and wanted to see the later ones. I told her that I could only give them up to either you or this Lebanese man. You became a central figure in my life for a while. I knew you would come."

We suddenly froze as the mysterious noise started up again. I slid my arm out from under her and sat up. "I have to go now," she said. She jumped lightly down and I turned to follow her movements through the dark as she looked for her cloak. She fumbled with its buttons for a moment. Then she turned toward me and flicked her wrist. A small notebook landed on my chest. She dressed and straightened her hair. Then she stepped toward me, leaned over, and kissed me.

"How do I get this back to you?" I asked.

"Don't worry about that. I have a copy."

I stepped out of bed and went with her to the door. She fumbled a bit trying to get the bolt to release but finally managed to slide it out.

I whispered to her, "I'm going to turn on the light so I can write down my telephone number in Muscat and my address in Egypt."

"No! Give me a pen. I can write in the dark."

Remembering that I had put my briefcase next to the door, I picked it up and rummaged inside until I found a pen. I handed it to her and she wrote down the details. Then she pulled open the door and slid away into the darkness. I tilted my head against the door and stood there listening. Hearing no strange sounds now, I turned on the light and studied the latch. I moved the bolt until its prongs fit into the holes, and I pulled to make sure it was shut. Then I sat in the armchair and flipped through the pages of the small, black-covered notebook and mulled over that handwriting—so challenging, so familiar.

Chapter Sixteen

THE EMPTY QUARTER, 1975

January 7

. . . We move on and on. Pack on back, camel in the lead. Kalashnikov over the shoulder. The transistor radio our most precious companion. Wide plateaus stretch out, dotted with flowers and verdant growth. The birds of the heavens in browns, reds, and blacks with long white stripes on their tails soar ahead beyond the flies. The highland roads are uneven paths marked by piles of rocks. Traces of camps set up by a local tribe that pitched its tents near the start. They migrated a month ago to the bottom of the mountain where they penned up their cattle. Were they escaping the bombing or getting ready for the rainy season? "Comrades, dear comrades," rang out. We looked around to see where it was coming from. A 10-year-old boy held a brass jug out to us, offering a drink of fresh milk. He looked over our clothes and weapons carefully, became excited. Turned to me and asked, "Warda?" He hugged me and kissed me on the cheek. He said to us, full of pride, "Drink. The milk has been boiled." When we started to leave, he coyly raised his fingers in a victory sign. All is not yet lost, then. This moment will not be forgotten. But does he realize we are retreating? At an oasis, we washed ourselves and drank. The cries of the birds. We dispersed into a field of high bean stalks. The water sources are targets for passing bombers. After the raids, the livestock that have been hit are slaughtered before they rot. We have made a habit of buying some of this meat to offset the losses of the local herdsmen. We met an old woman wearing a head scarf with tiny metal plates decorating the red cloth. A gold ring in her nose. She offered us tomatoes. She insisted that we take them, laughing invitingly. How long will these warm feelings last?

January 8

The Shah is in Cairo. Sadat rolled out the red carpet. Opposition voices have been silent. That's how Egyptians have always been: they are patient for so long, suddenly explode with zeal, then just as quickly it all dies out. In the end, everything goes back to the way it was before. I wonder what Rushdy is doing now?

January 11

Government forces west of the Hornbeam Line have overrun our headquarters and confiscated our cache of weapons and ammunition.

We spent the night in a cave that belonged to two married fighters with several children. I couldn't sleep. One of the children tossed around and coughed for several hours. We looked at him in the morning and he had the puffy eyes of a tuberculosis patient. The European advocacy groups have been collecting medicine, money, and surgical supplies. Now I wonder, will they ever make it here?

January 15

Gaddafi is talking about his Green Book as a serious contribution to a complete theoretical framework for revolution in the Arab world.

Reports of a new electrical line of defense that the Iranians have set up parallel to and just west of the Hornbeam line. They are calling it "Damavand." It stretches to the north, starting from Rakhiut. The goal is to pin our forces against the border with Yemen.

Estimates of our losses in the battle at Rakhiut are approaching one thousand.

January 20

Ahmad Muslim, an important figure in the militia with a son who is one of our fighters, hosted us. His wife lit the fire to cook the rice inside so as not to endanger us. Iranian ships spend the night flashing searchlights, then they call in coordinates to bomber pilots at daybreak. A green box sits in the corner full of Russian ammunition. Plastic netting and storm lamps lying on the ground.

We moved to a big cave where about 80 women and children stay. All their men are still away at war. There we could listen to the Front's broadcast, which the station Voice of the Revolution transmits every day on a different frequency. I explained to them the latest developments. Said Zinan, the militia's regional spokesman, followed me. He spoke of the popular committee's decision regarding accommodations, caves that would hide us effectively, and means to conceal cultivated areas. When he finished, he started to chant: "Long live the war of popular liberation and the struggle for democratic change." The others called back, and I joined in: "Long live the popular struggle of the Arab people in Palestine! Down with imperialism and reactionaries! Down with Zionism! Down with the client states and their mercenaries! Long live the people! Long may you live!"

Why? If only slogans could change the world so easily. Everyone left quickly without any discussion or even a single question. At this point, meetings that go on too long become dangerous. Rocket fire. Mortars. Bombs. Every type of weapon except napalm. Will that be next?

January 24

We kept going until nightfall. One of the comrades led us to a nearby cave where we ate with a family. Since the entrance was half a meter at most, we had to crawl on all fours to get inside. We sat down to drink red tea. As we waited for dinner, the flames from the stove warmed us. Some neighbors came to welcome us and join us in the food, tea, and milk. Mosquito bites. They made up a comfortable spot just for me and I fell asleep with ease.

January 28

Descended toward the coastal plain. Our scarves warded off the sandy winds that rushed in off the sea. Every house or cave in the area sheltered at least a few fighters taking an hour or two of rest. Bombing raids all day give way to cannon fire and naval bombardments at night.

February 1

Al-Hawf. Omani refugees squat in the caves surrounding the town. A mat on the ground, boxes, suitcases, and personal items stacked to the sides. A thermos, sometimes a transistor radio. We gather in the evening to listen to the Front's 45-minute broadcasts out of Aden. Sometimes we must walk a few hours to find a water source suitable for animals and humans. I stay with a family of 11 who lived near Dhofar with a herd of 25 camels and 50 goats. The British bombed their herd and destroyed their village. Starting tomorrow I will reorganize our forces out of the people that have retreated here. Fahd is in Mukalla waiting for a plane to take him to Aden so he can be treated for a serious injury to his vertebral column. Dahmish is in Ghaydah. Yaarib is in either Aden or Beirut.

February 2

In the camp named after the martyr Bakheet Bin Haijla. Ali commands 40 men. They all sleep in a big cave that holds up to 120. Also ammunition, weapons, and cans of tuna. Ali blows up when some cans go missing. He looks at me and says: "There are still petit bourgeois among us!" On a sheer cloth, a piece of camel meat dries in the sun. The camel was slaughtered in the morning. The choicest cuts have already been devoured: the legs, liver, heart, and rump. The meat was boiled and served over rice cooked with shortening from Holland. The time I tried it in Cairo, I hated the nasty smell that stuck to my hands and clothes. Now I don't notice. I consider us lucky. The animal is cut and distributed evenly so that everyone has two days' worth of food. Rice sautéed in tomato sauce. All the fires extinguished immediately. Only the flicker of lit cigarettes.

I spoke about the military situation using an example from Mao's struggle. When the Red Army was besieged in 1934, they had no choice but to retreat. Taking along 100,000 followers, they fled north. They walked a distance of 10,000 km, facing along the way hunger, thirst, disease, and skirmishes. The long march ended after a year. By then, only 5,000 men were left. Fourteen years later, Mao achieved ultimate victory and established the People's Republic of China. As I spoke, the number hit me: Another 15 years? 100,000, of whom 5,000 were left? Our own numbers barely made it to 5,000 . . . of whom at least 1,500 have gone back to Salalah. Besides, where will we go? North for us is the Empty Quarter. South Yemen is a foreign country. The enemy is to the east, and the sea is behind us. The Castro example might be better. He entered Havana 3 years after his first revolt ended in failure.

The most important thing right now is to raise the morale of the fighters. We must find a way to continue military operations inside Dhofar.

February 3

Um Kalthum is dead. A huge loss. She expressed all aspects of her epoch, moving from songs of feudalism to revolutionary anthems. She played such an important role in mobilizing the resistance after the defeat of '67.

We have put in place a strict regimen of military drills.

February 13

A Jordanian military delegation led by Zayed Ben Shaker, chairman of the joint chiefs, is visiting Muscat.

I've convinced the comrades to let me lead an attack on the Anglo-Iranian site in Sarfait.

February 15

We woke up before dawn and collected around the teakettle sitting on the wood fire. Each took a plastic or aluminum cup. I parceled out the bits of tobacco and matches we had left. (In the past, we handed out a bag of tobacco and box of matches every morning.) They rolled their own cigarettes.

I left ten comrades in the camp with Ali in charge of them — some to stand guard and the rest to serve the tiny community that still clung to us, depending on us for schooling, literacy centers, and security. As we marched off, we chanted: "Children of the nation are the army of liberation!" One of the comrades carried a Soviet-made mortar launcher on his back. Another carried its stand. The mortar rockets were distributed among everyone else. We have no more Land Rovers, nor Toyota trucks, nor camel caravans. We made our way in a line toward the plateau. Our group of 12 guerrillas jumped from one rock to another with the light, skilled steps of mountain goats, until we met a military transport vehicle carrying dozens of civilians on their way to visit their children in the camps across the border with Yemen, which was picking up passengers along the way. At the coast, piles of sardines. We waited for a motorboat that could take us close to Sarfait. The only way left to get there is by sea. We kept looking at the sky, our ears perked for the hum of airplanes. A group was waiting with us, women, old men, and children carrying wicker baskets and plastic bags. I tried to read the meaning of their stares but couldn't. Do they blame us for the misery they are living through? We waded out into the water to get on the boat. An old vessel, but it carried at least 40 people.

The base sat 10 km from the border, covering a large square area that held 800 Iranian soldiers and several dozen British. The base was guarded by four different well-armed batteries, with helicopters providing air support. It was this well-guarded fortress that mobilized the stream of attacks that rained down on civilian and military targets alike in western Dhofar.

The comrades assembled the rocket launcher inside a hollowed-out part of a rock. We spread out to see the camp from several angles. Bouarif stayed next to me with the walkie-talkie and the binoculars so he could pass along the coordinates of the targets. He handed me the binoculars. I examined the fortifications around the area. Bunkers of rock and concrete, shielding everything behind them. The operation started with a direct hit by an RPG on the biggest bunker, then rapid fire scattered all around. The enemy took the fire and didn't shoot back. Bouarif looked happy. He spoke with elation over the walkie-talkie to the men at the gun. After the next mortar was fired, we ducked under a protruding edge of the rock. Mussalem passed around some pressed dates. After half an hour, two Strikemaster jets appeared and started bombing. We all stayed in place with the jets flying back and forth above us—except for a comrade named Hussein. He sat in the open on a pile of rocks wearing a red shirt. He refused to take cover under our rock. He said that planes couldn't see fixed objects. I have a feeling that I'm the reason for his showing off in this way. He couldn't take his eyes off my breasts. Once the jets flew back to base, we started to make our way back. Bombs were landing around us as the base finally responded to our attack. I started writing up the report in my head: We hit the base for a full hour. Our goal is to fatigue the enemy until he pulls out, as he did in Thaqeeb two years ago. But at this point I found myself wondering—who will fatigue who?

February 17

Jordan has given Qaboos 31 Hawker Hunter fighter jets.

February 20

Government forces have managed for the first time to enter the area of Wadi Resham, after encountering light resistance.

Fighting has escalated between the Eritrean National Movement and the new Ethiopian regime. The military council has asked the United States for a shipment of weapons to buttress the campaign. Whoever gets caught in the trap of trying to put down the legitimate national-popular demands of their people always ends up running back to the embrace of the imperialists.

February 22

Ghaydah is 100 km across the Yemeni border. Along the dirt road, a flagpole waves the flag of Democratic Yemen. Yemeni soldiers. An area for schools. We were received by the director and a group of soldier-teachers. The old director, who had organized the children's protest against Soviet imperialism, died in battle some time ago. The primary school students stood in seven rows holding their notepads. Some had walked as far as 500 km to get here. Suddenly, they dropped the notepads and scattered. The older students and the teachers all rushed to man the defensive weaponry mounted around the school. An Iranian Jaguar jet came in low over the schoolhouse. The playground was covered with children who threw themselves on the ground. A massacre might have occurred, except that the jet never fired. Did the pilot hesitate at the sight of all the children? Or was he only here to gather reconnaissance?

I stayed with the family of Arjoun, a member of the Yemeni Popular Council.

Dahmish is taking care of something at the border and comes back tomorrow. I haven't seen him since Rakhiut fell. I am missing him.

February 23

In Ghaydah, 30 families combine their efforts to cultivate 100 hectares. The yield from the work is divided up according to need. The vagaries of the middleman are removed: everyone enjoys personal economic security. Our guerrillas offer farming instruction and provide tools. One of the leaders of the cooperative said to me, "Our only problem right now is security. The enemy strafes our fields with their firebombs during planting and during harvest."

February 24

Dahmish came back yesterday afternoon. I asked him if he missed me. He gave a shy smile. He doesn't express his feelings freely. I bathed and washed my hair with shampoo. Arjoun's wife gave me a splash of perfume with a wink and a smile. I massaged it in everywhere. She loaned me a white blouse with short sleeves, a colorful skirt, and proper sandals. Dahmish had dinner with us, then I took him outside. We walked along the dark, dusty paths. Dogs chased behind. I told him about my adventure in Sarfait. He talked about the efforts to regroup with retreating forces along the border. We discussed what might happen, then found ourselves outside town and stopped near a garden with no fence around it. I turned to him and asked, "Don't you want to kiss me?" He looked stunned, his dark eyes shining with a mysterious light. He showed not much experience at kissing. He just let his lips lie on top of mine, so I devoured them with my own. I sucked on his tongue and then stuck mine through to the back of his mouth. He held me until we stumbled over into the grass. When I started to climb on top of him, he insisted I be on the bottom. I was locked in by his grasp. I disliked being penned in. I resisted for a moment, then relaxed. I found some pleasure in being a woman, delicate and pliant and receptive. But I could also clutch him between my legs with force, and even keep him from moving. I helped him to enter me after his harried attempts showed his lack of experience. At that point I melted away, and he had to press his hand over my mouth to suppress my shrieks.

March 1st

New operations by the enemy in the central and eastern zones. We can no longer stand up to the government forces east of the Hornbeam line. The government's army now enjoys total freedom of movement.

Dahmish agreed with me that the situation is dire—perhaps even hopeless.

March 10

A crushing blow: Iran and Iraq have made a pact.

I discussed where we stand with some of the comrades. I argued that a guerrilla insurgency is a type of popular resistance and called for a transition toward that approach and against those pushing for a path toward certain destruction. Guerrillas work as a fighting vanguard for the people within a region, preparing the way for a series of militant operations with the strategic goal of taking power in the long run. But they must maintain the constant support of the peasants and workers in the area. I added that Guevara laid out in his 1961 book *Guerrilla Warfare* that the guerrilla insurgency is not the only mechanism for taking power in the Americas, but it is one of the most important tools currently available. Muhammad Ahmed, a member of the central committee, supported me indirectly. He said that the military struggle was limited to Dhofar for now. In the rest of Oman, the Front's fight was basically a political struggle. The people of Oman are not prepared to rise up against Qaboos after he has instituted his reforms. There is also the contradiction of the international support.

Said Masaud gave a sharp rebuttal: "We have said all along that we shouldn't depend on anyone else." I responded with a question: "Hasn't the heroism and sacrifice by our guerrillas been enough? This is not turning into another Vietnam." I went on, "We have to understand the demands of the people. We must embody their spirit and support their movement instead of dragging them into something. If the masses change their views for whatever reason, we have to assent to their will." Said Masaud fought back: "We must drag the masses and lead from out front, not be the dog's tail. If the masses change their views, we can spare no effort in raising their consciousness back up again. We have to always stay one step ahead of the people." His face colored as he became more worked up, and he started to shout: "What exactly do you want us to do about the fighters that are already in the hills right now? Are you asking them to surrender?" I answered that I was asking for nothing but an objective assessment of the current situation, followed by a commensurate plan for moving forward. He said he found my stance surprising.

March 15

Yaarib arrived from Aden. He brought me apples, 7 Up, and shampoo. He said that there were all kinds of products coming in from North Yemen now after the opening to the Gulf States. He's learned that Colonel Gaddafi will oversee the shipment of Soviet rockets to our forces. He also brought the new issue of *June 9* magazine. It included the text of a letter addressed by Gaddafi to Qaboos. Some very strange wording: ". . . We are surprised, my brother, by the fact that your sense of honor — personal, national, and popular honor alike! — permits you to let organized foreign armies occupy first Muscat, then Dhofar. We are asking you for the last time to order the immediate withdrawal of all foreign forces. And if they refuse your order, we will join with you to expel them by force. Or, should you join their side, we will ourselves take the side of our Arab masses. Please return to your senses, return to the hearth of the homeland, before you find yourself adrift and disgraced. We are warning you at the same time that we feel sorry for you. We are warning you because you are pursuing something wrong, and we feel sorry for you because it is leading you toward the fate of a scabies-infested camel. Both of these are the last things we would hope for."

I asked Yaarib about those taken prisoner in Mattrah. He blew up in my face. He showered me with abuse. He said I was the last person he expected this question from. "Do you think I betrayed my own comrades and gave them up to the authorities?" He caught his breath. Calmed a bit. Said he had probably been negligent in his planning regarding security, but nothing worse.

March 16

Yaarib's spirits are low in a way that reminds me of a time he came back from Muscat when we were living in Cairo. He talks about the situation in Aden. A struggle is going on beneath the surface between the right and the left within the Front. The right wing is gathering strength because of the economic situation. That's in spite of the Soviet Union forgiving its debt of 50 million dollars as of July '74 and Cuba sending aid money. Many of the power brokers there are looking to oil drilling along the border as a solution. Some of them see our struggle as an obstacle to this initiative.

The Sultanate has distributed a leaflet with my name in it. I'm worth a reward of 10,000 riyals to anyone who brings me in, dead or alive. I said to Yaarib: "My price has gone up by three thousand." He examined the leaflet carefully, then said, "They haven't even offered one riyal for me. I must not be worth anything to them." I felt uncomfortable. It was like it annoyed him that they gave me such importance.

March 18

Yaarib is ill at ease around Dahmish. He's cold to him. I haven't even told him anything about our relationship, but he has to have noticed that there's something between us. I remembered his attitude toward Shehab.

March 25

King Faisal has been assassinated. I wouldn't doubt the Mossad or the CIA having a hand in it. Possibly because they lost their complete control of him when he latched on to the idea of liberating Jerusalem.

Arab profits from petroleum sales last year surpassed 40 million dollars. All of it is invested in the banks of Europe, America, and Japan.

March 26

The Sultanate has set up new centers west of the Damavand line. There's a string of centers now that go from Sarfait to the sea, with barbed wire barriers lining the way. We are suddenly completely locked out of western Dhofar.

Our numbers are shrinking. Every day, we discover the disappearance of another guerrilla.

I prepared a report recommending a cessation of military activity and a pivot toward a focus on political work.

April 3

We published the following military communiqué: "On the date of April 2, 1975, a landmine exploded underneath a Bedford military truck carrying 20 Jordanian soldiers on their way from Salalah to the red line via the coastal road near the 8th km outside of town. The time was exactly 8 a.m." Dahmish gave a cheer and his spirits were raised for a while. I didn't want to bring him back down. I don't think this is a new initiative. Probably a leftover mine.

April 5

Discussions of my report are ongoing. There's much hesitation from the executive council. They are not ready to make this decision. Are they waiting to hear from the Aden comrades?

We arrived at a compromise. We will rebuild the movement in the north, starting with laying a political foundation. Dahmish, Yaarib, and I will take on the primary responsibility.

Observations on the situation inside Oman:

Control over state finances has transferred from the Sultan to an oligarchy of businessmen.

High administrative officials have replaced European officials everywhere except in the military.

Members of the ruling family have taken important positions no matter whether they are qualified or not.

Same for old officials of the Bou Said family like experienced clerks and scribes.

Same for important figures in the tribal structure.

Arab Omani merchants are given preference.

Kept at arm's length: Zanzibarians, because many only know Swahili or Swahili and English, but not Arabic, and also suspicion about their political leanings if they went to school in Tanzania; the Baluch, who have always been treated as second-class citizens and who tend to be uneducated; Omanis of Indian origin—mostly Hindus and Sikhs—who were once the backbone of Omani business and trade. They are wealthy and able to send their children away for schooling, but religious and ethnic distinction keep them from playing any political role. We will start our work among these groups of outsiders.

I am feeling anxiety and dread. This next stage is going to be hard . . . and possibly more dangerous.

April 6

He was on top of me. I had explained to him the time of the month for ovulation, but he never did get it. He put it all on me. Panting, he asked, "Is it safe?" I counted it out. "Today is the 13th day. That's the most dangerous. The egg is right there waiting, at its most lively, ready to be met." I started to say all of that, but caught myself. I inhaled deeply. Why shouldn't I? It's time. Instead, I whispered in the dark, "Yes, safe." I wrapped my arms around him.

April 7

Yaarib says that the coastal route is too far. It's as long as the highway that goes from Salalah to Nizwa, then on to Muscat, the one I took when I came the first time. Both routes are controlled by either the government or tribes loyal to them. The only other way is crossing through the desert. I pulled out an old map of the Arabian Peninsula. The southern spread of the desert takes up about half the area. It stretches a distance of 1,500 km from the Yemeni border in the west to the foothills of the Omani highlands in the east, and 800 km from the southern coast to the Arabian Gulf in the north. The majority is a desert known as the Empty Quarter. The only ones known to have crossed it are some British orientalists — Bertram Thomas in 1930 from south to north, then St. John Philby later the same year from north to south. Later, Thesiger in 1946 and again in '49. Yaarib thinks it's our best chance.

Dahmish says that talk about crossing the Empty Quarter is pure madness. He suggests we go to Aden, fly from there to Beirut, then come back into Oman through the Emirates. The streets of Beirut flashed before my mind's eye and I felt nostalgic. I thought Yaarib would welcome the idea, but he surprised me by taking a firm stance against. He said things are not like they were in the '60s. Every Gulf security agency knows about us now and circulates our pictures among themselves. Even the Iraqis can't be trusted after they signed their pact with the Shah.

April 8

I'm mad at Dahmish. I asked him what he was waiting for. Was it just about sneaking into Dhofar and doing simple little strikes now, like we did in Sarfait? Are we reduced to firing a few mortars and then running? That's if we're even sure we can still get in. Or will we just sit here and eat and drink, and do our drills as we wait for that promised day? Shall we give our lectures while our numbers dwindle and our challenges grow? Or shall we go to Aden so we can work in an office, publishing pamphlets and issuing communiqués about imaginary operations? We have given over our lives to the cause of Dhofar and Oman, I said, and we must keep up the struggle as best we can.

The sixth congress of the National Front in Aden has put in place a new internal order. Point 17 concerns respect for women's rights. An agreement has been reached to form one party out of the political organization of the Front, the Communist party, and the Baathist Talia party. The congress treated the call for unification of the two Yemens as an abandoning of the commitment to revolution, since it would close off the push toward that goal. In other words, if unification happened right now, the system currently in place in the north would prevail.

April 9

Back to the idea of the Empty Quarter. Yaarib explained that the journey would take us 3 to 4 months under the best of circumstances. There are two routes. One goes over the Qarra mountains north of Salalah, then veers right and skirts the edges of the Empty Quarter into Saudi Arabia at Wadi Moqshin and along a path to the sands of Gafa. You have to go into Saudi Arabia to get around the quicksand. From there, it's possible to skirt around Sheba and Sabakhat to the oasis at Liwa. Then we can turn left and reenter Oman just below Nizwa. The other route goes from Hadhramaut toward Monoukh in the north, crossing a 600 km stretch in the Empty Quarter with no water. Thesiger did it in 16 days. After that, we would be in Saudi Arabia, where we would head north, then turn right toward Abu Dhabi.

Clearly, Yaarib has studied all this carefully. Dahmish is still hesitant. He says the desert will be tough. The only water is bitter. The winds are full of sand. The extreme cold. The flaming heat. The bright, blinding glare with no trace of shade or clouds. Not to mention the isolation and the uncertainty.

There are constant disputes between the different tribes. For example, the historic feud between the Rawashid clan and the Daroua. Every family between Hadhramaut and the Omani border is loyal to one or the other of these competing groups. Some of the tribes will host a stranger for three days and guarantee a fourth day of protection. But always the tribal authority has to send an emissary to protect travelers after that. Our problem is that we don't know what allegiances we will encounter under these circumstances. We'll also need a guide who knows the hill country throughout Qamar and Qarra.

April 10

Dahmish has finally agreed to cross the Empty Quarter. We decided not to take the route through Hadhramaut and Monoukh because it crosses over an area controlled by the Saudi authorities who would love to get their hands on us. That only leaves the Wadi Moqshin route. It's true that this way also crosses Saudi territory, but only in an uninhabited area that is much less risky.

I must disguise myself. Either I can pretend to be a man by cutting my hair short and wearing a traditional wrap at my waist instead of khaki pants, or I can become a Bedouin woman by wearing a black mesh face veil with eyeholes. My decision: I'll do both.

Yaarib can't stay put. He is constantly in motion. Disappears sometimes for the whole day.

April 11

We overlooked something important. We were going to head from Shaiser to the edge of the Empty Quarter and move along its border to cut out 150 km between here and Moqshin. This route runs parallel to the highway between Salalah and Muscat about 30 km to the west. No major military activity there, but the whole route has fallen under the control of the government, so we will be likely to run into patrols. Even Moyshin, for that matter, probably has a checkpoint by now. If Yaarib was surprised to realize this, he didn't let it show. Dahmish and I agreed that the crossing was too risky, but Yaarib stood firm. He said that the route saves 150 km of crossing inside the Empty Quarter and wouldn't budge. We had to give in.

We started to prepare.

April 14

A Lebanese Phalangist militia in Beirut attacked a bus full of Palestinians and Lebanese. Twenty-nine passengers were killed in the attack, most of them children.

About 200 pounds of supplies: flour, rice, some maize, shortening, coffee, tea, sugar, canned goods (tuna, mackerel, vegetables, fruit). Should be enough for five people for at least two months.

The individual requires about a quarter gallon of water a day for drinking and washing. We have to start with enough for at least a month.

April 17

We made a deal with two comrades from the Kathir tribe, who were with me when we pulled out of Rakhiut. They will come along as far as Shaiser, then head back toward Ghaydah by way of their home villages. We never told them our real destination — just that we are going to the eastern zone to organize the resistance. Managed to get our hands on some fresh machine guns, still in their packaging. I inspected them and repackaged them in lubricated paper that protects them from the humidity.

April 18

I asked him what he does when he's not with a woman. He said, "Nothing." I told him that was impossible. He insisted it was the truth. I made it clear I didn't believe him.

He challenged me: "What about you?"

I answered: "I can say it. I'm not embarrassed by something so natural."

When I said what I did he blushed.

April 20

Beirut radio, 5 P.M.: "King Hussein announces that he has inspected his troops guarding the road to Thumrait during a visit to Salalah."

We are ready to go. Two small tents. Additional ammunition. Blankets. Heavy scarves. Radio batteries. An empty notebook. Books by Lenin and Mao. The Ostrovsky novel *How the Steel Was Tempered*, Fadeev's *The Defeat*, Sholokhov's *And Quiet Flows the Don*. A small box of medicine. Two cooking pots. Five water containers. A long rope. Ball of string. Box of matches. A penknife. A battery-powered lamp. Some Omani currency in a canvas bag.

April 22

Sadat is in Tehran. At 5:15, a broadcast from Cairo commented: "Iran's position has been an estimable one, standing with the Arab nation since 1967. It has taken a pro-Arab position toward Israel, and played an estimable role in the October War." How shameful! They have forgotten how the Shah rushed to save Israel with oil supplies in the first days of fighting. Sadat is showing his hand by pandering to the kings and emperors.

Dahmish has gone to the next village over. He's looking to buy or rent camels. We should rent our camels and then trade them in and rent new ones every time we cross into a new wadi held by a different tribe.

April 25

We rented five she-camels from the Mahra. We will exchange them in Habrout. I suggested we start out immediately so we don't get caught in the rainy season. Dahmish says by the time it starts we will be into the northern foothills at the edge of the Empty Quarter. The tribes will have gone to their caves and there won't be much movement. I threw out the khaki pants and replaced my bras with cloths to wrap around my breasts to flatten them. I put a big mauz around my waist that goes down all the way to my feet. Dahmish smiled mischievously when I sat on the ground and the edge of the mauz came up and exposed my thighs.

April 26

Feeling nauseous, dizzy. Pretty sure I am pregnant.

May 1

The Vietnamese Liberation Front has captured Saigon. The ultimate victory over American imperialism is at the threshold.

I prepped a leather bag big enough to take all my journals. I tied my shirt down at the waist with a leather belt strong enough to make a pocket from the shirt end that will hold the bag. We carried our weapons. I have a 9 mm Makarov. Its magazine holds eight bullets. Not very accurate on short-range targets. We started out at dawn, walking barefoot behind the camels. We walked for 3 hours. The craggy brush cast lines of shadow across the rocks. The camels couldn't seem to walk in a straight line—always curving slightly toward their home villages. We had to herd them back with our canes. Mine is compliant but takes very small steps. Earth became rocky. We all grabbed the reins of our camels. Tied mine to the tail of Dahmish's. Pounding heat. They mounted the camels, but I preferred to keep walking. At night we stopped by a small watering hole. We pitched camp among the rocks and bramble and let loose the camels to drink. We all helped make the rice. Drank tea after eating. We pitched one of the tents for me, but the men prefer to sleep in the open. Decided to preserve the radio by listening to less news. We scheduled our turns at night watch. Then I came back to my notebook.

May 3

Yaarib is absorbed in thought. He isn't talking like he normally does.

I feel urgent desire for Dahmish's body. But we have agreed to be discreet as long as we're with the comrades and Yaarib.

May 4

Habrout. Families from the Mahra tribe gather around shallow wells to water their camel herds near the date palm groves. Women in this area don't wear the hijab. Their clothes are dark blue. One was wearing a silver ring in her nose. Their children ate with us. We spent the evening cleaning our weapons.

I met Dahmish in the evening during his guard duty. I spent the whole time in his embrace.

May 6

We traded out our camels, but we couldn't find the extra one we wanted in case we lost one to accident. Or in case we need to slaughter one of them for food. Finally, we found a black camel that we could buy cheap. Here, people dislike the color black. African migrants have a hard time. It's a young camel with big, long strides, pregnant in its fourth month. It has eight more to go.

I told Dahmish that I think I am pregnant. He scolded me. We were supposed to be careful. To test him, I told him I couldn't give myself an abortion in the desert. He looked shocked. He shouted, "Are you crazy?" Then he hugged and kissed me. I will give birth either in Nizwa, Jebel Akhdar, or Muscat. We will be there in two months . . . maybe three.

May 7

He insisted that I ride my camel. Suddenly showing me keen sensitivity. He lowered it to its knees for me, then he lowered the head of his own camel and got on. He sat cross-legged on the saddle with his feet under him and his weapon resting under his arm parallel to the ground. I couldn't balance myself well enough to sit like him.

May 9

From Habrout, we moved up to the plateau. Several of the Mahra people were watering their camels there. A woman among them wore green face paint. Another had drawn blue and green lines around her face and chin. The green of the plateau was stripped off to reveal the grim surface of the rock.

I didn't mention that I was pregnant to Yaarib. Something makes me feel I shouldn't tell him.

May 10

A group from the Jedad clan challenged us, asking us to pay for the right to pass. We refused. We turned back around and, after a little bit, took a shortcut that runs along the border. That will keep us from having to cross the Qamar hills. We can cross the border at the foothills to their north.

May 12

The two comrades lead the way, followed by Yaarib. He's making a point of keeping to himself. This set-up allows Dahmish and me to stay next to each other. We talk constantly. I find myself able to open up about things I haven't discussed with others. I told him, "We always said that the two forces that drive the revolution were the workers and the peasants. We never stopped to ask who are these workers. We just thought that since we were the vanguard, no one else mattered."

May 13

I told him all about Shehab and Waleed. I kept a careful eye on his expression. That jealous look bothered me.

May 14

We passed by a camel herd tended by an old woman and a young boy. We asked for some milk. She shouted at the boy, "Hurry! Hurry!" He brought some of their finest reserves. "Welcome, welcome to our honored guests," she called out. She gave us a pail of milk. Its cover had brown sand on top. We all sat on the ground with her. We blew the foam off the top and drank. When she asked where we were headed, we answered vaguely, pointing to the mountains. Then she said with fervor, "God bring you victory." Did she already know who we were? Only a year ago, we would have come out and told her we were with the revolution.

She insisted on pouring extra milk into a small jug for us to take. She told us we should mix a little into our drinking water every day to make it tastier. We realized one of our water bottles had a small leak, and she fixed it with a little of the curd.

May 15

We turned right toward the east, following the wadis that wound around the high plains.

Yaarib asked what it was that I wrote every night. I told him I was committed to recording the events of the revolution—and that I had made it a habit to keep a diary since I was back in Beirut. He asked, "Can you remember everything?" I said I tried my best. He thought for a moment, then asked, "Do you remember people's names?" I said that when I can't, I just give people new names. He asked if that might not be dangerous. I didn't answer. Several times this has occurred to me, but in the end I just let it go.

May 16

"Just as soon as we make it there, we will be married," he said to me.

I answered that he was starting to think like the bourgeoisie. "We are already married. We don't need any paper to prove it."

He answered that we were entering a new phase that would require us to follow the old rules. We had to think of the child. He smiled that shrewd little smile of his that I love and said, "According to the traditions of the Kathir clan, if the wedding does not take place before the first month, your father is required to pay for the ceremony and all the preparations."

I told him if we were going to follow these conventions, he would also owe a sizable bride-price that should be paid half to my father and the other half to Yaarib.

May 21

I felt nauseous this morning. My nipples feel inflamed and my thighs are swollen.

May 23

We took two weeks to cross Wadi Ghodon after leaving Habrout. We stopped to rest during the afternoon near a palm orchard harvested by tribes of the Kathir clan every September. Some armed Kathir passed by us, carrying mostly English 303s. But there were also two carrying Russian machine guns. Their leader is an older man—short, with shining eyes, a dangling beard streaked with white. Full of life and moves around lightly. From the Moussan clan. They know Dahmish's family. I just turned away and went to the tent to rest. They didn't seem curious about me at all. I heard Dahmish telling them we were going to the eastern zone. They said fighting there had died down. They avoided saying which side they were on, but that in itself must mean they are with the Sultan. Sunset drew near, so they washed and performed the Maghrib prayer. Each set his weapon in front of him like it was a Quran as they prayed. They all recited the Fatiha, the only sura that many tribes know. They pray at dawn and dusk and skip the other daily prayers. While they pray their heads twist and turn, as they keep an eye out so they aren't surprised by enemies from rival tribes. Right after the prayer, they moved on. They mounted their camels and the leader turned on purpose to give me a look. I felt nervous.

May 24

We went north slowly following Wadi Ghodon, one of 5 dry riverbeds that come down off of the Qarra mountains. We had to pick our way through the piles of fallen rocks from the cliffs that filled the sides of the route.

May 25

We spent the night with the family of one of the comrades from the Kathir clan, settled under two trees without even a tent. Even though they were poor, they slaughtered a goat. The wife, who went without a veil, was very thin and coughed all the time. Their worldly possessions: some pots, a water jug, canteens, some dried sardines scattered on shreds of cloth, a bag made of goatskin half full of flour. I asked them about the Empty Quarter. They looked at me amazed. The comrade said, "You mean the sands?" I asked, "Is it true that there are no people there?" He answered that his cousin had once walked in it for 40 days without seeing anyone. I asked if it was possible to cross it. He said it was possible but only with a guide. Dahmish came at me later. He said that news in the desert travels like lightning. Like when one Arab meets another and the first question is always "What news?" and whatever the answer, everyone listens carefully to know the latest movements of this tribe or that.

May 27

We left our two comrades just as we arrived at Shaiser. We made camp away from the caravan trail. When we were sure they were both gone, I changed my clothes. I became a Bedouin in a flowing black robe. I completely covered my face with a black leather mask with two eyeholes. Went back into my tent while Yaarib and Dahmish left to explore the village. A cave nearby stored ancient statues of birds, and there were relics from an old stone fortress. This place must become a museum once we have won victory. There's also a 15-foot-deep freshwater well among the rocks. We each took a water jug to fill. Men and women come down from the mountains together, singing. They dump their pails of water into a leather trough that the camels rush to drink from. Rows of jars filled with water. By the time our turn came, the well had been emptied. We were taken to another close by. We started up casual conversation with the locals. They surprised us by asking where the rest of our group had gone. They also said they had been expecting us. A group of the Moussan that we had met while crossing Wadi Ghodon had already come by there. Their leader told them all about us. They had been told that we were four men and a woman. No point in disguises here. We told them the other two men felt ill and turned back. We asked which direction the Moussan travelers were heading, and they answered that they had set off toward Wadi Moqshin. That was unsettling news.

I gave my opinion that we needed to change course, that there was something suspicious about the Moussan clan's interest in us. Yaarib said it was normal behavior among the tribes. I said that we should be as cautious as possible. He went back to the argument that by going through Moqshin we gain 150 km. I repeated that government patrols present a danger. Dahmish took my side. Yaarib had to go along with us this time. I said we weren't stepping back from our commitment to cross the desert, only making it tough for anyone who might think about following us. We agreed to announce that we were headed to Moqshin and then change direction as soon as we had left Shaiser behind.

After dinner, I announced that I planned to sleep with Dahmish in the same tent. Yaarib did not seem surprised. Still, he wasn't happy. We arranged our guard duties. Dahmish and I shared a watch. When we lay together, I took off my robe and he covered my belly with kisses. I gave in to sleep with my head on his chest, inhaling the strong odor of his sweat.

May 28

Dahmish has gone to look for a guide. Yaarib is quiet, absorbed in thought. Is he angry with me? Will we pass the night in silence?

Dahmish came back downcast before sunset. No one is willing to cross "the sands." Many groups have lost their way there and perished. Besides, since there's only a few of us, we could get caught between tribal battles or come under attack.

May 29

Yaarib disappeared for the whole day. Dahmish is still looking for camels or guides. We need at least two of them to feel safe.

May 31

Yaarib brought back two guides. An 18-year-old who calls himself Ibn Najam. Long hair, full lips, shiny white teeth. He carries a British rifle. The other is Kheshaat. He is older and bigger. I don't care for his way of running his eyes over our things all the time. He has a Kalashnikov. I asked where he got it. When he laughed and didn't answer, I disliked him even more. We agreed to finish preparations tomorrow and then start out the day after.

June 1

We replenished our supplies. We have enough water for 20 days if we limit ourselves to a quarter of a gallon per day for washing, coffee, and tea, and another quarter gallon per day per person for drinking. Also, taking into account some evaporation and seepage. We decided that we should use only pure sand for washing our hands and cleaning off. We watered the camels one last time. Each drank between 10 and 12 gallons of water. Whenever they stopped drinking, we slapped them on the rump and spoke to them, urging them to drink more. A camel can go without water up to 20 days as long as they can graze, even if for only two or three of those days. We also have a case of dates. Our guides joined us, bringing their two camels and a few supplies.

June 2

We woke before dawn. The morning was harsh, with cold wind infiltrating from the northeast. Could cover our tracks if it continues. We ate the food left from yesterday. Drank tea and bitter coffee. Loaded our camels. When one buckled and spit at us, I wondered if she sensed the journey's danger. We tried to muzzle her, but it was no use. Kheshaat pulled at his camel's headdress and barked, "Down, down." She kneeled on her front legs and he bound her hind legs with her headdress, so she couldn't move while being loaded. He set our coordinates on the compass and called out, "God preserve us." Then we shot out toward the desert. I began to sing our anthem about the hour of liberation, and Dahmish joined in. Suddenly our companions began to belt out an old tribal song: "Our tribes thunder in a booming voice." That brought us back to reality.

Kheshaat pulled up after one hour in front of a pile of rocks on the right side of the path. He pointed to the right and said it was the way to Moqshin. We said we wouldn't go that way, that we intended to head due north instead. I felt nervous—we hadn't agreed with him on this beforehand. To my surprise, he didn't say anything. We walked another seven hours. The road was level and smooth. We ended up near some foliage where we pitched our tents and lit a fire. We brought the camels to their knees in front of it. Kheshaat measured out a pound of flour, added some water, and kneaded it until it rose. He divided it into small portions and laid it out on a cloth. Ibn Najam kept the fire going using the end of his kaffiyeh. He made a grill out of branches and they heated the balls of dough over the fire with it. After turning them over twice, he buried them in the sand under the ashes. We watched the sands and ashes rise before our eyes until they were done. Ibn Najam took them out, cleaned off the sand, and set them to the side to cool. They tasted like sawdust. After the meal, it was my turn to clean the dishes. I rubbed sand all over them. Then we sat around the fire drinking tea. Kheshaat took his tobacco out of his small leather bag that he carried under his shirt, filled his stone pipe, and lit it up. He took two puffs and passed it to his partner. I pulled the saddle down from my camel, carefully watching my feet, fearful of stepping on a scorpion or a desert horned viper. I used the saddlebag as a pillow. Kept the ammunition belt beneath it, the machine gun to my side. I dug a small hole in the corner of the tent to store my bag of journals until the morning.

June 3

Yesterday, the men sat for a long time by the fire talking. Still I heard them get up while I was half asleep and prod the surly camels from their resting place. I finally woke up all the way when one of them began to grind the coffee with a brass pestle. Then one raised his voice in a call to prayer. I stuck my head from the tent and spotted Kheshaat performing ablutions. When I realized what he was doing, rinsing his hands and feet with precious water that we had taken such care to store and transport, I leapt up. I asked him why he didn't use sand like we usually do. He said it was better to pray than to drink. Could barely control my anger.

We walked for two hours. I grew weary, so I pulled at my camel's headdress and lifted my leg to ride. I climbed into the saddle. Spreading my legs across the saddle and riding on top of it like they did was impossible. The borders of the saddle kept scraping against my thighs. After a short march, we could see the sands of the Empty Quarter stretching in front of us like a pink wall. We stood there stunned, regarding the view in awe. Then, slowly, we walked on. The fine-grained sand is easy on the camels, unlike the hard gravelly surface we had been walking on before. In the afternoon we pitched our tents next to some ghafs— trees with long, thick branches and very deep roots.

The camels spread out and started grazing. One suddenly called out a warning. A group of Bedouins was charging toward us on their camels, their rifles at the ready. We grabbed our weapons and spread out on the ground. Kheshaat shouted to us that these could be neither Daham nor Saar because of their saddles, and their clothes proved that they weren't Awamer either. He stood and advanced toward them slowly, his finger on the trigger of his rifle. Suddenly he lowered his rifle as one of them came running toward him. They hugged each other. We stood up and breathed a sigh of relief, then welcomed them and offered them coffee. They said they had looked for us along the way to Moq-shin, having heard in Shaiser that we were going that direction. I exchanged looks with Dahmish.

They wanted to untether one of their camels. She was in heat and was whipping herself with her tail and grinding at her bit until her lips were swollen and a pink foam bubbled up from her mouth. We brought over the young female. They pulled her to her knees and got her ready. One of them sat on the ground next to her to help. The male camel can't find the proper place by itself.

When Dahmish came to my bed that night, he asked, "Do you know what the difference is between humans and camels?"

I said, "We think."

He said camels also think. He turned on top of me and then whispered, "The difference is that male humans know the way. They don't need any help."

I smiled in the darkness, remembering our first time together.

June 4

In the morning, Ibn Najam explained how one recognizes a friendly tribe in a desert meeting: The way they've hung their ammunition belt. How they wear their kaffiyeh—hanging across their chest or tied around their head. The holster of their rifle. Inscriptions on their saddles. Their gait. Their accent. He was loading the camels and his long hair hung over his eyes. He pushed it back with his hand. My gaze came to rest on his bare chest. I had to force myself to look away. Dahmish noticed. Something in my look angered him and he gave me the silent treatment. We wrapped ourselves with robes and covered our faces with kaffiyehs so that only our eyes showed. The extra layer keeps sweat from evaporating and so helps keep the body cool as the wind passes through.

I am watching as the changes transform my body. Life's miracles, and the human species endures.

Nothing is more awe-inspiring than the desert at sunset when the sun coats it with a rose-colored curtain.

June 5

When we went to sleep last night, Dahmish was still angry. He turned his back to me. I stroked him. He turned toward me and gave me a forceful hug. Even in his arms, I could feel his anger. Why do men believe that a woman's feelings have to be limited in direction toward just one man. If something pleases me about another man's body, that doesn't mean passion has overtaken me or that I must sleep with him. Even if I did dare to want it, that would only mean that my body and my feelings are alive, vibrant, and active. I am a vital being. Dahmish must deepen his knowledge in this area. We have enjoyed being together. I wish that there were a pool nearby where we could have a swim. Honestly, Ibn Najam is only adding to the pleasure we are achieving. We have all the time in the world to explore all the hidden secrets of our desires, emotions, and feelings.

Receiving radio broadcasts is pretty hard. Good news from our comrades in Aden: the Suez Canal reopened for international shipping. Not as good: formation of an Egyptian-American commission for development of investment in Egypt made up of Rockefeller, the president of First National Bank in the US, the president of Mobil Oil, the president of Union Carbide, Fuad Sultan, Zaki Hashem, Adel Jezareen, and others.

We discussed Stalin and the personality cult. Yaarib defended Stalin. He argued that he had been able to lead his country during a challenging time, confronting the invasion of Germany and putting in place a socialist infrastructure. I answered that his crimes could not be whitewashed, that he had wiped out hundreds of faithful political and military cadres and instilled fear in the hearts of the common people. He was also responsible for the declarations of the ninth Soviet Congress that any statement that deviated from the party line would be considered traitorous. Dahmish challenged my critique, saying, "What would happen if Fahd, for example, announced publicly that he opposed a decision by the central committee to engage militarily or retreat?" I said that would be a special situation where military logic held sway and that military logic was by its nature dictatorial and not humanistic. I thought the issue went deeper and that it had a truly philosophical dimension. Is it possible for an individual to monopolize the truth? Dialectical thinking says it is not. Science as well. But then how do you convince a fighter to confront death if the cause that he is fighting for can be questioned or has two sides? Is death for a particular cause ever even necessary?

June 6

We happened upon a small underground well. Took two hours to get it clean. The water was coming up smelling of sulfur. When I first put it in my mouth, I spat it out without swallowing. The camels wouldn't drink it. We had to muzzle them and force it down their throats. I wanted badly to rinse the sweaty, sticky film off of me. We filled a water jug, carried it out into the distance. Dahmish unfolded a blanket and held it up to give me privacy. When I took off my clothes, he turned his head away in embarrassment.

I dropped the bag that had my notebooks. I bent over to pick it up and when I stood back up, I noticed Kheshaat watching me carefully. That sharp stare made me uncomfortable. Yaarib suggested I let him keep the notebooks for me at night in case Kheshaat could be thinking the bag has money or something else worth stealing. I told him I am capable of taking care of myself and my journals.

June 7

Just before noon we noticed a dust cloud bearing down on us from our right side. A group of mounted Bedouins came into view riding toward us quickly. We grabbed our weapons. Kheshaat fired two shots in the air. They waved their kaffiyehs in the air, and one of them jumped off his camel and threw some sand up in the air. We knew then it was okay. They halted at a distance and brought their camels to their knees. They walked toward us shouting out traditional greetings, and we answered. They touched their noses in salute, and Kheshaat and Dahmish approached them. I made a large pot of coffee and Dahmish spread out some dates. We drank and ate, and offered them more coffee. Then, the sharing of news began: marriages, divorces, births, and deaths. They asked us about the price of flour in Salalah. An attempt to know more about us? They sat motionless as their dark, active eyes darted in various directions, recording everything. They mentioned they were heading toward Shaiser, but said nothing else about what brought them to that remote spot. We watched them carefully until they had disappeared. Dahmish said that one of them kept looking at me, and he was sure he wasn't from around here. He had noticed his feet. Bedouin feet are not used to going up mountains. They usually curve in because of all the time they spend mounted on camels. Highlanders have feet that are bent a little backwards. Bedouins walk with straight backs, taking short steps. But our friend walked like the highlanders: bent forward, long steps.

June 8

We stopped for a few hours today trying to find something to hunt. We were wanting to celebrate tomorrow on the tenth anniversary of the revolution. Kheshaat tracked down a gazelle with the help of Dahmish. We grilled half of it and stored the rest on top of the tent to protect it from the sands. Ibn Najam cooked the rice.

June 9

The meat was gone when we woke up in the morning. Footprints in the sand of a desert fox gave away the culprit. Kheshaat followed them to the spot where what was left of the meat had been buried. We cleaned it off and boiled it.

I remembered the frankincense tree that we planted in our first camp in central Dhofar, ten years ago now. By now it would be starting to flower. I told Dahmish that it was a symbol of our success. We have truly achieved a part of what we set out to do. But has this really all been to create a better society, or did we do it just for ourselves? We will achieve victory by continuing the struggle with every possible means. I thought of another tree used for incense. Its yield is less and the quality not as good. It is the male tree that does the pollinating, and they call it the billy goat.

We managed to pick up a radio station from Aden. They broadcast statements for their anniversary celebrations from Abu Iyad, George Habash, Nayef Hawatmeh, Ahmad Jabreel, the Lebanese Communist party, the Armenian Brigade, and the Popular Fronts in Bahrain, Eritrea, Ahwaz in western Iran, the Popular Guerrilla Army of Iran, the Western Baluchistan Liberation Front, the Organization of the Iranian Popular Mujahideen, the Popular Front for the Liberation of the Western Sahara, the Cuban Communist party, the Afro-Asian Solidarity Committee, solidarity committees in Europe, Canada, and the United States, and other organizations. I was happy when I heard them read a letter from Michel Kamal on behalf of the Egyptian Communist party entitled "The Revolutionary Program in the Region Is Gaining Strength and the Working Class Is Seizing Its Independence and Achieving Renewal and the Latent Energy of the Arab Revolutionary Movement Prepares the Way for Fundamental Change."

Yaarib started a long discussion. He says that Marx foretold that proletarian revolution would spread outward after starting in the more advanced capitalist countries. Lenin had come up with the idea at the beginning of the October Revolution of proletarian revolution from the margins in order to justify a revolution in an outer periphery of the capitalist system like the economically backward nation of Russia. He raised the question of whether history had proven Lenin to be correct. I said that Trotsky supported the notion of skipping stages and reaffirmed that backward countries need not pass through all the same historical stages that the more advanced nations had already experienced. Instead, they can build on the existing potential of their society and thereby leap over intermediate stages of historical development. I said that I had my doubts about his theory. I could think of dozens of situations we had experienced that showed how hard it was for Dhofari tribal society to accept revolutionary ideas. I gave the concrete example of the Gulf. We had started to hear about massive construction projects raising urban housing in its cities funded by petrodollars. I raised the issue of the negative effects on a culture based in tent dwellings when citizens are suddenly placed in modern buildings, moving because they are compelled to and not from the natural evolution of their lives.

June 10

We stopped to feed the camels with dried plants called *zahra*. Kheshaat says that just a bit of rain will transform these dry plants into leafy green shrubbery with branches covered in flowers a mere month from now. And you can't kill these plants. Their roots are extra long. I thought to myself that revolutions are the same way.

The radio has stopped working. Did someone mess with it? Was it broken on purpose?

June 11

Kheshaat says that he crossed the desert two years ago. He talks of the amazing Orouq of Sheeba in the far northeast. It's a succession of hills made of sand built up from the blowing desert. If we can make it across those, it should take about a month for us to arrive at Liwa Oases, an area of date palms that stretches across a distance that takes two days to cover by camel. He said he is nervous about the camels. They're not in good shape. Probably can't make it across the Orouq. I asked if there is any way around them. He said the only other option would be to go way out west toward Dakaka where the sands are level. I asked what the extra distance would be. I had to listen to a story that took him half an hour about his experience crossing there. He covered his reason for going, the places he stopped, the noblemen he ran into along the way, the name of the camel he rode, its background, its mother's background, the person he bought it from, where it went after the trip, the weapons he carried back then, where he bought them, the food he ate, his fear of running into someone from a rival tribe that held sway in the deeper part of the desert and that trace their heritage back to the Prophet Muhammad and don't bother to pray because they say their lineage excuses them from Islam's obligations. He never even got around to telling me how far it was.

We are heading north toward the sands of Ghanem. I noticed our companions slowing down. Last night, we found some foliage and they let their mounts go and graze—several times. As a result, it took a day to cross a distance we could have made in an hour. I am starting to suspect that they want to draw out the trip. Are they afraid of the inner desert? Or is something else going on?

June 12

I spotted an oryx today for the first time. I never imagined it would be so beautiful. It was the same size as a gazelle, with a full body, two long horns, and a pure white coat. But the most beautiful part was its eyes. I know now why the ancient poets sang their praises. Yaarib wanted to shoot it. I stopped him. We have surely come close to the lands of the Harasis tribe. They have their own language and culture. Qaboos won them to his side three years ago. He made their region into a preserve covering 14,000 square km set aside to keep the oryx from extinction.

I told Dahmish I wanted a daughter with eyes like the oryx. He frowned and didn't speak. Lost in thought for some time. As we unloaded the camels, I asked him what was wrong. No answer.

June 13

I think I understand how Dahmish feels. Basically, he assumes the baby is a boy. It's not that easy to do away with centuries of conditioning to prefer the male.

Girl or boy? I heard once that pregnant women can detect the sex with certainty. If its head sits to the left, it is a boy—to the right, a girl. But when does the head take shape? I am ignorant of this most awe-inspiring process in human existence. I never gave it a thought before. I have not imagined I would be a mother. As soon as I can, I have to get hold of some books on pregnancy, giving birth, nursing, and child-rearing.

We passed by some strange tracks in the sands. I suspected they were very recent footprints that the winds had blown over. Dahmish says a camel made them, but Kheshaat strongly disagreed. He says it's a hyena. Yaarib seemed convinced. I wasn't. Dahmish said that Bedouins can tell what made a footprint with just one glance. The depth of a camel's hoof gives away whether it's carrying a pack or pregnant. From its droppings, one can tell what kind of feed it's been eating and what was the last thing it drank. From that, you can know where it came from and where it is going. Also, where it is right now . . .

I feel anxious.

June 14

We came upon a burgundy-colored sand dune more than 100 meters high. Had to go around because the camels couldn't get over it. The next dune was not as high, so we just went over, but were surprised by a steep incline coming down. The black she-camel hesitated, then suddenly fell over on her side. We ran to it and untied its burden. She rose to her knees with difficulty. Started to wobble. We gathered up strong branches and tied them to her legs as we sat around it shooing away flies. Kheshaat said there was no use, that she would become a new burden now instead of helping with the ones we had. We slaughtered her and cut the meat into strips. Planted some sticks in the ground and hung the strips up to dry. We put the bone marrow inside the stomach, tied it with a leather strap, buried it in the sand, and lit a fire over it.

The desert is overwhelming. The Bedouins believe that its sand dunes are a hiding place for the djinn. Our guides keep circling them and saying over and over, "God alone is eternal."

As we were talking about the Iranian incursion, Dahmish said it was actually their second invasion. The first time, Qaboos's grandfather had managed to repel them. Yaarib said that Qaboos is worried about the Shah's long-term goals. I asked how he knew. He said he has a contact: a cousin of the Sultan who hates the British and leans to the left. He's also a candidate for succession. Yaarib is trying to convince him to accept the revolution's principles. Were he to replace Qaboos, we would then achieve our goals in one fell swoop. I objected to the idea. We do not support palace coups. The revolutionary process comes from below with full participation of the people. It cannot be forced upon them no matter how much more difficult that makes it. He wouldn't argue with me.

Spiders are everywhere. One can grow as long as ten centimeters. They have red, furry legs and don't sting.

June 15

We dug up the camel's stomach. A mix of blood, grease, and floating bones. Kheshaat poured it out into an empty water jug. We sat to eat at sundown, all eating our fill even though the meat smelled rank and was tough.

I spent hours imagining what might happen to my daughter. I always think of the child as a girl. Is this egoism on my part? Will she be a revolutionary like myself? Or will there be no more need for us in a time when we're replaced by specialists and technocrats? I convinced Dahmish of a name that calls to mind revolution: Thaïra for a girl, Thaïr for a boy.

Yaarib's morale is low. Keeps to himself, brings up the rear most of the time. It's like he wants to go back. He complains of stomach pains. Kheshaat told him to try drinking camel urine. He himself washes his hands in it before he milks them. They believe the camel will withhold milk if it is touched with dirty hands or milked into an unclean bucket.

Kheshaat told us about a relative that had been killed by a rival tribe. His father carried the corpse to where he was told the killer lived. At the tent, he found a young boy of 14. The boy tried to escape, but the father caught up to him. The boy stuck his thumbs in his mouth to signal his surrender. He begged forgiveness, but in vain. The father dismounted and unsheathed his dagger. He plunged it into the middle of the boy's chest, who fell down screaming, "Father, O father!" The man stood over him until he stopped breathing.

Kheshaat says our camels are exhausted and we have to exchange them. But how?

June 16

A long debate around the issue of how best to transform a society: reform or revolution? I said we don't have to pit them against each other, although it's certainly true that reform can get bogged down before it gets to the point of foundational change—in other words, revolution. Still, Lenin wrote about the possibility of a society's peaceful transition to socialism. He never said that revolution could only happen through violence and bloody conflict. In fact, bloody conflict, historically speaking, has been the instrument of the reactionaries. Revolution need not equal violence. (Is it really me saying this?) On the other hand, not all reformists are revolutionaries. Many are content with bandages instead of fundamental change. From here, our debate moved to the true nature of the change we are calling for. Yaarib said it was a complete break with the past. I doubt he really believes that. Not everything in the past is bad. Lenin said that the dialectical correction of a dynamic should be distinguished from its total obliteration. Developing and advancing historical dynamics through the dialectic to a new reality can preserve all that is positive in it.

Dahmish asked me about my childhood. I can't remember anything about our home in Oman except when I lost a milk tooth. My father threw it to the sky and cried, "Orb of the sun, take the donkey's tooth and give back the tooth of a gazelle." I remember well our house in Sanaa. An old house in a bourgeois quarter. Peaceful, with plenty of shade from the cypress trees. Each house had its own garden with grapevines and fruit trees—apricot, almond, peach, and pomegranate. Quiet except for the sound of the whistling wheels and ropes coming from the wells. In our garden, there was a square pool with a fountain and a small covered sitting area in front. The servants lived on the ground floor. Women on the middle floor. A wide washroom with square tiles, a wash basin, and a coal furnace to heat the water. The runoff drained through small holes in the front of the house to the gutters in the street. Rooms furnished with mats, shelves lining the walls, and no furniture. Windows offered a view to the outside, with colored glass panes that kept out the bright sunlight.

June 17

Almost out of water. We decided we can start using the bitter water if we mix it with some milk. Also cut in half everyone's daily ration of drinking water. Kheshaat says the rains might come at any time. Then again, they might not come at all. The camels have to drink every two or three days. They can go a week without water as long as there's some shade. I asked him if he thought we might find some foliage and he answered: "God only knows." We heard a wolf's howl at night. It's an awful sound in this barren spot.

June 18

A cool breeze came over the desert, carrying along some sand. The stars are so brilliant. We pulled up some dry roots and lit a fire. After eating, I was still hungry. I asked Dahmish for tea and tried to distract myself by cleaning my gun. Yaarib, meanwhile, honed a new stick for herding the camels. Kheshaat started to probe the hard bottom of his foot with his dagger, searching for a thorn. He never stops chattering. He goes on about how to treat a rash on a camel, tribal invasions, the difference in prices of basic commodities between Sultan Said's time and now, or oil prospecting in the area controlled by the Harasis. Dahmish finally joined in. He told a story about a well-known sheikh of the Kathir clan who was stabbed in the stomach and began to scream "like a woman." His analogy made me mad and I challenged him. I looked into his eyes and thought his mind was filled with a complex of inherited beliefs that would take so long to exorcise. Our first fight.

June 19

We slept apart last night. I could toss and turn all I wanted. I fell into a deep sleep. The grinding of the coffee did not wake me as it usually does. Nor the movement of my companions as they prepared the camels. Once I stuck my head out from under the blankets in the morning I felt something was not right. I jumped up. I called out to Dahmish, who pulled himself up groggily. No sign of Yaarib nor the guides and their camels. All we could see was our two she-camels. Our weapons were gone as well. Where had they gone? Footsteps headed off to the right. Toward Jeddat Harasis? Is there a well in that area that they might be looking for? But if so, why didn't they say anything? And why take the weapons and supplies with them? Even the broken radio. They only forgot some dates and some tea. Are they kidnapping Yaarib? We found no signs of a struggle. But signs of digging at the spots where I put away my notebooks. Someone must have seen me doing it. Luckily, I was too tired to put them away last night, so I just put them under my head, next to my Makarov and the dagger. They didn't come near us. They were probably afraid they might wake us up. They could have captured us. We waited awhile in case they came back, then we thought about following their tracks. But if the wind kicked up and covered them, we would be totally lost. They took all the water except for a little left in my water jug. Did they forget that one or intend to leave it? Should we stay here until they come back? One liter of bitter water is all that's left for us . . . until when?

We stayed in our place until the afternoon and then started to walk. We portioned four dates and a half cup of water per day for each of us. The dates make me more thirsty. At sundown, we pitched our tent behind a sand dune that helped block the cold north wind. I felt engulfed in wilderness as the light receded. The desert stretches out endlessly—and menacingly.

We talked forever about what had happened. I started to remember things about Yaarib. I kept going back over the details of the Mattrah imprisonments. Did it make sense? Buried doubts came back to the surface. Dahmish had his own way of expressing my same thoughts, through a folktale about a warrior-hero from the Nejd. His enemies were looking for him, and his brother-in-law pointed them to his tent. He escaped to a hill and managed to shoot down several of them with his handgun. When he had run out of ammunition, they climbed up to him. He stabbed one with his dagger, and it broke off. Finally, he grabbed their leader around the waist and jumped from a cliff to kill them both. His wife heard that her own brother had betrayed the hero. She hunted him down in the enemy camp and shot him dead.

We agreed to rotate our night watch.

June 20

During my guard duty, I dozed off. When my camel suddenly jumped up, I came to. I touched Dahmish. He leapt to his feet and in one movement was standing erect, gripping his dagger. We stood back to back, looking all around, searching the darkness. We could see nothing. Heard not a sound. We shook the camel's headdress until it knelt back down. As we lay down again, I felt smothered in fear and dread.

We found a wolf's tracks near our tent the next morning. If our normal pace is 5 km per hour, fighting through sand and steep dunes slows us down to one per hour. I tied my camel to the tail of Dahmish's and rode together with him. Many times I had fantasized about making love with him in the saddle to the rhythm of the camel's gait. That was impossible when the others were with us. Now, we found ourselves alone in the universe, holding each other on top of his mount. Even so, I had no desire. By afternoon I felt hungry and nauseous. At night, the dunes seemed even bigger than during the day. Moonlight illuminated the slopes. The shadows contained a horrific blackness. What will happen if we ever come to one that our camels cannot climb? They could collapse at any time if we don't find water soon. We have not made it even halfway across our route. I started to tremble from the cold. I wanted something hot to drink. We pitched the tent. A small fire warmed us. Luckily, they left us some matches. What would happen if one of us became sick, was bitten by a scorpion, or had some other accident?

June 21

I awakened Dahmish before dawn. We raised up the camels as they spit and growled. We ate some dates without bothering to make tea or coffee. Then we headed toward the dunes. As we came closer, the sun started to fire up the sands. My camel gave a ferocious shiver. It refused to keep going. I felt dizzy and jumped off. My legs sank into the sand up to the knee. With great effort, I pulled the camel behind me. My heart started to pound and thirst became excruciating. It was hard to swallow. My ears felt plugged. I tried to make saliva to wet my mouth but only felt like collapsing on the sand.

Dahmish called for me. I said to myself: "We can't make it back, there's no place ahead for us to rest, and I can't climb over even one more of these crushing dunes. It's the end. If we go west, we fall into the hands of the Saudis; to our east are the Harasis. Even if we stay here, we're still vulnerable to whatever tribe or wild animal passes. Not to mention thirst." Dahmish said we could do like the Bedouins: put a stick down the camel's throat and drink its vomit. And we might find a wandering she-camel that still has a bit of milk.

Through all this: the feeling we are being watched persists!?

June 22

I dreamed last night that I opened the icebox in my flat in Beirut and a feral cat jumped out at me.

I poured the two camels half a liter each instead of their normal two liters. They are exhausted and have no food. The sun has been powerful, setting the sands aflame. The soles of my feet have such thick calluses that they cannot be harmed, but the tender skin on the side of the foot feels like it is on fire. I had to mount my camel.

I try to fight off hunger by reading, only to have my mind wander off to think of shawarma, falafel, hummus, lebna, fava beans, and kebab. I remember my father's house in Sanaa. I would wake up early with the predawn call to prayer. As the sun came up, the servants used manure instead of sawdust on the stairs and in the hallways so that it would not scatter while they swept. The strong odor spread everywhere but it was not an awful smell, and the area was quickly swept up with bundles of tree branches. After breakfast, the women took up the housework. They beat the rugs, shined the brass pots with a scrub made of lemon and ashes, washed the laundry, hung it to dry on the balcony and the rooftop, and prepared meals using a brick oven fueled by dung. An older servant kneaded the dough while another made vermicelli. A third sliced the vegetables. A fourth separated the milk and skimmed the top to make yoghurt. My father ate by himself and then went upstairs for a nap. The women then took his place. In the afternoon, the men came for their qat sessions carrying tobacco pouches and baskets of qat. Women went out in the streets, completely covered in Indian cloth of red, blue, and green. Over the face, a sheer black veil adorned with white and red medallions gave them the appearance of some type of insect. The garments had an elegance as they took their relaxed walks, in large shoes with raised heels, although sometimes they would untie them and wrap them around their head.

At midday, we stopped next to a dune. Two Bedouins appeared on a dune in the distance and looked toward us. Our feelings bounced between hope and fear. When Dahmish waved to them, they disappeared. We walked toward them but found no trace. Were they a mirage?

June 23

I woke up this morning craving food. I lay down on my stomach and pressed on it. That made me feel a little warmth and relief. In our house in Sanaa, breakfast consisted of eggs, yoghurt, and bread or pastry with honey and clarified butter. I felt another movement in my stomach. We had a track today that was about like yesterday except that some of the slopes were a bit steeper. We dragged the camels—trembling, hesitant—to the top of a dune. I suddenly heard a strange, low buzzing. It grew intense until it sounded like a plane flying low. The camels pulled at their headdresses in fear and twirled around. We descended a little and the sound stopped. Dahmish reassured me that it was just the sound of layers of sand collapsing on one another.

So far, we've been getting along well. But when I went back to writing in my journal, I found him mocking me. I said that Guevara was keen to record his daily activity up until the last day of his life. That's the only way we know exactly what happened to him, who broke away from him, and who murdered him. A daily journal is the only way to preserve events for a most accurate future study. It's our weapon against treachery and defeat. He said that they will disappear with us, and I answered that we have to preserve them at all costs. Otherwise, who can stand up to Yaarib and keep him from doing even worse damage? I asked him to protect them for me should I fall. Imitating my tone, he asked,

"And if we should both fall?" I looked around at the barren desert. I said I would find a hiding place for them. Suddenly I thought of Rushdy. He might be someone who could do something useful with them. Either him or Amad. I would hope that no one other than them would get their hands on them.

June 24

A daunting sandstorm and thick clouds. Will the rains make it this far, or just to the hills of Dhofar? I wrapped my face in the kaffiyeh. We walked alongside the camels, our morale flagging. What will happen if we don't come to a spot to graze? Neither hunger nor thirst frightens the Bedouins. They can stay on top of a camel for seven days straight without food or water. All they fear is the collapse of their camels. Once that happens, death is certain. But I . . . I feel our camels cannot survive another day.

Chapter Seventeen

SALALAH, 1992

1.

The Indian or Pakistani driver picked me up in the morning. Unable to focus from lack of sleep, I already felt anxious, and was made even more so by the piercing gaze of Abu Ammar staring at my briefcase as he bade me farewell. Only after the car left me in front of the hotel did I start to relax.

I picked up my key and found a message in my box from Khalaf asking me to call. The bed upstairs was calling to me, but when I made it to the room I found the door open, a cleaning cart in the doorway, and a young Indian in a hotel worker's uniform inside. When he caught sight of me, he rushed to leave, stuttering an apology.

I closed the door behind him, hooked the chain latch, threw my briefcase on the bed, and took a long look at the phone. Coffee or tea?

I noticed a bottle of beer on the desk. It seemed nice and cool, with condensation collected on it, and there was a tall glass and an opener next to it. *Beer in the morning? And why not?* I popped off the top, slipped out of my shoes, and raised the glass to my lips. When I opened my eyes again, I was prone on the bed, fully clothed, with a pounding headache.

Struggling to get up, I took off my clothes and tossed them on the floor. I went into the bathroom and filled the tub with warm water, then sank down into it. Although this made me feel slightly better, the headache persisted.

After drying myself off, I stepped out of the bathroom and ordered coffee from room service, repeating myself a few times to make sure they didn't bring juice instead. I had barely put my clothes on before there was a knock at the door, and I opened up for a new Indian waiter carrying my coffee.

When he stepped out, I grabbed my briefcase, opened it, and took out the case that held my medicines. I took out a Panadol, then put the case back where it belonged. But in doing so, I realized the notebook had disappeared.

Immediately, I dumped everything in the briefcase out onto the bed: two pens, a packet of Kleenex, my passport, a pad where I had written telephone numbers, a map of Oman, another of Dhofar specifically, a travel brochure, a piece of frankincense that Khalaf had given me, a piece of scratch paper on which I'd scribbled some observations, the medicine case . . . no notebook.

Trembling, I stood up and started to go through the bed covers. I looked underneath the bed, on the desk, in the drawers, on top of the television and under it. Then I sat on the edge of the bed going back over my movements, starting from the moment I walked into the room. The notebook was in my briefcase when I threw it on the bed. All at once, I thought of the other journals, and I slid the chair to the side, lifted the edge of the carpet—and found no trace of them. I stood in the middle of the room in utter confusion until my eyes settled on the desk. Both the beer bottle and the glass had disappeared, and there was no sign of them in either the wastebasket by the desk or the one in the bathroom.

A dream?

Yet the bottle opener I had used sat there in its place on the desk, bearing witness to the reality.

My gaze shifted between the cracked-open window and the door. The chain by the door hung down—but I remembered latching it as soon as I walked in. I also remembered not unlatching it when I opened the door for the Indian waiter. It was hanging down—and still was.

My headache grew worse and I took another Panadol. I threw myself on the bed and closed my eyes.

At first when the telephone rang, I didn't move. But the ringing continued, and I picked up the receiver. No one answered.

Zayed playing games?

I stayed stretched out staring at the ceiling until I rolled on my side and noticed a folded-up piece of paper stuck under the door. I rushed to the door, opened it quickly, and looked up and down the hallway. No trace of anyone; no movement at all. Whoever put the paper there was long gone.

The work of the new waiter?

I closed the door, picked up the paper, and unfolded it. It was signed by Zayed.

2.

At six o'clock I threw my wool sweater over my shoulders and headed down to the empty lobby. Out in the garden, I walked toward the tennis court, picking up my heels extra high for exercise. A European family with several children was enjoying the swimming pool as I passed. The tennis court was empty, so I kept going, around the fence toward the beach, but then turned right and made a wide loop to avoid going near Fendy's chalet.

At a thicket of thorny bushes, I picked my way through the fallen branches and proceeded carefully to the path that led to the main road.

Of course there were no pedestrians. In fact, the road seemed abandoned. The Sultan's walled-in gardens stretched along the opposite side. Looking off to the right, I estimated the hotel's main entrance to be about 200 meters away. A row of trees between the spot where I stood and the hotel partially blocked my view of the three taxis that were constantly parked in front, as they in turn blocked my view of the door.

I turned left and persevered with the same deliberate steps. A late-model Mercedes suddenly appeared, speeding from the direction of the city. I caught a glimpse of two men in European clothes inside, and I kept my eye on it until it curved toward the driveway leading to the hotel entrance.

Glancing at my watch, I continued on, and when I heard a car engine coming up behind me I fought the urge to turn around, holding to my steady pace until the car caught up to me. It turned out to be a taxi carrying a European man. Another full ten minutes passed before another car came along, this time a taxi full of men in white dishdashas. As it came close they stared at me, surprised and fascinated. I stared right back at them, but they kept staring at me until they had driven off toward the hotel.

Where the fence ended at the street corner, I crossed and followed the sidewalk to the main road. There an old Ford sat, near the next corner alongside Qaboos Street. As I drew near, I inspected the driver. His clothes suggested he was Omani—Dhofari in particular, judging by his complexion and highland features. He followed me with his eyes in the rearview mirror until I pulled up beside him, then he reached out and opened the back door without saying a word.

This violated all the rules. In clandestine political activity, two strangers never meet without a third acting as intermediary. Even in spy novels, strangers always exchange code words—in a totally unbelievable manner—mentioning the weather, for example . . . or one of them wears a red rose in his buttonhole while the other carries a folded newspaper under his arm. If either deviates from the script, that tips the other off that he's not the real contact. Yet here I was just stepping into an unknown car with no script at all.

The moment I closed the door, the driver fired up the engine and took off toward the intersection. A sign indicated that the street turned into a private road. He entered the intersection and turned left onto Qaboos Street. A memory then came to me of being caught in a similar situation exactly thirty-seven years ago. The time was evening; the place, a deserted square on the outskirts of Abbasiya district on the east side of Cairo. A black Fiat with its lights off appeared ahead of me in the dark. Suddenly, its headlights came on, blinding me;

the car crept forward and stopped right next to me. A familiar voice called to me from the driver's seat and I was handed a stack of pamphlets to distribute. Of course, there was no cause for such theatrics—and for that matter, they might even have called more attention to us.

Without saying a word, my driver started at normal speed down the paved road that ran along the coast. We made it as far as the bird sanctuary before I started to think that we were headed toward Salem's friend—the one full of all kinds of stories and tall tales. But instead of proceeding straight ahead, he turned first right, then left, and after a while the road started to ascend, and I realized we were headed toward the hills.

I spoke for the first time. "Where to?"

He didn't answer, didn't even turn toward me; my question just hung there in the air. So I reverted to silence.

Light faded, and the scents of the countryside proliferated. We overtook tractors in the road as we drove through villages. I sat back and decided to just enjoy the fresh breeze. After a few more kilometers we made a sharp turn to the right onto a bumpy path and our headlights shined onto a steep incline. Slowly at first, we edged our way up before settling back into a normal speed. At a sharp bend, we maneuvered outside to the widest turn possible. I could only trust my driver's skill to keep us going fast enough to continue the climb without spilling backward. By the time we made it onto the plateau, I wanted to congratulate him.

"Great job," I said.

Once again, he didn't answer.

Discerning or deaf?

We continued slowly until finally the car stopped. He set the handbrake and leaned his elbows on the steering wheel, staring out in front of him. Then he switched off the headlights, cut the engine, opened the driver's door, and stepped out. Without saying a word to me, he crossed the way to a clump of trees and disappeared behind them. I guessed he might need to relieve himself, so I waited a few minutes. The minutes became a quarter hour and then half an hour without him reappearing. I opened my door, stepped out, and walked around the car. The keys were in the ignition. I reached out, honked the horn, and looked around. I honked again, holding the horn down this time, then I stepped back and waited.

Finally, tired of waiting, I opened the door and sat in the driver's seat. I made sure the car was in neutral and reached for the ignition.

Whenever I get behind the wheel, I always put it in neutral and check that the headlights are working. When the lights came on, they shined out into open space, stretching as far as I could see. I leaned this way and that to try to see anything in the light before I released the handbrake.

That is what saved my life.

My hand trembled as I opened the door and stepped out of the car. I stood there and considered the abyss that stretched beyond the cliff at the very edge of which the front wheel had stopped.

Circling around the car carefully, I honked the horn again. I thought, "I'm calling the driver back, but what am I supposed to say to him? 'Hey. You. Captain.'" Or maybe an American *hiya*, like they say in their movies. I thought for a moment about trying to drive the car in reverse, but quickly abandoned that idea. It would mean releasing the parking brake, in which case the car might slide forward before I could completely control it.

I shut down the engine and turned off the headlights. I left the keys in the ignition and closed the door. Looking around, I could not make out any landmarks in the total darkness. A cold wave passed through me, and I put my sweater over my shoulders. A glare bouncing off the car helped me find the driver's footprints heading into a thicket where bushes became trees and any trace of light vanished. I groped through the shrubbery, enduring an assault by a swarm of mosquitoes. Fresh scents came out from the trees, which were so thick their branches almost grabbed me. Obscure noises that were impossible to distinguish circled around me. I tried to remember the different animals that had come up in Warda's journals. The hyena that Abu Ammar had wanted to feed me came to mind. I walked faster, looking around me as I went. Fatigue came on and I rested against a tree trunk, but moved on before getting settled, thinking of the great tree snake. I didn't dare plop down in the thick grass. I briefly considered going back to the car, but realized I wouldn't be able to find my way back . . . and even if I could, what then? Sleep until morning? How could I know it wouldn't slide off into the abyss before I realized what was happening?

I decided to keep walking until I made it to the main road—or a village, or a remote camp. I came to a hill and started to climb. Finally, a faint light appeared in the distance that I could head toward. But as I followed the road up and down, the distance between myself and the light seemed to stay the same. I felt so tired that I stopped, at which point I realized that the light had moved over to my left, having been on my right at the start. At that point I understood that I'd gotten turned in a complete circle.

I felt thirsty and wished I might run into a highlander who would offer me fresh milk. Then I thought of food, and the trees whose leaves could provide nourishment, although one also had to be careful to avoid poisonous ones.

Did Warda pass by here?

I managed to shuffle up to another plateau where the smell of animal dung came drifting. I came to stone houses next to livestock pens. They were empty, so I kept walking through piles of hay that came up to my waist until I made it to a grove of gigantic trees. A small abandoned hut came into view, and I went inside. The floor and walls were bare, and it was generally devoid of any sign of life. There were no ashes in the oven nor remnants of cooking fat from goat or camel. Even so, I had to rest there for a while.

Something jumped up and hit me in the head, making me stagger back and almost fall. In the faint moon glow nothing was visible, but I sensed movement in a corner and listened anxiously. A mouse or something similar? What if it was a scorpion or the great snake itself, waiting for a chance to strike and move on? I tried to remember what I had learned about insects and reptiles and how one deals with them, but my brain was totally locked.

I felt so exhausted that I had to sit. I plopped down in the middle of the hut to stay away from the walls. A breeze blew in and I wrapped myself in my sweater and lay down on my side. I longed for a steamy hot cup of tea. Then the mosquitoes arrived to attack my face and hands. I tried to amuse myself by randomly slapping at them, but it did no good. Then I felt a sharp bite under my clothes. Fleas? My nerves frayed as I imagined something crawling over me. Trying to think of anything else, I remembered Waad and our night together.

Playing a role in a movie or searching for a father figure?

The next thing I knew, bird calls stirred me. Dawn had arrived, and I found myself curled up next to the wall to keep warm. I collected myself and managed to stand. Every part of my body hurt, especially my back. Brightly colored birds greeted me as I stepped outside. I was on the top of a plateau covered in wild verdure, through which I could see some cattle in the distance. I decided to walk toward them, but in the light of day I realized a deep valley lay between us. I looked around but couldn't find any sign of the sea that Warda had used to orient herself as she moved through the mountains.

Did she pass by here?

I decided to keep walking, sticking to downward paths as a way to stay headed toward the coast. I threw one last glance at the hills and started my journey back.

Chapter Eighteen

MUSCAT, DECEMBER 1992–JANUARY 1993

1.

"Back to her old ways," I said.

I was commenting on Shafiqa's hijab as she greeted me. She waved her hand as if batting away the remark and said, "Look how observant you are."

I set my suitcase down next to the door and asked, "What's the story?"

"There's no story."

Piano music drifted in. I nodded to the next room and said, "Beethoven is at work?" But Shafiqa was absorbed in putting dinner on the table. Leaving her to it, I headed to the bathroom and washed up.

"What's going on?" I asked when I returned.

"Did you hear what happened to Sarah?" she said.

"Sarah who?"

"The Filipina maid who shot her master thirty-four times when he tried to rape her. The court had condemned her to seven years in prison and blood money to be paid to the dead man's family."

"And the dead man's son appealed, asking that she be condemned to death."

"Right. And now the appeals court has gone along with it and given her the death penalty."

"What's their justification?"

"No clear evidence of rape."

"Wasn't there a medical report?"

"Yes, but the new court considered it doubtful because the dead man was eighty-five."

"And will they really execute her?"

"God knows."

The music stopped and was replaced by the sound of Fathy calling to me. I stepped over to his room and pushed open the door to find him sitting at the piano. He started playing again and looked at me as though asking my opinion. Then he sat back and said, "I have decided to use the structure of the sonata as my model. Of course, you don't understand, sir. For your information, the sonata is the most elegant of musical genres."

I nodded to acknowledge the sonata's elegance. He continued without noting my response: "The symphony I am composing is visual in nature. It has no connection to the classical form. Not even modern classical. It would be impossible to follow the model of, for example, a Stravinsky, Schoenberg, or Bartók, with their highly acoustic approach. Nor would I be able to use their dissonant melodies. Even so, I did try to employ polyphony in some of the movements."

My mind wandered. I thought of Waad and her lovely breasts. Coming to, I realized the room was silent. His mind had also wandered.

I pointed toward the living room and asked, "What's made her go back to the dark ages?"

"The Lord works in mysterious ways." He ran his finger quickly over the keys of the piano, then added, "The director at the radio station told her yesterday that they won't be renewing her contract."

"Why?"

His eyes flickered in confusion before settling on my face. I detected in his look a hint of accusation, and I cringed.

"Work requirements are tough around here," he said. "It's not easy to find new work quickly, and it's even harder after the Gulf War. I still have a year to go, with an option to extend to two years. She would either go back to Egypt by herself or stay here next to me without work. Neither option is good."

"Why?"

"Neither of us is capable of living alone, but if she stays without work, she'll go crazy. You know her. I would go crazy too, for that matter. Plus, we have to keep making payments on our beach house on the northern coast and Heba's apartment."

He let out a laugh, but I didn't join in.

"What will you do?"

"I'll go back to Fendy. If he can't help me, I'll try the Sultan himself. The problem is what price he might exact."

2.

There was nothing too eye-catching in the Omani morning paper. One of the ministers announced that Oman would conduct the first census in its history at the end of the year. Current estimates were that the population would turn out to be around two million—a quarter of whom are foreign nationals. At the bottom of the page, there was an article about Israel moving 415 Palestinians back to the Lebanese border nine days ago. They were still in tents, and snow had covered them. The Lebanese prime minister had refused to treat the sick and the wounded in Lebanese hospitals, stating that the responsibility for treatment should fall to Israel. Both Arafat and Hamas supported the PM's position, arguing that the Palestinians should stay where they are until they can return to their homeland.

Fathy stuck his head around the door and signaled for me to wait a bit because he hadn't quite finished his work. I turned to Salem, who was putting a tape into a VCR. "I'll show you an Omani dance that's just like your *zar* that Egyptian mystics do," he said. "They gather in the central square of the village with all the people who've come down with infections and want to be cured."

He pushed the play button and a row of men appeared on the screen next to some women sitting with their heads wrapped in sheer black scarves. One carried a large conga drum that covered half his body, and another held across his knee a small, elongated drum that he beat with both hands from either side. The two drummers circled the square while the row of men approached the women, inviting them to dance.

He pressed fast forward, then paused the tape. "Here's another dance you might be interested in. It starts with a poet standing and reciting a poem where every line starts with the next letter of the alphabet, starting with *aleph* in the first line and going all the way through to the *ya'* at the end of the alphabet in the last line."

"He composes it himself?"

"Yes, of course. It's all about the poet's skills."

A large circle of men with raised swords appeared on the screen. The swords had thin blades and the men fell in behind one whose sword was raised in his right hand. He recited his poem as they marched, and at each stopping point he shook his sword ostentatiously while his followers chanted: "O king! May God preserve thee," drawing out the word *king* for emphasis.

The accent and local dialect made it hard for me to follow the poem, so Salem repeated for me what he was saying: "*Aleph* starts the word for the creation of speech. *Ba'* is the word for remembrance of God. *Tha'*, for revolution and the good fight. *Jeem*, wonderment in time and space. *Kha,'* creation of the people of all nations. *Dal*, sustenance of home and hearth. *Za'*, time that shapes daily life. *Sin*, the flash of the blades. *Shin*, the spread of knowledge and wisdom. *Waw*, a *warda* rose for all time."

He stopped the tape before going on. "Fendy is going to invite you to a New Year's Eve get-together."

"You've never really told me about him."

"You haven't asked," he said. He was silent for a bit, then went on: "Do you remember back in 1977 when a congressional investigation in the United States revealed that some prominent figures in the region, like King Hussein of Jordan, had worked in the service of the CIA? There was an oil distribution company called Ashland Oil whose president, Atkins, revealed to congressional investigators that it had operated as a CIA front in various countries, including Iran. After the Shah fell Ashland started looking for deals in the Arab world, and a Libyan came into the picture named Yehya Amer. Alongside him was an unnamed Canadian with strong contacts in Muscat, and a third figure, who happened to be our friend. The result was a contract to buy Omani oil at a rate of twenty thousand barrels a day. The payoff to the Libyan for the deal was in the range of 5 million dollars. So just imagine what our friend took home."

"That's normal," I said.

I flipped through the pages of the newspaper until I came to a special page devoted to poetry. At the top there was a proverb written in calligraphic script: "If the king of kings showers favor, do not ask why."

"Rumors had circulated that he might be the next PM," Salem continued, "but now it sounds like it will be the Sultan's cousin instead. If that comes to pass, Fendy will be pushed aside because the new candidate is a personal friend of Harith Bin Ayesha, who is the sworn enemy of our friend."

"Who is that?"

"Bin Ayesha? He's an advisor to the Sultan who works behind the scenes."

He put a new tape in the machine and, without raising his eyes, asked, "Did you hear what happened after you left Salalah?"

"What happened?"

"They found a body in the nearby mountains. An Omani of African descent."

I tried hard to show no sign of emotion. "Murdered?"

"He seemed to have fallen from a high place. Maybe lost his balance or something."

After a moment I asked, "Any news about Zakariya?"

Without looking up, he answered, "No."

"There are so many things I don't understand," I said.

He smiled and repeated my words back to me: "That's normal."

3.

Based on what I had seen and heard more than on his tendency to show off his wealth, I had certain expectations about what I would find in Fendy's house on New Year's Eve: carpeting, ceiling fans, central air conditioning, colored mats, a Coleman refrigerator, a coffee roaster, a teapot, a juice pitcher, and a special seating area for men only, or at best a curtained-off area to the side for women. Thus, I was not ready for what I actually found.

We stood before an iron gate in the middle of a high stone fence. The Indian servant opened up for us and escorted us over a walkway paved with fine marble that led to a huge garage. From there, we took a different walkway that passed by a large swimming pool. The Indian stopped in front of a thick wooden door, which he opened with a remote device. We entered a crowded hallway lined with shelves holding antiques and with enormous chandeliers hanging over-head, then climbed the stairs to the second floor before coming to a giant hall full of plush leather furniture.

I stepped over a thick layer of oriental rugs and sat in one of the chairs. Sha-fiqa sat next to Fathy on an adjoining couch. She softly kicked at the rugs, whis-pering, "Tabrizi." She took out the chic eyeglasses that she brought especially for the occasion and put them on to get a better look at the opulence hanging over us, then said in the same whisper: "Those are Czech."

She moved her gaze to the various corners of the hall, her face filling with expressions of admiration and wonder. In truth, she had refined taste when it came to clothing, furniture, art, and interior design. She even had a collection of valuable paintings in her house in Cairo. I followed her lead and looked around, not doubting for a moment the elegance and expense of the pieces sur-rounding us. But unlike her, I did not find them beautiful. It was all too much.

A Filipina servant with a wide frame and a confident gait appeared in the doorway and announced in broken English that Madame would be down in a few minutes.

A wooden box next to me held a cluster of art objects. I took the opportunity to practice a ritual that I perform at times when I want to polish my skills as a writer. This involves picking up objects and searching for the perfect words that might best name or describe them. I did okay with a small metal horse, even though I couldn't tell if it was brass or gold. It was about the size of a fist. There were silver plates and antiques with Chinese or Japanese inscriptions. The one thing I couldn't identify at all in terms of its materials and artisanship was a small piece carefully preserved inside a glass box.

The appearance of our host and his wife rescued me from my quandary. He wore a dark-colored dishdasha that combined with a dark skullcap to highlight the whiteness of his face. His wife was darker—an elegant woman in her thirties with a modern look and fashionable clothing. She had a straight posture and wore a beautiful locally made black dress with a floral pattern that went down just past her knees.

The gathering was semifamilial, with just ourselves and a younger sister of the wife as guests. She seemed to be around twenty-five and wore jeans. She had studied engineering and worked for a foreign company. Then another woman joined us—an Iraqi in her late twenties named Suad, the daughter of a friend of Fendy's, who worked in an oil company job that our host had arranged for her. She wore a light, colorful dress with short sleeves, the top part consisting of two sections that connected without any buttons or clips to hold her ample breasts in place.

Khadija, Fendy's wife, asked what we would like to drink. Shafiqa immediately requested orange juice. I asked hesitantly what was available, and Khadija said, "We have everything."

"Have a gin and tonic if you want something stiff," said her husband.

Shafiqa threw a harsh look at Fathy, who hesitated. I came to his rescue by saying, "Have a whiskey. Shafiqa can do the driving."

He nodded his assent while giving her a sideways glance. Our hosts joined him in his selection, while the two younger women sided with Shafiqa.

The Filipina forewoman brought us a small table of hors d'oeuvres—Iranian pistachios, green olives, boiled shrimp, and Syrian sunflower seeds. Then she came around with the drinks she had made at the bar off to the side.

I picked up my drink, which was adorned with a slice of key lime hanging on the glass, and I stirred the contents with a plastic stir stick. As I raised it to my lips I gave Shafiqa a malicious look over the edge of the glass.

Feeling responsible for getting some cocktail chatter started, I commented on how impressive the house was. That started the hosts explaining its special features—how it overlooks the sea on one side and the mountains on the other, and so forth. Once we exhausted that topic, I asked Fendy how he starts his day. He answered with delight: "First thing after getting up, I have a glass of spring water imported from Switzerland to rinse my kidneys, then I do some Swedish calisthenics in my private gym, followed by a little relaxing in the Jacuzzi. Then ten minutes in the sauna, and ten more in the steam bath. After that, a light massage and a cold shower. I then put on a cotton robe and drink a cup of fresh orange juice. After that, I relax awhile in the barber chair as two of my Filipino servants give me a shave, a manicure, and a facial massage."

This summary caused him somehow to remember his origins: "My father was a fisherman from Batinah. I don't remember my mother because she died of tuberculosis when I was still a small child. We lived in a hut made of palm fronds. Father would wake me up before dawn and give me some dates and a ladleful of water, then I followed him to the beach and helped him shove his skiff out into the sea. At night we ate boiled fish left over from the morning's catch. Then my father became sick and couldn't go out anymore, so he stayed home and worked his small garden, which I helped out with instead. I got up early and went out to the garden and worked our skinny little ox to fill the irrigation tank."

I broke in: "When did you find time to go to school?"

"School? No one in my village knew how to read or write. Children ran around barefoot and almost naked. No doctor, no hospital. Everyone died young because of malnutrition and disease. The things we've seen! My father had to pawn his garden to a merchant who loaned us two hundred piasters, but he didn't even have time to make all the payments before he, too, died of tuberculosis. I had a hard time selling the watermelons, cucumbers, and parsley that I picked from it. There was no other way except to sell the garden. The pawnbroker offered one hundred piasters and deducted the outstanding debt, leaving me with twenty piasters. An official wrote up a deed of ownership transfer and charged ten piasters."

My glass was empty; I signaled to the Filipina standing at the doorway to refill it.

He went on: "Some other young men managed to slip into Saudi Arabia and Kuwait. We heard there were schools there and hospitals that treated patients for free. I snuck off one night without telling anyone, trying to avoid the local *wali* because the government jailed anyone they found trying to run away. Hiding my small bit of money in a pouch under my clothes, I headed for the border, and when I made it to Shinas I met a friend who had an extra donkey. He said he could get me a passport from Fujaira, so we went there and spent the night on the outskirts, then rode in with the call to prayer at dawn. We took refuge in a mosque and sold our donkeys, using the money to buy two passports for two hundred rupees. They called them passports, but they were just pieces of paper with the insignia of the Fujaira emirate. Then we bought tickets on the ferry that came from India and continued toward Kuwait and Basra. It took a week, but we did make it to Kuwait. There we saw for the first time a real city with tall buildings, bustling crowds of people, and cars that sped through the streets at an insane speed. The people spoke with accents that we didn't understand. In Ahmadi, we asked where the Omanis lived. Finally we found a countryman who took us in."

He raised his glass and smiled. "I still remember the taste of the fresh orange juice that he offered us—my first taste of it in my life. He offered us meat as well, something we never had in our village unless it was gifted to us at Eid al-Adha. He told us there were sixty thousand Omanis there doing menial work, like digging ditches or sweeping streets. The lucky ones found jobs with the oil companies. Only rarely would you find someone from Hadhramaut, Palestine, or Egypt in a menial job. Those people had education and could get jobs as engineers or doctors or find work in government offices or international firms. They lived in nice houses and drove cars."

I noticed that the two women — Khula, the sister-in-law, and Suad — were listening in silence, and I guessed they might have heard this story so often they'd memorized it. Soon they slipped into a womanly conversation with Shafiqa. Khadija, meanwhile, stayed attentive to her husband, even though she too must have heard the story often.

The young man found work in an oil company. He took a night class offered by literacy advocates with forty other young Omanis. A long-suffering Egyptian man taught them as though he were doing a service to the nation. After seven years, he earned a high school equivalence degree. During that time he got used to wearing sandals. But he never had to put up with the special mistreatment and abuse reserved for his countrymen, summed up in the phrase "an Omani welcome." He finagled introductions at the Iraqi embassy by way of Baathist friends and managed to travel to Baghdad for university studies in economics. He returned to Kuwait after graduating and signed on with an oil company. Then Qaboos took power, and he responded to the new sultan's call asking Omanis abroad to come home and contribute to building the country.

He spoke simply, with no self-consciousness, enjoying his comprehensive review. I thought he might go on forever, but his wife's turn came and I finally understood the secret of her patience.

"I was the first woman to enroll in the School of Education at Sultan Qaboos University. From the beginning, I really liked business. My father had an import company, and I asked if I could work with him afternoons. He said yes, thinking it was a phase I was going through that would end soon, but once I graduated I made myself a place in the company. At first I worked under a British manager, then I took over from him. I was a quiet young woman, but my life changed once I realized that I had talents I'd never known about. I managed to put together a deal for an American-style mall funded by a Kuwaiti investment of five million riyals. Next door, we set up a hotel and a hospital with a cancer ward that treated children."

She could see I was impressed, and her pride swelled as she spoke. "Omani women have a long history of working in the public sphere. Have you heard of a woman named Ghalia Bint Nasir who ruled Oman during the fifteenth century? She also commanded the army and led them to victories in wars."

Her husband broke in: "The status of women is improving rapidly. Just the day before yesterday the Oman Commercial Bank announced it would set up services exclusively for women."

My face must have given something away because he quickly added: "That's just the beginning. We have to start slow because of strong resistance from sheikhs and traditional elements in our society."

Our talk was cut off by a beautiful, dark-skinned girl who might have been about six. She broke into the room and threw herself into the embrace of Khadija, urgently pulling at her arms. Khadija asked what she wanted, and the girl, looking adorable, muttered something under her breath.

"Why don't you watch a Tom and Jerry cartoon?"

"Mama, I'm tired of them!"

"Okay. What about Pink Panther, then?"

"That's no good."

"We have Ninja Turtle tapes."

"I don't like it."

"Play with your toy trains then."

This last suggestion met with no resistance, so the mother called out, "Melissa!" A Filipina woman of about twenty with a full face appeared right away, wearing a blouse, jeans, and Reebok sneakers. The mother gently asked her to bring in the toy train, then she turned and said to us, "Melissa is my private servant. She's been with us for a month and she's doing wonderfully."

I asked Fendy about the Filipino man-servant with the earring. He watched Melissa as he answered: "We fired him."

Khadija explained, "On his day off, he came back drunk and an hour late. The next morning we put him on a plane back to his country."

A cute two-year-old boy appeared in the doorway sucking his thumb. Fendy's face lit up as he called out, "Bush! Come here." But the child was shy, and instead of running to his father he turned and reached up for his Indian or Sri Lankan nanny, who bent down to pick him up.

Fendy looked at me: "We had him right at the end of the war to liberate Kuwait, so we named him after the American president."

Melissa set an electric train car on the floor near the doorway and got down on her knees to turn it on. Her back was to us and I noticed that Fendy's eyes were fixed on her bottom. I looked at his wife and found her eyes locked in the same place.

The woman finished turning on the train and it ran off along the track, crossing bridges and passing stations. She lay on the ground next to the girl and played with her for a while, until suddenly she seemed to notice her master and mistress and sat up. As she started to rise, her mistress waved her over; she went next to her chair and sat cross-legged on the floor, her head level with the arm rest.

Khadija rested her hand on Melissa's head and stroked her hair as she started telling Shafiqa stories of her trips to the British capital. I saw that Shafiqa was mesmerized. It was not the sights and sounds of London that enraptured her, however, but rather the nonchalance with which Khadija described her lack of enjoyment: "Breakfast in the morning, then the dentist all afternoon. After that, looking for a restaurant where no one will bother or harass me. I have to hire a taxi but pass several by until I find one that gives me special treatment when I get in. After all that, back to the apartment to watch television by myself."

Fendy, perhaps guessing the question Shafiqa wanted to ask, said, "I prefer Singapore. It's two hours closer than London."

The Filipina announced that the food was ready and we all stood. Suad let out a gasp as, despite her hurried attempt at adjustment, her breasts came jumping out the top of her dress. Khula ran off to look for some safety pins to fasten her friend's top more securely. We moved to the next room, where a large rectangular table was covered by a spread that included meats, fish, poultry, grilled vegetables, stuffed vegetables, and more. We filled our plates, then went back to our places and sat eating silently while some strange light music played in the background.

By the time we were done, the hour was approaching midnight. We all exchanged best wishes and shook hands, except for Suad, whose hands never left her chest area. Fendy suggested that we have some tea in another room.

We followed him to a wide room set up as a traditional salon, with broad stuffed pillows on the ground and paintings with oriental motifs on the walls. Completing the picture was a wooden platform at the end of the room surrounded by sheer curtains, like a stage where a bridal couple would sit. Fendy slid in and, using a pillow, propped himself on his right elbow while bending his left leg. He invited me to sit next to him, so I lay down as well, propped up on both elbows with my legs stretched out in front of me.

Shafiqa sat down delicately, making an effort to fold her legs. Suad sat next to her, pulling Khula into her lap. Khula leaned toward Shafiqa and said, "Just barely touch her dress and you'll be able to see her nipples."

Tea came in on silver trays, and Khadija played background music on a cassette player: first a Tunisian singer named Bushnaq, then Warda, the Algerian songstress, singing "I Have Fun with You."

"Come on, Suad," she cheered. She started clapping, and we all joined in with gusto. Suad played along a little, but then begged off because of her dress, which was starting to come undone again. Khadija offered her a different dress, but ended up bringing metal clips instead, as well as a silk dancer's scarf to wrap around her middle. Suad finally gave in, getting up and walking toward the middle of the room, her hand never leaving her bosom. She started to shake to Warda's song as she looked at the ground bashfully. In no time, she was caught up in her dance and began to move her waist skillfully, completely forgetting the issue of her chest; she let her hands drop, barely noticing when a clip popped off and the tops of her breasts were exposed.

Fendy stood up and said to me, "Come over here. I want to show you something."

We left the room and climbed some steps up to the fourth floor, where we entered a room that was arranged as an elegant office, its walls adorned with rows of books set in glass-fronted bookcases. In the middle of the room was a big-screen TV and a video player. Waving for me to sit down on the nearest couch, he opened one of the bookcases and took out a video cassette, which he inserted in the player; he then sat down next to me and pressed play on the remote.

There were no opening credits or even a title. A rather shaky image occupied the screen, showing a long rectangular table with three people sitting together near one end of it. One was short, stocky, and bald with a nervous face. As the camera turned from him to the door, some other men entered carrying leather briefcases, and they spread out around the table. They all had Arab, or at least Middle Eastern, facial features. There was a nervous air in the room, but they also seemed to have a personal connection of some kind. Then an armed guard wielding a machine gun and carrying a briefcase walked in and went to the head of the table. Another guard behind him brought in a thermos filled with tea. The first armed man placed his briefcase on the floor next to the empty chair at the head of the table, while the second guard set the thermos down in front of him. Then, after taking one step toward the door, the first guard turned suddenly, raised his weapon, aimed it at the back of the bald man, and fired down at him. The second guard started firing as the other men fled under the table, pulling out their handguns and firing at the guards.

The film came to an end as suddenly as it had started; the whole thing was over in a matter of minutes. I stared at the screen like an imbecile. *A scene from some mafia movie? A training film for a terrorist operation?* As I replayed in my head what I had seen, I decided that it had the feel of a scene acted out rather than being a recording of a real event.

"You don't know what it is?" he asked.

I shook my head no.

"Have you ever heard of the politburo massacre in the People's Democratic Republic of Yemen?" While I was still trying to remember my history, he said, "Aden 1986."

I found myself excavating deep memories as he continued: "You've forgotten, or you're acting as though you have? An intellectual like yourself should know all about such a famous act of bloodshed in our local history."

"But who videotaped it? A hidden camera?"

He laughed without answering, turned off the video player, and stood. Ejecting the cassette, he put it back in its place in the bookcase and locked the case with a key. Then he opened a safe next to the case, took out three notebooks, and handed them to me, saying, "See if reading this will refresh your memory." As I took them, he added, "Did you ever find your two friends?"

Are there no secrets in this country?

I answered no.

As he led me to the door he said, "I might be able to help you. We could make a little deal. What do you think?"

He turned to me and put his hand on my arm. I looked at him in confusion.

"I don't have any experience with commercial transactions," I said.

He laughed. "The matter doesn't require any experience. There's just one principle in this business. It's called give and take."

Will you take my heart and soul—or are you after the notebooks that I have lost for good?

He turned toward the stairs and started down them, with me following. We found Shafiqa and Fathy standing somewhat tensely, as though they wanted to leave. The lord of the manor and his mistress accompanied us to the front door.

Shafiqa got behind the wheel and drove skillfully through the empty streets while commenting on the evening. "Those poor girls. Do you know what Khadija's sister said to me? She asked if I took off my glasses when I . . . when I . . ."

To toy with her, I said, "When you do it?"

"Watch your tongue. You've had way too much to drink."

She smoldered in silence and doubled her speed, but had to slow again when we approached a square where small groups of Indians had gathered. It was two o'clock in the morning by then, and I asked, "What's going on? Is it a demonstration?"

Fathy answered: "Nothing like that. They just celebrate out in public, where they don't have to spend money on a drink as they would in a cafe. Most only make about fifty riyals, and they try to live as cheaply as possible so they can send money home to their family." After a pause, he added, "Poor guys. They live forty to a room and they have no rights here, even if they've been here for fifty years. At any moment, they might find themselves on a flight home."

Shafiqa decided to speak up again. "Did you hear what the Indian ambassador to the Emirates said when he was asked about the difficulty of communication between Arabs and Indians? He said there was no real problem, since 60 percent of the population here is fluent in Urdu."

A few minutes later, her thoughts returned to the party. "Melissa seems very anxious and fidgety. I wanted to calm her down, so I told her that Madame is very fond of her. Know what she said?"

Fathy had been well trained in his wife's style of conversation. He said the words she was waiting for: "No. What did she say?"

"She asked, 'And what makes you think Madame is so fond of me?' The poor thing is in love with a boy from her country who lives here in Muscat, and her mistress forbids her to see him. She says she dreams of the day when she can return to her country. She's astounded by all the wealth here. She went once with Fendy's family to a wedding at one of the big hotels that cost 160,000 riyals. The singer alone cost 30,000. She asked me, 'If you had all that money, would you spend it on that?'"

I took a turn and asked her, "That's a good one—how *would* you spend your money if you had that much?"

Her voice had a dreamlike quality: "I would buy a one-way ticket to London."

4.

I woke up abruptly, drenched in sweat, flipped on the nearest light switch, and drank from a glass of water on the nightstand next to the bed. I then got up and went to the window, setting my sights on the wild, huddling mountains in the distance. That bloody scene came back to me. It had played out in just a few minutes but had resulted in a deep, historical wound that festered for years.

Stepping away and sitting on the couch, I picked up one of the notebooks that Fendy had given me, which I had been reading obsessively for the past four days. They presented various and conflicting points of view, but they also stirred up suppressed memories, filling in as they did so the general outlines of events around the scene of the massacre.

From the beginning, the PDRY government in Aden had faced economic challenges. Still, the leadership believed in the ability of their revolutionary path to bring about a profound change on the Arabian Peninsula. That's why they supported the various revolutionary movements—especially the one in Dhofar. Therefore, it must have been a particularly hard blow when Sultan Qaboos announced to a throng of fifty thousand Omanis that the resistance had been wiped out on December 11, 1975. After that came the announcement of a general amnesty that led to two thousand revolutionaries surrendering themselves in exchange for "gifts" from the Sultan—everything from color televisions to packages of candy showered down from above by the Sultan's air force. It took only another three months for the Sultan to pull off what would have seemed a miracle just a short time before, by entering into a cease-fire agreement with South Yemen. The Saudis reportedly paid off the Yemenis handsomely and promised to finance the building of an oil refinery.

In reality, South Yemen was in dire need at the time, and that created tensions between the revolution and the state. Only three years earlier, the government had prioritized the nationalization of commerce in fruits, vegetables, fish, and meat, and the people came out in support, demonstrating and chanting, "Salmin don't stop! Take the taxis and other shops!" Times were difficult then as well, but the popularity of President Salmin wasn't affected by the difficulties. He presented himself as a simple man of the people, spending time with common folk and trying to find solutions to their problems. He drew on his long experience mediating among tribes, and he hated bureaucracy, embracing any opportunity to circumvent it and make direct decisions. At the same time, this strategy entrenched his power and caused anger and resentment among the other leaders. In September '76, they confederated and managed to persuade a majority of the executive council to pass resolutions challenging his authority. But they could not settle the issue entirely.

By the next summer, Ali Antar, an important independent leader, had returned from Moscow after finishing a course at a military training academy. (He had only recently learned how to read and write.) He found that the conflict between Salmin and the majority of the politburo members, including Ali Nasir and his group led by Abdelfattah Ismail, had become worse. This group attempted to bring Ali Antar over to their side by nominating him to the position of defense minister, but Salmin strongly opposed the move, fearing that the army would be taken over by his opponents. Ali Antar was well known for being both naive and excitable. Reports circulated that Salmin had been telling officials, "Ali Antar is crazy and could end up making a mess, just like Tschombé." Ali Antar had always loved Salmin and been enchanted by his style, but when he heard what he was saying, he reportedly went to him and said, "Either you go, or I go."

So the power struggle between the two sides escalated. Many commentators described it as a battle of ideas. Sometimes the battle played out between a pro-Soviet faction led by Abdelfattah Ismail, who considered himself a theoretician and put on airs of being an Arab Lenin, and a pro-Chinese faction led by Salmin, who had never tried to hide his affinity for the Chinese way. At other times, the line was between those who wanted revolutionary change and those who threw themselves into the embrace of the reactionary Arab regimes. But events disproved all of these explanations, because as the most crucial arguments erupted, foreign policy was pushed completely out of the picture.

Likewise the question of Yemeni unity, since all Yemenis in the south wanted it, and for that matter, so did the north. The only concern of the leadership in Aden was that the issue not be resolved in a way that would benefit the forces of reaction in North Yemen. But the coup d'état that Colonel Ibrahim al-Hamdi carried out in June of 1974 in North Yemen changed the calculus. Al-Hamdi was enlightened in his opposition to feudalism and the tribal mentality, and he also had a long-standing connection to Salmin, whom he had met in the earliest meetings of the then-fledgling Movement of Arab Nationalists. Now they came together again out of mutual self-interest to solve their respective problems: in the one case, strengthening al-Hamdi's position against the rule of reactionaries and tribal leaders taking support from the Saudis, and in the other, reinforcing Salmin in his confrontation with his rivals.

Statements by both presidents aspiring to unification were issued, and it suddenly seemed within reach. This prospect provoked anxiety in capitals both on the Peninsula and in the region as a whole, especially after al-Hamdi issued a statement about securing the waters of the Red Sea and making sure they did not fall under the control of imperialist and reactionary forces. The anxiety came to a head when the colonel decided to visit Aden on October 11, 1977, to announce new steps toward unification. It was a visit that was fated never to happen.

On October 10, his vice president, Colonel al-Ghashmi, invited al-Hamdi to his house. When the president arrived, having driven himself in his personal Volkswagen, he found that his brother, who had arrived earlier, had been killed. Quickly he met the same end. Later, some said that he had been lured to the house by the prospect of meeting two young French women, whose dead bodies were also found on the scene. Other stories claimed that al-Hamdi was assassinated in the presence of the military attaché of a neighboring Arab country and of a Yemeni Alawite leader, who would become a prominent figure in the years that followed. All of this was only one month before Anwar Sadat's inauspicious visit to Jerusalem, and that coincidence meant the incident not only connected with regional events but also signaled what was about to happen. But first, the bloody incident was temporarily put aside, as Colonel al-Ghashmi quietly became the new president of North Yemen. In only a few months, the American secretary of defense traveled to Saudi Arabia to sign an agreement providing North Yemen with American tanks and F-5 fighter jets worth $300 million — accompanied by American experts, of course. But no worry: it was all paid for by the Saudis.

On June 21, 1978, Salmin called al-Ghashmi and told him that he would be sending a group of detained tribal sheikhs back to him, transported by private plane and accompanied by an emissary who would deliver to him an important message.

On June 24, the plane arrived with the sheikhs and the emissary, who carried a briefcase that he insisted on delivering personally to al-Ghashmi. He was led to the president's headquarters, where he delivered the briefcase. When al-Ghashmi opened it, the case exploded, killing both men.

North Yemen immediately accused Salmin of carrying out the assassination as revenge for his murdered friend. President Ali Nasir Muhammad, on behalf of the government in the south, condemned the killing. Then, the next day, Fadhillah Mohsin, a member of the southern politburo and the brother-in-law of Abdelfattah Ismail, flew to the north with two colleagues to meet Salih Muslah, the north's interior minister. His aim was to clarify the southern government's new position against Salmin. The air during the meeting was filled with extreme tension, with each side keeping its eyes on the hands of their opposites to be sure they didn't reach for their gun first. Fadhillah told Salih, "I will not leave this spot until you and I have found common ground." Salih insisted that Salmin pay the price for his operation to kill al-Ghashmi, which he believed he ordered to bring about unification. He accused Salmin of personally picking an emissary who was an old militant (his name was Mahdi and they nicknamed him "Hajj Tovarich," which meant "comrade" in Russian, because he had gone to Moscow for a training course). He believed Salmin had charged this man with carrying the briefcase after convincing him to martyr himself for the noble cause. He claimed a video had even been made of a special ceremony celebrating his sacrifice, his commitment, and his dedication.

Once back in Aden, Fadhillah Mohsin headed directly to the presidential palace with Ali Antar and Muhammad Salih Mutia. They offered to let Salmin resign to stop the cycle of bloodletting, convincing him with the promise that he could go into exile in a dignified manner. The central committee then held a meeting to appoint an executive council to act as president, made up of Ali Nasir Muhammad as chair with Abdelfattah Ismail, Muhammad Salih Mutia, Ali Antar, and the communist representative Ali Badhib. The council issued an order stripping President Salmin of all his political and governmental powers and charging Ali Antar, Salih Muslah, and Salih Mutia with personally supervising his departure from the Aden airport.

Later, it was said that Ali Salih Abad, who had helped Salmin plan the revolt against Qahtan al-Shaaby in 1967, walked out of the meeting and immediately called Salmin to let him know that the moment was ripe to get rid of all his rivals in one fell swoop. Another version of the story had an officer in the republican guard called Um Zarba exploding in anger at the decision to strip Salmin of his power and acting on his own to carry out the bloody response.

In any case, when the meeting of the central committee ended, Abdelfattah Ismail, Ali Antar, Ali Nasir Muhammad, Salih Muslah, Muhammad Salih Mutia, and Fadhillah Mohsin all headed to Ali Nasir's house to celebrate the victory over Salmin. It had not been easy to extract his resignation, but once obtained, it would now settle the problem with the north that al-Ghashmi's assassination had caused.

As they were still toasting their victory, gunshots and cannon fire erupted at two o'clock on the morning of June 26, so they issued orders for planes and naval vessels to besiege the presidential palace. The assault continued until six o'clock that evening, when all resistance was finally exhausted and the palace was surrounded. When the president's surrender was demanded from a bullhorn outside the palace, he came out accompanied by a politburo member and a member of the central committee. All three were taken to politburo headquarters, where they were quickly tried and executed. The central committee announced to the people that a coup engineered by Salmin had been put down, finishing off the announcement with the traditional slogan: "Long live collective rule. Down with the cult of the individual." Salih Muslah, meanwhile, made no attempt to interfere, and all other allies of Salim Rubai went to jail, including Ali Salih Abad, who ended up spending five years behind bars.

After that, the first founding congress of the Yemeni Socialist party took place. The party accepted a proposal from Ali Nasir Muhammad that Abdelfattah Ismail, the secretary general of the party, be made president in order to reinforce the central role of the party along the Soviet model. A politburo was established made up of Abdelfattah Ismail, Ali Nasir Muhammad, Muhammad Salih Mutia, Salih Muslah, Ali Salem al-Baidh, Fadhillah Mohsin, and a few others. Ali Nasir was appointed prime minister. To put to rest the rumors circulating about ideological differences in the area of foreign policy, the congress committed to peaceful coexistence with the Gulf states. Ali Nasir Muhammad came out of the meeting the number 2 man in the government.

Still the power struggles continued. The following months witnessed feverish preparations for the next round on all fronts—local, regional, and international. Every mechanism for gaining the upper hand, from bribery to calling in tribal and regional loyalties, was employed. Finally, things came to a head around the question of military intelligence: Was it the province of the defense ministry (run by Ali Antar) or state security (Mohsin)? It seems Ali Nasir convinced Ali Antar that Mohsin was working to take control of the military so he could reinforce Abdelfattah Ismail's power, whereas he—Ali Nasir—was fully supportive of Antar. Meanwhile, he was also telling Mohsin that he was on his side. The problem was eventually resolved through the formation of a national security council, reporting directly to Prime Minister Ali Nasir, thus securing him a position of power at the center of the military establishment.

Rumors then began to circulate anew about ongoing power struggles, forcing Abdelfattah Ismail to announce in March 1980, "All our decisions are made by consensus, and anyone waiting for a new power struggle in Aden will have a very long wait."

But the wait was not so long; in fact, Abdelfattah Ismail himself was a victim of the next round.

Ali Nasir had managed to convince Ismail that several of the other leaders were not equipped to bear the burdens of the coming challenges to the nation. He named among this group Ali Antar and Salih Muslah, calling both members of "the barbarian bloc." At the same time, he was going back to these two and whispering to them that Abdelfattah was a cultured and effete theoretician, a poet living in an ivory tower, and that he wouldn't do as a head of state or a party leader. He told them that Abdelfattah had surrounded himself with authors and poets and that he considered the other members of the party leadership a bunch of beasts.

Once April rolled around, Ali Nasir informed Abdelfattah Ismail that a group had formed in the politburo that sought to remove Abdelfattah and replace him with none other than Ali Nasir himself, but Ali Nasir told Abdelfattah he could not take a position out from under him, and so he said he planned to resign. Abdelfattah understood from this that he had no more allies left in the politburo; he therefore decided to resign and ask Ali Nasir to take his place.

On April 20, 1980, the central committee held a meeting, which they barred Abdelfattah Ismail from attending. In an atmosphere clouded by threats of violence, Ali Antar chaired the meeting, in which the committee accepted the resignation of Abdelfattah Ismail from both the position of president and that of secretary general, "for health reasons." Ali Nasir was then charged with assuming both positions, on top of his duties as prime minister. A new position was created for Abdelfattah; following the Iraqi model, he was named president of the party. In a private ceremony, Ali Nasir awarded him the October 14 Revolution Medal. Also following the Iraqi model, the ceremony was followed by a trip to the airport in a private limousine and a flight out of the country to exile in Moscow. At that point, Muhammad Salih Mutia, who was foreign minister, a diplomat, an intellectual, one of the most prominent heroes from the war of liberation, and a staunch supporter of the efforts to oust both Salmin and Abdelfattah, became the number 2 man in the party.

Finally, Ali Nasir Muhammad took total power. Still, he felt uneasy. After all, Muhammad Salih Mutia was still there. So after four months he informed the politburo of a conspiracy between Mutia and a foreign government that was organizing a coup. Mutia was arrested, though Ali Antar tried to defend him.

Even then, Ali Nasir still considered the presence of a few of the older leadership in the politburo a thorn in his side. He set out to rid himself of them completely, calling an extraordinary congress of the party two months after Mutia's arrest. Cunningly, he arranged for delegates to the congress to be elected by his supporters. As the congress convened, he let the politburo members know that the results of the delegate elections reflected the general loss of confidence in the current politburo members among the base. Abdelaziz Abdelwali, a highly respected older member with a reputation for honesty and fairness, requested the floor, saying: "Respected Secretary General, I personally would like to submit my resignation from the politburo and would like to suggest that we in the old guard make room for new faces." The others acquiesced, and a new politburo was formed with only Ali Nasir and Ali Antar remaining from the previous membership.

Abdelwali's noble gesture could not save him, however, for as he prepared to leave for Damascus, a letter turned up from him to his friend, the ambassador of South Yemen to Syria, in which he wrote that spitting on some of these members of the new politburo would be too good for them. The politburo responded with an immediate decision to relieve him of his ministerial position and expel him to East Berlin to pursue advanced academic study. There he died from poisoning in 1983.

Seven months later, it was Ali Salem al-Baidh's turn. He faced a charge of violating family law that now forbade polygyny. He was removed as a result from both the central committee and his position as vice premier.

The following month, the moment of Ali Antar's trip to India was seized as an opportunity to execute Mutia without trial. Ali Antar rebelled upon his return, attacking Ali Nasir for his attempts to monopolize power and for arranging meetings with military officers to discuss the need for a corrective movement to bring back collective rule. Once Ali Nasir heard news of this, he went to work to isolate Ali Antar from the army. He used the old "kick them upstairs" strategy, appointing him vice premier and minister of local government affairs. Then he gave the position of defense minister to Salih Muslah Qasim, who was known for his discipline, his aversion to factionalism, and his tendency to resort to the position of mediator.

What happened next led directly to the final confrontation. Hussein Qamata, the former leader of the militia forces and a member of the party's central committee, was arrested on multiple charges, none of which were made public. Before the trial, he was killed in his prison cell. Ali Nasir's opponents felt endangered, and to protect themselves they began to meet. They sent a message to Abdelfattah Ismail in Moscow. Ali Nasir responded with an attempt to win over Ali Antar, appointing him vice president. He also brought Ali Salem al-Baidh back, giving him the position of minister of local administration, thus throwing aside the old concern with the marriage law.

The result was a whole new set of alliances and rivalries that brought back into play old regional and tribal loyalties. Ali Nasir found himself facing the same charges that had been leveled against Salmin of capitulationist policies toward the Gulf states. And indeed, certain signs supported such accusations. For example, products began to appear in the local market that had come via Saudi distributors, such as American apples and 7 Up (exactly as had happened in Egypt at the time of the open-door policy). Ali Nasir also issued an order that shipments arriving from the north would not be inspected, and televisions, appliances, and even suitcases filled with money came flooding in. By the fall of 1983, Ali Antar was headed to Moscow to engage in self-critique before Abdelfattah Ismail, and he was followed the next year by Salih Muslah. Ali Nasir, in an effort to cut the two of them off, also flew to Moscow to try to set up an alliance with Ismail by offering him safe return.

This series of contacts led to a decision by the politburo in February 1985 to bring back Abdelfattah Ismail and appoint him to the modest position of secretary to the central committee. Additional members were also brought into the politburo, giving Ali Nasir's rivals a majority. Haidar Abubakr al-Attas, an ally of Abdelfattah Ismail, was elected prime minister, replacing Ali Nasir, who had served in the position for fourteen consecutive years. It was announced that Ali Nasir had resigned the position to free himself up for his duties as party leader and president.

But these changes still could not undercut the ongoing tension among the rivals. Long negotiating sessions were held, some of which were attended by Habash and Hawatmeh, the prominent leftist Palestinians who had been active in Yemen. And in preparation for the party's general congress, Ali Nasir floated a suggestion of having set lists for the elections of delegates, run along Soviet lines, with prior review of all eligible candidates by party leaders, ensuring the election of the approved delegates even if a majority opposed them.

The election of delegates went forward in this irregular manner, allowing the two main factions to select their own supporters. The result was a deepening of the conflict, rather than a resolution or softening of it. A showdown loomed on the horizon. Leftist and communist delegations from around the Arab world visited to try to mediate. The Soviet embassy, which meticulously maintained complete neutrality between the two sides, also participated in the attempts at mediation.

On January 9, 1986, the politburo met to discuss a proposal from the supporters of Abdelfattah Ismail to transfer authority to them by making Abdelfattah the number 2 man in the party. But they were unable to agree, and the discussion was adjourned until Monday, January 13, at 10 A.M.

The members of the politburo all gathered at the headquarters of the central committee at the appointed time. When Ali Salem al-Baidh arrived, he found sitting there all the members who opposed President Ali Nasir: Abdelfattah Ismail, Ali Antar, Salih Muslah, Salem Salih, and Ali Hadi. The only one missing was Haidar al-Attas, who was on a trip to India. None of Ali Nasir's supporters were in the room. This didn't seem problematic, though, since they had all seen Ali Nasir's car parked in front of the building when they arrived. His bodyguards were in the building, and his personal secretary had told them that he was finishing an important meeting and would join them right away.

After a while Hassan, one of Ali Nasir's bodyguards, entered the room carrying the secretary general's briefcase, which he put down on the floor near the seat reserved for him. He then turned around, pointed his machine gun at the back of Ali Antar, and opened fire. All the other politburo members immediately dove under the table, pulling out their handguns and firing away at Hassan and another guard who pretended to be putting a thermos of tea in front of Ali Nasir's chair, but then quickly joined the gunfire.

The surviving members—Abdelfattah Ismail, Ali Salem al-Baidh, and Salem Salih—took refuge in an adjoining room, where they tore up the window curtains and then tied the strips together to make a rope that they could use to pull in more guns brought to them by one of Abdelfattah's guards.

During all this, the personal guards to most of the politburo members were being executed in the square in front of the building. At the same time, other mass killings along the same lines were targeting meetings that had been called at all levels of government—including the ministries of defense, interior, and state security—to discuss the possibility that an Israeli attack on Aden was under way. Forces loyal to Ali Nasir occupied key roads in and out of the capital, which they took control of, arresting or killing anyone associated with other factions. Navy and artillery began bombarding the homes of prominent figures, destroying the house of Abdelfattah Ismail in the process.

In sum, Aden came under the complete control of forces loyal to President Ali Nasir, who then embarked on stage 2 of his plan. Wrapping one of his arms in a bandage as if he were injured in a gun battle, he drove his car to Abyan province, where at 3 P.M. he made an announcement in the name of the politburo, declaring that an attempted coup had been put down. The goal of the insurrection, he said, had been to assassinate the president, overturn the party system, and tear up the constitution on which it was based. An order had been issued to assassinate the following plotters: Abdelfattah Ismail, Ali Antar, Ali Salem al-Baidh, and Ali Hadi.

Later, Ali Salem al-Baidh reported that Abdelfattah Ismail had escaped from the headquarters in an armored car but perished inside it when it was bombed. Meanwhile, al-Baidh himself had set off in another armored car, but abandoned it after going only 30 meters. He then hid in the area Monday evening and all of Tuesday. On Wednesday before dawn, he managed to telephone comrades and put together resistance. Ali Nasir had already taken control of the navy, but tanks and artillery began to defect to his opponents. The conflict then spiraled out to the point that fire was being traded between the tanks occupying the city and the ships docked in the port.

The fighting continued for nine days. The official tally listed deaths at 4,330 and material losses at the equivalent of 39.6 million dinar. In the end, Ali Nasir lost control of the capital. As soon as he was sure of his defeat, he escaped to Sanaa where he joined Ali Salih Abad, and from there, they continued on to Ethiopia.

The eruption resulted in the surviving ideological rivals of Ali Nasir, led by Ali Salem al-Baidh, taking power. Al-Baidh immediately announced that they would maintain the same foreign policy that Ali Nasir—and Salim Rubai before him—had followed. The official statement from the office of the president made this clear: "Our nation will adhere to its efforts to reinforce strong ties with its neighbor Saudi Arabia based on principles of fraternity, mutual respect, and nonintervention. This is equally true for our fraternal relations with the Sultanate of Oman, based on the previous agreement of principles entered into by the two governments. . . ."

5.

Fathy came back before lunch from downtown so he could take me to Sultan Hospital: my back pain had turned so severe that it was impossible to sleep. Jawhar helped him get me from the elevator to the car seat, and to fasten my seat belt. As we exited out to Qaboos Street, he said, "I met Fendy this morning and asked him about work for Shafiqa. He told me, 'The matter is out of my hands.' It's a strange choice of words, don't you think?"

Ignoring the question, I asked, "So what will she do now?"

He lowered his voice. "I'll try the Sultan."

The hospital was in a new building and was packed with patients, most in obvious pain. They wore distinctive clothes, sunglasses, and other accessories that suggested they had come in from the hinterlands. I walked gingerly past rooms packed with the latest instruments. We took the elevator up to the third floor. A Malaysian doctor met us. He seemed annoyed by me, and we had a hard time understanding each other's thick accents as we tried to converse in English. He had me strip, gave a quick exam, then referred me to the x-ray room. When I returned, he gave the images a look, then wrote me a prescription for Voltaren tablets and several physical therapy sessions. When I asked him to explain what was wrong with me, he muttered a few words of which I understood nothing. To round things out, he became angry when I pointed out that he had written my name wrong.

Fathy accompanied me to the physical therapy department, then left me there to go pay a visit to an acquaintance. I sat in a short hallway waiting my turn, passing the time by reading the newspaper. There was nothing new in it: communal riots between Hindus and Muslims in India, between Serbs and Bosnians in Yugoslavia—and those Palestinians, still stuck at the Lebanese border. A short piece covered a report by the Arab League about the twelve thousand Palestinian children that had become disabled because of the actions of the Israeli army. This included six thousand children under the age of sixteen who had lost either one of their limbs or their sight or hearing after being hit by rubber bullets or asphyxiated by tear gas, including babies still in their mothers' wombs.

I kept flipping through the pages until I was struck by a prominently featured ad:

"DUNHILL PRESENTS: UNITED BEAT, TREMENDOUS PARTY
    FEATURING MUSIC AND DANCE.
PEPSI CO IN COOPERATION WITH AL-FALAJ HOTEL.
8:30 P.M. FEATURING THE WORLD FAMOUS MUSICIAN/
    DANCER:

SHIAMAK DAVAR.
Tickets available at Pizza Hut, the Ice Rink, and other outlets."

I heard an accented version of my name called out and an Indian doctor appeared in the doorway to one of the rooms. She was of average height, middle aged, somewhat pretty with a dark, round face decorated by a traditional red dot on her forehead. But her features had a lifelessness that suggested she was in an emotional state I knew very well. Once it came out that I was Egyptian, however, a glimmer of interest flickered in her eyes.

She led me to a small area surrounded by curtains, spread me over leather cushions with an extension cord attached, and walked out. Immediately, I found myself enjoying a warmth spreading through my back.

Through a crack in the surrounding curtains, I could see her desk. A recent picture of the Sultan hung over it, with children's drawings of trees, houses, and cars attached at the bottom. After a few minutes she came to me and adjusted the cords. I asked her about the drawings and her face lit up. She said her daughter had made them and told me that she was in second grade back in Bombay. I asked no more questions, to avoid opening the wound lurking in her eyes.

She wanted to make an appointment for me to come back at the beginning of the next week, but I told her I was leaving the country in a matter of days. She advised me to spend as much of the coming days as possible lying on a flat, hard surface and to continue with the physical therapy as soon as I could.

I offered her a present of an ink pen with pharaonic inscriptions on it, which she received with the merriment of a child. She asked that I write down my address in Egypt, and she gave me her own addresses in both Muscat and Bombay.

On the way to the apartment, we picked up a free dose of medicine. Back home, Fathy spread a blanket over the rug for me to lie down on my back and placed some books and today's paper next to me. He said he could make me some lunch, but I insisted we wait until Shafiqa came home, so he brought me a radio and went back to work.

I didn't use a pillow, the idea being for my head to stay on the same level as the rest of my body. This made reading a challenge, so I turned on the radio. I switched from station to station until I landed on one playing old Abdel Wahab songs.

If beer and similar illicit materials were prohibited by Shafiqa, music like that of Abdel Wahab was the only thing not allowed by her husband. For Abdel Wahab — according to Fathy — was solely responsible for demolishing the Arabic music tradition and turning it into a mess, cut off from its roots and randomly stealing from the music of the West in either its classical or pop manifestations.

Personally, I had connected as a youth with the deep emotion of the songs he made famous in the '40s and '50s that mourned abandonment and loss at times, and yearned for it at others. As I grew older, I found myself setting them aside for his older songs, which were marked by a sweetness of lyrics and melodies and an overall simplicity, notwithstanding the intensity and purity of his voice. Fathy's absence gave me a chance to spend an hour listening to his songs, starting with the ones I loved best from the film *Al-Warda al-Baidha / The White Rose.*

Shafiqa returned from the radio station in the midafternoon. I called to her, and she came in the room and her eyes peered down at me from her face swathed in that hijab. When she saw me stretched on the ground, she asked what had happened at the hospital.

"They told me to lie here like this for one month," I said.

She looked surprised, then laughed, and I said, "Don't worry. I'm leaving as scheduled."

6.

I counted out the 5 Omani riyals for the exit tax and bade Fathy farewell. I put my briefcase and suitcase through the security screener, then crossed through the metal detector. On the other side, I picked up the briefcase and looked around for the desk that would check my luggage. A customs official came to my aid, pushing my bag to the side and lifting it up onto a rectangular table, then set to inspecting its contents in detail. He then turned the same attention to my briefcase, focusing particularly on my papers. When he finished, he led me to a wooden booth where he ran his hands over my chest, my back, and between my legs.

Finally he let me go, and I followed behind an Asian worker who carried my briefcase and placed it on a scale. I handed over my passport and headed toward the immigration desk, taking my place in the line for multinational nonresidents. My turn came quickly and I gave my passport to an officer who carefully flipped through the pages then left his chair without speaking and disappeared.

I felt the looks of the others on me, but I calmly stepped back and occupied myself by paging through an Indian newspaper that a traveler had left on a chair. A section devoted to news of Oman included coverage of the foreign minister's statement committing to support any action that would help bring about an end to the Arab economic boycott of Israel. Another article covered negotiations between Oman and Britain over a weapons sale worth 227 million dollars, which the paper described as a significant boost for British military production that would save eighteen hundred British jobs.

A full page was devoted to an excerpt from the memoir of General Peter de la Billière, who had led British forces during the Gulf War. Selections were taken from the important stages in his life. And it was indeed a rich life, lived by someone who had been in key places at the most important times: the Suez Canal and Jordan in 1956, Jebel Akhdar in Oman in '59, Aden in '64, Dhofar from '69 to '74, Sudan in '77. And when he left the military after the Gulf War, he became an administrator of a major financial securities firm. Remnants of a civilization in one life!

The passport officer returned and spoke to me warily, asking that I follow him. I grabbed my briefcase and followed him down a quiet hallway with fluorescent lights running the length of the corridor. He stopped in front of a door with no marking or signage of any kind and gave a gentle knock. Then he turned the knob, pushed the door open, and stepped aside for me to enter.

The room was small, with a metal desk in front of two chairs that faced each other. Powerful beams shone down from a square glass light mounted in the middle of the ceiling. The walls were bare except for an air conditioner grille and two pictures of the Sultan—one in a frame, the other on a decorative hanging calendar. There was no filing cabinet, nor any other indicator of what sort of work was carried out there. It was a room with no identity—like the ones where suspects are interrogated or prisoners meet their visitors.

The officer who had led me in shut the door behind me, leaving me standing before a man who sat at the desk concentrating intently on the pages of my passport. He wore a white dishdasha and a headdress of the same color, and he had on tinted glasses that were almost completely black. Still, I recognized him from his stark white eyebrows and his mustache.

He gestured for me to sit without looking up from the passport. I set my briefcase on the floor and sat down delicately, concerned about my back. I noted the handle of his dagger protruding from the multicolored belt with adornments wrapped around his waist. I felt like his eyes were attacking me even as they continued to scrutinize the passport.

He tossed the passport on the desk next to a small black intercom, then took off his glasses and set them down next to the device.

My heartbeat had started racing the moment I entered, overcome as I was by fears and expectations. But I had become calm now, and felt relaxed by the rustle of the air conditioning unit in my ears.

Can you imagine!

The waving hands, the Marlboros, and the scholarly tomes were gone, and in their place a dagger, a turban, and a bright red jewel inside a thick gold ring.

I was speechless. He gave me a moment, then broke into a faint smile. "You weren't expecting me?"

I couldn't manage an answer, so he went on: "I've heard that you've been searching for me."

Wrinkles surrounded his eyes, which projected a cold, calculating look. As I stayed silent, he continued: "Thirty-four years since our last meeting? A lifetime, wouldn't you say? But you haven't changed that much."

I finally found words. "You have turned into Harith Bin Ayesha."

He set his hands flat on the desk and pushed himself back in his chair. "Harith is one of my forefathers. He was a sheikh who led a whole tribe. And Ayesha is my mother's name. You might not know it, but the Bedouins . . ."

"I know," I interrupted. "I read the Sultan's encyclopedia."

He broke into laughter. I got the feeling that he, too, was a bit nervous.

"But why?" I asked.

He answered in a slightly mocking tone, "A corrective move! The necessities of the new stage." Now he seemed surer of himself. He went on: "Tell me, why were you looking for me?"

"I wanted to know what had happened to you, and . . . to Warda."

"Well, now you know, right? I mean, you read her journals."

I gathered myself and answered, "There are still a few matters that aren't so clear."

He pushed himself further back. "Like what?"

Suddenly, a rush of anger came over me. "Like, what exactly happened to her in the end and why you abandoned her in the desert."

He studied me for a moment with something like concern, then spoke slowly: "What is your theory?"

"Either you feared for your own safety or you went looking for the way out and became lost—although I doubt it was that because you could have just told them what you were planning. Most likely the whole thing was planned from the start."

His eyes narrowed but he made no comment. I went on: "When did you start working with the government? Was it back when they first arrested you in Mattrah?"

He didn't answer, but I kept on without slowing down. "You were set on being done with her. Then at the last minute you hesitated. Maybe you felt sorry for her, or you discovered she was pregnant, or you thought it would be more strategic to just leave her in the desert for the wolves and the tribes."

Devastatingly measured, he said, "You're talking about my sister?"

"I realize you loved her. Maybe even more than you should have. In spite of that—or maybe because of that—you abandoned her. One of the tribes must have taken her in—her and Dahmish—and sheltered her until her daughter was born. She called her Waad instead of naming her Thaïra like she had wanted. She wanted to protect her, or to remind the tribe of the commitment she had drawn out of them to deliver her safely to her father's relatives. Of course, I have no idea what happened after that. Maybe she had some kind of accident in the desert or the authorities caught up with them. Most likely, the tribe finished them off but kept the child alive. Then they fulfilled their promise by giving Waad to her uncle, who kept the whole thing secret. What do you think?"

"Not bad. Keep going."

"The important thing is that you played your role. Everything could have played out with no problems if the journals hadn't surfaced. Someone found them, or maybe members of the tribe wanted to benefit from them somehow. In any case, you had to know what they said about you."

He opened the desk drawer and pulled out the last of the notebooks with its black cover. He held it up and waved it in front of me. "Everyone was chasing after this. Your friends, for example, fighting among themselves as usual, with every faction wanting to use them against the others. My friends too . . . You met Fendy? Then there are the sheikhs and the brotherhood. Also, our neighbors and our neighbors' neighbors. Do you know why? Can you believe that the desire to know what happened to Warda is the real reason?" He leaned forward. "It's me they want."

"But why now?" I asked.

Gathering himself, he settled back into silence. I asked, "Is it because your friend, the Sultan's cousin, is about to be prime minister? I doubt it."

The look that flashed in his eyes clued me in. Slowly I said, "You're getting ready for something even bigger."

He stole a glance at the intercom, giving away that the machine had another function and that my arrow had hit its target.

Suddenly, he grabbed the journal with both hands and started ripping its pages into small pieces. We both stared at the paper scraps, piled now on the desktop like so much black and white confetti.

"No one will be able to use this to their advantage now," he said.

"Unless there's a copy," I responded.

His hands froze over the pile of scraps and he concentrated his gaze on me. "You do not have a single sheet of paper from any of this. We've done a complete inspection. And you haven't been near a copier since the moment you arrived in the Sultanate." He leaned forward again and studied me carefully. "Where?"

"With Waad."

He suddenly erupted. "That little bitch."

"She wants only one thing," I said.

"What's that?"

"To go to college. Here or abroad."

"What about you?"

"My cousin's wife."

"What about her?"

"They want to end her contract. You must know about it. All she's asking for is a two-year extension until her husband is done with his project."

He tapped his fingers on the desk, keeping his eyes fixed on mine. "Two years, then. And not a word from you."

I nodded my head.

Just two years. Then we'll see.

I looked at my passport and his eyes followed. He considered it for a moment, then reached for it, picked it up, and handed it to me. I took it, picked up my briefcase, and stood.

I turned. Finally, I was leaving.

ADDENDUM

At the beginning of 1990, Ali Salem al-Baidh made an announcement on behalf of the leadership of the People's Democratic Republic of Yemen. The name of former president Salim Rubai, aka Salmin, would be rehabilitated. On May 22, 1990, the two Yemens were united, with Ali Salem al-Baidh becoming vice president as well as head of the Socialist party of Yemen. After a series of assassinations of party leaders allegedly carried out by elements working with North Yemen, al-Baidh locked himself in his headquarters in Aden, refusing to travel to Sanaa. The situation deteriorated until armed clashes between the two sides broke out and by April 27, 1994, devolved into full-fledged civil war. On May 21, 1994, Aden announced that the PDRY would come back into existence. The war continued for another two months, ending with victory of the north over the south, tens of thousands of casualties, and 11 billion dollars in losses. Al-Baidh took refuge in the Sultanate of Oman, where he settled. Ali Nasir stayed in Damascus. Ali Salah Abad became head of the Yemen Socialist party. In 1999, Osama Bin Laden, a Saudi of Yemeni origin, gave an interview to a French investigative journalist in which he admitted that he had personally supervised the assassination of 158 Yemen Socialist party cadres in Aden between the years 1990 and 1994.

May 2000

SELECTED SOURCES

Arkless, David. *The Secret War: Dhofar 1971–1972.* Kimber, 1988.

de la Billière, Gen. Peter. *Looking for Trouble: An Autobiography from the SAS to the Gulf.* HarperCollins, 1994.

Hawley, Donald. *Oman and Its Renaissance.* Stacey International, 1984.

Janzen, Jorg. *Nomads in the Sultanate of Oman: Tradition and Development in Dhofar.* Westview Press, 1986.

Lowi, Miriam R. *Water and Power: The Politics of a Scarce Resource in the Jordan River Basin.* Cambridge University Press, 1995.

Journal of Oman Studies 6, no. 2 (1983). Ministry of National Heritage.

Le Nouvel Observateur. 1975 and 1995.

Sources in Arabic

حصاد ندوة الدراسات العمانية. المجلد السابع, وزارة التراث القومي و الثقافة, سلطنة عُمان, 1980

وثائق الجبهة الشعبية الديموقراطية العمانية.

من فنون عمان التقليدية. وزارة الاعلام, سلطنة عمان, 1990.

الرمال العربية. ويلفرد ثيسجر, ترجمة ابراهيم مرعي, موتيف ايت, أبو ظبي, 1992.

الأعمال الكاملة. أرنستو جيفارا, دار الفارابي و دار دمشق, 1982.

كنت طبيبة في اليمن. كلود دي فابان, دار الكلمة, صنعاء, 1985.

مناضل من عمان: محمد امين عبدالله 1915–1982. حسين درويش, 1990.

البلاد السعيدة, برترام توماس. وزارة التراث القومي و الثقافة, عمان, 1984.

صورة الفتى بالأحمر. فواز طرابلسي, رياض الريس, 1997.

وعود عدن. فواز طرابلسي, رياض الريس, لندن, 2000.

الصراع على الخليج العربي. عبد الرحمن النعيمي, دار الكنوز الأدبية, بيروت, 1994.

حرب الشعب في عمان. على فياض, الاتحاد العام للكتاب و الصحفيين الفلسطينيين, 1975.

الحزب الشيوعي السوداني و انقلاب 5 مايو. محمد سعيد القدال, الخرطوم, 1986.

الصراع في عدن. شاكر الجوهري, مكتبة مدبولي, 1992.

الصبح الدامي في عدن. حميدة نعنع, دار المستقبل العربي بالقاهرة, 1998.

الواقع التاريخي و الحضاري لسلطنة عمان. خالد يحي العربي, 1985.

دولارات الارهاب. سعيد اللاوندي, دار نهضة مصر بالقاهرة, 2000.

ACKNOWLEDGMENTS

Author's Acknowledgments

Thanks to Omani friends who opened their hearts even before their homes and gave me the gift of the glowing light of their ancient civilization.

Thanks, too, to those who gave generously of their deep knowledge: Mark Pellas and his French comrades who have championed the cause of the Arab people and preserved the history of their struggle; Jarallah Omar of the Yemeni Socialist party's political bureau; Haidar Ibrahim, director of the Center for Sudanese studies in Cairo; Hanya Sarour, who allowed me to screen her film *The Hour of Liberation Has Arrived*; Fawaz Trabulsi, who made available to me his essays and papers; Amin Radwan, Ali Mohsen, Hussein Moussa, Salah Zaki Mourad, Hosna Mikdashi, Ibrahim Farghali, Ferial Ghazoul, Walid Qazhia, and Nabil Darwish. And to those who assisted so generously in other ways: Mohieddin Labbad, Salah Hazeen, Ahmad al-Qaseer, Ann Harlow, Wael Abdelfattah.

As always, the comments of Laila Awais and Nadia Mohammad al-Gindy on the manuscript, catching mistakes and polishing the final product, were invaluable.

Thanks also to Abdel Menaam Saudi at Dar al-Mustaqbal al-Arabi in Cairo for his felicitous copyediting.

Translator's Note and Acknowledgments

The entry for September 5 in chapter 9 includes two quotations from the Quran. For these quotations I have used the following: *Al-Qur'an: A Contemporary Translation by Ahmed Ali* (Princeton, NJ: Princeton University Press, 1993), [34:34], [30:41].

The entry for January 1974 in chapter 14 includes a poem by Bertolt Brecht, "General, your tank is a powerful vehicle," originally published in German in 1938 as "General, dein Tank ist ein starker Wagen," translated by Tom Kuhn. Copyright 1939, © 1961 by Bertolt-Brecht-Erben / Suhrkamp Verlag. Translation copyright © 2019, 2015 by Tom Kuhn and David Constantine, from *Collected Poems of Bertolt Brecht*, translated by Tom Kuhn and David Constantine. Used by permission of Liveright Publishing Corporation.

The final sentence of the novel in the original version cites a French text, M. Tabachnik's *Les Cercles de l'enfer*, which does not mention Bin Laden. The author and translator have agreed to delete this citation. Bin Laden's involvement in assassinations of leftists in Yemen during the period referenced is described in Lawrence Wright, *The Looming Tower: Al-Qaeda and the Road to 9/11* (Vintage, 2007), pp. 173–76.

For inspiring this effort and/or keeping it alive, my thanks to Sonallah Ibrahim, Richard Jacquemond, Fady Joudah, and Samah Selim.

SONALLAH IBRAHIM, one of Egypt's most prominent living authors, has written fourteen novels as well as multiple volumes of travel writing, young adult books, translations, and reportage. His career has been characterized by his independence and innovation in both his writing style and his public stances. As a young man during the early 1960s, he spent time as a political prisoner. In the later 1960s and 1970s, he spent time in exile, working as a journalist in East Germany and studying film in Moscow. Considered to this day a voice of conscience in Egyptian society, he has lived modestly in the middle-class neighborhood of Heliopolis in northeastern Cairo since his return to Egypt. His work has been translated into multiple languages, reviewed in the pages of *Le Monde* and the *New York Times*, and adapted for film and television.

HOSAM ABOUL-ELA is a writer, translator, and literary critic. He was born in Alexandria, Egypt, and now teaches English at the University of Houston. His writing has appeared in the *Huffington Post*, *Words without Borders*, npr.com, the *Houston Chronicle*, the *New York Times Magazine*, and several academic journals. His most recent translation is Sonallah Ibrahim's novel *Stealth*.